Hostage Situation
An Alexis Parker novel

G.K. Parks

Copyright © 2024 G.K. Parks

A Modus Operandi imprint

All rights reserved.

ISBN:
ISBN-13: 978-1-942710-46-2

For my mom and dad

ONE

I knocked and waited. No answer. I tried again. I turned the knob and slowly pushed open the door. "Hello?" No response. "I'm here to clean the room." Still nothing.

Hoping I wasn't about to see someone parading around in his birthday suit, I peered inside. A man remained in the tub, facing away from me. He was slumped down, his arms around the edges, keeping him from going under.

"I'm sorry, sir. I didn't mean to intrude." I took a step back, bumping into the cleaning cart and knocking over a mop. For a former federal agent trained in tactical maneuvers, one would think I'd be less of a clutz. I grabbed the mop and shoved it back into the bucket and secured the handle in the slot at the top.

He didn't respond or turn. I glanced back at him. He hadn't moved at all.

"Sir?" His lack of response sent a chill through me.

Leaving the cleaning cart where it was, I approached him. Since the tub wasn't filled with ice water, I assumed this was for flotation therapy or washing off the gunk from one of the other procedures.

"Are you okay?"

When he didn't answer, I pressed two fingers against his

neck. He jumped, which startled me. I stepped back, an unprofessional yelp escaping my lips.

"What the hell do you think you're doing?" The look of disdain at my uniform spoke volumes.

"I knocked, but no one answered."

"What?" Annoyed, he pulled the tiny earplugs out of his ears. "What are you doing in here? I was meditating. Why are you disturbing me?"

I backed toward the door. "I wanted to make sure you were okay."

"Do I look okay?" He glared at me with angry eyes. "I've never seen you before. The rest of the cleaning crew knows to stay away from clients."

"It won't happen again." I let myself out of the room and closed the door. My heart pounded in my chest. He wasn't dead. That was a good thing, or so I told myself as I pushed the cart down the hall to the next room. But he could have been nicer. Had he been in real danger, I would have helped. After all, I wouldn't be investigating the spa if there wasn't a reason. And since the owner had just quadrupled his liability insurance, it must have been one hell of a reason. Death of a client didn't seem beyond the realm of possibility.

I was halfway through cleaning one of the massage rooms when I heard the man telling someone on staff how I'd ruined his treatment. On the bright side, if I got fired, Lucien Cross, my boss and head of Cross Security, would have to send someone else to handle this investigation. The last place I wanted to be was here.

As if on cue, I sneezed. The diffusers and essential oils had been wreaking havoc on my allergies. My eyes teared, and I went to the window and tried to open it. Like most of the windows in this place, it didn't budge. The tiny glass rectangles served one purpose, allowing soft light to filter in. That was it. Airflow be damned. The frosted glass mocked me.

I should have been relieved that was my current nemesis and not some psychopath hell-bent on killing me. But then I sneezed again, and I couldn't help but think my chances might have been better with the psychopath.

After I finished disinfecting the room and grabbing the

used linens, I returned to the hallway. Kathy Walters, Spa Alive's manager, stood outside the door, her arms folded over her chest, an annoyed expression on her face. Maybe this undercover assignment would be cut short. How would Cross take it? Would he accuse me of sabotaging it on purpose? Probably. I had done just about everything I could to get out of it, but given our new dynamics and my new designation as a full-time employee, Cross reminded me I didn't have a choice. And I reminded him, we'd been there, done that, and more than likely, this wouldn't end well for either of us.

Walters took one look at my puffy, red eyes and tear-stained cheeks, and her expression softened. "Alex, are you okay?"

I sniffed, not to be dramatic, but because my nose was running. "I take it you heard what happened. I didn't know he had earplugs. I thought he may have had a heart attack."

She considered what I said and sighed. "It's okay. Better safe than sorry. I smoothed things over by comping his session. But from now on, unless the door is open or a staff member specifically asks you to clean up, stay away. Spa Alive has policies regarding interactions. They are meant to protect our clients' privacy and modesty."

"Yes, ma'am."

"I can see this has upset you. Everyone makes mistakes. It's okay, but don't do it again." She nodded to the bathroom door. "Why don't you take a minute and get your faculties in order? After that, finish the laundry, mop the floors, and call it a night."

Instead of correcting her, I went into the bathroom. After blowing my nose a few times, I washed my face, hoping the cold water would get rid of the puffiness, before returning to my duties. By the time I came out, the cosmetologists and massage therapists had gone home. Walters remained in her office, making it impossible for me to search it. The only other member of the cleaning crew who had been assigned to work today met me in the laundry room.

"Is everything okay?" Ellie Danver asked.

"Uh-huh." I loaded the washing machine and pressed the button.

"It's only your third day. You'll get the hang of it. Don't let these rich jerks get to you."

"That's not the problem."

"It isn't? From what I heard, you nearly gave Mr. Chesterfield a heart attack."

"Has anything like that happened before?"

"Support staff pissing off clients?" She grabbed the towels out of the dryer and started folding them. "No. You're the first."

I found that hard to believe, but that wasn't what I wanted to know. "I was asking if medical emergencies are common."

"They aren't." She kept folding. "As far as I know, there's never been a problem. Were you hoping to cause one?" She glanced at me, her eyes teasing.

"Only after I convince one of these rich jerks to name me as beneficiary on his life insurance."

"Good luck with that. The chance of that happening is a zillion to one. Now, if you were one of the regular staff who makes them feel or look great, I'd say you might have a shot at it."

Hoping to gain usable intel, I chuckled to myself. "How many staffers does this place lose every month?"

"None. I'm assuming that means they aren't that great at their jobs. Well, except for maybe Damon."

"Damon?"

"The massage therapist. Big guy, ripped, dark hair, beard. He's the hottest thing in this place." She looked around, afraid her voice had carried. "He gets booked up weeks, if not months, in advance."

"Maybe he's good at massages."

"Or something else."

"Are you serious?"

"I don't know, but I've heard he's gone out with a client or two."

The intel I'd pulled said Damon Thoreau had worked at Spa Alive for five years. There had never been any complaints. His background check came out clean. "Did you ever see it happen?"

She shook her head.

"Have you ever seen him ask anyone out or exchange numbers?"

"No, but I wish he'd ask if I wanted to exchange numbers."

I left the washing machine to do its thing while I put the rest of the cleaning supplies away, emptied the bucket, and wrung out the mop. By the time I finished with my chores, Ellie had put the towels away and taken off her pink smock. She folded it a few times and put it down. The heather gray tank top she wore underneath had sweat stains around the collar and arm holes.

"I'll see you tomorrow, Alex," she said.

"Good night." I waited for her to leave before ducking into the employee locker room. After taking off my own pink smock, I shoved it into the locker, pulled out my lock picks, and searched every locker in the place. No contraband. No drugs. No weapons. No recording devices. Nothing indicated anyone on staff was doing anything illegal, or they'd been smart enough to take the illicit items with them when they went home for the night.

Unsure what I hoped to find, I pulled out my RF reader and scanned, but Spa Alive didn't have much in the way of surveillance cameras. When I couldn't find anything emitting a signal, I tucked the device away, grabbed my bag, and went to wait for the laundry to finish. Once it was done, I folded the sheets and towels and put them on the shelves. Then I locked up the storage closet where the cleaning supplies were kept and headed toward the front.

The sound of rapid typing echoed in the otherwise silent interior. Cautiously, I approached Walters' office. She didn't notice me lingering in the doorway. Instead, she continued to type.

Pulling out my phone, I took a few shots of her screen and tucked my device away. "Ms. Walters?" I knocked on the open door. "Is there anything else you need me to do?"

She turned at the intrusion, immediately minimizing the window on her screen. Whatever she was doing, she didn't want me to see it. I resisted the urge to make a joke about searching for pornography. Instead, I pretended to remain oblivious to her behavior.

"That's it for today. The offices get cleaned Friday nights, so expect to work late then. Other than that, once you finish tidying the treatment rooms, you're free to go."

"In that case, good night."

She waited until I was halfway down the hall before she started typing again. Every cell in my body wanted to sneak another peek at what she was doing, but I'd already taken a few photos. That should give me some idea of what she wanted to keep secret. Hopefully, it connected to the reason the owner wanted to drastically increase his liability coverage.

As soon as I got into the car, I locked my doors and took out my phone. Walters had been working on a spreadsheet. The columns weren't labeled, so I wasn't sure what it was. It could have been this month's P&Ls or an order form. I studied the information, but I couldn't make heads or tails out of it. Maybe someone at Cross Security could.

TWO

After giving the spreadsheet photos to the techs working on the floor above, I settled behind my desk at Cross Security. While they figured out what Kathy Walters tried to hide, I'd see what deep, dark secrets Damon Thoreau was keeping. But I'd already done extensive research on Spa Alive and every one of its employees. No one had a record. They were all clean.

Damon Thoreau didn't have any social media accounts that I'd found. I tried reverse image searches, but the only things that came up were connected to his profession. His photo was on the Spa Alive website, his website, and on several job sites. That was the closest thing this man had to an online presence, and it told me next to nothing about him.

But I couldn't be deterred that easily. So I ran down each and every bullet point on his online resume. I searched for his name at his alma mater. He'd made the dean's list several times, graduated with honors, and had a degree in physiology.

I dug deeper, but it led nowhere. I tried looking up his classmates, people who graduated the same year he did with the same major, but it was nothing more than a fishing expedition. For all I knew, I could be looking at his best friend or ex-girlfriend and not even know it. But I didn't have the time it would take to go through every social media post that had been made a decade ago in the hopes of finding a younger Damon Thoreau engaging in questionable activities. Honestly, I wasn't even sure what good that would do me.

Forcing my hand off the mouse, I read the intel in the files. What was I doing? Maybe instead of searching for dirty details on Damon, I should see if Spa Alive's clientele had any salacious photos of the massage therapist in compromising positions. But given the dozens of clients who visited the wellness center during any given month, that would be just as pointless. Was that even why the owner wanted to up his liability insurance? Did Damon take liberties which could result in a lawsuit? If he did, he should have a record or prior accusations.

I found the owner's name, Ralph Lively, and pulled up the background check I'd already run on him. No criminal record. No pending lawsuits. Hoping I'd get lucky, I searched online for allegations and rumors that he was involved in something that was about to blow up. When that failed, I resorted to reading online reviews.

Nowadays, everyone was a critic. You couldn't get a ride from point A to point B without worrying how you'd be rated, either as the customer or the driver. That mentality should have made my job easier, but I didn't find anything new since the last time I checked, four days ago. Perhaps the guy in the tub hadn't gotten around to sharing his negative experience with the world yet. Or maybe what Kathy Walters said was true. Spa Alive had policies to protect its clients' privacy. Maybe the clients didn't want to be associated with the wellness center. After all, several of them were famous enough that any leaked photos or stories could turn into fodder for late night TV or click-bait for gossip sites.

Checking the client list again, I only recognized a handful of names. The others were minor celebs, online influencers, and ex-spouses of actors and models. Maybe that's why Cross made us take this case. It wasn't about the insurance. It was to sign more famous people as Cross Security clients.

Pulling up the intake form, I read the contract my boss had signed with the insurance company. Our job was simple. Determine if Spa Alive suspected it'd be targeted with a lawsuit or if it was actively violating practices that would result in such a lawsuit. The only thing I knew for sure was they followed guidelines for keeping the place sanitary. Everything had to be wiped, washed, and properly disinfected. The linens had to be laundered at a high temperature. The glass cleaned. The tubs and cushions disinfected after every use. Everything checked out. But maybe that level of cleanliness was a recent development.

I was making a note to ask Ellie if Spa Alive had always been so stringent with their practices when someone pushed open my partially closed office door. I didn't bother to look up. The telltale throat clearing gave it away.

"What do you want, Lucien?" I asked.

"Have you made any progress?"

"No."

"I was informed you brought photos for the techs to analyze."

I clicked the icon, but I had no new messages. "Do they know what kind of data Walters was enthusiastically typing into the rows and columns?"

"No." He moved closer, peering down at the files and papers I'd been consulting between my internet searches. Picking up the blank legal pad, he cocked an eyebrow at it before putting it back on my desk. "You usually have notes and theories by now."

"This isn't a typical case." I closed the tabs on the computer screen and looked up at him. "I hate insurance cases. Without a claimant, this is a waste of time."

His expression changed. "Is everything okay?"

"I'm frustrated. I've been cleaning this place for days, searching what I can, when I can. I haven't found anything. The staff won't talk to me, unless it's to tell me to clean something. It's too elitist. It's making it difficult to gain intel, and the members of the cleaning crew who will talk barely have any gossip or rumors to share. Today, I finally got a juicy tidbit out of Ellie, but even that wasn't particularly useful." I slumped back in my chair and rubbed my eyes.

"I'm not talking about work." Cross scrutinized me. "Are you okay?"

"Since when do you care?"

"Always. I am not your enemy, Alex. I'd think by now, after everything, you would have realized that." He dropped into the chair in front of my desk. "Why have you been crying? Is this about your adoptive father?"

"I haven't been crying."

"I'm an investigator. I can see the signs all over your face and hear it in your voice."

"It's called allergies."

He looked like he didn't believe me.

"Why are you bringing up Don? Did something happen?" My adoptive parents had been moved into WitSec. If something had happened, SSA Mark Jablonsky would have gotten word before my boss. Mark would have contacted me. The OIO and U.S. Marshal Service had a working relationship. Cross Security was a private company, nothing more than an interloper.

Cross held up his hands in surrender. "I was just asking. It hasn't been that long. The scars from that are fresh. I'd think they'd still hurt."

"I didn't end up with any scars, for once."

Cross snorted. "What are you allergic to? Manual labor?"

"Essential oils. Not all of them, but most of them. Anything floral, especially the damn lavender they use all the time."

"It's calming."

"It's lethal."

Cross chuckled. "You didn't cite that as a reason not to take this case when you tried to beg off of it."

"I didn't know. Would that have made a difference?"

"No, but I'll have the medical staff upstairs get you some allergy medicine. I'd hate to make you extra miserable."

"You're enjoying this."

"Oh, so you think I'm a sadist?"

"Justin thinks so."

"Why are you discussing me with my executive assistant?"

"No reason."

He wasn't buying it. This conversation was making him uncomfortable, possibly nervous. He ran a hand through his hair. "If I were a sadist, we'd get along better. It'd feed into your masochistic tendencies."

"I'm reformed."

"Yeah, okay." He didn't buy that either. Reaching over, he grabbed the copy of the contract off my desk. "I asked Almeada to keep his ear to the ground in case whispers circulate about a pending lawsuit or threats of one."

"Would he share that intel with you? He could be disbarred for violating privilege." I thought for a moment, recalling my law school days. "Actually, wouldn't that be a conflict?"

"He wouldn't report on his clients or his firm's clients. But he may hear chatter around the courthouse and in those private clubs he likes to visit. It's possible he'll hear something we don't. Lawyers tend to travel in tight circles."

"Well, I guess it's only fair since he makes us dig up dirt for his cases." I was still sore about being asked to look into a police investigation and find a way to tear it to shreds for Cross's attorney. But that was my hang-up. Most of my friends carried badges, either local or federal, so I didn't want to draw any unnecessary lines in the sand. "Since you asked Almeada to work on this, does that mean I'm free to do something else?"

"This is the only case I've assigned you. You're not freelancing, are you?"

"I'm confused. Am I required to disclose that to you now that my employment contract has changed?"

"Are you working on something else?" he repeated.

"No, but you could assign me something else. In fact, I'd be more than happy to give Mr. Almeada my office. I wouldn't mind using his. I bet he has a window."

"We have better snacks and our own medical staff."

"I can buy my own snacks."

"I've been to your apartment. I've seen what you eat. You'd starve to death if you didn't work here."

"Now you sound like Martin."

That made Cross smile. "I'm glad he has a reason to be pleased you work here."

"Stop. The two of you are done. You got what you wanted from him, Lucien. You got the research you needed on biotextiles. Leave him out of the rest of your plans for world domination. He doesn't like getting involved in things that require government oversight or testifying before a committee. He tries not to involve himself in government contracts when he can avoid it. And you don't play fair. You used me, my relationship, to get him to cave."

"You're wrong. James Martin loves you. He came to me to find ways to keep you safe."

"That's right. I forgot about that tracking chip you gave him. I never asked. Did you pick out the charm on the necklace, or did he?"

"Alex—"

"I don't want to know." That was an old fight. Martin had his reasons. I had mine, which was why I chipped his watch. But that dysfunction hadn't lasted too long. Now we tracked each other the much more normal way, with an app on our phones.

Cross tapped the files on my desk. "This is your priority. Support staff is here to assist. I'm here if you need me."

"You need to send someone else in."

"We've been over this."

"I don't mean to replace me." Though, I wasn't opposed. "I mean as a client. Spa Alive has a caste system. The cosmetologists and massage therapists won't give the cleaning crew the time of day. I can't get them to talk when they won't even look in my direction."

"I'll see what I can do, but you've worked cases like this before. Don't let them treat you like an outsider. Find a way in."

THREE

Find a way in. That was easier said than done. But I'd worked undercover enough to know that I could change the play. I'd also done this enough to know that some missions had to be scrapped. At this point, I wasn't sure which way things would go.

Since Ellie had mentioned Damon Thoreau had a reputation, I thought I'd try exuding some sex appeal. Instead of putting the vastly oversized smock on over a pair of khaki pants, I decided to dress it up a bit. A few strategically placed safety pins kept the fabric from billowing everywhere. And instead of wearing the khakis which further washed me out and made me look like a beige ghost, I wore a skintight black skirt with a tiny bit of shimmer. The skirt was long enough to cover the scars on my thigh but short enough to make me wonder if I'd be reprimanded or fired.

Instead of leaving my hair in a sloppy ponytail, I had gotten up an hour early to curl and style it into some fancy updo. I even went through the trouble of expertly applying my makeup, as if Martin was taking me to a gala. The mascara I put on was waterproof, but I doubted the promise on the label would be enough to ward off my overactive tear ducts. So I filled my purse with everything needed to wash this off and reapply. Worst case, I'd end up looking like a raccoon. So it'd be best to approach Damon before that happened.

Since Spa Alive got scrubbed at night, the mornings were always quiet. I hung around the break room, waiting for the first set of appointments to conclude before I cleaned the rooms. Two of the cosmetologists sat at a table, drinking kombucha and chatting over their oat bran muffins.

"Morning, ladies." I smiled at them over the rim of my teacup. Coffee would have been better, but chamomile tea was the only recognizable item available for consumption in the kitchen.

The two women nodded in my direction, but they didn't want to affiliate with me. I didn't realize we were back in high school. Since I'd never been invited to sit at the cool kids' table back then, this was no different.

Five minutes later, Damon entered with a travel cup in hand. According to the schedule, he didn't have his first session until ten. But he always showed up to work forty-five minutes early, which is why I was waiting in the break room. He wished the women a good morning before opening the fridge and peering inside.

"Would you like some tea?" I asked.

He turned, noticing me for the first time. His eyes traveled up my legs, and a smile tugged at his lips. He'd never seen me before, and if he had, he didn't recognize me without pants. "No, thanks." He shook his cup and glanced back at Willa and Terri. "Is Ms. Reynolds getting a seaweed wrap today? I passed her on my way in. It sounded like she hoped to have a full-service experience. My schedule is full, but Erica could rub her down after you finish. How many procedures does she have on the books?"

"Dammit." Willa got up, tossing the wrapper from her muffin into the garbage. "So much for my calm tranquility. She does this all the time. She thinks we can fit her in when all she requests is a facial or a cut and color."

"I'll go with you and see what we can move around." Terri shrugged at Damon. "Thanks for the heads-up. My horoscope said it'd be one of those days."

"I bet." He winked, waiting for her to leave.

"You sure know how to clear a room," I said.

He gave the teacup in my hand an intrigued look. "I've

never seen you around here before. Is this your first day?"

"Why? Is the cleaning crew forbidden from coming in here? The clients aren't supposed to see us, but I didn't know the same was true for the rest of the staff."

He tilted his head to the side while he reached around me to grab a banana from the fruit bowl. "You're Alexandra, right?"

"Alex," I corrected, hating that Cross hadn't come up with something more unique for my cover identity.

"I'm Damon Thoreau." He put the banana down and offered me his hand. "I heard you caused quite the ruckus yesterday afternoon. Apparently, you thought Mr. Chesterfield was dead in the bath."

"I knocked. He didn't answer. I assumed the worst. Is he one of your clients?"

"No, but I heard all about it."

"Great." I rolled my eyes. "I'm surprised I didn't get fired. Ms. Walters was so mad."

"Don't worry about it. We all make mistakes."

"Even you?"

Damon grinned, but he wouldn't fall for the bait that easily.

"Yeah, I didn't think so." I helped myself to an orange.

"He's Willa's client. Because of you, she didn't get tipped. That's why she and Terri were giving you the cold shoulder." He indicated the table they vacated. "You've got a real knack for making friends."

"I thought they were being distant because I'm part of the cleaning crew."

Damon's brown eyes sparkled. "Are you saying we're too snobby to associate with the pink smock brigade?"

I looked down at my outfit. "These are pretty terrible. I wouldn't want to associate with anyone wearing one if I could avoid it."

"Which do you hate more? The outfit or the tea?"

"Whatever do you mean? I love herbal tea." But that's not what my expression said. I'd done my research. Damon Thoreau stopped for a caramel latte with a double-shot of espresso every morning on his way to work. He always kept his drink covered, and when asked, he'd tell his coworkers it was organic chicory root with honey. I didn't know if they were dumb enough to believe him. But since he called me out on the tea, I'd return the favor. "Isn't that what you're drinking?" The emblem on the cup was from a famous tea brand.

"Oh yeah. All the time." He glanced around, but we were alone. "So how come I've never seen you before? When did you start working here?"

"Monday. I'm supposed to be a ghost. You make a mess. I clean it up."

"I'm known to make quite the mess." The way he said it sounded filthy. "How have we not crossed paths until now?"

"This is a big facility. Thirty treatment rooms, saunas, quiet rooms, salon services—"

"I don't need you to quote the specs off the website." Damon moved a little closer. "Where have you been hiding?"

"The laundry room, mostly."

"I should go in there more often." He studied my left hand while I peeled the orange. "Did you take your jewelry off before starting work?"

"How about you ask what you really want to know?" I peered down at his hand, but he didn't have a wedding band, which I knew he wouldn't. Damon Thoreau had never been married. As far as the research showed, he wasn't in a relationship, and unless I had reason to believe he was the cause of the increased liability insurance, Cross didn't want to waste the time or resources setting up surveillance.

"Are you seeing anyone?" he asked.

"No."

"How much do you hate herbal tea?"

"So very, very much." I looked down at his cup. "I can smell the espresso from here and something sweet."

"Caramel." He held out his cup. "Do you want some?"

"I'm sure those are grounds for immediate firing, and I'm already on thin ice. Thanks anyway." I finished peeling the orange, split it in half, and offered him a slice.

He shook his head. "Do you like fruit? Or are you desperate?"

"Are you saying the skirt's a bit much?"

"I like it. It might make you the most fun thing to look at

in this place."

He was on the border of inappropriate comments, but I'd been pushing the envelope. I couldn't bust him on that when I instigated. However, I wondered how many lines he'd used on the other people who worked here. Given his interactions with Terri and Willa, I didn't catch any inappropriate vibes. Maybe my attire had brought that out in him.

"You have nice legs. Strong. Toned. Do you run?" he asked.

"All the time."

"Me too. I like the paths at the park." He opened an app on his phone to show me the course he usually ran.

"I'll have to check it out."

He returned his attention to the yellow fruit he'd left on the counter. "When's the last time you had a massage?"

"Trying to drum up new business? Because it won't work. I'm a cleaning lady. Massages and pampering aren't in the cards for me."

"It's a shame." He tossed the peel into the trash and headed for the door. "I'd love to get you on my table."

After he left, I searched every inch of the break room, but I didn't find anything. What would anyone even hide in here? Narcotics? Subpoenas? Hidden cameras? Aside from tofu wraps and a pitcher of kombucha, there was nothing sinister to be found. The only place I'd find anything would be in one of the offices, and I'd have to wait until Friday to gain access. In the meantime, I had to play the part. Hopefully, my new mark would be willing to shed some light on the spa's inner workings since my coworkers on the cleaning crew hadn't been particularly helpful.

I spent the rest of the day scrubbing every surface and doing my best to make friends. Since Damon had spoken to me, I hoped the others would follow suit. After all, he was big man on campus, the quarterback, so to speak. Pushing too hard could compromise my cover, but the employees had no reason to think Spa Alive was under investigation. Cross had created the perfect background story for Alexandra Bradley. No one would suspect me of anything, so it wouldn't hurt if I painted myself as an extrovert, even if that was the farthest thing from the truth.

By the end of the day, I'd introduced myself to most of the staff again since many of them were leery or rude the first time I tried. Ellie insisted that was because I was an outsider—part of the cleaning crew. But that didn't seem to be the case today. They weren't as rude, but most of them didn't want to chat or audition for the part of my new best friend either. They kept their distance, unsure what to make of me. However, Janet, who ran the salon side of the spa, stopped me on my way back from cleaning the sauna.

"Your mascara's streaked," she said.

"I should have known better than to wear makeup to work. I just felt so blah. Thanks for letting me know." I ducked into the bathroom, surprised when she followed me. She had a makeup bag with her and unzipped it while I checked the damage in the mirror. "I won't make the same mistake again. Waterproof can't hold a candle to my allergies."

"What are you allergic to?"

"Everything."

She poured remover onto a cotton ball and handed it to me. "Try this." After I rubbed off the black streaks, she forced me to face her. "Damon said you were having trouble making friends."

Everyone loved gossip. "He's the massage therapist, right?"

She nodded, her focus on applying eyeliner and shadow to my eyes. "I thought I should welcome you to the Spa Alive family. We're a tight bunch. We don't do the best job of warming up to outsiders."

"Ellie's been here for years. She says she still gets the cold shoulder."

"There are reasons for that."

"Oh?"

Janet grabbed a brush and some mineral foundation and applied it beneath my eyes to hide the discoloration. "About a year ago, the cleaning crew threatened to strike. They accused us of deliberately making more work for them. They wanted raises and recognition. More privileges. Management didn't listen until they stopped working. Half the rooms were unusable. Eventually, they got raises, more time off, and more help. But the way they did that screwed us over. We had to cut down on our clients. We took the hit. It hurt our pocketbooks and our reputations."

"I never heard anything about that." Cross Security hadn't either.

"It wasn't publicized. It was an internal issue. But our clients knew something was wrong when we had to cancel appointments or reschedule things. We lost several."

"That sucks. I didn't know."

"Why would you? You just started here."

"True, but for the record, I'd never hang anyone out to dry."

Janet smiled. "There. Good as new." She indicated the mirror, and I turned to see that she'd expertly done my eyes, making the blue pop against the smoky dark colors. She also covered up the red puffiness and dark remnants from beneath my eyes with concealer and foundation.

"Is there anything else going on around here that I should know about? A civil war brewing? A strike? Something scandalous?"

"That skirt you're wearing is the most scandalous thing around here. Where'd you get it?"

"The department store on Tenth. It was hanging in the window, and I had to have it."

"I don't blame you. I'm pretty sure I need one too." She checked her watch. "After work, a few of us are going out for drinks. Do you want to come?"

"More kombucha?"

She laughed. "No. It's just me, Damon, and Courtney. We don't really follow the healthy lifestyle protocols like everyone else around here."

"Sure. I'd like that."

"Great. We'll see you there."

FOUR

Liquor was a great way to loosen lips. Once the booze started to flow, I hoped to gather dirt on Spa Alive. But the three other people at the table only had fun stories to share. Most were work-related. A few had to do with classes they'd taken or books they'd read. Unlike the majority of the staff, Damon, Courtney, and Janet didn't buy into a lot of the more outlandish wellness practices and theories.

"Do you want another drink?" Damon put his hand on my knee, as if on accident, testing to see how I'd react. He was smooth to the point it could bleed into criminal.

"Sure." I wondered if he'd try to roofie me. But he didn't.

"How did you end up a cleaning lady?" Courtney asked.

"I needed money and couldn't find anything else." Alexandra Bradley didn't have an extensive cover story. She dropped out of college, worked a bunch of part-time gigs, and bounced around to make ends meet. "What sold me was the medical and dental." I sipped my drink. "What made you decide you wanted to touch naked people for a living?"

Janet's unexpected laugh caused her to choke. She sputtered a few times, wiping her face.

Courtney scowled. "I watched a family member suffer terribly, so I was always curious about pain management and alternatives to pharmaceuticals and surgical interventions. Originally, I thought I'd be a chiropractor, but it wasn't in the cards."

"That's admirable. So the urban legends aren't true about

massage parlors being fronts for brothels?"

"Spa Alive isn't like that." Courtney's eyes narrowed. "I don't know about any other place."

"I've heard some things about the less reputable establishments." Damon rested his elbow on the table, turning to face me. "When I worked at a few of them, I may have been propositioned a time or two."

"No way." Janet's eyes went wide. "Who asked? What did they ask?"

Damon shook his head. "It's not worth repeating. Client privacy and all."

"You were never tempted?" I asked.

"If you'd seen the people who asked, you'd understand."

"That's the only reason?"

His brows knit together. "I've never been that hard up for money."

"Or that hard up," Janet teased.

Damon laughed good-naturedly.

This was getting me nowhere. "Where did you work before Spa Alive?" I'd checked his resume, but none of his previous jobs had triggered red flags.

"A couple of places. It doesn't matter."

"Did any clients follow you when you left?"

"A few. Why are you so fascinated by this?"

I indicated the empty glass. "Alcohol takes away my filter which means it's time I go home before I say or do something I'll regret. Thanks for inviting me out. I had fun." I reached into my bag and pulled out enough cash to cover my share of the drinks. "I'll see you guys tomorrow. I'll be the one in pink cleaning up your messes."

"You're not driving, are you?" Janet asked.

"No. I'll call for a ride."

"I'm heading out too. How about I wait with you?" Damon offered. He looked at Janet and Courtney. "Behave yourselves. It's not the weekend yet."

"Spoil sport," Janet said.

Damon pushed the door open, holding it while he waited for me to walk through first. "Why were you asking all those questions?"

"You said you wanted to get me on your table." I turned

up the flirtation. "I wondered who else has been on your table. There are a lot of adult videos dedicated to things of that nature."

He gave me a sexy grin. "That's not a service clients pay for."

"Shame. I bet it'd pay better than whatever you're making."

"I make more than enough. I don't charge for experiences like that."

"You ever date any clients?" I ran a hand down the center of his button-up shirt. Hopefully, he'd think I had some kind of fantasy I wanted to play out, as opposed to gathering intel.

"No."

"That's not what I heard."

"Spa Alive has rules against sexual relationships between clients and staff."

"They also have rules against caffeine on the premises."

"That's different."

I could see it on his face. "You dated a client." The flirtation was gone. "Did you get in trouble?"

"Not exactly. She found another spa when we hooked up."

"You don't give massages off the books?"

"I do, but it wasn't about that."

"Who was she?"

"Someone I thought I knew a lot better than I did." He shook it away. "Let's not talk about that. It's ancient history. Why don't you come back to my place, and I'll show you exactly what the fuss is about."

"I shouldn't."

"But you want to."

I didn't. But I had a job to do, so I let him call a car to take us back to his place.

Damon Thoreau lived in a nice townhouse in a quiet neighborhood. I half-expected to find a bachelor pad, but he didn't have the den furniture or big screen TV. The place was furnished nicely. Not a lot of clutter or knickknacks. Copies of his degree and certification were framed on the wall beside a few photos of graduation day with his parents.

He didn't have any other framed photos. He had a few

decorative pieces, mostly metal art, which hung on the wall. The surfaces were clean, except for the desk in the corner. I wandered over, noticing a stack of mail.

"May I have some water?" I asked.

"Sure." He went into the kitchen. "Have you always lived in the city?"

"Yeah, pretty much. How about you?" I flipped through the envelopes. Most of it looked like junk or bills. No letters. No summons. No legal documents. Moving away from the desk, I examined the graduation photo. "Your parents look proud."

"They are."

"If I had told my mother I wanted to be a massage therapist, I would have been kicked out of the house." I took the offered glass. "I was raised to believe professionals had to wear suits and sit behind a desk. They've never approved of anything I've done. I was always their biggest regret. A disappointment."

Damon brushed a strand of hair out of my face. "That sounds like the first real thing you've said all day."

The context was fabricated, but the sentiment wasn't. Was he onto my other lies? The last time I worked undercover, I'd been playing a version of myself. Maybe I'd gotten rusty pretending to be someone else. "I have problems letting people in."

"I believe that too."

"Takes one to know one." I put the glass down. "Tell me who the real Damon Thoreau is."

He ran his fingertips up my arm. "What you see is what you get." He moved to kiss me, but I turned my head. "Would you like that massage first?"

I shook my head. "This was a mistake. I should go. I'm sorry."

"What's wrong? You seemed into this earlier. We flirted in the break room. You came out for drinks. What changed?"

"I don't know a single thing about you, other than what you do for a living."

"Does that matter?"

"It might. You could be a serial killer."

"I'm not."

"How would I know?" I gave him a pointed look. "For all I know, all your exes are dead."

"You're acting a little crazy."

"Prove me wrong."

He sighed dramatically. "Lorna Pagano. Look her up. She's alive and well."

Giving him a suspicious look, I entered her name into my phone. Her family owned a brewery. They weren't the Rockefellers, but her social media accounts led me to believe she took the family jet for the weekend to visit Ibiza. "She's the client you dated."

"As you can see, she's alive and well." He slid his hands against my sides before pulling me closer. "Now how about that massage?"

"Can I use your bathroom first? I'd like to freshen up." I stood on my tiptoes and nipped at his ear. "Maybe we'll skip the massage part."

"Whatever you want, babe. But I'd be happy to work out your kinks." He pointed to a doorway. "Bathroom's right there."

"Thanks." I headed for the door, my heart hammering in my chest. I had a name. It may not lead anywhere, but it was a start. If there was dirt on Damon, it'd trace back to her. It had to. But I couldn't worry about what kind of dirt I'd find once I started digging. Right now, I had to figure out how to get out of here without blowing my cover or ruining my chances of gaining additional intel from the mark.

Shutting the door, I took a few deep breaths, searched the entire bathroom, and texted Cross. *Call me in seven minutes with an emergency.* I stared at the screen, but he didn't reply. He better not have my number blocked. I needed an out. Briefly, I thought about texting the same request to my cop friends, but they were liable to send a tactical team to storm the building. Martin would follow through, but I didn't want to tell him why I needed him to call. If he found out I had gone back to a strange man's apartment under the pretext of having sex, he might send out his own tactical team to handle the situation.

Just as I flushed the toilet and finished washing my hands, Cross replied to my text. *You got it.*

A part of me wondered if he waited that long because he wanted me to sweat. Letting it go, I checked my reflection in the mirror and stepped out of the bathroom. Dropping my purse on the chair, I wandered back into the living room where Damon was waiting. He had unbuttoned the cuffs on his shirt and rolled up his sleeves. When he saw me, a smile tugged at his lips.

"Have I mentioned I like that skirt?" he asked.

"I wore it for you."

"Really?"

"You are the best looking thing at work. I wanted to get your attention. Until today, you never even noticed me."

"We didn't cross paths."

"We did, but I blended in."

"That's why you were making a big deal about how the staff wouldn't speak to you. It all makes sense now."

That had nothing to do with it, but small talk would delay the inevitable, and I needed to waste time for the next five and a half minutes. "That probably sounds a little crazy, but then again, you already said I was crazy."

"I like crazy." He took my hand and led me toward the couch. He sat down and pulled me onto his lap, forcing me to straddle him. The skirt hitched up my thigh, but he didn't notice the end of my scar peeking out from beneath the material. I smoothed it back in place before he noticed. His hands went to my low back, his fingers digging in. "You're tense. Relax."

"Is that what you tell your clients?"

He grinned. "Are you sure you don't want that massage?" His fingers ran up my back. The pressure and paths they took were the result of years of experience. He knew the human body, but he didn't know mine.

My breath hitched when he hit a sore spot, and I winced.

He moved his hand downward, gentler now. "Does that hurt?"

"Are you playing doctor?" What was taking Cross so long?

"No." He cocked his head to the side, feeling along the bottom of my shoulder blade and ribcage. "Something feels like it's out of alignment."

"You're not a chiropractor, remember?"

He ignored my joking tone and slid his fingers around my shoulder blade, making me hiss. "Let me get my table. It won't take more than twenty minutes to rub that knot out."

"I thought you said it was an alignment issue. Do I need my tires rotated too?"

He didn't say whatever devious thought came to mind. For the briefest moment, he reminded me a little of Martin. "The knotted muscle fibers are what's putting pressure on your shoulder, causing you to compensate, which is making your side and back hurt."

"I'm pretty sure that's from mopping."

"Twenty minutes." He extricated me from his lap and went into the other room to grab a black, cushioned contraption that he unfolded into a portable massage table. "Hop up."

"Aren't you supposed to tell me to take my clothes off first?"

"I thought you might let me help you with that after."

Before I could say anything else, my phone rang. It was about damn time. "One sec." I held up my hand before grabbing my bag and taking my phone out. I gave the caller ID a bewildered look.

"Who is it?"

"My brother." I waited for it to ring again. "He never calls."

"You should take it." Damon went to grab the coconut oil, convinced the call couldn't have been planned as an escape since he had to insist I answer it. *And that's how you do it, ladies and gentlemen.*

FIVE

"Lorna Pagano's name isn't in our records." I stared at the data on the screen before double-checking the printed copy. "We don't know about any of Spa Alive's former clients. We don't have those details. And we never even noticed. We only have the client data from the last six weeks. Nothing before."

"They must have purged former clients from the system. Which computer did you plug that drive into?" Amir asked.

"The one in the lobby. It's the only computer I could access. I haven't been inside the offices yet."

"They must have those records stored elsewhere. They couldn't destroy them."

"Even with changing privacy laws?"

"No, they'd need that data, especially if they're facing a lawsuit."

"Unless they wanted to get rid of it before being compelled to turn it over. Discovery can be a bitch." I slid away from the workstation I was using to see what was on Amir's screen. "Did you get anything off that spreadsheet?"

"I'd say it's a money thing. Earnings versus expenses. But they aren't quarterlies. I think Spa Alive is considering raising its prices. This looks like market research."

"That doesn't help us."

"Do you think every piece of intel you find should be useful?"

"Yes." But that'd never be the case. "The most likely

source of a pending lawsuit would be a former client who was harmed. We've been looking at this all wrong."

"That would make the most sense, but wouldn't they have filed by now? We know everyone who's been to the spa in the last six weeks. Why would they wait so long?"

"It depends on the statute of limitations, how long it takes to find an attorney willing to take the case, and the research she has to do. At least now I know what to look for when I search the offices tomorrow night."

"Shouldn't you have figured this out sooner?" Cross asked from the doorway.

I turned, surprised to see him still at work. He wasn't in his usual suit. He had on jeans and a t-shirt with his hair spiked and gelled. I'd seen him like this once or twice before. Every time, it was a shock to my system. "I was following your lead. You said dig through what we had. You missed it too."

His eyes narrowed. "Why did you need the rescue call?"

"I didn't want to have sex with Damon."

Amir nearly choked. But he covered it in a cough and kept his eyes glued to the screen in front of him.

"My office. Now." Cross didn't wait before heading for the stairs.

"I get out of trouble with one guy only to get in trouble with another." I looked at Amir. "Any chance I can get you to call my phone in four minutes and claim there's an emergency?"

"I'm sorry, Ms. Parker."

"Me too." Leaving the expert to build a profile on Lorna Pagano, I took the stairs and met Cross in his office. The executive level was empty. Even Justin had gone home for the night. Noting the time, I wondered if Martin would be home from work yet. I doubted it. He worked almost as many late nights as I did. Maybe more.

Cross poured a drink from the cart in the corner and took a sip before folding his arms over his chest. He wasn't pleased.

"Did I do something wrong?" The sarcasm bled from every word.

"We are operating blind. We have no idea what kind of

lawsuit the spa could be facing or what allegations may be surfacing. Why would you put yourself in danger like that, Alex?"

"Danger? I went home with a guy, one with no known criminal record. I don't see what the problem is." I eyed him up and down. "You sure as hell aren't the morality police. It looks like you had every intention of picking someone up tonight. Let me guess, you're mad because I cut your night short." He opened his mouth to speak, but I didn't give him the chance. "I didn't ask you to come back to the office. All I needed was an excuse to leave. I told you that before we disconnected."

"You said you had a possible lead."

"So? Don't you think I'm capable of running it down on my own?"

He drained the contents of the glass, put it on the tray, and approached me. "I need you to be more careful."

"This isn't a dangerous assignment. The biggest risk to my well-being is anaphylaxis when my allergies go into overdrive." Every conversation we had and every worried look I'd seen on his face played through my mind. "You're worried about me, about my safety. Why?"

"You don't have the best track record."

"That's been going on since the day we met, since the first case you gave me. This is something else. What's going on, Lucien?"

"Nothing. But now that you're a Cross Security employee—"

"I've always been an employee." Even if I preferred the term private contractor. It was a game I played with myself to ease the commitment-phobe anxiety. "Nothing's changed, unless you're terrified I'll drop dead before you get your money back. If you're so worried, Martin will pay back the remaining balance on my debt."

"I don't give a shit about the money." He circled, his hand running through his hair. "I gave you this case. The last case I forced you to take, the one you didn't want, the one you fought me on—"

"This is about what happened in L.A.? I didn't know you cared."

"Of course, I care. James Martin's bodyguard was nearly killed. You and James could have been shot."

That's what this was about—Martin. I should have known. "Should I dredge up the other plum assignments you've given me that have resulted in bloodshed? Because I've been in much worse scrapes and much worse danger, and you never batted an eye afterward. If I remember correctly, you once told me getting shot wasn't that big of a deal. So tell me, what do you want from Martin this time?"

"Nothing."

"That's not true. Admit it. Your concern about the danger of me being alone with Damon has nothing to do with your fears and everything to do with what Martin will think. You're afraid he won't approve of his girlfriend dating someone else to satisfy the requirements of a case you assigned me."

"Watch yourself. I sign your paychecks."

"Feel free to stop anytime you want." I stared Cross down the same way I would any suspect on the wrong side of an interrogation. "Tell me what you want from Martin."

"He owns the proprietary rights. I can only move ahead on the body armor with his permission. It's best that I don't piss him off."

I wasn't surprised, but the truth hurt, just a little. "I'm a pawn to you. A means to an end, and a worker bee for the interim."

"Alex, that isn't the whole story. You're twisting things."

"Are we done?"

"No."

"Too bad. I have work to do."

Leaving his office, I stopped by the lab, checked to see if Amir had found anything important, told him to leave whatever he had in my dropbox, and went home. I could look into Lorna Pagano and her father's company from the comfort of my apartment. Right now, this building was the last place I wanted to be.

When I got home, no one was there. I sent a text to Martin to make sure we hadn't gotten our wires crossed. He assured me we were staying at the apartment tonight. We'd go back to his house next week, but with the international calls and meetings he had scheduled, he preferred staying closer to the office. It saved time on the commute, and it gave us more time together. Even though, it didn't feel like it.

After opening and closing every cabinet at least twice and checking the pantry and fridge four times, I stopped pacing. Lucien Cross always had an ulterior motive. That was old news. This shouldn't bother me. He hired me as a way of getting into Martin's good graces. He sent me to open the L.A. office so I'd be close to Martin. Everything else that happened wasn't his fault. I didn't blame him, not anymore. Bruiser was on the road to recovery. Martin and I were fine. All's well that ends well. But Cross couldn't leave it alone.

Maybe it was because he'd finally fooled me into thinking he cared. He showed up when I needed him. He had my back, even if he bitched about it. He said he trusted me, valued me to handle things for him. But none of that was about me. Could I trust him if Martin wasn't in the picture? My gut said yes, but the broken and bruised part of me said no.

"Fuck." Tears threatened to fall. This wasn't just about Cross. It was about everything. It hadn't been that long since I confronted my adoptive father and finally closed the book on that. For the last few weeks, everyone had been tiptoeing around me, expecting me to fall into old patterns. But I was fine. Or I thought I was. I wanted to be. I wanted to be done. It shouldn't matter.

Mark Jablonsky's words came to mind. If I called Mark now, I'd cry. And I didn't want to.

Instead, I forced myself to get back to work. After an hour of looking into Lorna Pagano and her ties to Damon Thoreau, I closed my laptop lid and crawled onto the couch. After flipping until I found a classic cartoon, I stared at the screen. I could wallow tonight. Tomorrow, I'd get my ass back to work. Nothing had to change.

An hour and a half later, the key scraped in the lock. I thought about reaching for my nine millimeter but decided against it. Instead, I remained where I was, my eyes on the screen. The door opened, and Martin stepped inside.

"Sweetheart, you didn't have to wait up." He locked the

door, securing the various bolts before putting his bag down and dropping his jacket and tie on top of it. He gave the TV a concerned look before bending down to kiss me. "Is everything okay?"

"Yep."

His green eyes spoke volumes. "What happened?"

"Lucien and I got into it." He glanced at my knuckles to see if they were bruised, which made me snicker. "I didn't hit him."

"What did you fight about?" Martin stood in front of me, unbuttoning his shirt while we talked.

"You."

"Did you tell him I'm already spoken for?" he teased.

"He knows."

"But he has a hard time not getting what he wants." Martin pulled his shirt free from where it was tucked in. "I know the type."

"You are the type."

"So are you, sweetheart." He gave me another uncertain look, aware I hadn't moved. "Did you eat dinner?"

"It's two a.m."

"Fine. We'll have breakfast together in the morning. I don't want you to starve." He cocked his head to the side. "I like the skirt. But you don't look comfortable. Why didn't you get changed?"

"I could say I kept it on so I'd look nice for you, but the truth is I couldn't be bothered taking it off."

"You don't usually wear that to work."

"I had a date."

"Oh?" Martin headed for the bedroom. "Was he hot?"

"He's a massage therapist."

"You didn't answer my question, so I'm guessing the answer is yes."

"He reminds me a little of you."

"Shit. Should I be jealous?"

"He's a massage therapist," I repeated.

"So he's an Adonis with great hands. It's weird. My parents never told me I had an identical twin."

I sat up. "You know I don't like people touching me."

Martin stepped out of the bedroom. "He touched you?"

Though we'd been teasing, the look in his eyes said he might kill the guy.

"No. He's a mark on the case I'm working. Before any touching could occur, I had Lucien get me out of there."

A thought crossed Martin's mind, and he smirked. "You kissed me when I got home."

"So?"

"That means you didn't kiss him."

"I had no intention of kissing him."

Martin smiled. "Good."

"You know I'd never—"

"I know, sweetheart. Neither of us likes to share. As far as I remember, that's the only hard and fast rule you had when it came to us."

"You don't have the same rule," I said. Martin's stipulation was that I always made it home alive. Lying was also frowned upon.

"Because I know you'd never do that to me." He grabbed my plush pajama shorts and one of his t-shirts and brought them into the living room. "Are you sure you don't want something to eat?"

"My stomach's in knots."

"Because of Lucien or the case?"

"The two are inextricably linked." I shook my head and returned to my previous position. "How was your day?"

"I have a few things I need to check. Why don't you go to bed? I'll be there in a few minutes."

"I'm not ready for bed yet."

Normally, Martin would make a suggestive quip. Instead, he patted the clothes he brought out. "In case you'd rather be comfortable. You don't even have to get up to change."

He knew me so well. And he knew whatever happened tonight had left me a little worse for wear.

"I love you."

He pressed his lips to my temple before grabbing his belongings off the chair. "Give me twenty minutes, tops."

While he was gone, I shimmied out of the skirt, tugged on the plush shorts, and changed into his t-shirt. It was the purple one he always hid from me. Tossing my clothes onto the chair, I went back to staring at the screen.

When Martin returned, he climbed onto the couch, wedging himself between me and the backrest. "I don't deserve you," I said.

"Hey," he slid his hand across my waist, forcing me to turn toward him, "we're not doing that. You know it isn't true."

I disagreed, but I wasn't stupid enough to argue. Instead, I kissed him. "Does that mean I get to keep your shirt?"

"Just for tonight."

I turned back to face the TV. He reached behind us and turned off the table lamp. After tossing the throw on top of us, he wrapped his arms around me. Martin hated sleeping on the couch, but tonight, he didn't argue or suggest otherwise.

SIX

I showed up to the morning meeting late. Part of me didn't want to go, but this was work. I couldn't skip it. Not anymore. Not when I was indebted to Cross, despite what he did or how much he tried to hold things over my head.

The conference room was almost full. I sat in the only empty chair beside Kellan Dey and looked at the items piled on the table in front of me. Cross met my eyes, but he didn't berate. He continued speaking, never missing a beat.

Kellan tapped his pen against the sticky note on the folder which had my name on it.

I nodded my thanks and opened it to find intel on Lorna Pagano and Damon Thoreau. The techs had been busy digging up dirt. Given the nature of the photos, I didn't think these had been on the internet. A computer or phone had been hacked, but it was best that I not ask those kinds of questions.

"All right. You have your assignments. Get to it." Cross's gaze bore into me. "Ms. Parker, hang back a sec. I need to speak to you."

"Don't leave me," I whispered to Kellan.

He snickered. "I'll see you later, Alex." He moved around the table, pausing behind Cross and mouthing, "You'll be fine."

I didn't think so, but Kellan didn't know what transpired the previous night. Even if he did, he was under the misguided belief Cross favored me. He didn't understand why, but that point had been hammered home last night.

"Sir?"

Cross waited for the last investigator to file out and the door to close before he let out a sigh. "Don't start that. Things got twisted last night. The point I was attempting to make was misconstrued. I want you to know your safety is important to me." He nodded at the N95 face mask and prescription pill bottle. "The medical staff assured me that should help with your allergies. Most cleaning crews provide personal protection equipment for handling chemicals and hazardous materials."

"It's a spa."

"That doesn't make them exempt." He jerked his chin at the mask. "It'll help."

"If nothing else, it'll keep Damon from getting too frisky." I held up one of the photos of him and Lorna in a compromising position. "Is she the reason Spa Alive wants added liability insurance?"

"I don't know. That's your job to figure out. But she had a torrid affair with the massage therapist. She stopped going to Spa Alive around the time they started dating. If you flip to the back cover, you'll find an interesting photo."

I wasn't sure I wanted to see what other Cirque du Soleil sex positions they'd tried. But I flipped to the end anyway. Several photos of Lorna Pagano which had been scraped from various sources, including social media, were included. Her skin was badly blistered, especially her face and neck. A few other photos showed the damage ran along her collarbones and covered her hands. I checked the dates the photos were taken. "This happened while she was a Spa Alive client."

"We believe she had a bad reaction to a treatment. Amir's checking to see if anyone else has made any claims or reports."

"She posted this on her social media account?" I indicated the square photo.

"She took it down almost immediately. It's why we didn't find it and why it didn't ping when we did a deep dive on Spa Alive's reviews. She never tagged them or anyone who works there or goes there."

"I didn't find any negative reviews anywhere. At least nothing actionable or indicating injury to this extent."

"Like you pointed out last night, we were looking in the wrong place."

I checked the dates again. It was months ago. "This is around the same time the cleaning crew threatened to strike and stopped working. Could that be the cause?"

"Until we get a look at Pagano's medical records, we can't rule anything out."

Those were difficult to access. "If this was a cleanliness issue, some sort of bacteria or fungus could have contaminated the place. She wouldn't be the only one affected. Spa Alive could be facing several lawsuits or even a class action suit."

"I'm aware. But until we know the actual cause and diagnosis, we can't jump to conclusions."

Turning back to the earlier photos, I examined the images and limited correspondence we had between Lorna and Damon. "Do you think she was using him to get dirt on the spa?"

"Possibly."

I thought about the things I'd asked and the conversation I had with Damon yesterday, but it left me with more questions than answers. "According to everyone I've spoken to, there have never been any incidents or medical issues that arose from the procedures or treatments at Spa Alive."

"People lie."

"No shit."

He cleared his throat. "You should know, I worry about your safety, just like I worry about the safety of every person who works here. That has nothing to do with James Martin or my desire to remain in his good graces."

"You don't want to get sued either."

"That is not the reason." He ran a hand through his hair before placing his palms flat on the table. I'd struck a nerve. I could see it in the way the fire burned in his eyes. "This case is making me twitchy. I don't know why. There's no reason it should. But it is, and every time I get twitchy, bad things happen. Very bad things. Something about this is making you uneasy too. It's why you called me last night.

Under any other circumstance, you would have found your own way out."

"I'm trying to be a team player."

"Do you think I'm wrong?"

"I don't think Damon's a predator." I indicated the file. "Given what your techs uncovered, that seems even less likely now. But something isn't right with that place." I checked the time. "I have to go. The manager won't like it if I'm late."

"While you're cleaning the offices tonight, make sure you plug that into every computer you find. We need their files." He pointed to the USB sitting beside the folder. "Amir made it simple. Plug and play. Just make sure you take it with you when you leave."

"I have done this before." I tucked the drive into my pocket and picked up the rest. "Allergy medicine makes me sleepy."

"It makes everyone sleepy. But I don't want you to go into anaphylaxis. I would like you to remain alive and breathing, if possible."

"Is that so you can boss me around?"

"I do rather enjoy it."

"I know. Justin warned me."

"I'll need to remind him not to speak to you." Cross held the conference room door open for me so I could exit. "Hey, Alex," he said before I escaped into the elevator, "be careful. I'd hate to have to find someone to replace you."

I snorted, unable to hide my grin. "You're such an asshole."

"I've been called a lot worse. You've called me worse."

I stepped into the elevator. "You'd only know that if you have my office bugged."

"Touché."

*   *   *

Fridays were busy days at Spa Alive. Dozens of clients had sessions booked. A bachelorette party had plans to spend the afternoon primping and preparing for the big day. It was all-hands on deck for the cleaning crew. Despite having the extra help, we were slammed.

"Hey," Damon snuck up behind me while I was on my way to clean the sauna, "is your brother okay?"

"He's doing better. I sat through a meeting with him this morning." Which wasn't a lie. "He had a bad night." Also not a lie. "He's back on the straight and narrow. Working the steps. Doing what he needs to." That may have been a stretch.

"He's lucky to have you," Damon said. "Doesn't he have a sponsor?"

"What can I say? He called me instead."

"You two sound close."

"You have no idea."

Damon snickered. "No wonder you carry around so much tension in your shoulders. Having an addict in the family must be tough. Keeping secrets is always hard."

"Speaking from experience?"

Damon shook his head.

"Really? You aren't hiding anything?" I wheedled.

"No, but maybe you'd like to come over tonight, and I can work that knot out of your back."

"I can't. It's Friday. I'll be working late."

"Okay. How about sometime this weekend?"

"You have my number. It's probably best if we play it by ear." I had to figure out how to grill him on Lorna Pagano, but brilliance hadn't struck yet. It may have been on account of the fumes from the cleaners or the damn essential oils.

Damon flicked the mask, which hung loosely beneath my chin. "At least you're doing something for your allergies. That should help, but for it to work, you have to wear it."

"Yeah, I got it." Lifting it up, I reached for the strap and adjusted it. Once I was properly outfitted, I opened the door and was immediately assaulted by lavender. Fortunately, the scent was drastically dulled. The mask wasn't perfect, but it made a significant difference. My eyes didn't water. I didn't have a sneezing fit. And my sinuses didn't immediately clog. At least my fight with Cross resulted in a tangible benefit. Maybe we should argue more often.

The next few hours flew by. The dull roar which had been coming from the salon finally quieted. The bachelorette party must have left. I thought about poking my head inside to say something to Janet, but I had two rooms waiting to be cleaned.

Opening the first door, I froze. *Not again.* Someone remained in the tub. I must have gotten my room numbers confused. Quietly closing the door, I went in search of Willa to see what I was supposed to clean instead. But the hallways were empty. Had everyone been abducted by aliens? Maybe they'd all gone home and forgot to tell me it was quitting time.

I looked at the clock on the wall. It was definitely too early for this kind of lull.

Peering into the break room, I found Willa unconscious on the floor. Rushing inside, I checked her pulse and made sure she was breathing. "Hey, I need help," I called, but no one answered.

I pulled my cell phone from the front pocket of my smock, glad I'd worn khakis instead of that dumb skirt. I dialed 9-1-1 and pressed send. Nothing. Pulling the device away from my ear, I noticed I didn't have a signal.

Getting up, I hurried to the lobby. That was the nearest landline. I nudged the door before my mind caught up to the scene in front of me. Four armed men wearing gas masks had taken up positions inside the main room. Two of them were securing the front door. The other was checking the computer. The woman assigned to work the front desk was slumped to the side.

A masked man gently slid her off the chair and onto the floor. The sound of me bumping the door made one of them turn toward me. I didn't wait to see what would happen. Instead, I ran down the hallway.

On my way, I spotted several of my coworkers unconscious. *The gas masks.* Those creeps must have pumped knockout gas through the ventilation system. Why wasn't I affected?

Almost as soon as the thought hit, I felt lightheaded. I needed oxygen, fresh air, before I passed out. The N95 must have filtered out enough of the contaminant that I hadn't gone down for the count yet. But I would soon enough.

Think, Parker, where are the windows that open? I kept

moving, even though it was getting harder to concentrate. Whoever heard me at the door would see me if I didn't get out of the hallway. The outer room which contained the sauna had a window that opened. It was a security feature.

Pushing the door open, I stumbled to the window. I had to stay upright. The small rectangular window had a crank that caused it to push out a few inches. Once I had it open, I pulled the mask down and stuck my head in the opening, using my forearms to anchor me in place.

My head spun. The desire to lie down and not get up was becoming harder to resist. My limbs felt heavy and sluggish. My head weighed a thousand tons. I sucked in more air until I felt strong enough to fight the sedative. Then I took deeper breaths, filling my lungs until my chest ached before releasing it and repeating the process. Ever since my surfing debacle, I'd been working on increasing my lung capacity. Some people could hold their breath for minutes at a time. I hadn't timed my attempts, but I had to be past three minutes. The breathing exercises forced enough fresh air and oxygen into my system to counteract whatever I'd inhaled.

When the dizziness abated, I took another deep breath from the window and pulled out my phone. Still, no signal. Those bastards must have jammers. I tried switching to Wi-Fi, only to remember Spa Alive didn't believe in such things.

I scanned for surrounding networks, but I couldn't find any. The jammers could have been blocking them too, or none of the other businesses were close enough for me to pick up their signals. The spa was self-contained with lots of greenery surrounding it.

I had to get my priorities in order. Four men had invaded the building. As far as I knew, everyone inside had been knocked unconscious. Since I didn't know what was being piped into the building, I hoped it was non-lethal, but I didn't know. Everyone's best bet at survival was to get out of here as soon as possible.

What did those men want? This was a spa. I'd searched the entire building except the offices. The spa didn't keep a lot of cash on hand. There were no narcotics. No controlled substances of any kind. The place was lousy with oil, essential and massage, not crude or anything worth a damn. So what was this about?

I thought about the clients. Who had appointments today? Spa Alive's customers were wealthy. Could this be a kidnapping? What if it was a hostage situation or robbery? Did this have anything to do with the liability coverage?

Shaking the thoughts away, I had to get out of here. I had to determine the situation, and I had to get help. I put my mask back on and crept to the door.

I'd seen four hostiles in the lobby. But only one followed me into the hallway. He was checking each room as he went. Had he seen me? Or was he making sure everyone was sound asleep? Maybe he was taking a headcount.

I watched as he entered the room where I'd found the first victim in the tub, but I hadn't realized that's what I was seeing. Stupid privacy rules. If I hadn't been reprimanded that first time, I would have caught on sooner. Maybe I could have done something before they breached.

My lungs burned, and I went back to the window to catch my breath. I wouldn't last long like this. I had to find a way out. The thought of leaving everyone else behind bothered me, but the only way I could help anyone would be to get out of here.

A sound outside the room told me he was close. I looked around for a place to hide. He had a gun and a gas mask. I didn't. In a fight, my oxygen would be depleted too quickly, assuming he didn't shoot me first.

Hastily, I pulled the mask off, tucked it in my pocket, and got on the ground. I waited until the door creaked open before I closed my eyes. Don't breathe. Don't move.

He walked in, checking every nook and cranny. Opening the doors to the sauna, he peered inside, but the steam room was empty. He left the door open and approached me. He leered down at me. I could feel the weight of his stare. Would he put a bullet in me to make sure I wasn't faking?

Don't move, the voice in my head reminded me. After another ten seconds, he gave my thigh a gentle kick. I didn't react.

He circled. Deciding I was down for the count, he approached the window. When I heard the squeak of the crank, I climbed to my feet and pounced. My head swam, maybe from lack of oxygen or the crap being pumped into the air. But I wouldn't let that stop me. Jumping on his back, I wrapped my legs around his torso and yanked the mask off his face.

He tried to fight me, but he hadn't been expecting the surprise attack. The Glock 17, which had been in his hand, he had tucked into his holster when he went to close the window. While he bucked, grabbing for me and knocking me against the tiled walls, I pulled the gun free. Before I could cold-cock him, his knees buckled.

I fell to the side when he crumpled. Scrambling away, I fought the urge to suck in air. My lungs burned, my vision becoming dull, the edges disappearing into darkness. The rational part of my brain told me to check him first, make sure he was down for the count, but survival instincts demanded I prioritize breathing. So I launched myself at the window, pushing it a few inches outward before sucking in several ragged gasps.

Slow, deep breaths, my inner voice said. But I couldn't control my breathing. Right now, I needed oxygen. Once I felt stable, I turned, relieved to find him passed out on the floor.

The gas mask had obscured his features, but now that it was off, I got a good look at him. Dark, greasy hair. A week's worth of beard growth. A small scar on his cheek. Instead of committing those things to memory, I snapped a photo and saved it on my phone. The useless device had to be good for something.

Scooping up the gas mask, I pulled it on over my face, adjusted the straps, and took a tentative breath. I couldn't detect anything in the air. I took another breath. When I didn't feel woozy, I decided to keep it. It was nice he brought me a present.

SEVEN

The armed men outside would eventually come looking for their missing pal. The longer it took for them to find him, the better the chances were of help arriving before things turned ugly. But it wasn't like I could stick him in a coat closet or stuff him in the washing machine.

First things first. I searched him. No wallet. No ID. No phone. Not that it would have been much use anyway. The tactical vest he wore could come in handy, so I unstrapped the Velcro and tugged it free from beneath him.

He grunted, but he didn't open his eyes. Realizing my mistake, I closed the window. Since everyone else was conked out, I didn't see why this guy should get special treatment. I just hoped I wasn't signing everyone's death sentences, including his. What were they piping into this place?

Stripping out of my smock, I strapped on the tactical vest and moved the items from the smock into my pants pockets. I checked the magazine in his gun, chambered a round, and tucked it at the small of my back. I'd prefer my nine millimeter, but that was in my locker. I wasn't sure if I'd be able to get to it or even if I should try. But I'd figure that out later. First, I had to move this guy.

Grabbing him beneath the arms, I dragged him into the empty sauna and closed the door. With any luck, whoever came looking wouldn't bother to check in there. But I didn't hold out much hope. Unfortunately, that was the best I could do.

"Hey," I said, giving him a shake, but he didn't wake. Part of me wanted to grill him for answers on what was happening and why he was here, but given the unknown situation and lack of restraints, that would be a dumb idea. Plus, I wasn't sure if fresh air would be enough to rouse him. If this was some kind of aerosolized anesthetic, which is what I assumed, it could take hours for the effects to wear off.

My goal had to be getting out of the building. Once I was out, I'd call for help. That was the plan. Easy peasy.

I cracked the door open and peered into the hallway. Since three of the men had set up shop in the lobby, going out the front would be a fool's errand. Instead, I'd try the back door.

Since I'd been working here, no one had used the back entrance for anything. There was a good chance it had an alarm. Should I risk it? Maybe I could disable it. Why hadn't I paid more attention?

I crept down the hall. Movement from the other side of the salon doors caught my eye. People were lying everywhere. The bachelorette party hadn't left. They'd blacked out. Janet and Terri were on the floor, along with a pair of legs that I didn't immediately recognize. One of the men was pilfering through the women's belongings.

Don't engage. But I wanted to. I wasn't used to doing nothing. Fleeing felt like cowardice. But I had to be smart. I was outnumbered and outgunned. I had to get help or even the odds. *Go out, call for help, and come back in. Hurry, Parker.*

I stopped where the hallway split, pressed my back against the wall, and peered around the side. Two armed men stood in front of the back door. One had an assault rifle hanging at his side. I couldn't tell what kind of hardware the other was carrying, but he was armed. I was a good shot, but taking out two guys would be difficult even if they weren't wearing tactical vests and gas masks. The noise would surely attract the third, who'd come at me from behind while I was trying to get the door open.

Every seminar and lecture I'd heard said that escalating

the situation was not advisable. Gunfire would be met with more gunfire. Even if the armed men didn't kill me, they could retaliate against any of the dozens of unconscious and helpless people inside the spa. I needed a better plan. Any plan.

If these two were at the back and the third was in the salon, the front should be clear. Reversing course, I hurried toward the lobby as quickly as I could without making too much noise. My biggest fear was the rubber soles on my shoes letting out a squeak. So I had to be careful how I moved.

Once I made it to the lobby door, I peered inside. *How many of you assholes are there?*

One guy paraded in front of the door. Another man remained at the computer, a gun on the desk inches from his hand. He kept his eyes on the screen. He had the details of the security system open in front of him. The red buttons indicated the system was armed. A few chairs had been stacked in front of the doors as a makeshift barricade. These bastards had no intention of going anywhere. They were holing up. But why and for how long?

Since the front and back doors were out of the picture, I'd have to find another way out of the building. None of the windows that opened were large enough for me to climb through. A few of the picture windows might suffice, but that was thick glass. I'd need something heavy to break through. And that would make noise.

Letting that thought stew, I crept past the lobby and down the side hallway toward the offices. I hadn't explored them. But they had phones and computers, hardwired computers with internet access. Hoping the bastards hadn't done something to disable the internet, I went into the manager's office. Kathy Walters wasn't passed out at her desk. In fact, I had no idea where she was. Had she left for the day? Stepped out for lunch? Or was she in one of the many rooms I hadn't explored with Damon, Courtney, and the rest of the staff?

I closed the door and turned the cheap lock. It wouldn't keep the men out for long, but it would have to be long enough. At the least, it'd give me a chance to return fire and take a few of them out.

I picked up the phone. No dial tone. "Come on." I checked the cord, finding it had been cut. Someone had already been in here. "Dammit."

Maybe the other offices had a working phone, but that'd take time, and since these guys had disabled this one, I had to assume they disabled all of them. The computer was my only remaining option. Clicking the icon in the corner, I let out a sigh of relief when I saw the internet connection. They hadn't gotten around to disabling that yet.

Calling 9-1-1 would be the best plan. After opening the program, I dialed. The "all lines are busy" message came on. "You've got to be kidding me." I didn't hang up. A 9-1-1 operator would get to me as soon as he could.

In the meantime, I opened Kathy Walters' e-mail and hit compose. I didn't have time to log into mine. This would have to suffice. I had several e-mail addresses memorized, Detectives Heathcliff and O'Connell and Lucien Cross. In the subject line, I put "Hostage Situation – Alexis Parker." If anyone marked that as spam, I'd never speak to him again.

I wrote out the pertinent details, everything I knew, and hit send. In case that wasn't enough, I plugged the USB into the slot. Doing that would allow Amir to see what was happening on the screen in real time. Hopefully, the techs in Cross Security were paying attention. Cross hated the police, but he'd call them. Situations like this didn't come with that many options.

A noise outside the door told me I was in trouble. Disconnecting the internet call, I closed the windows I had opened, left the drive where it was, and looked for a place to hide. The office wasn't large, but there was another door in the corner. I pulled it open, hoping to find an emergency exit. It was a tiny, cramped closet.

The doorknob rattled. Unsure if my chances were better hiding or fighting, I forced my way into the closet and closed the door.

I didn't have much room to maneuver. In the pitch black, I couldn't see what I was doing. The closet had been filled with winter clothing. I didn't know why Walters had this stuff in here. Maybe they were donations for a fundraiser or she didn't have any closet space at home. Perhaps, she wore different winter coats to work every day and never took them back. I had no idea, but as I tried to move behind them, things kept falling off the hangers and landing in a pile at my feet.

The door to the outer office banged open. Whoever was here was seconds away from opening the closet door. Dropping to all fours, I tossed the heavy coats on top of me, pulling more off the hangers and adding them on top. I had no way of knowing if I was covered or if the giant lump at the bottom would be recognizable as human, but I was out of time.

Holding the gun, I curled onto my side, my knees pulled up to my chest. Between the dark and the heavy coats resting on top of me, I couldn't see anything. I'd shoot him in the ankle and then the head once he went down, assuming he didn't kill me first. But since I couldn't see him, I hoped he wouldn't be able to see me either. With the tactical gear, the chances of being killed or killing someone greatly decreased. I gave myself a fifty-fifty chance. Those weren't terrible odds.

The door creaked open. I searched, but I couldn't see the light from the office. Too many layers prevented that. Of course, the gas mask didn't make it any easier to see. The hangers above me shifted from side to side.

Don't look down, I thought. Five seconds later, the door creaked closed. I didn't move. Instead, I waited, wondering if he'd left. The last thing I needed was for an incoming e-mail to alert him to my presence. Whoever these guys were, they had a plan. They didn't want trouble. The knockout gas was meant to make sure they didn't encounter problems.

I had a habit of making lots of problems. Ask anyone I'd ever worked with or dated. And these guys were next on my list. I'd already set the ball rolling. Only their unconscious buddy knew what was in store, and he wasn't talking.

When I couldn't take it anymore, I freed myself from the pile of winter coats and fumbled for the knob. I aimed as I opened the door. But the office was empty. The armed goon had turned off the light, but he left the door open. If I closed it, they'd know they weren't alone.

As silently as possible, I opened Kathy Walters' e-mail provider. There were two waiting messages. One from Cross. The other from O'Connell.

Ignoring my boss, I started with my favorite detective. O'Connell had the specifics, so he didn't waste time with questions. All he wanted to know was if a tactical team should come in loud.

Too many unknowns. These guys could kill a lot of people in a short amount of time. Quiet would be better, if possible. Again, I reiterated that I didn't know what was being pumped in through the ventilation system, but time could be running out and lives could be in danger. It was his call.

While I waited for O'Connell to reply, I opened the message from Cross. Thankfully, he didn't say I told you so. All he said was, *What do you want me to do?*

Sure, now he had no problem letting me call the shots. *Talk to O'Connell.*

Cross replied immediately. *Amir said if you can plug the drive into the other computers, he may have a better view of the system. If they're using it, maybe we can figure out what they want.*

I'll try, I replied.

O'Connell sent his response a moment later. *ESU is being briefed. We'll set up close by. We'll try not to alert them until we have a plan to move in. Can you stay in touch?*

Cell jammers are messing with my signal.

What if we get you a radio?

Window in the sauna room. I told him where the room was located.

Stay safe. Someone will come to you. We'll get you out, Alex. I promise.

I closed the e-mail and pressed the power button on the monitor. I'd come back to check later, if I could. In the meantime, O'Connell had a plan. And since I was still working on coming up with one of my own, I'd do what he said.

Unplugging the USB, I left the office and headed for the next. Spa Alive only had four offices. Ducking into the next one, I checked the desk phone to find another sliced wire.

While I waited for the USB to do its thing, I searched the room for anything useful. But this was the accounting office. I'd have to be Macgyver to turn the calculators and staplers into weapons of mass destruction.

Once the drive finished installing, I pulled it out of the slot and headed for the next office. Heavy footsteps sounded from within, and they were getting closer. I didn't have time to run back to the room I left. Instead, I pressed my back against the wall and waited.

A man in a gas mask exited. He had a binder in his hands. I didn't know what was inside of it, but he scanned the pages as he went, his handgun holstered at his side.

As soon as he cleared the doorway, I spun around the corner and disappeared into the room. The retreating footsteps stopped. Did he see me?

We'd been so close, I didn't think it was possible he missed me, but the gas masks impaired peripheral vision. I remained motionless, afraid he'd hear me if I moved deeper into the room. Surely, he must have realized I was here. After all, someone had gone into the manager's office to cut the phone cord. That person left the door open. When this guy came to check the room again, the door was closed. If it was the same guy, I was doomed.

The footsteps resumed a second later, growing fainter as he headed toward the lobby. Since I didn't know how many unsubs there were, I couldn't risk an altercation. Not yet. Not unless it became absolutely necessary. At last count, there were six. Only five were mobile, but there could be more. Lots more.

Not wasting any more time, I booted up the computer and plugged in the USB. This was Ralph Lively's office. As far as I knew, he hadn't stopped by this week. The intel we'd pulled suggested he rarely made any appearances at the spa, preferring a hands-off approach to daily operations.

On the bottom shelf was a row of binders. None of them were labeled. I grabbed the one beside the empty slot and flipped through it. I couldn't make heads or tails out of it. On a whim, I reached for the phone. But that did me no good.

The pages inside the binder were written in code. I

snapped several photos. Whatever was contained within the pages could be the reason these armed men had taken over the spa. I scanned for networks again, but the place wasn't equipped with Wi-Fi. If only I could find the jammer and disable it.

After checking the time, I went into the last office. This one looked like it was nothing more than a storage room. No computer. The desk was basic, the drawers filled with useless supplies, or so I thought until I found a bag filled with different types of cables. Among them were several phone cords.

EIGHT

"I don't know how long I have," I whispered.

"All right. Tell me what's going on?" O'Connell said.

"I don't know. There have to be at least six hostiles. I incapacitated one of them. I don't think they found him yet."

"I can barely hear you."

I moved the phone closer, but the mask muffled everything. Sucking in a deep breath, I lifted it off my mouth, reminding myself not to breathe. "They're guarding the doors. The front's barricaded. Armed men are at the back. One of them is monitoring the security system. I don't think they realize I'm here, but maybe they do. Or they're looking for something." I lowered the mask and took a breath.

"Are you safe?"

That last attempt made me a little dizzy, so I left the mask in place. "No, but neither are they."

"Do not engage."

"I won't if they won't."

"How many hostages?" O'Connell asked.

"I don't know. The staff made up twenty. I'm sure we had just as many clients."

"Where is everyone?"

"The majority are in the salon, but bodies are spread all around." I regretted using that word. "I didn't get a chance to check everyone I passed, but I think they're alive."

O'Connell made a noise. "I'm looking at the blueprints and what's been filed with the fire department. ESU will find somewhere to breach. They're setting up a mobile command center a few blocks from the spa, out of sight. A member of the team will move on foot to the rendezvous point and bring you a radio. Do you have any idea who these guys are or what they want?"

"No, but I took a snapshot of the guy I knocked out. If you ID him, you might learn something."

"Okay."

A noise in the distance made me cringe. I ducked behind the desk. "John McClane didn't make this look easy."

"Are you wearing shoes?"

"Yeah."

"Good, you're already doing better than he was."

The noise grew louder and closer. "I have to go." I pulled the cord out of the phone, rolled it up, and tucked it into my pocket. Until my radio arrived, I couldn't risk letting these bastards destroy my only means of communication with the outside world.

The noise turned out to be voices, two of them. One of the men carried the binder. I had to assume that had been my close call from earlier. I wasn't sure who the other man was. He could have been the one from the lobby, or the salon, or even guarding the back door.

"It was in here," Binder Boy said.

"Show me."

As soon as they disappeared inside the owner's office, I ran down the hall. With no cover positions, it'd be best to get out of sight as quickly as possible. Maybe the blur of the gas mask and tactical vest would make them think I was one of their own.

Slowing near the lobby, I peered through the door. The room was empty. The two masked men were gone, and the two customers who'd been waiting for their appointments were no longer passed out in the chairs. Afraid of what had happened to them, I resisted the urge to go inside to check. The men from the offices would be coming back soon.

Instead, I took a left and started searching the treatment rooms. On my third try, I found Damon and his two o'clock appointment. Damon was on the ground. A small pool of blood had collected beside his head.

Fear gripped my insides. Had they shot him?

"Don't be dead. Don't be dead." I pressed my fingers to his neck, relieved when I felt a strong and steady pulse.

Carefully, I rolled him onto his side. He must have hit the floor or the edge of the table when he lost consciousness. Grabbing my phone, I turned on the flashlight and lifted his eyelids. His pupils were equal and reactive.

"Damon?" I shook him, but he didn't wake. If anything was to bring him out of it, it would have been the bright light in the eyes. Grabbing one of the clean towels, I wiped his wound. Head wounds always bled a lot, but it didn't look too bad. I folded another towel and placed it beneath his head. "Help's on the way."

Before leaving, I checked the woman on the table. Her face rested against the pillowed sides of the open circle while she faced the floor. Her breathing was steady. Her pulse even. After opening another towel and draping it over her, both so she wouldn't get cold and to protect her modesty whenever help arrived, I checked the rest of the room and pocketed a lighter I found.

I checked the other treatment rooms, finding more staff and clients. Afraid I'd miss the rendezvous, I skipped the break room, the supply room, and a few other places. I needed to share the intel I had and get that radio.

The hallway remained empty. I wasn't sure where the men had gone or what they were doing. Carefully, I took the long way around the salon, spotting two men in tactical gear. They paced back and forth, as if they expected something to pop off at any second.

The thought left me unsettled. What would happen if everyone woke up? Would they start shooting?

My shoe squeaked, and I swore, ducking down the next corridor. I waited ten counts, but no one came to investigate. More than likely, they hadn't heard me. Double-timing it, I dashed toward the sauna room. I was almost there when a man came out of a room across the hallway.

Surprised to see me, he fumbled for his weapon. "Hey. Stop right there."

I lunged for him, knocking him back into the room from which he came. His gun went off, a wild shot that lodged itself in the wall.

I grabbed for his mask, but he had it strapped on too tightly for me to pull it off from this angle. He swung his gun, hoping to clock me with it. The weapon impacted against the side of my mask, which lessened the blow.

Grabbing his arm, I stepped into him, spinning and throwing an elbow. The filter on the left side fell off his mask. But I didn't let that distract me. I kicked into his knee and knocked the gun from his hand. It slid across the floor. He grabbed me around the hips and threw me to the ground. My back hit hard. Luckily, it wasn't my head, or my skull would have cracked open.

He landed on top of me. I shoved both hands beneath his chin, forcing the mask upward. It scraped against his skin, leaving deep red marks in its wake. His eyes were hazel and badly bloodshot.

Unlike my previous foe. This guy didn't go down. He must have been holding his breath.

He went for my mask, and I struggled beneath him. But I couldn't get my legs free. I threw wild punches, swatting and scratching at his face.

Almost out of oxygen, he let me push him away. While I scrambled backward, he secured his mask back in place. The gunshot he fired had attracted the attention of his friends. Three men stormed into the room, guns at the ready.

I raised my hands in surrender. "Take it easy."

"Who are you?" the one with the blue shirt asked.

"The cleaning lady."

Blue Shirt didn't buy it. "Try again."

"It's true."

"Where did you get the vest?" the one to his left asked.

"I found it."

"And the gas mask?" Lefty asked.

"Found that too."

"Take it off."

"I'd rather not."

"Take it off." He aimed more emphatically.

I held up my hands. "All right. No problem. Give me a sec." Without the mask, they could do anything to me. Taking it off wasn't an option. Four to one weren't great odds. In fact, they were pretty damn shitty. Reaching for the straps, I pretended I couldn't get them loose. "My ponytail's stuck. Can one of you help me?"

Lefty nodded to the third guy. "You do it."

"Careful," Hazel Eyes said.

"Did I hurt you?" I asked. "I mean, you did try to shoot me."

"You weren't supposed to do that," Blue Shirt hissed at him. "Go see what's taking so long."

Hazel Eyes went out the door. He didn't want to hang around to see what was going to happen. That left me with better odds.

"What do you guys want?" I asked as the third man approached. "Why are you here? Is this about a ransom?"

"Who are you?" Blue Shirt asked again. "Are you a cop?"

"Cops can't afford spas like this. Like I said, I'm the cleaning lady."

"What'd you do before you started cleaning?" the third guy asked, now within striking distance and blocking me from view of his two buddies.

"A little of this and that." I didn't wait. Instead, I grabbed the handgun from the small of my back and fired twice into his chest. Before he even hit the ground, I sidestepped, shooting the other two. One shot each, dead center. Depending on the type of rounds in the gun, they could be dead. But I didn't think so. I didn't see any blood on the clean floor. But they went down.

The impact and shock would delay them for a few seconds until the adrenaline kicked in. I had to get out of here, but the third guy returned fire. He shot me in the back of the shoulder, propelling me forward with the blast.

Stumbling, I dashed out the door. Hazel Eyes rushed toward me from the other end of the hallway. This was bad. *You had to screw it up, didn't you, Parker?*

Ignoring my internal voice, I darted down the next hallway. This place had a million rooms and hallways that branched out in different directions. I'd gotten lost and turned around several times when I first started, which was why I spent a great deal of time figuring out where everything was. I hoped these guys hadn't performed that much recon.

A few bullets chipped away at the corner of the wall as I turned down another corridor. The third door led to a couple's massage room, which had two different exits. I ducked inside and pulled the door closed behind me. That bought me some time.

Using the phone cord in my pocket, I tied it around the handles of the door, making it even more difficult for anyone to get in that way. But it wouldn't keep them out forever. If they were smart, they'd go around, but I'd be long gone by then.

I went out the other door, relieved to find the hallway empty. Not waiting, I went into the supply room. A few of the cleaning supplies were flammable, but starting a fire seemed like a terrible idea, particularly when the air was already compromised. A single spark could result in the entire place getting blown sky high. Instead, I went to the shelf near the back. Several large boxes blocked the area behind it from view.

I shoved the oversized cardboard boxes aside, my arm and back screaming in protest, before ducking down behind them and moving them back into place. I kept my back against the wall, realizing this wasn't a great place to hide. But the spa didn't offer many defensible positions. All I could hope was they wouldn't spot me when they came looking.

My heart hammered in my chest. This was bad. Would these assholes threaten to kill hostages if I didn't reveal myself? Would they kill me on sight? The bullets in the wall suggested that was their plan, but Blue Shirt said they weren't supposed to do that. What were they supposed to do? What did they want?

My fingers cramped, but I resisted the urge to release my grip on the gun. My hands were shaking. I just hoped I wasn't. Surely, they'd notice if the shelving was rocking back and forth or doing the Tarantella. *Brilliant, pick the dance of the spider*, my internal voice mocked. *It's not like they want to squish you like a bug.*

For the next five minutes, I waited. No one came to the door. I never even heard anyone outside the room. Did they know I was here? Were they planning to jump me as soon as I stepped outside?

When I couldn't take the not knowing, I abandoned my hiding spot. Cautiously, I approached the door. The light pattern didn't appear to be blocked or partially obscured. Still, I feared that opening the door would lead to my brains getting splattered against the nearest wall. On the bright side, someone else would have to clean up the mess. I'd be exempt.

Twisting the knob, I cracked the door open. But I didn't move. I remained with my back against the wall. No one tried to enter.

I pushed the door open a little more. Still nothing.

Keeping the gun pointed at the opening, I pulled out my phone, turned on the camera, and held it in front of the opening, recording as I manipulated it from side to side. Pulling it back in, I replayed the footage. The hallway was empty.

Half-convinced this was a trap, I left the supply room. Considering where the firefight took place, I didn't believe it was possible for me to get back to the sauna room. So I needed another plan.

Tiptoeing down the hallway, I entered the locker room. At first glance, it appeared empty, but I couldn't be sure given the number of possible hiding places. Resisting the urge to lock the door, I checked the stalls and every nook and cranny. Unless one of those bastards was thin enough and committed enough to lock himself inside a locker, I was alone.

Before doing anything else, I took out my nine millimeter, tucked the assailant's gun into my purse, draped it diagonally across my body, in case I needed a backup, and tucked my gun at the small of my back. If I'd known this was going to happen, I would have packed my shoulder holster.

Quietly, I crept out of the room and entered the laundry room. The steady whir of the machines reassured me I was alone. After performing my due diligence, I unhooked the hoses and plugs, bent over, and pushed one of the heavy machines in front of the door. It let out a shriek as it scratched the tile, but keeping those bastards out was my only concern. I didn't care if they knew I was here. I wasn't planning on sticking around much longer.

The ache in my back and shoulders told me I pulled something. I rubbed the spot where I'd been hit, but I didn't find any blood. The bullet hadn't pierced the vest. At least these jerks had decent equipment, except that would make things harder when the police tried to resolve the situation.

I had to get out of here. I had to tell the cops what I knew so everyone else could be rescued. Grabbing the fire extinguisher from the spot on the wall, I approached the thick, frosted window. The damn thing was solid, double-paned. I held the extinguisher near the top, making sure I had a firm grip before ramming it into the glass.

The first hit left a small chip. So I reared back and threw my hips into it. The inner pane of glass shattered, sending shards flying toward me. Luckily, the gas mask protected my eyes from the sharp pieces. With one final thrust, the window broke.

I ran the heavy red container around the sides, knocking off the sharp daggers. Once that was done, I double-gloved with the rubber cleaning gloves, hoping for as much protection as possible, before gripping the frame and pulling myself out. I fell over the edge and landed in a bush.

Lifting the mask off my face, I tossed it to the side and peered around the exterior of the building. I didn't spot a getaway vehicle. How did these guys get here? More importantly, how did they plan on escaping?

Remaining in a crouch, I circled around the side. The HVAC was in a fenced off area. Two canisters were nestled beside it. Hoses ran from the canisters directly into the intake. I couldn't determine what kind of gas it was, but the lack of skull and crossbones gave me hope it wasn't lethal.

Before I could do anything else, someone snuck up behind me in full tactical gear, assault rifle at the ready. "I wouldn't do that if I were you."

NINE

He grabbed the gun from the small of my back before I could reach for it. That left the backup in my purse. I moved to get it, but he said, "Don't even think about it."

I turned around. The gear wasn't the same. The exposed Velcro and missing patch indicated one thing. I just hoped I wasn't reading the situation wrong.

"ESU?" I asked.

The guy with the assault rifle didn't have a gas mask, he had the masks tactical wore to conceal their identities. He kept his gun trained on me while he peered at the tanks. "Who are you?"

"Alexis Parker."

"Parker?"

"Are you here to bring me a radio?" I nodded at the one clipped to his belt.

"I thought you couldn't get out." He lifted a flap on his vest, flashing me his badge. "I need a SitRep."

"You're not gonna like it." I filled him in on everything that happened while I led him back to the window I'd broken through. "They know they aren't alone. I was sure they'd come looking. They tried to kill me, but I lost them somehow. I don't know how. It makes no sense."

"When was this?"

"About ten minutes ago."

"There are dozens of rooms inside. They could still be searching for you."

"Maybe." But I wasn't convinced. "Now that they know they're exposed, the hostages are in even more danger."

He radioed for his team and pulled a printout from another flap. "Where did it go down?"

I indicated where I'd encountered trouble. A few seconds later, four people in full tac gear appeared behind us. He instructed them to monitor the front and rear doors and to find a way to get a line inside.

"How many hostiles?" he asked.

"I don't know. At least six."

"All armed?"

"Yes. Mostly handguns. One had an assault rifle."

"Only one?"

"I can't say for sure." I pointed to my nine millimeter. "Can I have that back?"

He gave me an uncertain look. "Let me see your phone. O'Connell said you had intel."

I gave him the device. Once he was certain I was who I said, he unloaded my weapon and gave it back to me. "We have a command center set up four blocks in that direction." He pointed. "Get yourself clear. We can handle this."

"I've been inside. I know my way around. I can help."

"I'll have you escorted."

"That won't be necessary."

The look in his eyes said he didn't trust me. Given the givens, I wouldn't have trusted me either. But a major crimes detective vouched for me. That should have meant something. "I think it is." He nodded to one of the men in tactical gear. "Get Parker secured. Head back once we know she isn't going anywhere."

"If you're planning to detain me, you should have kept my weapon. How do you know I won't try something?"

"Get going," he said.

The other member of the team gripped my elbow. "Ma'am, let's move."

He led me off the premises. Half a block later, a uniformed police officer intercepted us. The ESU team member handed me off and disappeared back the way we came.

"Do you want to frisk me?" I asked.

Officer Richards gave me a sideways look. "I remember you."

"Yeah?" I quirked an eyebrow. "Is that good or bad?"

"Let's get you squared away." He walked me back to the mobile command center, opened the door to the oversized monstrosity, and waited for me to go up the steps.

Upon entering, I hoped to spot a familiar face. But O'Connell, Heathcliff, and the rest of the guys from major crimes weren't on the scene. Maybe they'd show up after the fireworks. I'd have to remember to give them a hard time for missing the fun.

"Alexis Parker," the man in charge approached and extended his hand, an earpiece clipped to his ear, "you reported a hostage situation inside the spa." He eyed me up and down and signaled for the female officer to join us. "Where'd you get the vest?"

"I took it off one of the hostiles."

"Officer Gimble will collect whatever evidence you have. Afterward, we'll chat."

She led me to a small alcove about four steps from where I'd been standing. "Ma'am," she pulled on a pair of gloves and reached for the straps on the vest, "how did a bullet get lodged here?"

"Someone shot me."

"We'll get medical—"

"I'm fine."

"Ma'am?"

I held my palms up higher, shrugging backward. "It's Alex or Parker. Not ma'am."

She pulled the vest away and placed it into an oversized evidence bag. "What else?"

"I found a lighter. I don't believe it belonged to any of them." I pulled it out of my pocket, and she tucked it into a baggie.

Staring down at the bullet lodged in the vest, she eyed me curiously. "That's gotta hurt."

"I'm used to it." I nodded at my purse. "Inside is a handgun I took off the guy who gave me the vest. It's his. It was fully loaded when I got it. It isn't any more."

"You shot them?"

"They started it."

"Anything else?"

"Everything else I left at or near the scene."

"What else was there?"

"A gas mask."

She jotted something in her notebook before turning back to the commander. "Sergeant Wu, she's all yours."

The sergeant pulled out a chair from where it was tucked beneath the makeshift desk and patted the back. "Fill me in on everything I need to know about this situation, Ms. Parker."

Taking a seat, I rested my elbows on my thighs and leaned forward, examining the aerial map while I told him everything that happened. "I don't know when they arrived. I don't even know when they took control of the ventilation system. The first indication I had that anything was wrong was finding a client asleep in the tub, but since that had happened earlier this week, I thought I'd gotten my rooms confused. That's when I spotted an unconscious coworker. When I went for help, that's when I saw the men."

"How many?"

"Four."

"You said six."

"Later on, I encountered two others. There could be more than six. I have no idea."

Wu tapped his radio. "Use heat signatures to get a look at what we're dealing with." He turned back to me. "Was anyone else conscious besides you and the hostiles?"

"No."

"You're absolutely sure?"

"No one else on staff wore a mask. It's unlikely they would have lasted long enough to find one or put one on, and even if they did, without filtration or access to a window, they would have gone down by now."

He considered what I said. "Where are the windows that open?" He shoved the building's blueprints closer to me.

I pointed them out. "It's possible there are others that I don't know about, but almost every room has frosted glass to provide ambient light. Those windows don't allow a view outside or any airflow in."

He relayed the details over the radio. "Why were you wearing a mask?"

"Allergies."

"Do you always wear one?"

"Today was the first day. My boss insisted."

"That's lucky."

"Uh-huh." I knew what he was thinking. But I wasn't involved.

Wu was becoming less trusting by the second. "So you go for help, see armed, masked men, realize the air is contaminated, and run to one of the only rooms with a window that opens. When one of the hostiles happens to poke his head inside, you take him out by yourself, steal his vest and weapon, and go Rambo on their asses?"

"John McClane."

"What?"

"Never mind."

"Don't be cute."

"I can't help it." Whatever points I may have earned with Wu vanished with that last statement. "To answer your question, he didn't poke his head into the room. He was clearing the rooms in the hallway." Now that I had twenty-twenty hindsight, I had a few theories as to why. "Originally, I thought he heard me outside the lobby and wanted to make sure everyone was unconscious, that they wouldn't encounter any surprises, but," I continued before he could interject, "he may have been looking for something."

"What?"

"I don't know. They took a binder from the owner's office. They went back in a second time. They want something."

"Is that why Cross Security sent you in as a cleaning lady? Were you looking for something too?"

Wu knew more than he let on. Someone had filled him in. My money was on O'Connell. Cross never liked to speak out of turn.

"We were hired to investigate an issue involving the spa's insurance policy," I said.

"Wouldn't details like that be kept in a binder in the owner's office?"

"I don't know."

Before he could say anything else, the radio went off.

"We have tons of heat signatures. None of them are moving. Permission to breach," a member of ESU asked.

Wu gave me an uncertain look, but this was his call. "Go ahead."

We listened to the radio chatter. After an eternity, the all-clear came over the radio. "We found the victims. No hostiles to report. Request for ambulances, as many as you can spare. We're looking at forty-two victims."

Wu made the request. "Where did the hostiles go?"

"I don't know." Six armed men couldn't vanish, but after I used the phone cord to secure the doors, no one pursued me. I thought I'd gotten lucky, but maybe that's when they decided to haul ass. "Do you have any visuals from outside the spa? They could have left after the firefight." I reached for the radio and pressed a button. "Did you find the man I left unconscious in the sauna?"

"Parker?" the ESU team leader asked.

"Did you find him?" I repeated.

"No. The sauna was empty."

I put the radio down. "They took their buddy and cleared out."

"They could have tossed their gear and disguised themselves as victims. They could be waiting for us to walk them out of there." Wu picked up the radio. "Every victim gets fingerprinted and photographed. No one gets released until we verify their identities and their reason for being at the spa."

"They won't like that," I mumbled.

"Excuse me?"

"Spa Alive is an elite wellness center. They do everything to maintain their clients' privacy, including limiting security cameras and forcing people to turn off or surrender their phones upon arrival. You're going to piss off a lot of people and their high-powered attorneys."

"What do you suggest I do instead? I won't risk letting armed shitheads walk away."

"Um, Sergeant," the radio squawked again, "notify the ME's office. We found one dead. The paramedics will have to declare it, but there's no point in waiting for verification."

"Who is it?" I asked, but I didn't get an answer since I didn't speak into the radio.

Wu glared at me. "Like I said, no one's walking, especially now that this is a homicide. Best you get comfortable, Ms. Parker."

TEN

I stood in the doorway, watching as CSU and the medical examiner worked the scene. Detective Nick O'Connell stood beside me as they tested the temperature of the water before checking the temperature of the body. I wasn't sure what that was going to tell them, but given how serious they were about it, I figured it'd factor into time of death.

"I never checked her pulse," I said. "This may have been where it started. Someone could have snuck in, killed her, and covered his tracks with the gas. When I opened the door and saw her there, I thought I had the wrong room. I let myself out. I should have done more." I'd gotten yelled at for doing that earlier in the week, but I knew better. Instinctively, I knew better.

"It's not your fault, Parker. You couldn't have known anything was wrong." O'Connell peered around the room. "What is that smell?"

"Lavender and freesia." Saying the names made me want to sneeze. I wiggled my nose and sniffed, keeping the tickle at bay. My eyes watered. I wiped them with the back of my hand. "I don't know why they need both."

O'Connell watched me from the corner of his eye. "No wonder you had a mask."

"Cross insisted."

"Does that mean I should bump him up on my suspect list?"

"Only if you think he sent me here to perform a hit." I stepped closer to the body, making sure not to get in anyone's way. "Is that bruising around her neck?"

The ME pointed to the purple marks. "Good catch. We'll know more once we get her on the table, but nothing indicates drowning. It could be cardiac arrest, brought about by whatever knockout gas was utilized."

"Do we know what they used?" O'Connell asked.

"We're working on it. It appears to be an inhalation anesthetic. None of the other victims presented with serious adverse effects."

"What exactly are you thinking?"

"Possibly something pharmacological, used for general surgery."

"It wouldn't have been concentrated, like in an OR. So is that even possible?" O'Connell asked.

"Given the forty-two people who got carted out of here, I'd say so." The ME pointed to the victim. "It's also possible this woman wasn't that lucky. The dosage or the chemical itself could have triggered cardiac arrest. She could have had a pre-existing condition or an extreme adverse reaction."

"That doesn't explain the bruises," I said.

The ME examined them closer. "These could be older or superficial. It's too soon to speculate."

"Superficial? I don't let people put their hands around my neck and squeeze for the hell of it. Do you?"

"Rough sex," O'Connell suggested.

I gave him a look. "What you and Jen do is none of my business."

He scowled at me. "I'm stating a fact, not sharing personal experiences."

"Whatever you say."

"Even after everything, you're gonna bust chops?"

"Sorry." I peered around the rest of the room, giving the tub a wide berth. On the table was the victim's purse. Someone had already checked her ID and left it open in an evidence bag. I read the name. *Tabitha York. Forty-two. 5'7. 141 lbs.*

"This is going to be a mess." O'Connell rubbed his eyes. "Parker, take me through the rest of this place. Show me everything I need to see and every place you spotted these chuckleheads. We'll go from there."

"Hey, Nick," I said when we stepped out of the room, "is everyone else okay? Damon Thoreau sustained a head injury. It appeared accidental, the result of the gas, but I wanted to make sure no one else was seriously hurt. Sgt. Wu didn't share much with me."

"The hospital's checking everyone out, but nothing's been reported besides a few minor contusions, headaches, and nausea."

"Are we sure the gas wasn't toxic?"

"The doctors said no."

"They don't always get things right."

"You sound like my wife, but I spoke to Jenny. She said everyone's fine."

"What about bruises? I shot three guys. They had on vests, but if they tried to hide among the victims, that'd be one way to identify them."

"No bruises indicative of gunshot wounds. What's going through that head of yours?"

"Wu made it sound like I was working with them, like I let them escape. That I'm making this up."

"It's my investigation. You aren't even on my suspect list."

"Not that I'm complaining, but shouldn't I be?"

"Do you want to help me figure this out or not?"

"You know I do."

"Then stop asking such asinine questions." He stopped in front of me and peered into my eyes. "Are you sure you're okay? You're the only one who didn't get checked out."

"I'm fine." I shook out my shoulders. "Just dealing with post-action jitters."

"Once we finish up here, we'll head back to the precinct. I'll get you some coffee. That should help."

"Thanks." The confused look on his face made me chuckle. "For coming to save the day. I can always count on you. That's why you're my favorite," I said.

"It's not like I did much of anything. You took care of the situation before we got here, except the cleanup." He fell into step beside me as we headed to the lobby. "And to think, you were hired to be the cleaning lady." He made a tsk noise. "Someone should have provided you with a more detailed explanation of what that entailed."

"Tell me about it."

I'd taken O'Connell on enough walkthroughs in the past that we fell into old habits. He followed me as I retraced my steps, sometimes backtracking. A member of CSU joined us in Ms. Walters' office. I indicated the closet while O'Connell gave the computer a cursory glance. Since no windows remained open and the ones I'd accessed didn't lead to a smoking gun, he let that be while he examined the items inside the closet.

"Why does she have so many winter coats?" he asked.

"I wanted to know the same thing, but they came in handy. If they weren't there, we may not be having this conversation." I peered over his shoulder at the massive pile I'd hidden beneath.

He scribbled furiously as we went down the hall to the owner's office. He examined the shelves, but the binder the masked men had taken remained missing. "Is anything else gone?"

I didn't spot any obvious gaps, but I couldn't say for certain. "I don't think so."

"We'll have someone go over everything."

"The owner will be able to tell you for sure," I said.

"If he cooperates."

"You think he knew he'd be targeted?"

"You were hired because the insurance company got nervous. My gut says someone in charge of this place knew what was coming, feared the worst, and wanted to know everything would be covered."

"The worst being Tabitha York dead in the tub?"

O'Connell shrugged. "Unless you can come up with something worse than that."

I could come up with forty-two things worse than that, but as far as I knew, everyone else survived. "Not for her."

O'Connell finished looking around before I led him to the storage room. "This is where you phoned me?" he asked.

I nodded. "I found a cord in there." I indicated the drawer. "Thanks for answering and for checking your e-mail."

"Serve and protect. That's the motto."

"Remind me to give Heathcliff shit for that."

"Today's his day off."

"Oh sure, give him an excuse."

O'Connell chuckled. "Hey, Sarvin, make sure you inventory everything in the offices. The masked men searched these rooms for something. Let's make sure we don't miss anything. And dust everything for prints, collect fibers, shoeprints, whatever you can get."

"Yes, sir." The tech glanced down, but we were properly outfitted with booties and gloves, even if I'd already touched everything in this place during my first go-around. But my prints were in the system. They'd be disregarded as scene contamination, unless O'Connell changed his mind and decided I'd make the perfect suspect.

After our tour of the offices, I led O'Connell to the scene of the firefight, took the path of my attempted escape, and led him around to the other side to show him where I'd secured the doors with the phone cord. The cord remained in place. None of the masked men had tried to enter. In fact, nothing indicated they'd pursued me beyond the few gunshots that had gotten lodged in the wall.

We concluded the walkthrough in the laundry room. It took both of us ramming the door to get the washing machine pressed against it to budge. Once it did, I slipped through the crack and strained to push the machine a few more inches away from the door so O'Connell could join me.

"They never came looking for you," he said. "We'll pull whatever security footage we can, but my guess would be, once you shot them and ran off, they cleared out in a hurry."

"They jammed the cell signals. They had no reason to think outside help was on the way. They should have assumed I was trapped, like everyone else."

"The landlines still worked, and the internet never went offline."

"There's no Wi-Fi."

"Maybe they didn't know that."

Something told me they'd done their research, but I didn't know enough yet to prove it. Right now, I wasn't even sure what they wanted. "Do you think they knew I called you?"

"Maybe, or they figured it was only a matter of time. Even if you couldn't call for help, they couldn't guarantee you wouldn't find a way out. After all, you'd already taken out one of their own. They must have gone searching for him. Once they found him, they decided it was best to get out while they could."

But the look on his face told me he didn't believe that. "You think they accomplished whatever they set out to do, and that's why they left?" I asked.

"The binder's gone, and a woman's dead. I'd say it's a damn good possibility."

O'Connell passed along orders to the techs and officers we passed. Once we were outside, he led me to the HVAC system. The canisters had been removed. CSU was processing the scene. Security cam footage from the area was being collected. As of yet, the scene hadn't been released, so no one was on site except the police and yours truly.

"Nothing's labeled on the tanks?" I asked.

The crime scene tech looked up. "The markings and warnings have been scraped off. Besides flammable and contents under pressure, the rest of it was removed. We'll be able to take a sample, run it, and figure out what was inside."

"Once you do, we'll need to track down where it came from. That should give us an idea of who these guys are." O'Connell tucked his notepad away, put his hands in his back pockets, and surveyed the area. "I wouldn't have expected this place to be so secluded. The surrounding greenery makes it less likely anyone would have seen something. It's not like the property can be seen from the street, not with the way the building's pushed back with the private drive."

"I can't say for sure, but I'm almost positive they came in through the front door. You should have footage of that," I said.

"Yeah, guys with masks," the ESU commander said, joining us. He nodded to me. "Alexis Parker, former FBI agent, part-time police consultant, and current Cross Security employee."

"And I don't even know your name." I stared at the

exposed Velcro where his name should have been.

"Dominguez. Rafael." He held out his hand. "You can call me Raf."

We shook. "Does this mean I can have my bullets back?"

Raf glanced at O'Connell. "What do you think, Detective?"

"You better, or I'll never hear the end of it."

Dominguez undid one of the pockets, reached inside, and held out his closed fist. "Try not to shoot anyone else today, Ms. Parker."

"I'll do my best, but no promises." I tucked the loose bullets into my bag, not wanting to waste time reloading with a tactical unit nearby. "When did you have time to run my background?"

"After we finished clearing the building." Dominguez turned his attention to O'Connell. "Isn't this a little out of your jurisdiction?"

"Blame Parker. She called me. Since I got things rolling, the commissioner said I should stick with it." O'Connell hadn't mentioned that, but we hadn't had a lot of time to catch up. We'd been focused on business.

"All right. Whatever you need, let us know. You'll have our reports on your desk before we go home for the night," Dominguez said.

"Thanks." O'Connell pointed in the direction of the broken window. "Do you have any idea how the masked men got out of the building? All I've seen is your breach point and Parker's makeshift exit."

"The alarm on the back door was disabled. They could have gone out that way. When we forced our way inside, we had to find a way around the barricade they set up at the front. That's why we used the large window. There's no way they went out that way. And none of the other windows were broken. The back door's the most likely scenario. It wasn't blocked."

"Any idea how they disabled the alarm?"

"They turned off the sensors."

O'Connell nodded a few times. "All right. Get those reports to me as soon as you can, and thanks for making sure Parker was safe."

"I'm his favorite police consultant," I said as we went past Dominguez and headed for the street. "He worries."

"I never said that," O'Connell insisted.

"You have another police consultant you prefer?" I asked.

"No."

"See, that makes me your favorite."

O'Connell rolled his eyes. "Why is it every time I turn around you find a way to get yourself into trouble?"

"I like to keep you on your toes."

"Please don't."

"Trust me. I've tried." I got into O'Connell's car. Cross would send someone to collect mine later. Right now, I was too shaky to drive. I'd just never admit it. "You know, yesterday, Lucien told me he assigned me this case because he thought it was safe."

"What else did he tell you?"

I knew I wasn't supposed to say anything, especially now that I was a full-time Cross employee without the benefit of moonlighting or consulting without his direct approval. But I didn't care. O'Connell might as well be family. I owed him everything. "This case made him twitchy. Something never sat right with him when it came to our investigation. That's why he arranged for me to get hired as a cleaning lady."

"Because you attract trouble like a balloon to static cling?"

"He said it's because I have this dogged determination to get to the bottom of things."

"I call that a death wish."

"Hey, I worked on my issues."

"And yet, you still had to e-mail me an SOS."

ELEVEN

"You're in my chair." Detective Thompson put his hands on his hips and stared down at me.

"You weren't using it."

"I was running an errand." He jerked his head to the side. "Move."

O'Connell grabbed a straight-back chair and placed it beside his desk, hoping that would keep me and his partner from bickering. "Here, Parker. Problem solved."

"More protecting and serving?" I got up and offered Thompson his desk back. "Shouldn't you play music? Isn't that how musical chairs works?"

Thompson rolled his eyes and sat down. "Now what has she gotten us involved in this time?"

O'Connell snorted. "A homicide that came out of what may have been a hostage situation."

"Where?"

O'Connell gave his partner the spa's address while I sipped the white chocolate mocha he'd picked up from the coffee place on the way here. The caffeine and sugar helped, but it also made me queasy. At least, I was no longer wired or on the verge of crashing from the adrenaline roller coaster. Instead, the back of my shoulder ached to the point I had to use my other hand to drink my coffee. So far, no one had noticed.

"That's all the way across town. Isn't that out of our jurisdiction?" Thompson typed something into the computer.

"Yeah."

"So why are you in charge of the investigation?" Thompson turned his icy stare on me. "Let me guess. You made the request."

"I didn't make a request. I sent an e-mail. I wouldn't have had to do that if 9-1-1 wasn't busy. Do you realize how screwed up that is? I had an actual emergency to report." Thoughts of the dead Tabitha York came to mind, making me feel lightheaded on top of the queasy. But that may have been the caffeine or the aftereffects of the gas.

"An e-mail?" Thompson turned his attention to O'Connell, hoping his partner would elaborate.

O'Connell shook his head. "It's been an interesting afternoon."

"Parker's fault, no doubt."

"Hey," I said, "you missed me when I went to California."

"I never said that." Thompson glared at me before turning his focus back to his partner. "What do you want me to do?"

"Nothing. I got it. The commissioner put me in charge of overseeing things. I'm liaising with the other precinct. They're in charge of evidence collection and witness statements. I'm coordinating with them and reviewing reports, but they know what they're doing. This shouldn't be anything more than a formality. The only thing I need you to do is stay on top of our other cases," O'Connell said.

"Commissioner Cross?" I eyed O'Connell. "How did he hear about this?"

"I'll give you one guess," Thompson muttered.

"Seriously?"

O'Connell shrugged. "You only CCed three of us on that e-mail, and Lucien and the commissioner share a last name. Make of that what you will."

I rubbed my face and sat sideways in the chair, leaning my good side against the backrest. "Did I jam you up?"

"Nah. We're good." O'Connell gave his screen another look. "Now that I've taken your statement, let's go over it one more time. Then we'll get you out of here."

"Are you trying to get rid of me?"

"Yes," Thompson said, his eyes on the monitor.

"You're not consulting, Alex." O'Connell kept his focus on the words in front of him, afraid I'd protest.

"You're not even going to ask?" I looked in the direction of Lt. Moretti's office. "Maybe with the proper amount of cajoling—"

"You told us that was off the table for the foreseeable future."

"Yeah, but—"

"You're a material witness. I have another forty-two statements to review." O'Connell wasn't mad or annoyed. I wasn't sure what he was, but he was putting some distance between us. Whether that was professional or personal, I couldn't tell. "Run through it one more time."

I did as I was told. By the time the Ts were crossed and the Is dotted, ESU's reports had flooded O'Connell's inbox. While I signed the forms and collected my things, I tried to read over his shoulder, but it looked like nothing more than an after-action report. Dominguez had already filled us in at the scene.

"Hey, keep your phone handy," O'Connell said. "I'll be in touch if I have questions."

"You know where to find me." I glanced back at Thompson. "Next time, I'll remember the jellies and bear claws."

"It won't matter. You still can't have my desk."

"We'll see." I was halfway to the door when a new thought came to mind. "Hey, Nick, should I call Derek?"

"You better."

I waved goodbye and pushed my way through the double doors. I didn't remember the door being that heavy, or I had hurt myself with all the lifting and dragging earlier.

Before taking the stairs down, I sent Detective Derek Heathcliff a text. *Hey, in the event you check your e-mail, please disregard. The situation has been handled. Nick's got the details. I'm okay. Crisis resolved.*

I tucked my phone away, figuring it was bound to ring in the next three minutes, after Derek checked to see what I'd sent and realized he'd missed something big. While I waited, I went down the stairs, surprised to find my boss making himself comfortable at the intake desk.

Cross leaned over the counter, chatting with the gray-haired desk sergeant. She jerked her chin in my direction when I let myself out of the gate that prevented unauthorized access up the steps. "Speak of the devil," she said.

I'd seen her before, but I couldn't remember the context of our prior encounter. It had been that kind of day. Instead, I tossed my empty coffee cup into the wastebasket and faced my boss. "I assume you're here for me."

"I'll see you, Sara." Cross's brow furrowed as he assessed me, but he didn't inquire. "C'mon, I'll give you a ride back to the office."

We made it as far as the door when my phone rang. *Heathcliff.* "Hang on a second." I answered, turning my back to Cross and moving off to the side. "Hey, Derek."

"What the hell happened? Are you okay?"

"I said I am."

"That doesn't mean you are."

"I'm okay," I repeated, answering his question. "Masked men invaded the spa, knocked everyone out, and—"

Cross grabbed the phone from my hand before I could say another word. "Detective Heathcliff, this is Lucien Cross. Ms. Parker has already provided her statement and everything else the police need to conduct their investigation. If there's something you want to know, ask one of your buddies in blue. In the meantime, we have business to discuss, and since Ms. Parker is on the clock, I'd prefer if she tells me what happened instead of you." Cross's expression soured. "Uh-huh." He paused. "Yeah, you do that." He disconnected and held out my phone.

I snatched it away from him. "You did not just do that."

"Alex, let's go." He held up his palms, seeing the fight in my eyes. "We have to get ahead of this. We don't have time to waste. The police are lucky I didn't storm upstairs and demand they release you."

"They weren't holding me. I'm not even a suspect. I'm a witness."

"A witness to what?" He led me to a waiting town car and opened the back door. "A robbery? A hostage situation?

Ransom demands?"

"All of the above, but you left out murder."

"Shit." He waited for me to get in before closing the door and going around to the other side. After instructing the driver to take us back to the office, he ran a hand through his hair. "Tell me everything."

"You first." I glared at him, pissed about the phone and whatever situation he'd forced upon O'Connell.

"I received your e-mail. I had to act."

"You called your father?"

"O'Connell wouldn't have had any control of the situation. Given the circumstances, ESU would have taken over the scene. After things resolved, it would have been investigated by the detectives from the nearest precinct. I believe that's the 18th. I had to assume the worst. You needed a friendly voice on the other end of the line, someone who would make sure ESU didn't go in hot and get a lot of innocent people killed."

"O'Connell's not a negotiator."

"No, but I made sure he was primary."

"That wouldn't have given him any authority over the scene commander."

"It would have given him some. And the only thing I know for sure is he wouldn't let them do anything to jeopardize your life. This is the part where you thank me."

"Thank you?"

Amusement flashed in his eyes. "It shouldn't sound like a question. But you're welcome."

I wanted to kill him. "ESU didn't do anything. It never came down to that."

"How was I supposed to know that?"

"You wouldn't."

"That's right."

I hated being reprimanded, almost as much as I hated it when Cross was the voice of reason. "Thank you, really."

He cupped his hand around his ear. "Sorry, I didn't quite catch that."

"Thank you, Lucien," I said louder, even though it came out more sarcastic than I intended. "As you can guess, I'm not having the best day."

"Join the club." He gestured that I go ahead. "Fill me in on everything."

So I did.

By the time we reached the office, Cross knew everything I did, possibly more. The wheels in his head hadn't stopped turning, which was a good thing since my brain had short-circuited somewhere after the walkthrough but before finishing my fancy coffee concoction. "I'll find out what the police know, see what the hospital's saying, and pull up everything we have on Tabitha York." He stepped out of the car, confused why I was struggling with my door. Coming around to my side, he held the door while I slid out. "Did EMTs check you out at the scene?"

"No."

"What about at the hospital?"

"I didn't go."

He led the way inside and pressed the button for the elevator. "Our medical team will give you a proper assessment. With any luck, whatever chemicals they pumped into the air are still floating around in your system."

"How is that a good thing?"

"It'll give us some idea what we're dealing with, and it'll save me from having to get that information through other means."

"I don't want to know."

"You really don't."

"What do you think was in the binder?" I asked.

"It could have been anything, but more than likely, something related to Spa Alive or the employees. Maybe billables. Possibly something to do with Tabitha York."

"Do you think any of this has to do with the injuries Lorna Pagano sustained?"

"It might. I'll need you to dig into that connection, see if you can link the homicide victim to Pagano or Thoreau. For all we know, York could be another of his dalliances."

"He said Lorna was an ex-girlfriend, not a dalliance."

"She's fifteen years younger than York. I'm not saying Thoreau has a type, but that's a big age gap. York could have been a one-time thing. A dalliance, if you will."

"The age-gap wasn't that big. Not for him. He falls in the

middle."

"Despite the double-standard, societal norms allow men to date younger without any associated stigmas. The same isn't true when they date significantly older."

"York is seven years older. Is that significant?"

"It could be."

"Damon Thoreau was out cold. He hit his head on the table when he went down. There's no way he knew what was going to happen to York or anyone else inside the spa," I said.

"Don't jump to conclusions. Someone on the inside could be involved. We don't know enough yet to rule anything out."

"Have you spoken to Ralph Lively? He owns the place. More than likely, this situation has to do with him and the enemies he has."

"The police want to question him. It's best that we don't overstep. He is not our client. In fact, I'm hoping our involvement at the spa won't come to light. Hopefully, the police know better than to bring up our investigation while asking about theirs. How much did you tell O'Connell?" He held up a finger before I could answer. "You told him everything, didn't you? Why do I even bother?"

"I didn't tell him everything. I only told him why I was there."

"Not about Lorna Pagano or any of our working theories?"

"No." But I couldn't remember. My brain kept glitching.

"Good. We have a duty to our client. The insurance company will want a detailed report on everything that happened. They'll want our assessment as soon as they're contacted. Given everything, my guess would be we have until the morning to figure things out," Cross reasoned.

"It depends. O'Connell wants to review the victims' statements first. The police may hold off on contacting management."

"Half the victims are Spa Alive employees. The management will hear all about it whether the police reach out or not. They'll be on top of this. That's why I have to get ahead of this." Cross pointed to the medical wing. "Get checked out and get back to work. We're on a clock."

"Yes, sir."

The medical staff were used to dealing with injuries, which was why Cross had an entire wing outfitted with equipment they'd need to do a decent assessment. They were trained. He even had a few former trauma surgeons on the payroll, not that I needed anyone that specialized for a bruise, but it was nice to know they were around. Cross had a habit of hiring the best, even if almost everyone on staff had fallen from grace, including yours truly.

"I always say we're the land of broken toys." I winced when the doctor poked at my back. "I didn't realize I meant it in the literal sense."

"Nothing's broken, Parker." He indicated the scans. "You've been shot enough times to know what to expect."

"Yep."

He poked lower. "Is that tender?"

"If by tender you mean white-hot fire, then yeah, it's a little tender." I looked at him over my shoulder. "What's the damage, Doc?"

"You strained your lats and intercostals, which may have exacerbated an old injury."

I reached for my shirt. "I'll tell you what. I'll trade you the allergy medicine for some high-dose ibuprofen you keep in the cabinet."

He unlocked the cabinet and scanned the bottles. "All right. See how you do with this. Muscle relaxers would work better, but I know how you are. The best thing you can do is rest."

I looked down at the band-aid taped to the crook of my elbow. "What did the blood tests reveal? Any idea what was pumped into the air?"

"I don't have those results yet, but I haven't observed anything troubling. You insist you feel fine. Your lungs are clear. Is there something I should know?"

"Brain's a bit foggy, but other than that, I'm good. Great even."

"It could be due to the stress and trauma."

"Yeah, maybe."

"Make sure you ice your shoulder, and take it easy for the

next few days."

"You got it." Grabbing the offered pill bottle, I slid off the exam table and headed for my office.

TWELVE

I went over everything, but I couldn't think straight. So I reverted to muscle memory. After-action reports weren't required at Cross Security, but that's how we handled things at the OIO. And unlike most of my fellow agents, I'd always been a stickler for getting everything down as soon as I could. Starting at the beginning, I detailed everything that happened in the order I remembered it happening.

When I was done, I reread it. I'd already gone over this with O'Connell, but there was so much more to it. Somewhere in this mess was the reason those men forced their way inside. Grabbing my notepad, I wrote down the one question I hadn't been able to shake. *What would they have done if I had been passed out like everyone else?*

Getting up, I circled my office a few times, my legs stiff, my body sore, and my head heavy. Two masked men were at the back. Four were at the front. When did the two at the back enter the spa? Were they the first to arrive or the last through the door? Did it matter?

Too tired to pace, I dropped onto the sofa and curled up on my good side. Tabitha York was dead in the tub. We needed to know her TOD. I scribbled that on the pad. The bruises around her neck replayed through my mind. She'd been strangled or held down. No one had heard her scream, unless everyone had been passed out. But she would have been passed out too. So why kill her?

Maybe the ME was right. Maybe she died from a heart attack. Maybe the bruising was unrelated. But damn, if

Mark Jablonsky hadn't pounded it into my head that coincidences didn't happen, and that would have made one hell of a coincidence. However, bruises indicated murder. Were those men planning on killing everyone inside the spa? The weapons they carried indicated that was a strong possibility, but that one guy had been annoyed when the other one opened fire. What had he said? *It's not supposed to be this way.*

Closing my eyes, I tried to recall the tiny details. Usually, unrelated tidbits would jog my memory. It's how I'd gotten witnesses to recall things during interviews. Instead of thinking about the big things, I tried to focus on something less significant. I recalled their clothing.

What kind of shoes did the man who spotted me have on? Sneakers? Dress shoes? Work boots? I remembered white laces. Streaks of green. They had to be sneakers. Did they squeak? He ran after me. We fought. He slid. I slid. I tried to recall the sounds, their voices, the feel of the air. My thoughts drifted until they were nothing more than gibberish.

"Hey, Alex, I heard—" Kellan Dey's words forced my eyelids open. "Were you asleep?"

"No."

He didn't believe me. Instead, he picked up the pill bottle. "These aren't supposed to make you drowsy."

"I wouldn't know. I haven't taken any yet." I winced as I sat up.

"Maybe you should."

"Yeah, but I have to eat with them or they'll rip my stomach apart."

"And you're too queasy to eat." He headed for the door. "Say no more. I know just what you need."

"Kellan," I called after him, but he was halfway to the break room. When he returned, he had a plate of toast, a sleeve of crackers, and a bottle of ginger ale. "How do you know me so well?"

"I spy on you."

I sighed and took the plate.

"Still too soon for that to be funny?" he asked.

"It'll never be funny." I nibbled on the toast while he read my notes from the chair beside the sofa. "Does Cross have you looking into this too?"

"Everyone at the office was told to drop everything and gather as much intel as they can. It's not often Lucien gives us orders like this. Well, he never used to. Then you started working here."

"Are you saying I'm a lot of work?"

"It's not you. It's the cases you get." He put down my notepad and held a printout in my direction. "Upstairs finished analyzing the chemicals. It was a combination of three different compounds used during surgery to keep the patients under. That may explain why you're so sleepy."

"I wasn't at first. Shouldn't I be more alert now that it's metabolized?"

"Delayed reaction?"

"That's now how the drug works." It was the adrenaline crash and the trauma of being shot. No matter how many times it happened, I'd never get used to it. It always took a toll.

"No, it isn't," Cross said from the doorway.

"I'm getting a bell to put around your neck," I muttered before reaching for the ginger ale and swallowing a pill. Something told me I'd need it to deal with the giant pain in the ass that just entered my office. "If you're here to check on my progress, I haven't made much headway."

Cross tucked his hands into his pockets, reading over Kellan's shoulder. "The police department's forensics lab determined what drugs were piped into the spa. A contact notified me. I passed that information on to our medical team. Your blood tests verified it. The lab upstairs found trace amounts of medical-grade anesthetics in your system." He gave the pill bottle a look. "You're crashing. You're no good to me like this. Let me take you home."

"I'm fine."

"That wasn't a suggestion." Cross stared at me, waiting for me to get off the couch and grab my things. But I didn't budge.

"Wouldn't you rather sleep in your own bed than on that crappy couch?" Kellan asked.

I glared at him. *Judas.* "I thought we were on the clock,

Lucien."

"We are, which is why I don't appreciate you wasting my time. Get your stuff. I'm taking you home."

Grumbling to myself, I tucked the legal pad I'd been using to make notes under my arm and went to get the rest of my things off my desk.

"Kellan, perform a deep dive on Tabitha York. I want to know everything, from what the weather was like the day she was born to every person with which she interacted. And I want that on my desk by the time I return."

"I can find another way home," I said.

The look on Cross's face told me he wanted to discuss something in private. Considering this was his office and these were his employees, I wondered why he didn't want to discuss these things in their presence. "I have to check on something. Your apartment is on the way. If not, I wouldn't offer."

"Fine." I stuck a piece of toast in my mouth, pocketed the sleeve of crackers and the pills, and grabbed the soda. Once I was situated, I took the toast out of my mouth. "Thanks, Kellan. I'm sorry to stick you with this."

"You're not sticking him. I am," Cross said.

"I wish." Kellan winked. "Night, Alex. Feel better."

I was a few steps beyond the door when Cross thanked Kellan and told him he could go home once he pulled everything on York. While we waited for the elevator, I ate the toast and tried not to leave a trail of crumbs in my wake.

Once the doors closed, Cross's eyes found mine in the shiny metal reflection. "The ME hasn't performed the preliminary on Tabitha York yet."

"The body's still warm. You know how backed up they get."

"I need to know the verdict."

"I don't work for the coroner. And I don't know anyone at OCME who owes me any favors."

Cross turned to face me. "Do you think her death was accidental?" He'd seen my notes. He knew my answer.

"No."

"Why not?"

"She had faint bruises around her neck."

"How old?"

"It's hard to say. They could be fresh. They may not have fully developed yet. It's also possible they're in the final stages of healing."

"You've seen plenty of brutal attacks. Which is it?"

"They were fresh."

"Any idea if she was killed before or after everyone's naptime?"

"No idea." I could read the next question on his face. "The police don't know either. They speculated she had an adverse reaction to the anesthetics which caused cardiac arrest."

His jaw dropped. "Who the f—"

I held up my hand to stop him. "I know. I thought the same thing, but the room was clean. No signs of a struggle. Nothing violent or out of place. And like I said, the bruises were faint."

"Did you take any photos?"

"In the middle of a police crime scene?"

"You should have."

"Next time," I said.

"York had a full day scheduled, starting with flotation therapy and ending with a full body massage."

"Flotation therapy? It's a tub with Epsom salts."

Cross smirked. "I didn't come up with the name."

"The salt content would have made drowning unlikely. The only way that would work was if she was face down, and the way the tubs are set up, with the cushioned neck and headrests, no one would have bought that, unless she had been getting out when the attack happened, got dizzy, and collapsed into the water face first." I tried to think through the jumble in my brain. "If killing her was part of their plan, it would have been difficult to fake a drowning or make it look accidental."

"Instead, someone found her in the tub and strangled her."

"I don't know if it was a strangling. The bruising was too faint for that."

"That's why we need photos."

"Yeah, I heard you the first time." I shook my head,

hoping to clear out the cobwebs. "Maybe they held her under the water after she blacked out. But it doesn't fit. Her hair wasn't wet. She could have been suffocated." I thought about the folded towels.

"If the coroner suspected cardiac arrest, she could have been injected with something. Did you notice any needles or puncture marks?"

"No, but I didn't get to do a thorough search, y'know, on account of it being a crime scene." I studied him. "You think she was murdered?"

"I'm deferring to you."

The elevator doors opened. Being upright had kickstarted my brain, that or it was the leftover exhaust fumes from the parking lot. Cross led me to his sports car. Before unlocking the door, he gave me a careful look.

"What?" I asked.

"I wanted to make sure you weren't hiding another piece of toast."

"Afraid I'll mess up the upholstery?"

"Actually, I've seen you nearly get carsick. I'd prefer a few crumbs to the alternative."

"Good thing I have crackers and soda."

"If that's not enough, tell me to pull over." The look in his eyes told me he was teasing, but his tone didn't convey it.

"Why do you think they murdered York? Was she the reason they took over the spa, or was she an unfortunate casualty?"

"I was hoping you could tell me."

"I don't know."

He checked the rearview before backing out. After turning out of the garage and onto the main road, he said, "As soon as you figure that out, I need to know."

"Why? What's so special about Tabitha York?"

"I'm not sure yet."

"That's bullshit. Talk to me, Lucien. Is she a client? A friend? One of your lovers?"

"How many do you think I have?"

"At any given moment?"

He growled. "Y'know what, don't answer that. My private life is none of your business."

"So you don't know York?"

"No."

"But you're worried why she was killed."

"I'm worried why she was at the spa."

I hadn't expected that. "Isn't she a regular? That's what our research showed."

"Only for the last six months."

I'd read her background, but it hadn't sent up any red flags. Reaching for my phone, I was going to search for her when I realized reading in the car under current conditions was not recommended. Instead, I swallowed uneasily, took another swig of ginger ale, and stared out the windshield. "Tell me what I'm missing."

"Tabitha York married well. Before that, she worked as an investigative journalist for an online news outlet. She wrote a lot of exposés, received several death threats, and made a lot of enemies."

"None of that turned up in her background. I would have remembered it."

"That's because she didn't write under the name Tabitha York. She wrote under Talia Greene. After she became Mrs. York, she vanished from the news scene. The reasons she cited were to focus on having a family."

That put a pit in my stomach. "How many kids does she have?"

"Four."

"Fuck." I wanted to hit something, but Cross wouldn't take kindly to me slamming my fist down on his dashboard. Instead, I knocked against the window. "I'm awake now. Take me back to work."

Instead, he pulled to a stop outside my apartment building. "Tomorrow."

"Don't you want to know if those men staged that elaborate quasi-hostage situation to cover up her murder?"

"No." He looked me right in the eye. "That's for the police to decide. What I want to know is what she was doing at the spa."

"You think she was investigating them?"

"We're investigating them. It stands to reason she may have been trying to get back into the game. Finding something juicy, like an upscale spa involved in making people sick and covering it up, would be a great way to get back into the thick of things."

"She had a family to raise."

"Her youngest started school last year. A woman like that wouldn't sit at home all day." A spark ignited in his eyes. "Are you going to tell me this is a coincidence?"

My boss never bought Jablonsky's theory, but he had no trouble turning the tables on me. He liked to push buttons and boundaries. Unfortunately, my gut said he was right.

"If that's true, any of her enemies could have planned this out and had her killed. You said there were death threats. We should look into them. Starting there would put us ahead. Maybe then we can find these bastards."

"You're not listening." Cross shook his head from side to side, as if hoping the gesture alone would somehow translate into knocking some sense into me. "Cross Security does not involve itself in murder investigations. You've seen what happens when we do."

"I've seen you dragged away in handcuffs. That may have been the highlight of my year."

He glowered. "Until now, you were acting as a private contractor. The cases you took without my permission couldn't bounce back. I was indemnified, but things are different now. You are not investigating her murder. We," he pointed at me and then at his chest, "are not investigating her murder. That is a job for the police. Let O'Connell deal with it. He works major crimes. Surely, he can solve a homicide. After all, he has two precincts to pitch in and help."

"Lucien—"

"The only thing I want to know is what York found."

"What if it was the reason she was killed?"

"Then we better figure that out before the police do. We were hired to determine why Spa Alive needed the extra coverage. We have our suspicions, but we don't have evidence or many leads, except the masseur you're hoping to honeytrap."

"I was getting us answers."

"Sure, Alex. Whatever you have to tell yourself."

"You're a piece of work. You know that?" I opened the car door, waving off the building doorman. "Where are you going now?"

"To speak to York's former editor. He owes me a favor."

"Do I want to know?"

"Maybe one of these days, I'll tell you."

THIRTEEN

I went over everything again, writing out page after page of notes. If what Cross told me in the car was accurate, the men who took over the spa could have been hired to perform a hit. The rest of the takeover could have been a misdirect—knocking everyone out, stealing the binder, all of it.

When the pounding in my head and my aching back became too much, I changed into the shirt and shorts I wore the night before, found the ice packs which were tucked on the freezer door, and settled onto the couch. Every part of me wanted to call O'Connell. He deserved to know what was what, but the way he acted said he wanted to distance me from the investigation. I wasn't sure why, but I had to assume he had a good reason.

I scrolled through my contacts. The OIO didn't owe me any favors. In fact, I owed them, specifically Mark. I could get my old partner, Eddie Lucca, to do some checking on hired hitmen and Tabitha York, but Lucca had a big mouth and an unhealthy obsession with following regulations. Asking for his help would come with too many strings.

I thought about calling Heathcliff. I owed him an explanation, but whatever I said to him would get back to O'Connell. Until I knew more about the police department's stance, I had to tread lightly. Instead, I sent him a text, apologizing for Lucien's behavior and telling him I'd fill him in the next time we had drinks.

Out of ideas, I put my phone on the side table, propped

myself up against the pillows, turned on the TV, and fell into oblivion. At some point, Martin came home and carried me to bed.

"You could have left me," I mumbled. "I was comfortable."

"We slept on the couch last night. We're not doing it again." He pressed his lips to mine, but I was already back in dreamland.

My heart raced, the sound of gunfire jolting me upright. I gasped, expecting to feel the bullet's impact, but I didn't. My limbs tingled, and I fought to see through the darkness. Where was I? The power hadn't gone out. Where were the men shooting at me?

"Alex, what's wrong?" Martin sat up beside me.

"Nothing." I pressed my hand to my chest, hoping to slow my breathing and prevent the beginnings of the panic attack from becoming full-blown. It was a dream or a memory. "Go back to sleep. I didn't mean to wake you."

A theory formed, courtesy of my subconscious. Tabitha York didn't die from the gas. I had entered the room around the same time everyone started dropping like flies. If she was having an adverse reaction, there would have been signs—spasms, gasping, something. Either she was already dead when I mistakenly went to clean up, or someone went into the room after everyone was knocked out and killed her. The masked man who came looking for me, the one I'd fought in the sauna room, had gone into Tabitha's room. Did he kill her? Did I let him get away with murder?

Turning toward the nightstand, I felt a sharp pinch beneath my shoulder blade. "I need my phone. Have you seen it?"

"Sweetheart, what's going on?" Martin reached for me, but I grabbed his hand before he could touch my shoulder.

"Give me a minute." I sucked in some air. Who was I even going to call with this revelation? Cross made it clear he didn't want us getting involved in the murder investigation, and contacting O'Connell at this time of night wouldn't be polite. It'd have to wait until the morning. My chest felt tight, the walls closing in around me. I was at home. I was safe. But I'd been there. I could have stopped it. I should have stopped it. I didn't know. There was no way I could have, but why didn't I check? Maybe I could have saved York. Maybe I could have gotten to him before he got to her.

Martin flipped on the bedside lamp. Despite the blinding agony, it erased the mental image I had of the woman in the tub and the man in a gas mask, gun raised, bullets flying. Martin rubbed the grit from his eyes and brushed his dark, almost black, hair back. He needed a haircut.

"My phone's in the living room," I said.

"Do you want me to get it?"

"No." I squeezed his hand, trying to ground myself. "It can wait." York was dead. The men were gone. The PD had the killer's photo, if my assumption was correct that he killed her, but maybe not. Maybe the two other men, the ones I hadn't noticed until I tried to escape out the back, had already been inside the spa before the gas was released. They could have killed York without anyone being the wiser. Dammit. Why didn't I check on her when I had the chance?

"Did you go to work today?" Martin asked.

Oh god, did he know? Was it on the news? Did O'Connell call him? "Yeah." The bile rose in my throat, but I swallowed it down, my entire body shaking. I didn't want him to worry more than he already did.

"I wasn't sure." His tone didn't sound accusatory. He was doing his best to keep it light, conversational. "When I got home, you were sound asleep on the couch, watching the same thing you had on when I left for work this morning in the same clothes. I thought you may have stayed there all day."

"I wasn't watching the same thing."

"Are you sure? How many orange cats wear fedoras?"

"It was a different episode."

Martin smirked. "I like the one with the penguin and walrus better." Gently, he brushed the hair out of my face, careful not to make any other contact. My heart rate slowed. I smiled, cupping his hand against my cheek before kissing his palm. Martin watched cartoons and classic sitcoms because that's what I needed on particularly rough days. But I didn't think he had a favorite. The point of the conversation was to distract me from my nightmare, and it worked. "Are you feeling better now, sweetheart?"

"You're magic."

His green eyes twinkled. "Do you want to see some tricks?"

"Not tonight, handsome." I settled back onto the mattress, wondering if he noticed the ice pack on the couch. "What time did you get home?"

"After three."

"What time is it now?"

He turned to look at the clock. "4:15." The smile fell from his face. "Do you want to tell me what your nightmare was about?"

"No."

"Alex—"

"If you're about to suggest I go to a meeting, you should know I'm okay. It's not that." I winced, hoping he didn't notice. "I had a bad day at work. That's all. I'll be fine once I find someone to share my theories with."

"Do you want to talk through it?"

"It's the middle of the night."

"It doesn't matter."

"No."

"Alex—"

"I'll tell you what happened in the morning. But right now, my head hurts, and I want to go back to sleep."

He got out of bed, flipped on the bathroom light, and left the door cracked open so I wouldn't be trapped in the dark before turning off the lamp and crawling back into bed. He scooted closer, planning to wrap his arms around me. Instead, I grabbed his arm, wrapped mine around it, and held it against my chest. Since we were both on our sides, I let my forehead rest beneath his chin.

"Are you sure you're okay?" he asked. Usually, I slept on his chest or pressed against him. This was different. He wasn't used to it. "Your heart's beating awfully fast."

I kissed his fingertips. "It's because I love you. You know that, right?"

"I love you too." He scooted closer until our arms were wedged between us. "But this is something else. I'm worried about you."

"Don't be. I'm fine." Tabitha York wasn't, but there was nothing I could do about that now. I needed a clear head to think through everything. Then I'd find the bastards responsible.

*   *   *

When I woke up, Martin wasn't in front of me. The clock said it was almost eight. Since he'd been working late on account of foreign meetings, he'd been showing up to the office later than normal. By now, he should be halfway through his workout, in the shower, or making breakfast. But the bathroom door was open, and I didn't smell coffee.

Tentatively, I stretched, gasping when a sharp pain shot across my shoulder blade, down my lats, and through my ribs. "Shit."

"Easy, sweetheart," Martin said from behind. "Your back is black and blue. Mostly black. I wouldn't even call it bruised. That seems too tame."

"That explains why it hurts so much." Rolling over seemed like a bad idea, so I didn't turn to face him.

"This is why you wouldn't let me touch you last night." Martin climbed off the bed and came around to the other side. Since I was a captive audience, he made sure he could look me in the eye. "Dammit, Alex. Why didn't you say something when I asked?"

"I'm fine."

"The hell you are."

"I am." Thoughts of Tabitha York came to mind. Maybe she hadn't been strangled. Maybe she'd been suffocated. The folded towels would have done the job. I remembered seeing them on the chair. They didn't look as neat or pristine as when we first folded them. I hadn't given it much thought until now. CSU needed to check for saliva. I wanted to grab my phone to see if I had any messages. If not, I'd make plans with O'Connell. Cross would kill me. Maybe I should call him first, but he said we weren't investigating the murder. Cross wouldn't like my theorizing, but by now, he should know I couldn't let this go.

"Tell me what happened," Martin insisted.

"Later."

"No. Now." He nodded to my shoulder. "I've seen marks like that too many times before. I know what it means. Someone shot you yesterday. It's why you had the nightmare. It's why you were freaked out. It's why you were asleep on the couch when I got home. Is that why you wanted to sleep out there the other night too? Did you think something like this would happen? All you've said to me about your assignment is random shit about some hot guy and how your allergies are acting up. What about that bullshit about Cross not wanting to give you anything dangerous?"

"It wasn't bullshit." Starting the day like this was asking for trouble. Martin knew better than to come at me first thing in the morning, which meant he'd been up for a while, dwelling. The dark circles beneath his eyes indicated he may not have gone back to sleep. "This was an insurance case. Plain and simple. We had no idea armed men were going to gas the place and take over."

"What?"

I told him about the quasi-hostage situation, leaving out the part about the dead woman. And that's when the bigger question came to mind. "They took off after they fired on me. They disappeared. It was a ten minute window, at most, but it may have been closer to five. I don't know. I'm not sure how long I hid in the storage room, but they had to go back to the sauna and carry their guy out. How did they know that's where he was? Locating him would have taken forever with all those rooms. They must have already found him before they found me. The guy coming out of the other room, the one who caught me, he must have known to be on the lookout. They knew someone else was awake inside the spa. They must have suspected the cops were on the way. They were already planning on leaving when things took a turn. That's how they got out so quickly." Were they planning on doing anything else? How many other people did they plan to kill? They'd dragged enough hostages into the salon, and they'd gone through whatever personal effects they could find. Did they rob the victims? Was that another misdirect or a bonus?

I forced myself to sit up, fighting against the stabbing around my shoulder blade and ribs. The medics were right. I aggravated an old injury. I ran my hand along my bottom ribs, making sure nothing was out of place. The repaired dislocation was sore, but that was a muscle and tendon thing.

Martin's expression softened while he watched me suck in shallow breaths. "What can I do?"

"Stop yelling at me."

"Stop getting shot. Don't we have an agreement?"

"The asshole with the gun didn't give me time to explain that."

Martin sighed. "Ice. Arnica. What else?"

"The pill bottle on the side table in the living room."

He disappeared while I dragged myself out of bed. Moving made it better. Sleeping in one position had made my sore muscles stiff. I stretched a little, shifting my hips in one direction and my upper body in the other. Eventually, the stabbing dulled to a familiar ache associated with working out too hard and lifting too heavy. But I didn't dare stretch my shoulders or back. The bruise wasn't something I could work out. It was going to hurt, and it was going to hurt for a while.

Martin returned with a fresh ice pack and the prescription bottle. He read the label before handing it to me. "Do you want pancakes and eggs or French toast?"

"I can eat cereal."

"Pick one, or I'll make both."

I moved closer, putting my hands on his biceps. "I'm okay. It was no big deal."

"The fuck it wasn't." He pulled away from me, running a hand down his face. "I could have lost you."

He had no idea how true that was. I'd left out the more gruesome details of the chase and what I thought was a narrow escape at the time. "I'm fine. I had a vest. ESU was on the way."

"You should have told me last night. Actually, you should have called me. You promised. No more secrets."

"I didn't break my promise. I swore I'd always come home, and I did. But yesterday was crazy. It was one thing after another. I forgot to call."

"That doesn't make it better, sweetheart."

I hated it when he said sweetheart in that tone, like it was a curse instead of his preferred term of endearment. "Fine. Pancakes." I tugged open the dresser drawer with my good arm, grabbed some clothes, and slammed the bathroom door. I didn't want to fight with him, but I couldn't deal with this right now.

"Alexis," he rested his hands against the door, his face so close to it, the wood vibrated with his words, "I'm not going anywhere. We need to talk about this."

"We already have." I finished brushing my teeth. "What do you want me to say? I screwed up again. By now, you should be used to it." Images of Tabitha York floated through my mind. It wasn't my fault she was dead, but a tiny part of my subconscious disagreed.

"Why didn't you call me after it happened? I would have met you at the hospital. I am your emergency contact. Getting shot counts as an emergency."

"I didn't go to the hospital."

"Fine. I would have picked you up at Cross Security."

"I was working."

"You were hurt."

"Not according to the medics." I opened the door, surprising Martin who would have stumbled into the bathroom if he wasn't so agile. "Lucien wanted me to get started on an assessment. It was only after I proved to be useless that he drove me home. By then, I had other things on my mind."

"I wasn't one of them."

That was the real reason we were fighting. My behavior last night made him suspicious. He saw the bruise, got scared, and things spiraled. Given that he was the stable one in our relationship, I often forgot he could be just as neurotic and insecure as me.

"You're always on my mind. But worrying you so we can fight about this isn't something I ever want to do. If I was really hurt, I would have called you or someone else would have. This isn't that serious. It's a bruise. It's no big deal."

"It is a big deal." He stared at me. "A woman died."

The bastard had read my notes. "That's not why I had the nightmare, if that's what you're thinking."

"So what was haunting you last night?"

I couldn't lie to him. He'd see it on my face, and we'd never stop arguing. "That the men in the masks were going to kill me."

His face contorted. "But it wasn't serious," he said sarcastically.

I shoved the tube of Arnica into his hand, spun, and pulled the shirt off over my head. "It wasn't, or that bruise would be a hole in my back."

"Sweetheart—" His tone was softer now.

"The reason it hurts so much is because I aggravated my ribs. But it's nothing. It's a bump. The men had no interest in me. I went into the wrong room at the wrong time. They got spooked. I got spooked. We exchanged fire, but everyone walked away. That was it."

He rubbed the ointment over my shoulder and down my side. I forced myself not to react. Once he was done, he capped the tube and pressed his lips against the nape of my neck. "I'll get started on the pancakes."

"Hey," I spun around and grabbed his arm, "I never want you to worry. I have every intention of always making it back alive." I looked down at the ring on his finger. "That will never change."

He moved closer, took my face in his hands, and kissed me like he may never see me again. "It doesn't matter how many times you say it. I will always worry." He kissed me again. "I'll warm up some maple syrup to go with the pancakes."

It wasn't an apology. We were both too stubborn. But we were done talking about this for now.

FOURTEEN

"Where's Lucien?" The door to his office was closed, but that didn't mean he wasn't hiding inside.

"I don't know." Justin checked the calendar. "He should be here any minute. Have you tried calling him?"

"You know he doesn't like to answer when I call."

"Do you want me to call him?"

I thought about it, but Cross would find me. I didn't need to go looking for him. This way, I could say I tried to ask permission before diving into the deep end on something he prohibited. "That's okay."

"Ms. Parker," Justin hesitated, "I heard about yesterday. Everyone heard about yesterday. It's a good thing you were there."

"Hoping to get rid of me?" I teased.

"No. I kind of like the way you make Lucien crazy. What I meant was your presence may have kept things from escalating."

"Is that what Lucien told the insurance company?"

Justin turned back to his computer. He was loyal to the boss. He wouldn't talk out of turn unless he believed it was in Lucien's best interest to save him from himself. "I'm not sure he's spoken to them yet. Did you finish your report?"

"What report?"

"You might want to finish your report. The details should be in your inbox."

"Is there anything else I'm supposed to do?"

"Stay out of trouble."

"I'll work on that."

Justin waited until I was almost to the elevator. "I'll tell him you were looking for him."

"Give me the heads-up when he arrives."

"Whatever you say, Ms. Parker."

"You know, you can call me Alex."

"Lucien doesn't want us to get too chummy."

"Too bad." I winked at him. "I'll catch ya later. Maybe we'll do lunch."

Martin had insisted on dropping me off at work. I didn't argue since I didn't have a car, and the last thing I wanted was Cross to pick me up. Though, I distinctly remembered him mentioning that last night, which made me wonder why he hadn't been banging down my door first thing this morning and why he'd been radio silent all night. Had something happened to him?

Justin hadn't seemed concerned, which made me think he knew where the boss was and didn't want to tell me. Still, it would have been nice to know what he learned from Tabitha York's editor. If what happened yesterday was a hit and not a robbery gone wrong or a hostage situation that crumbled before it got off the ground, then I had to assume one of York's enemies was responsible. I wanted to find out what the killer's motive was. That would be the fastest way to ID the guy.

The elevator doors opened on my floor. I stepped out, finding the woman at the reception desk swamped with calls. She snapped her fingers at me and pointed to a stack of files at the edge of the desk. *Take those*, she mouthed.

I leafed through the files, unsure how they related to the Spa Alive investigation. Shaking it off, I carried them into my office, surprised to find O'Connell waiting inside.

"Close the door," he said.

"You're just the man I wanted to see. You could have turned the light on. Did you sneak in?" I put the files down and clicked my mouse, but O'Connell hadn't turned on my computer. From the looks of things, he hadn't searched my desk either. Unlike me, he respected boundaries. Snooping through his things was a favorite pastime. That and annoying Thompson by sitting at his desk.

"I thought I'd stop by on my way to work." He pointed to the coffee cup. "Cappuccino?"

"Sure." I pulled the cup out of the drink carrier. "No donuts?"

"Cross has better options available."

"Did you sneak into the break room too?"

"No."

"Do you want me to grab you a breakfast sandwich or something?"

"I'm fine."

That made one of us. I sat beside him on the couch. "How did you get past the receptionist and building security?"

"Security didn't have a choice. I have a badge."

"And the receptionist?"

"She wasn't at her desk when I got here, and I didn't wait around to ask permission."

"Did Heathcliff teach you that trick?"

"You really think we have nothing better to do than talk about you?"

"I don't think it. I know it." I sipped the coffee. "Thanks for this."

"How are you feeling?"

"Lethargic. Sore. I almost called you at four a.m. But I refrained since you seemed like you didn't want my help on the investigation."

O'Connell gave the closed door another look. "Cross had you blackballed from helping the department on this."

"He did what?" No wonder he wasn't upstairs. He had gone into hiding because I'd kill him.

"The commissioner said in no uncertain terms that the department is to keep things under wraps. No outside help. Nothing beyond the norm of collecting statements and interviewing witnesses."

That bastard. Since Cross knew he'd never be able to keep me on a tight enough leash, he had his father do it for him. "I didn't think Lucien got along with the commissioner, not enough to call in those kinds of favors."

"I don't know, but that's the word from on high and why I didn't want you saying or doing too much once we got back to the precinct. It wasn't personal. But since eyes are on me, I figured it was best to play ball for both our sakes. You've consulted so many times. I'm sure this will blow over eventually."

That explained a lot. "Are you sure it's not because I'm a suspect?"

"Not as far as I'm concerned."

"Thanks, Nick. For the record, I had nothing to do with any of this." But the evidence against me didn't look good. In fact, given the conversation I had with my boss yesterday morning, we could both be considered suspects. Cross said the investigation made him twitchy, like he knew what was going to happen before it did. He gave me the N95 to wear, which was the only reason I didn't black out when everyone else did, and together, we placed O'Connell into the thick of things, a cop with which we had a history and working relationship. I didn't know how much Lucien had disclosed to his father, but visiting the inside of an interrogation room sometime in the near future didn't seem that farfetched. "Is Lucien a suspect?"

"Why would he be a suspect? He was nowhere near the spa."

"Everyone's a suspect, right? For the record, he wasn't involved either." I had no way of knowing that for sure, but my gut said it was true. He had no reason to want Tabitha York dead or the spa to be threatened, even if my mind could come up with scenarios where we came out as heroes and Cross Security signed dozens of A-list clients because of it. But that was my overactive imagination running amok. That wasn't reality. Damn, when did I decide I trusted my boss?

"Okay, so why did you want to call me at four in the morning?"

"I'm guessing Tabitha York was the target. The rest was window decoration. CSU should check the room. She could have been suffocated or strangled. Being held down or restrained would explain the bruises. Has the ME gotten back to you yet? Something tells me she was killed before everyone else went nighty-night. But if she wasn't, they waited for her to pass out, entered the room, and suffocated her. The guy I photographed, the one I incapacitated, he had gone into that room. He could be the killer."

O'Connell jotted down a few notes. "All right. You saw the room. Nothing indicated there had been a struggle. How can you be sure her death wasn't an accident? The ME postulated it was an adverse reaction. What's your basis for thinking they killed her? The bruises?"

"For starters." I ran through my late night revelations and subsequent theories. "Have someone check the towels. They didn't look right. Spa Alive has rules about how everything should be done, including how the towels are folded. Also, you should know, Tabitha York wasn't another socialite. She used to be an investigative reporter. She wrote under the name Talia Greene. She had plenty of enemies. Lots of people wanted her dead. Cross believes she was hoping to make a comeback and was looking for something juicy on the spa. If word got out that she'd be writing scathing exposés again, someone may have decided now was the time for a little revenge or to silence her before she could air more dirty laundry."

"Do you have anything to substantiate this?"

"Not yet. Cross spoke to York's former editor last night, but I wasn't invited. We haven't touched base today." I went to the computer and logged in, but the report Justin referenced was something basic for the insurance company, detailing the progress we'd made on the assignment thus far.

"You were sent into the spa to find dirt on them too." O'Connell tapped his fingers against his thigh. "If York was doing the same thing and was killed because of it, the takeover had to be an inside job. Tell me what kind of dirt you were looking for on Spa Alive."

"Anything actionable. We didn't find the smoking gun, so we're still looking. But if someone on the inside is involved, that would explain how the men gained access to the place. They acted like professionals with the way they barricaded the doors and took over the security system. But things fell apart, so maybe they haven't done this before."

O'Connell got off the couch. "Is there anything else I should know?" He looked over my shoulder at the computer screen, but there was nothing concerning the hostage situation or subsequent murder.

"These are just theories right now. As soon as I have something concrete, you'll be my first call. Are we allowed to call? Do I need to send smoke signals or use Morse code instead?"

"A call will be fine, but don't leave a message or text if you're worried how it'll make you or your boss look." He narrowed his eyes. "I know you, Parker. You've been inside Spa Alive for a week. You must have some inkling as to why this happened."

"I'm not sure yet. All I know is York is dead. She was killed, more than likely, by the man I left in the sauna. I should have done more. I should have found a way to keep them from escaping. I shouldn't have fled. I should have stayed and fought."

"They would have killed you."

"I shot them."

"Alex, it's never that simple. You did the best you could with the facts you had. Retreating was the right move."

"I should have figured it out sooner, realized what was going on."

"Figured what out? Is there something or someone I should be questioning?"

"No."

"Are you sure? Someone must have sent your spidey sense buzzing."

"No."

He didn't like that answer. Truthfully, I didn't either. Keeping things from him bothered me, but siccing him on Damon Thoreau and Lorna Pagano would only confuse matters if the murder wasn't about the affair, and that didn't seem big enough for an investigative journalist like Tabitha York.

"All right. I'll be in touch." O'Connell gave me another look. "If you find something, let me know."

"Absolutely." I walked him to the door, wondering how he'd sneak out.

"Alex, be careful. These guys shot at you. They know you can ID them. If York was killed because she was investigating the spa, you could be next on their list if they find out you and Cross Security are doing the same."

"I'll be fine. Plus, I already gave you the photo to ID the guy." I palmed my phone. "Did you get a hit in the database?"

"Not yet. We're working on it. Facial rec takes time. But no one in the department recognized him, so he's not a frequent flyer."

"What about his prints? I had his gun, vest, and gas mask. There must have been a usable print on something."

"We're working on it."

"This information sharing thing goes both ways. Don't forget that."

"I have orders. You're not investigating, remember?"

"We'll see."

O'Connell gave me a look. "I'll do what I can to keep you in the loop, but try not to cause any more trouble." He pulled open the door, revealing Lucien Cross waiting on the other side.

"What's going on in here?" Cross asked.

"Nothing," I said. Justin didn't warn me, or he didn't know Cross was back yet. I wasn't sure which. "Nick stopped by to check on me and apologize for kicking me out of the precinct yesterday. Apparently, your father doesn't want me poking around."

O'Connell slipped past him. He eyed me over my boss's shoulder, but this was my fight. Once the detective was sure I could hold my own, he disappeared down the hall and into the elevator.

Cross entered my office without invitation. "My father?"

"The police commissioner. Is the no consultant request your doing?"

"It is not." Rage burned in his eyes. "That bastard."

"You didn't ask him to preclude me so I wouldn't get involved in a murder investigation?"

"No." Cross ran a hand through his hair. "It doesn't matter. What else did the detective want? What exactly did you tell him?"

"Nothing."

"I have a hard time believing that."

"Why don't you tell me what you found on Tabitha York?"

"So you can share it with the police?" Cross picked through the files I hadn't had time to read. "I was right. York was working on a piece. She didn't tell her editor much, just that it would shake things up. I had the techs track her internet history." He picked up a file. "This is research on Lorna Pagano." He picked up another file. "This is research on flesh-eating bacteria. And this," he picked up a third file, "is everything on the art of shiatsu massage. I'm working on gaining access to Pagano's medical records. In the meantime, the techs are analyzing everything on Spa Alive's network and in their database."

"You think their clients were exposed to something deadly?" The thought made my skin crawl, or maybe that was the necrotizing bacteria chomping away at it. "If that were the case, why would York put herself at risk?"

"First off, I don't think that. York may have. It's her research. Second, if there was a risk, maybe it was removed. Or York suspected Pagano was running a con and planned to expose her."

I leafed through the folder, finding several personal injury lawsuits filed by the heiress, some of which had been settled, others dismissed. From the brevity of the text, I couldn't tell if they were frivolous or lacked evidence. "Did York research these?"

"I assume so. That's what I found in her browser history."

"Are you planning to warn the insurance company that Spa Alive may be in Pagano's crosshairs?" I asked.

"No. This is conjecture. We have nothing solid. I won't risk my reputation, crying wolf until we know more."

"What about the binder taken from Ralph Lively's office? Do you think there's proof to these claims?"

"I don't know. I haven't spoken to him. Doing so would tip our hand. I'd prefer not to do that, if it can be avoided. But the police will want to question him. I was hoping you could convince O'Connell to share what he knows. At least, I was hoping that until you said the commissioner issued a decree." The rage returned with a vengeance. "That fucking bastard."

"O'Connell will share, but he'll want something in return." I waited, but Cross appeared lost in thought. "Why doesn't the commissioner want us involved? Does he think we're responsible?"

"I never know what that man is thinking, other than wanting to show he's top dog. He knows I'll burn everything down. He doesn't want that. To have a private security firm, my security firm, show up his police force would be the biggest slap in the face, especially if we expose dark secrets in the process." An ugly smile tugged at Cross's mouth. "But we avoid murder investigations for a reason. With the stakes this high, the commissioner would have us arrested to make his point. Instead, we'll stick with our case—the insurance case—because whenever whatever dirty secret Spa Alive is covering up comes to light, it'll burn everything to the ground. And he won't be able to do a damn thing about it."

"What about Tabitha York? Finding her killer should take priority over your family feud."

"Don't you have faith in Detective O'Connell?"

"That's not what I said."

"Do you think he's capable of solving a murder without your help?"

"Lucien, stop twisting things. If we keep things from him, we're hamstringing his investigation. I won't do that."

"In that case, I suggest you work out an arrangement. Unless one of York's other enemies killed her and just so happened to do it at Spa Alive, my guess would be the motive for her murder is the same reason the spa wants increased liability. We figure out what that is, and we'll find the people responsible."

"That's what I think too. O'Connell's already on board."

Lucien sighed. "I hate overlap, but part of the reason I hired you was for your ability to work with the police department. We can work side by side, but no crossing the streams. Almeada has better things to do than get us out of jail."

FIFTEEN

Cross set everything up in the conference room on the executive level. He wanted to keep tabs on me. Justin helped move in boards, easels, and file boxes.

"Anything else?" Justin asked.

Windows took up one wall of the conference room. "A way to get these open in case I decide to jump," I said.

"I'll see what I can find at my desk. If you need anything else, I'll be right over there." He pointed, reminding me he could see me.

"Don't you ever miss not having windows?" I asked before he could leave.

"I miss having walls. Eight years ago, I was promised my own office. I'm still waiting."

"You can have mine. I wouldn't mind camping out in front of the boss's door."

"He would."

"That's the point."

Justin stifled a chuckle and returned to his post.

I stared at the three blank boards. Two white. One cork. Since I couldn't make this look like a murder investigation, I had to be careful how I presented the information. The last thing any of us needed was Cross taking over my investigation or the police arresting us. Just another reason why this new work arrangement wasn't working.

Starting with the corkboard, I tacked up a photo of the victim—Tabitha York, a.k.a. Talia Greene. The techs had already dug up the articles she'd written, but most dated back a decade. Some were fifteen years old. Whoever she exposed or ruined should have gotten their revenge years ago, but I'd be remiss if I didn't rule out every possibility. So I started with the first article.

Most of the people and companies she'd written about didn't suffer any lasting damage. A few changed their business practices and supposedly repented. Some even came back stronger after issuing statements and altering whatever harmful practices York exposed. However, a few CEOs had been forced to resign, sell their companies, or declare bankruptcy when they couldn't turn things around.

I tacked their names and details to the board under potential suspects. After running background checks, I found most had taken positions as CEO of other corporations or had embarked on other endeavors. Those who flourished were less likely to want to harm Talia Greene's alter ego, Tabitha York. So I ruled them out and focused on the few who had hit rock bottom or never bounced back.

Only four names remained. I checked for overlap, but I didn't see anything that connected these potential suspects to Spa Alive or the spa's staff. No familial connections. No work connections. Nothing obvious.

Instead of wasting time digging deeper, I made a request for Cross Security's crack team to build complete profiles on those four individuals. Once they did, it might lead to whoever had her killed. But again, I was reminded that wasn't my job. I was to find out what Tabitha York was investigating. Right now, we didn't even know if she'd been murdered, but my gut said she had, and O'Connell seemed pretty certain too.

I left the suspects pinned to the first board, grabbed a marker, and turned my attention to the blank whiteboard that stared at me, waiting to be filled with my brilliant theories. There was only one problem. I didn't have any brilliant theories.

Collecting the notepad I'd been scribbling on since the attack, I scanned the details and wrote my unanswered questions on the board. Now they were bigger and easier to see but just as difficult to tackle. Sitting on top of the conference table, I swung my leg back and forth while I tapped the capped marker against my chin.

Grabbing another colored marker from the pack, I drew a line and wrote down every questionable fact and rumor I possessed about Spa Alive. That included everything from Lorna Pagano's affair with Damon Thoreau to the cleaning slowdown to the number of winter coats Kathy Walters had in her office closet.

Once that was done, I picked up the notes and research Cross had gathered the previous night, drew another line, and wrote down every theory that came out of that. Did Spa Alive cause the rash and blisters on Lorna Pagano? If so, was that an adverse reaction to a treatment, or was that the result of an infection due to unclean practices?

"Hey, Lucien," I called, wondering if he could hear me from his office. When I didn't get a response, I turned. "Justin?"

"Hmm?" The executive assistant looked up. At least someone heard me.

"Can you get the boss?"

Justin pressed the button on the intercom. "Hey, Lucien, Alex wants you."

A moment later, Cross appeared in the doorway. Justin and I exchanged a look. This could be fun. The boss eyed my handiwork, the argument forming on his lips, but I pushed ahead before he could scold me for what I'd hung on the corkboard.

"Did Lorna Pagano's medical records come back yet?" I asked.

"No."

I pointed to the photos. "Do you think you could ask the doctors on staff to take a look and tell us what we're seeing?"

"Don't you think I already tried that?"

"Did you?"

Cross glared at me. "The photos aren't close enough to make a definitive determination."

"I don't need definitive. Speculation works for me."

"I prefer facts."

"I prefer not wasting time."

"Yet, you do a lot of it." Cross tucked his hands into his pockets and moved deeper into the room. He stopped beside the corkboard. "It could be an infection, fungal or bacteria. It could also be chemical burns."

"Like a sensitivity to the products used? That looks more like a rash. Wouldn't chemical burns be uniform over the entire application area?"

"Not if she was splattered with something." Cross examined the photo. "My money's on an infection. Why else would York have that in her search history?"

"Millions of reasons."

"You mean to tell me I finally broke you of that stupid *no such thing as coincidences* mantra?"

"No, but if York had gotten wind of a potential pending lawsuit, she could have been looking into the possibilities. It doesn't mean she was any better at guessing these things than we are."

"That's why we need Lorna Pagano's medical records."

"If it was necrotizing bacteria, Pagano would have had to seek treatment. Something serious like that should require a hospital stay."

"She could have had someone come to her, if all they needed to do was administer medication and keep an eye on the infection."

"Check with the CDC. Something like that would be reported. They wouldn't divulge the patient's name, but they'd mention a case popping up. Infections like that are often communicable. They'd want to make sure no one else was afflicted."

"I checked but didn't find anything."

"Then this isn't flesh-eating bacteria." I crossed that off the list. "It must have been a reaction of some sort." I scanned the rest of York's research, wondering if that was everything or if we were missing something. York could have used a different computer, maybe one at work or masked her search using a VPN or something untraceable. However, speculating didn't help matters. "My gut says Lorna Pagano's issue and Tabitha York's death aren't connected. Unless we find more cases like Pagano's, one isolated incident wouldn't make enough of a splash to get York's career back on track."

"We don't know if it's isolated. Our people are looking into it," Cross said.

"Don't you think if this was about what happened to Lorna Pagano, Tabitha York would have spoken to her directly?" I picked up everything Cross had pulled on Pagano and York, including their phone records. "They had zero interactions."

"That can't be true. York looked into Pagano. She had a file on her, the list of Pagano's previous lawsuits, and all sorts of dirt."

"That sounds like York may have been working on a story about Pagano, not the spa."

"They could have had a go-between. They both used Spa Alive's services. Why would York go there if it wasn't about the spa?"

"I don't know." I resisted the urge to say coincidence. Cross had me so twisted around, I was forgetting the fundamentals of conducting an investigation. Commonalities were rarely coincidences. "York and Pagano were never members at the same time. Pagano stopped going to Spa Alive before York's first visit." I pulled up Lorna Pagano's home address. They weren't neighbors. "Have you checked their purchase histories? I doubt they shopped in the same places. Like you pointed out, there's a fifteen year age gap between the two. Pagano exudes heiress vibes. She's about being flashy and getting spotted in hot, trendy places. York tried to stay out of the public eye. She wanted to keep a low-profile. Whether that was for her safety, I don't know." I scrolled through the images on my phone. "York and her husband have been seen at several upscale venues, but they mostly blended in. He's in the public eye more than she was since he's some big shot producer. In fact, I'd go so far as to say she used his fame to hide her own and maintain her anonymity as nothing more than his doting wife." I tried to do the same thing whenever I was out with Martin, but it got harder the longer we were together. People started recognizing me from other events, even if I was usually credited as the unnamed girlfriend or his unknown female companion, which was how I liked it.

"Was Lorna Pagano at any of those events?" Cross asked.
"I don't know."
"I'll look into it."
"I bet I can get answers faster." Putting the marker down, I patted my pockets. "Did someone pick up my car?"
"It's in the garage. Building security has your keys." Cross looked unsure if he should ask any other questions, but curiosity won out. "Where are you going?"
"Directly to the source."

*　　*　　*

Lorna Pagano's name afforded her internet fame. She had hundreds of thousands of followers and her own lifestyle brand, based off her family's fortune. She never wanted to let her followers down and posted photos several times a day. Her latest was taken from a rooftop restaurant. She'd positioned herself perfectly to frame the skyline as her backdrop. The sun made her skin glisten and her eyes pop. There wasn't a single scar or imperfection. Whatever happened to her at Spa Alive had healed nicely.

The elevator let me out on the top floor. The people who'd been in the elevator with me didn't stop with the side eye, even as they exited. I wasn't dressed for this place. I wasn't even dressed for a normal day at the office, but given that it was Saturday, I had gone with the basic jeans and a t-shirt. Now, I regretted that decision.

"Excuse me, miss," the host said in that snotty way which indicated he was itching to have me escorted back to the lobby and kicked out of the building, "we enforce a strict dress code here."

"I know. I've been here before."

"As what? A dishwasher?"

"As a guest." Martin had gotten us reservations one night. The food hadn't been worth the price. It was the view that impressed everyone. But since heights and I didn't get along, we hadn't been back. "I have no intention of causing a scene, but I will if necessary." I looked behind him, smiling and waving as if I spotted a friend. "Two minutes." Instead of waiting for him to tell me to leave, I pushed past him and

G.K. Parks

entered the dining area.

"Miss, I'm calling security." The host trailed behind me. As of yet, he hadn't touched me. He must have been told doing so could result in a lawsuit or, in this case, getting his ass handed to him.

"Lorna," I sat down across from her, "I knew I'd find you here." I offered her a bright smile, ignoring the host who sputtered an apology while doing his best to force me to vacate.

"What's this about?" She looked up, expecting him to answer.

"I wanted to talk to you about what happened at Spa Alive." I pushed a printed copy of the photo she'd deleted from her social media account toward her.

She snatched it off the table and crumpled it up before anyone could get a look at it. "How did you get that?"

"You posted it."

"I deleted it."

"Funny thing about the internet, once it's out there, it never goes away."

Two security guards arrived. The host pointed emphatically at me. "Remove her."

"Ma'am," a guard grabbed my upper arm, "we need you to come with us."

"We're having a conversation." I stared at Lorna. "You should hear me out."

"Ma'am." He jerked harder, pulling me out of the chair. That sent a wave of pain through my shoulder, and I yelped. He loosened his grip but didn't let go. "Come on."

"What caused that reaction? Was the spa at fault?" I asked.

"Of course they were," Lorna insisted. "They did that to me. After that, I never stepped foot inside the place again."

"But what caused the reaction?"

"It was a paraffin treatment. I don't know if the wax was too hot. But whatever it was, those bastards were negligent."

"Are you going to sue them?" I asked as the two men hauled me away from the table.

"I don't know."

I dug in my heels, but they yanked me backward, making

me hiss and groan.

"Why not?" I asked through gritted teeth. "Did someone threaten you? Was someone else looking into this? Don't you have a history of suing places for causing injury?"

She looked around. By now, every eye was on us. A few people had pulled out their phones. I didn't know if they were recording, but I wouldn't put it past them. Lorna looked embarrassed. "Get that crazy woman away from me. I have no idea who she is, but she's ruining my lunch."

SIXTEEN

When she exited with her oversized hat and sunglasses, I pushed away from the side of the building, aware of her waiting car and bodyguard making his way toward us. If she wanted better protection, she should have invited him to lunch.

"Ms. Pagano," I said, "I wanted to apologize. I shouldn't have approached you like that. I was hoping we could start over." I kept my distance, my hands raised to shoulder height to keep her bodyguard from getting rough. Building security had already caused more than enough damage. "I was hired to find dirt on Spa Alive. I'm looking into them. I thought we could help each other."

She spun around, her expensive handbag clutched against her side. "Why should I believe you?"

"That's up to you. But I'm telling the truth. I was hoping you could tell me what happened and if you know of anyone else who's been harmed by Spa Alive."

She shook her head. "I already told you it was a paraffin treatment. After that, I stopped going."

"Paraffin, on your face?" That didn't make sense. Paraffin was for hands and feet, or so I thought.

She sighed. "No. The paraffin was on my hands. I was getting a facial at the same time. They mixed them up or together. I don't know. But you saw what it did to me. They should pay."

"Do you remember who did it?"

"Willa something."

"Why haven't you filed suit yet?"

She headed toward the car, waiting for her bodyguard to open the door. "It's complicated."

"You dated someone who works there. Are you still seeing him?"

"Why are you bothering to ask questions when you already have the answers?"

"Is he the reason you didn't file suit?"

"I have time to decide." She slid into the back seat. "The next time I see you, I'll be filing harassment charges. Stay away from me."

The bodyguard closed the door and gave me a menacing look. I took a step back. He got into the front seat, and the car pulled away.

Admittedly, I could have handled that situation better. Cross wouldn't be happy about this. However, we now had a better idea of what may have happened, assuming what Lorna said was true. It sounded plausible. At the very least, I was sure she hadn't contracted a skin-eating infection, so that ruled out the possibility Spa Alive was a petri dish of deadly diseases, which made me feel better. Now I wouldn't have to go home and scrub my skin raw. That was always a plus.

Since I already made one mess, I figured I'd lean into the chaos and called Damon.

"Are you okay?" I asked. "I wanted to call sooner, but with the police and the hospital and everything, I couldn't tell which way was up."

"Yeah, I'm okay. Are you?"

"A little bruised. Nothing too serious."

"Tell me about it. One minute I'm reaching for the oil, and the next I'm waking up in the hospital with police officers around me. I'm not convinced this isn't a terrible nightmare."

"Did they let you go home?" I hadn't asked O'Connell, but I didn't think anyone had been kept for observation.

"Yeah."

"Me too. Do you want to do something? I'm driving myself crazy, and since you know I'm already a little crazy, being left to my own devices is bound to end in disaster. It'd be nice to talk to someone who's in the same boat."

Damon laughed. "I was thinking of going to the park, if you want to join me."

"I'm not up for a run today."

"Me neither, but we could go for a walk and get some fresh air."

"Fresh air sounds great. I'll meet you there."

Before doing anything, I called Amir and asked him to keep an eye out for any suspicious activity regarding Lorna Pagano. The brewery heiress may have changed her tune after my confrontation, so it'd be best to stay on top of things in case photos were posted, comments were made, or she phoned her attorney and had him file suit against the spa. Hoping I'd performed enough damage control, I got back into my car and headed for the park.

On my way, I picked up a couple of coffees, remembering Damon's preference. Since I ran out on him the other night, coffee was the least I could do, but I hoped yesterday's insanity put a damper on whatever romantic notions he had. Our phone call hadn't been particularly flirty, but it never hurt to be cautious.

Damon arrived ten minutes after I did and found me waiting on a bench. He had a small bandage on his head. After handing him the coffee, I pointed at his temple. "Did that happen yesterday?"

"Yeah. I must have hit something on my way down." He gave me the once-over. "You don't look worse for wear."

"My shoulder's pretty banged up."

He indicated the path, and we started out at a leisurely pace. "Did the police tell you what happened?"

"Not in very many words. They had more questions than answers. What did they tell you?"

"They said men invaded the spa, knocked everyone out using the ventilation system, and robbed the place."

I nodded, as if I'd heard the same thing. "I don't find that comforting. I don't think they have any leads as to who the men are or exactly what they wanted."

"I'm sure it was just a robbery. They cleaned out our clients. Wallets, phones, the whole shebang." He sipped the coffee. "This is exactly what I needed. I've been groggy all day. Spending the night in the hospital isn't conducive to sleep, not with all the back and forth and everything. Thanks for remembering."

"No problem."

"We were lucky," he said. "The police said someone died."

"Tabitha York. They asked me about her, but I didn't have anything to say."

"No one does. We were all passed out." He stopped, resting his forearms on the railing and staring into the trees. "Can you believe this shit? These are the kinds of things you hear about on the news. They always happen somewhere else, to someone else. I can't believe this happened here. To us. Never in a million years would I have expected this, not at Spa Alive. The place has an impeccable record."

"Does it?"

He gave me a cockeyed look. "What do you mean?"

I mimicked his posture, focusing on a bird in the branches. "Every workplace has an occasional incident. It's like those signs they have in factories. Y'know, the ones that say x days since our last accident. Since Spa Alive never had any issues whatsoever, maybe this was karma's way of evening things up."

"You have a screwed up sense of the world. I didn't peg you as a pessimist."

"It could be the lethargy. I've been off all day. But you see my point, right? Nothing's perfect. That's life."

"Spa Alive was never perfect. But c'mon, a group of men knocking everyone out, robbing the place, and killing someone is about as far from perfect as you can get."

"True."

We remained silent for a time, sipping our coffees. A squirrel scampered across the grass and up the tree.

Damon bumped against my arm. "Are you okay?"

"Not really. A woman died. What are we supposed to do? Go back to work on Monday like it didn't happen?"

"I don't think anyone's going to work on Monday. Kathy told the staff to cancel our appointments for the week. The police have to give us the go-ahead before we can get back to business. Until then, the place is shuttered."

"I haven't heard from her. In fact, I haven't heard from anyone. I had no idea we weren't supposed to show up for our normal shifts."

Damon looked surprised. "I thought everyone had been given the heads-up. Maybe she only spoke to the regular staff since we have appointments and clients." He looked a little uncertain. "Maybe I wasn't supposed to mention it to you, but I can't imagine why it'd be a secret."

"The spa wouldn't want the bad publicity."

"That makes sense. We were told to keep everything under wraps. Spa Alive doesn't want news of what happened to get out. If it did, the place would go under."

That was an angle I hadn't considered, but that wouldn't connect to Tabitha York's death or her possible investigation into the spa, unless she had ties to Ralph Lively. Making a mental note to look into that later, I asked, "Is that the policy for everything? Not to diminish this in any way, shape, or form, after all, I can barely process it, but when the cleaning crew threatened to strike, that was kept hush-hush too."

"Everything always is," Damon muttered.

"So Spa Alive isn't perfect."

"Of course it's not fucking perfect."

I backed away. "Easy."

He rubbed a hand down his face. "I'm sorry. This is crazy."

I waited, hoping he'd say something. But he didn't. "I didn't even think to ask. Did you know the woman who died?"

"Not well. I gave her massages. We made small talk. She seemed nice."

"That's got to be rough. I'm sorry."

"Thanks."

"Did she tell you a lot about herself? Maybe we should send flowers to her family."

"I can't remember her mentioning anything specific. She usually asked what was going on in my life. She reminded me of my aunt, even though she was a lot younger, but she always wanted to hear about my dating life, who I was seeing, the kinds of things we'd do. It's like she never got out much or wanted to live vicariously through me. I got the sense she was searching for something."

"Huh." I wasn't sure where to go with that. Grilling him would lead to him shutting down. "Maybe she was hoping you'd ask her out."

"I didn't get that vibe. She was interested in the details, not in me."

"That's hard to believe." I moved closer until my forearm rested against his, but he was too lost in thought to catch the flirtation, which meant I didn't have to keep up the pretense.

"I don't like thinking about people getting hurt or dying. The point of wellness centers is to bring comfort and peace." He stared into the distance. "I don't think I can work there anymore."

"I was thinking the same thing."

"I'm not sure what to do. This could happen anywhere."

"Any idea why those men would target Spa Alive? I know I sound like the police officers who questioned us, but the armed men had a reason for taking over the spa, besides robbing everyone. Maybe they wanted to get revenge on someone. The owner, the manager, one of the staff. Do you think someone wanted to hurt Tabitha York?"

"I have no idea."

"When you worked on her, did you ever notice any bruises, like someone roughed her up?"

"No. That's crazy to think about."

Not in my line of work, but I couldn't say that. "I keep trying to make sense of it, but I don't know. With all the questions the police asked, it's gotten stuck in my head. Has anyone on staff ever harmed someone?"

"Not intentionally."

"But something comes to mind?"

Damon pushed away from the railing. "That has nothing to do with this."

"How can you be sure? Maybe the aggrieved sought revenge. Maybe he or she planned this."

"Lorna wouldn't do something like this."

"Your ex-girlfriend?" I gave him a look, like I thought he was joking. "What did you do to her?"

"I didn't do anything. It was Willa, but it was fine. Everything turned out okay. Lorna was fine. More importantly, she would never be involved in something like this. She doesn't have a violent bone in her body."

Maybe she didn't, but her bodyguard did. Lorna Pagano may have had reason to hire a team to infiltrate Spa Alive and steal files or proof that Willa had messed up and caused her temporary disfigurement, but Lorna had no reason to want Tabitha York dead. Or did she? I wasn't getting love triangle vibes, but it was too soon to dismiss the possibility. Was Lorna Pagano the jealous type?

"Forget I said anything." Damon forced me to turn and face him. "Promise me, Alex."

"On one condition. You tell me what Willa did to Lorna."

SEVENTEEN

"Willa never meant to hurt her. It was around the time the cleaning crew threatened to strike. Half the rooms were unusable. To make up for it, the cosmetologists were booking as many procedures as they could per session, so they wouldn't have to clean the rooms in between."

"That makes sense," I said.

Damon's cheek twitched. "Yeah, except Willa got careless. Lorna wanted the works, so Willa had everything going at once. A seaweed wrap, a facial, and a paraffin treatment. On top of that, someone on the cleaning crew left a bottle of solution on the counter."

Every single bottle came with a hazard label, which is why we always wore gloves. No contact with skin or eyes. That was the rule. "Tell me Willa didn't get that mixed up with something else."

"I don't know. I wasn't there. But I heard Lorna screaming. When I entered the room, she was saying her skin was on fire. Willa got everything washed off as quickly as she could, but Lorna had all these blisters on her face and arms. It took weeks for them to heal. That's when Lorna swore she'd never go back to Spa Alive."

"You weren't dating then?"

"We flirted. She always requested me as her massage therapist. She came in once a week for a rub down. Toward the end, she was coming in twice a week."

"She wanted to see you."

He smiled. "Yeah."

"It must have been awkward for her to date you after what happened at Spa Alive."

"That incident is what brought us together. Kathy Walters wanted someone to check up on her, make sure she was doing okay, send over gift baskets, comp her treatments, cover her medical expenses, the whole nine yards. I volunteered. Once her blisters healed, Lorna had no desire to step foot in Spa Alive again, which meant we could see each other. Things were great. We had a lot of fun. But she couldn't get over what happened. She'd ask me if Willa had been fired and why she hadn't. Her obsession made our relationship toxic. I told her that, and she said she'd try to let it go. We stopped talking about the spa, which meant I stopped talking about my day and my friends. After that, we didn't have much to say to one another. That's when things fizzled between us."

"That sucks."

Damon gave me a suspicious look. "Who are you really?"

"What do you mean?"

"You've been obsessed with finding dirt on Spa Alive and sussing out my relationship with clients. Did management put you up to this?"

"No. I was hired to clean. That's it." I didn't want to argue. After all, he was right. For another thing, the more I protested, the more suspicious he'd get. It was best to deny it once and hope he dropped it. "Do you want a pretzel?" I pointed to the cart. "I'm kind of starving."

"Sure."

When I returned with our bounty, I handed him the salty twist. "I didn't mean to bring up bad memories. The police made me paranoid, like someone was out to get us. With the questions they asked, it's as if they suspected someone intended to kill Tabitha. But I mean, she was in the tub. She passed out like the rest of us and drowned. Sure, that's felony murder or manslaughter, or I don't know, but it has me twisted around, kind of like this pretzel. Too many true crime podcasts, I guess. I'm sorry to pry. Can you forgive me?"

Damon chewed thoughtfully. "I guess. It's been a weird

couple of days."

"Yeah." We headed back to the entrance, eating our pretzels in silence. "Thanks for agreeing to meet. I didn't want to be alone."

"No problem." He checked the time. "It's early. You want to catch a movie or get a bite to eat that doesn't come in a paper wrapper?"

"I'd love to, but I'm about to crash. It hit me all of a sudden."

He brushed his fingers through my hair and studied my eyes. "Are you okay to get yourself home?"

"I'll manage." I stood on my tiptoes and kissed his cheek. "Call me if you want to do this again. Next time, I'll have happier conversation topics picked out."

"I'm holding you to that."

Damon and I parted ways. He didn't offer to walk me to my car or wait for a rideshare to pick me up. I'd pushed too hard. Unless he called, I planned to let things settle. I'd gotten as much out of him as I could.

On my way back to the office, I called O'Connell and filled him in on the few tiny tidbits I had. "Have you spoken to Tabitha York's husband yet?" I asked.

"He was first on my list."

"Did he say anything useful?"

"Parker, we're not working together on this."

"C'mon, Nick, you know it's not that simple." But I found a better way to rephrase the question. "Does Mr. York have any idea what his wife was investigating or what her big comeback article was going to be about?"

"He says he doesn't."

"Would you mind if I spoke to him?"

"Since when do you ask permission?"

"I'm trying it out to see how it goes."

"Does it matter what I say?"

"Probably not, but Cross warned me his father would have us arrested for interfering in your investigation, so I'd like to know if I need to be prepared with the bail money."

"I won't arrest you, unless you leave me no choice. I can't speak for anyone else in the department."

"All right, good to know. Did Mr. York mention who

would want to harm his wife?"

"No, but I'll follow up with him again tomorrow afternoon. Make of that what you will."

Spouses were always prime suspects. "Do you think he's involved?" I asked.

"Not really. He has an alibi for the time of her murder, but given everything I know about the botched takeover, I wouldn't expect him to be there. However, I'm checking into the possibility he hired the team to do it for him and make it look like an accident."

"So it was murder. CSU and the ME hadn't seemed sure yesterday."

"More than likely, but the autopsy report hasn't come back yet."

"You'd tell me if it did?"

O'Connell let out a grunt. "We're not officially working together, remember?"

"Don't give me that."

"Now you sound like my wife."

"What about prints?"

"Parker."

"It's my last question. Then I'll let you go."

"We pulled several partials, but they aren't enough to run through the system. We can compare them to a suspect once we have a suspect, but that's about it."

"What if you combined them together? Cross Security has experience doing things like that. We have several experts in the field, and with our own lab—"

"Do you hear yourself?"

"Right, not officially working together. Got it." I pulled into the garage beneath the building and parked in my usual space. "Have I mentioned I hate this new arrangement?"

"You should have thought about that before you e-mailed me," O'Connell teased. "I know it goes without saying, but be careful. If you stumble upon something, let me know. Don't hesitate. Finding these guys is my job, not yours."

"We'll see."

When I stepped out of the elevator, Cross was waiting in the conference room. "Shut the door," he said.

I knew that tone. I was in trouble. "What's going on?"

"What did you do?"

"Nothing."

"Right, so Amir didn't waste the last two hours scrubbing videos of you off the internet." Cross didn't wait for me to respond. "Tell me you didn't confront Lorna Pagano for no reason."

"I definitely had a reason. The rash and blisters weren't caused by an infection. Willa Garrison messed up Lorna's treatment and burned her skin. Damon verified it."

"What else did Lorna say?"

I told Cross everything I'd learned. "York wasn't investigating Spa Alive. She may have been investigating Damon, but given her research, I'd say she had her sights set on—"

"Lorna Pagano." Cross stole my thunder. "Did you mention this to Lorna?"

"No."

"Make sure you don't. In fact, you are not to go near that woman under any circumstances. Do I make myself clear?"

"I told you I was going to the source. If you had a problem, you should have objected sooner."

"I didn't think you'd make a spectacle."

"It doesn't matter. She doesn't know who I am."

"She could find out."

"How? Amir pulled the videos."

"Stay away from her," Cross repeated.

"Fine. But at least now we know what's what. We can stop wasting time speculating what dirt York was hoping to find on the spa. Her interest was Pagano."

"Assuming no one lied to you, which is a big fucking if. Like I said, York and Pagano could have been working together. They could have had a go-between. Damon Thoreau would have been perfect. They could have passed intel or messages to each other through him."

"Wow. Did you buy a one-way ticket on the crazy train or is it roundtrip?"

He cleared his throat. "Tabitha York had research on Lorna Pagano. Since we've discovered Pagano has a history of questionable legal situations, it's possible she and York were working together to bury the spa."

"Spa Alive wouldn't be a big enough fish, not if what happened was truly an isolated incident. Did you find any other injured parties?"

"Not yet, but we're still looking."

We'd performed our due diligence before I ever stepped foot inside Spa Alive. No one else had been harmed. It had been a good theory when we thought Lorna Pagano had contracted an infection, but now that we knew that wasn't the case, I didn't see this turning into anything on a grand scale unless it had to do with worker conditions, and none of Tabitha York's research had involved the cleaning crew, work environment, or federal guidelines. "Did York have any files on Willa Garrison?"

"Not that we found. What are you thinking?"

"I'm not sure. Do you think Willa harmed Lorna Pagano intentionally?"

"I'm not sure why, but I'll see what I can find." Cross picked up his phone and sent a text. "Anything else?"

"My gut says Damon told me the truth. York was careful what she asked him and how she did it. He wasn't passing notes. He may have provided intel to York, but he didn't realize it. He didn't know who she was or why she wanted to know so much about his dating life."

"Too bad she's dead. You could have learned a thing or two from her."

"Probably, but I didn't screw up. I didn't do anything wrong. I'm investigating this case the way I see fit. You assigned it to me. Let me handle it the way I want."

Cross studied the corkboard. "I would if I thought you could follow instructions. But you're not interested in the reason we were hired. You're looking into why York was killed. That's why I'm overseeing things."

"We agreed this morning that the two are connected."

"That was this morning. You just got through telling me York wasn't looking to dig up dirt on the spa, which means we should turn our attention elsewhere. We'll look into Willa Garrison, but if nothing shakes loose, we'll focus our attention on the binder taken from Lively's office. York's death may never have been the goal of the takeover."

"Lucien, please. I found York in the tub and didn't check

to see if she was okay. Now she's dead. The men responsible have vanished, and the only thing you're worried about is saving the insurance company a few dollars. I can't do this. I can't work like this. I can't pretend the bottom line is the only thing that matters."

"It isn't."

"Really? Because that's how you make it sound."

"We can't get into the thick of things. Finding out Spa Alive's dirty secrets is the only thing we can do. I'm almost positive it'll lead to the team responsible. Meanwhile, the police will build their case. Maybe what we find will be the icing on the cake."

"Do you mean that?"

"Look into my eyes. Am I lying to you?"

"You're a poker player. I can't read you when you're guarded like that." I studied him, searching for the telltale nervous tics—his hand through his hair, his clenched fists or jaw, the clearing of his throat. But I wasn't getting anything from him.

"I'm not guarded. I'm telling you the truth." He nodded to the corkboard. "The coroner finished his preliminary report. I took the liberty of printing a copy for you. Don't make me regret this."

"I just spoke to O'Connell. He said the report wasn't back."

"That's because he hasn't gotten it yet."

EIGHTEEN

Tabitha York didn't have an adverse reaction to the anesthetic. The ME didn't find so much as a trace of it in her body. That meant she'd died before the knockout gas had entered the ventilation system. The rest of her toxicology report came back normal. She hadn't been drugged or poisoned.

I scanned the next page. Her lungs were clear. That ruled out drowning, in case anyone had any doubts. So what killed her?

Her eyes showed signs of petechial hemorrhaging. Cotton fibers had been found in her nostrils and down her throat. I was right. She had been suffocated.

The attached photos didn't indicate any defensive wounds. No foreign DNA had been found beneath her fingernails. From what I recalled of the room, there hadn't been any blood droplets. No puddles on the floor. That's why CSU believed she suffered cardiac arrest. They speculated it had been quick and painless. But I had doubts.

Someone had entered the room, held a towel over her face, and didn't let go until she was dead. They probably cleaned up any tub spillage with the same towel before they left. The bruises around York's neck had darkened slightly, but she hadn't been strangled. Just to make sure, I checked the autopsy report again, but her hyoid bone remained intact. Whoever killed her held her down while they suffocated her. That's what caused the bruises.

After writing a few cryptic notes on the blank whiteboard, I paced the length of the conference room while I visualized the attack. Someone snuck up behind her. Either she hadn't heard her attacker or assumed it was someone on staff. She didn't bother to turn, which would explain why she didn't scream or initially fight back.

Whoever did this must have grabbed the towel off the chair and attacked her from behind. That would explain why she never got a piece of her killer. Moving behind an empty chair, I pantomimed suffocating someone from behind. The slant of the tub would have made it even harder for York to gain traction. The thought made me sick.

I checked the report again, but the TOD window didn't help me. York was already dead when I checked the room, which meant I'd been minutes behind the killer. I could have passed him or her in the hallway and never realized it. Did I pass anyone? Did I see anyone suspicious?

I'd replayed that afternoon on repeat during the walkthrough and while providing my statement. For the life of me, I didn't remember anyone leaving the room. But I'd been told the room was empty, that I should clean it. That's why I went in. Maybe I hadn't gotten it wrong.

Think, Parker. I resumed pacing, desperate to remember who told me the room was ready to be cleaned. I was ninety-nine percent sure it was Willa Garrison. Scribbling on the board, I wrote, *Did I get the wrong room?*

That had been my assumption up to this point. Even after assuming York had been murdered, I held on to the belief I made a mistake by stepping inside. But what if I hadn't? That changed everything. That meant Willa believed York had finished her flotation therapy and vacated the room. What time did her session end?

"Justin," I stepped out of the conference room, "do we have Spa Alive's appointments handy?"

"What dates?"

"The day of the incident."

"One sec." He clicked his mouse three times and slid his chair closer to the printer. Once the contraption spit out the paper, he snatched it out of the tray, but I crossed to him and took it before he had to get up.

"Thanks." I peered into Cross's open office door, but it was empty. I scanned the list of appointments as I headed back to the conference room. "Hey, do you think—"

"Right here." Justin held out another sheet of paper. "You were going to ask for the session details."

I went back to his desk and took the second sheet from his outstretched hand. "Are you a mind reader?"

"I've learned to anticipate Lucien's requests."

"That's a scary thought."

"You have no idea."

I tapped my temple. "Now what am I thinking?"

"You want me to do a Carnac impression."

"Okay, now you're freaking me out. Stay out of my head. It's a dangerous place. I don't want you to get hurt." I returned to the conference room, grabbed the legal pad, and sketched out the appointment blocks.

Based on the prescribed treatment duration as established on Spa Alive's website and Tabitha York's appointment time, she should have finished her flotation therapy twenty minutes before the men entered the spa. However, the place had been swamped. Fridays were always busy, and with the bachelorette party, everything had gotten backed up.

"Justin," I called again, not bothering to get up from the table, "do we know what time Tabitha York checked in?"

"She arrived at 1:35 according to the data entered in Spa Alive's system."

"What time did her treatment begin?"

"It doesn't say."

"Who was in charge of setting up the room for her flotation therapy?"

"That should be on the sheet I gave you."

I checked again, but the cosmetologist box was blank. "It's not here."

"Hang on." A moment later, he said, "Willa G."

"It wasn't a mistake."

"What?"

"I didn't make a mistake, which means I miscalculated." I wrote more notes on the third board. Willa was responsible for the mishap with Lorna Pagano. If York was investigating that or helping Lorna get proof the spa had been negligent or intentionally inflicted harm, Willa may have had reason to kill York. But if she was responsible for York's death, why would she send me into the room to find the body in the tub? That made no sense.

I wrote her name in big letters on the board and surrounded it with question marks. Instead of bothering Justin again, I left the conference room and headed for the elevator. We had run background checks on every employee. But I had to make sure we didn't miss anything.

"Where are you going?" Justin asked before I could press the button for the elevator.

"To my office."

"I thought you preferred working up here with the windows."

That's when I heard it. "Cross told you to babysit me."

"It's not like that."

"What's it like?" The elevator opened, but I didn't get in. Instead, I apologized to the three people on their way to another level.

"Lucien said you can use his office."

"I need my computer."

"Use his."

"Really?"

"Sure."

"What about the files he has? Am I allowed to access those?"

"You mean in the cabinets?"

Justin was an expert at playing dumb. If he wasn't Cross' righthand man, his boyish features and innocent eyes would have convinced me he was naïve. But I knew better.

"If I go in there," I pointed to the open office door, "I can't be held responsible for my actions. So are you sure Cross wants me to work from here?"

"That's what he said."

"Okay." Calling his bluff, I went into the boss's office. A part of me wanted to search the place, both out of curiosity and because it'd serve him right for keeping tabs on me, but I had more important things on my mind. "How do I log into his computer?"

"It's networked. Use your own credentials."

That explained it. Cross didn't think I could gain access. With enough time, I could but not with his guard dog a few feet away. So I stayed on task and dug up everything I could find on Willa Garrison.

The woman didn't like me. After what Damon said, I had to assume she didn't like anyone who wore a pink smock because she blamed the cleaning crew for the incident with Lorna Pagano. Idly, I wondered if someone on the crew had left the bottle of cleaner out on purpose, hoping something like this would occur. Could revenge have anything to do with what happened on Friday?

People were motivated by all sorts of things. Perceived slights could turn into huge feuds. But stealing from the clients and killing York wouldn't harm the cleaning crew. Why would Willa retaliate like that? And why would she send me to find a fresh kill if she was a murderer? No matter how I turned the facts, they didn't make much sense, unless someone hoped to frame Willa. Did she have enemies?

While I searched for trolls who hated her or stalked her online, Cross returned from wherever he'd gone. He didn't ask why I was in his office or using his computer. Instead, he went to the bar cart, made himself a gin and tonic, and took a seat on the sofa.

"Ralph Lively provided a statement to the police," he said when I stopped my maniacal mouse clicking.

"For someone who wanted to use me for my connections to the police, you seem to have plenty of connections of your own."

"I have a few, but that's not how I got the ME's report or Lively's statement."

I closed my internet search. If Willa had an enemy, I couldn't find that person on the internet. "How did you get them?"

"You really want to know?"

"I really want to know."

Cross smirked. "The backdoor into their databases."

"But O'Connell didn't have the ME's report. If it was floating around their system, he should have been able to access it."

"It wasn't in the PD's system. It was in the ME's."

"How did you get access to that?"

"Who do you think designed their internet security protections?"

"No wonder you're afraid of getting arrested. They have enough to throw you in prison for decades."

"Be that as it may, greasing palms and exploiting contacts would be worse. I'd hate to get a good cop in trouble, assuming it's possible to even find one."

"What about the desk sergeant you're so fond of?"

"She's the exception, not the rule." Cross pointed to the cart. "If you'd like a drink, help yourself."

"It wouldn't mix with the pain meds."

"You're wrong. It'd serve as a nice chaser." Shaking away my comment before I could even voice it, he picked up the tablet. "Lively claims to have no idea who's responsible for Friday's attack. Nothing sensitive is kept on the property. It's a place of business. They don't deal with cash, so they didn't have any cash drawers or safes to clear out. Since it's not a medical facility, there were no drugs to steal." Cross looked up at me. "I assume if this was one of those places that encourages microdosing and the use of hallucinogens, you would have mentioned it."

"As far as I know, it isn't."

"So no drugs?"

"Only whatever the clients had with them. Same with cash and other valuables."

Cross went back to reading Lively's statement. "Which is why he told the police he believed the men wanted to hurt his customers instead of him."

"Did he say hurt?"

Cross nodded. "The officer asked if Lively knew of anyone who wanted to hurt him. Lively replied using the same verbiage. Is that significant?"

"Aside from Tabitha York, no one else was harmed." I put air quotes around the word. "The minor injuries were just that. They weren't intentionally inflicted."

"Everyone's lucky the armed men didn't take any liberties. With the entire place knocked out, they could have done anything they wanted to anyone they wanted. No one would have been the wiser."

"True, but they weren't there for that. They had an agenda. Killing Tabitha York was part of it, unless she was dead before they arrived." I told him what I realized. "Willa Garrison could be what ties everything together. After I left you, I had Amir do another deep dive, but she came up clean. No suspicious calls, internet searches or posts, and no weird financial activity. As far as I can tell, she didn't communicate with the masked men or hire them to perform a hit or take over the spa."

"She could be a scapegoat. I thought someone may have wanted to frame her, but if she has an archnemesis, that person isn't trolling her online."

Cross considered what I said. "What do her coworkers think of her?"

"She has an ongoing feud with the cleaning crew, but she seemed chummy with the other cosmetologists."

"This is according to your buddy Damon?"

"He's not my buddy."

"Sure." Cross almost winked, or I'd imagined it. No doubt, a residual from the knockout gas. "Damon said the bottle of cleaner was left on the counter in the treatment room when Lorna was injured."

"If that was done intentionally, someone may be targeting Willa, hoping to get her fired or worse. That gives us several new possibilities to explore."

"But you don't think Friday's takeover and Tabitha York's death have anything to do with Spa Alive's insurance policy or the binder taken from the office?"

"I'm not sure. The easiest way to find out why Spa Alive wanted the increased coverage would be to ask Ralph Lively about it."

Cross held up the tablet. "I hoped the police would do it for me."

"Did they?"

"No."

"I could ask."

"No. But maybe you could convince O'Connell to do us a favor."

"Fine." I picked up my phone and sent O'Connell a text. I

didn't know when or if he'd spoken to Lively, but he would eventually. A moment later, he replied with a response I wasn't expecting.

"What is it?" Cross asked, nodding at my phone.

"Lively told O'Connell the increased coverage was Kathy Walters' idea. She thought it'd be a good idea since they had so many valuable clients. Does that make sense to you?"

The wheels turned in Cross's head. "In a way." He picked up the tablet and checked something. "The spreadsheet you found Walters working on was a price assessment. They planned to bump up the cost of their procedures and offer a subscription plan. Assuming those proved to be lucrative, Spa Alive's earnings would have increased, which could have made them more susceptible to lawsuits. Still, increasing liability coverage now would be premature. They must have feared someone would sue or something would happen."

"Did Ralph Lively tell the police what was in the binder?" I asked.

"Pricing strategies, order sheets, things like that."

"What about client information?"

Cross shook his head. "The police report didn't go into details. I don't know if that's because Lively didn't elaborate or the cop asking the questions didn't think it was important."

"The other binders were in code, a shorthand of some sort. Why do that?"

"Only one reason comes to mind." Cross took another sip of his gin. "Cooking the books."

"If that's what Spa Alive is doing, we could be looking at an embezzler."

"Or they inflated their worth and raised their insurance for a bigger payday or payout." Cross reached for his phone. "We could be onto something."

I sent a text to O'Connell suggesting if the attack was orchestrated by someone on the inside, he should start at the tiptop and work his way down. "Lively wanted to make the business appear more lucrative so anyone who sued would seek a bigger payday, and the insurance would have to turn it over. He could have had a shell planted inside who claimed injury, and then they'd split the payout. Is that what you're thinking?" I asked my boss.

"It wouldn't be a bad way of saving a dying business or shutting down a business that was no longer operating in the black without facing a serious backlash or bankruptcy. No one would blame someone for a situation that was beyond his control. This could be Lively's way of getting out and saving face." Cross peered out his open office door. "Justin, pull Spa Alive's financial records and tax information for the last few years. I want to see how they were doing before the cleaning crew threatened to strike and how things were going during the feud and after."

"Give me a sec," Justin called back.

"Janet told me they lost clients. Everyone on staff took a financial hit. She made it sound like that was short-term, but it's possible they never bounced back," I said.

"It's hard to get a former client to return." Cross leaned toward the door again. "Justin, get the full client list to compare from before to now."

"Amir should be able to get that now that he has access to their entire network," Justin replied.

Cross picked up his phone and sent a text. A moment later, he received a reply, read the message, and put his phone down. "We'll find out soon enough."

NINETEEN

"It looks like we may be on to something." Cross put down the highlighted sheets. "Prior to the slowdown, Spa Alive had nearly twice as many clients. They hit their lowest point around the same time Lorna Pagano was injured."

"That would explain why Kathy Walters was determined to do everything in her power to keep her."

"Don't forget the bad publicity. Spa Alive couldn't have weathered a scandal like that, not from a lifestyle influencer."

I leafed through Pagano's file. "How long was that photo posted online?"

"Long enough. About ten thousand people saw it."

"Jeez." Viral photos and videos traveled fast, but this photo had been up for less than an hour. "How much business did Spa Alive lose because of it?"

Cross skimmed the client list. "I don't think any."

Rocking back in my chair, I wondered what made Lorna Pagano take the photo down. Was it vanity? Did Damon have something to do with it? "With that kind of reach, it sounds like she could have single-handedly made the wellness facility go bust."

"Someone in legal or PR could have told her that would hurt her case or reputation if she left the photo up."

"Maybe." I checked the other suits Pagano had filed. The ones that hadn't been dismissed were settled. Gag orders were part of the deal. But Pagano was the heiress to an empire. She didn't need the money, so why go through the trouble?

When I looked up from my notes, Cross was staring at me. "According to Spa Alive's records, business picked up, but they never returned to their previous numbers. Supposedly, they're in the black, operating at a healthy profit level, but the numbers don't add up."

"Did they raise prices or lower wages?" I asked.

"I'll have to do more digging into that, but since those binders were written in code, I'm sticking with our previous theory." He eyed me curiously. "What are you thinking?"

"Lorna Pagano has a history of suing places. When she stopped going to Spa Alive, Kathy Walters did everything she could to keep her former client happy. Lorna refused to go back, but as of yet, she hasn't filed suit against them."

"Do you think it's because she got Damon as a conciliation prize?" Cross put the tablet down.

"Lorna liked him. Everyone at Spa Alive knew it. She was booking massages with him twice a week. Walters asked him to do whatever he could to make things right with Lorna." The look on Damon's face played through my mind. "He was clearly into her too, but he could have been urged to trade in sexual favors. I don't think he was opposed, but—"

"When did they break up?"

"I'm not sure."

"Did anyone know about their affair?"

"Damon never broadcast it, but they all knew."

"Which means everyone knew when it ended. Depending on when that was, Walters may have feared Lorna would move forward with the lawsuit since she and her beau were no longer on speaking terms. Spa Alive may have been desperate to make a quick cash grab or shut down before that could happen, hence the insurance increase and Friday's incident. Or they saw the writing on the wall, knew what was coming, and wanted to do the best they could to remain operational after having to dish out a settlement." Cross got up. "I'd ask you to find out when Lorna and Damon broke up, but it might be best if I handle that one."

"For once, we're in agreement."

Cross quirked an eyebrow. "Do you feel that?"

"Hell freezing over? Yeah."

"Good, for a second, I thought it was just me."

*   *   *

The only thing I wanted to do was find the men responsible for York's murder. I paced the length of the conference room. It had gotten dark hours ago, but I couldn't make heads or tails out of the hodgepodge.

My back ached. I gave the ibuprofen bottle another look. Usually, I'd knuckle my way through these things. But I was reconsidering my stance. Was I getting soft?

"Alex," Cross said from the doorway, "it's time to call it a night."

"Too late. Night's already fallen."

He entered the room and looked at the three boards. Two hours ago, I gave up the pretense of doing what he wanted. Damon and Lorna broke up recently enough that it fit perfectly within our timeline. Regardless of Spa Alive's motives, they knew they'd need the extra coverage for one reason or another. While Cross was looking for proof they knew what was coming, I returned my attention to who the men were and why they killed Tabitha York.

Now, all three boards were covered with details of the murder, the takeover, and the few facts I possessed on the team responsible. The techs had the photo I'd taken of the one assailant and a description of the other one that I'd fought with. Even without the red marks from the too tight mask, I was pretty sure I'd recognize the guy with the hazel eyes who fired that first shot. Too bad I didn't know what his friends looked like beneath their masks or even how many of them were involved in the takeover.

"Have you made any progress?" Cross folded his arms over his chest.

"Not unless Amir has something for us."

"Amir went home three hours ago. It's late. You should do the same."

I went to the second whiteboard and pointed to the one tidbit that had nothing to do with the attackers. "Are you sure Damon and Lorna broke up two months ago?"

"That's what their phone records indicate. It may have been longer, if they didn't have a clean break." Cross took the marker from my hand and bent down to write on the bottom portion of the board. "Damon and Lorna break up. It takes a week or two for the news to travel. Damon wouldn't want to broadcast it."

"Or he wasn't sure they were over for good. Sometimes, it takes a few weeks for reality to set in."

Cross glanced up at me. "Feel the urge to share something personal?"

"I'm just stating a fact."

He went back to writing. "We'll say Walters finds out three weeks later. She's concerned what it means for the spa."

"Or she suggested Damon should take one for the team and beg Lorna to take him back."

"That would give him grounds to file suit." Cross considered it. "Either one would explain why she thought increasing their liability wouldn't hurt. Figure she had to pitch it to Lively, who would have taken a few days to consider it before contacting the insurance agency."

"Which puts us right on track."

Cross straightened. "It's sound. We may not have concrete proof, but circumstantial evidence is still evidence. It's also possible Spa Alive's hemorrhaging money. Lively could be covering it up, possibly with Walters' help, and one or both of them set this plan in motion, filled the spa with people they trusted who were willing to split the insurance payouts, and figured they'd cash out before the shit really hit the fan."

"Except—"

"Don't." He pointed the marker at me.

"Tabitha York was killed. Were they responsible for that too?"

"That is not our problem," Cross said, but I ignored him.

"You really don't think the two are connected?"

He studied the boards, not meeting my eyes. "This is more than enough to take to the insurance company."

"Why does it even matter at this point? Spa Alive is a crime scene. Even without our insight and theories, the insurance company knows what's coming down the pike. There's no way they'll sign off on the added liability coverage without a massive premium hike. They're already expecting to issue payouts for damages—physical, emotional, and psychological."

"That isn't our concern. The only thing I'm worried about is proving we can do the job. I don't want to get blamed or accused of brushing off the research due to recent events. Cross Security does what they say. It's about keeping our word and maintaining our reputation."

"Rah, rah."

Cross gave me a sideways look. "Go home. That's an order."

"I don't follow those particularly well."

"I'm aware." He capped the marker and put it on the table. "I can have you forcibly removed."

"I'd never come back."

"I'll keep that in mind in the event I decide to get rid of you. But Detective Heathcliff is waiting downstairs. I suggest you walk him out of here. He won't like it if I do it."

Checking my phone, I had several missed text messages. According to this, Heathcliff had been downstairs for the last fifteen minutes. "Why didn't you tell me he was here when you first came into the room?"

"I told you to go home. On your way out the door, I would have mentioned it. But you wanted to be stubborn."

I grabbed my things and took a few photos of the three boards in case Cross decided to do something with my hard work, like erase it. Then I grabbed the legal pad I'd been using to make notes. "You're washing your hands of this, aren't you?"

"Cross Security will contact the insurance company in the morning. I'd like you to join me for the meeting. We'll turn over our report and answer whatever questions they have. After that, we'll see what happens."

"What time?"

"Tomorrow's Sunday, Alex. I'll be lucky to leave a message. I'm assuming the earliest we'll be able to speak to them is Monday."

"That gives me one day to figure this out."

"That's not what I said."

"No, but you don't want to miss anything either. You have a reputation to protect." I didn't wait for him to retort before leaving the conference room and pushing open the door to the stairs.

The elevator would have been preferable, but waiting for it to arrive would have given him more time to issue orders. One was more than enough, but he gave me two. Drop this and go home. I didn't care for either of them. Luckily, when I stepped onto the thirtieth floor, I spotted Heathcliff waiting near the reception desk.

"Is everything okay?" I asked.

"You tell me." He glanced around, but the surrounding offices were dark. Everyone had gone home for the night. "Between the e-mail, the call, and everything going on at the precinct, I thought I should check on you." He nodded at the phone in my hand. "Any reason you didn't respond to my texts?"

"It's been that kind of day." I checked to see if I had any other missed messages. Luckily, Martin hadn't called. "You didn't have to come down here."

"O'Connell said someone died." Heathcliff gave me that annoying look of his, like he could read my mind or see into my soul. "You were there."

"Uh-huh."

"How are you holding up?"

"I'm fine."

"The circles beneath your eyes say otherwise."

"You sound like Martin. For the record, I get enough of this at home." I stabbed at the button for the elevator. "Since you want to act like him, you can pay for dinner."

Heathcliff let out a sigh and followed me into the elevator. "Parker, talk to me. That's why I'm here."

"Did Martin put you up to this?"

"No, but there are only a handful of reasons you'd ask that question."

Being abrasive or petulant wouldn't get me anywhere. "My back hurts. My ribs hurt. Martin and I fought this morning. Cross wants us off this case. Nick won't let me help, not officially. It's a mess."

"I know." Heathcliff stared at his shoes while I studied his reflection.

"Did Nick send you to update me?"

"I came to check on you."

"And to update me."

Heathcliff smiled. "On one condition. You tell me how you are."

"I just did."

"No, you didn't. You came up with a few excuses why you're being bitchy and hoped I wouldn't notice the difference."

I hated how well he knew me. I'd spent years keeping people at arms' length, needing that distance to protect myself or them. But those carefully constructed walls to keep people out started to crack when I first went to work at the OIO and met Mark Jablonsky. After things took a turn, I wanted to reinforce them with steel girders and an alligator infested moat, but Martin came into the picture, then Nick and Derek. Now I had a support system I never intended, which may have made me as close to a normal human being as I'd ever been, but it also meant the annoying men in my life wouldn't let me push things aside or focus on what I wanted.

"I kind of hate you," I said. The elevator opened in the lobby. "Did you park out front?"

"Two blocks that way." He pointed.

"Do you feel like driving or drinking?"

He pulled out his keys. "Where to?"

"Our usual place."

Heathcliff didn't push. Instead, he waited me out, like any good detective conducting an interrogation. The silence didn't bother me, but he could go all night. Another thing he and Martin had in common. Thankfully, Martin was a talker when it came to these matters, or we'd spend months locked in the apartment staring at one another. However, since I didn't have that kind of time and wanted the detective's help, I had to open up.

"Tabitha York, wife, mother of four, former investigative reporter allegedly looking to make a comeback, was murdered yesterday afternoon. I walked into the room minutes after it happened and didn't do a damn thing about it."

"You are now," Heathcliff said.

"Cross doesn't want me involved."

"The commissioner or your boss?"

"Both, but I meant Lucien. I don't know what the deal is with his father. He's never intervened before."

"That you know of." Heathcliff shook his head before I could ask the question. "We'll circle back to that. You first, remember?"

"York was suffocated. The ME's report proves it. Her attacker used one of the towels to do it. He probably used the same towel to clean up whatever mess he made and left it on the chair, folded, to mock us. Had I known, had I not been so preoccupied with keeping my stupid cover intact and making a good impression with the spa's manager, I would have gone into the room and checked her pulse. I'd done the exact same thing only a few days earlier. If I had, maybe I could have resuscitated her. Maybe she'd be with her family now." I stared out the window and leaned harder into the seat. The sharp sting at the back of my shoulder helped keep my emotions at bay. I didn't want to freak Heathcliff out by crying. He would make me go to grief counseling.

"It's not your fault."

I sucked in a breath. "Yeah. I know. I've told myself that a dozen times."

"You know, they have a meeting on Monday."

"I'm not going. I'm not blaming myself. I'm...not." I adjusted in the seat. "Right now, I'm pissed. I want to find the crew responsible. I spent the day going over things, looking for motives, hoping to find something, but I haven't come up with anything brilliant concerning who these men are or what they wanted. We have theories. Too many theories, all of which are feasible, and yet, we have zero proof."

"Brilliance takes time. It only happened yesterday."

"Which means the killer and his five buddies could be anywhere by now. And that's assuming my headcount isn't off. There could be more. I don't know. Does Nick have any leads on where they got the anesthetic?"

"A medical supply warehouse reported a break-in three days ago. Several canisters were taken. We reviewed the footage. We have a partial plate and the color of the getaway vehicle. The men were covered, head to toe. We can't get an ID from the security footage."

"How many robbed the warehouse?"

"Four, plus the driver."

"There were at least six inside the spa. But it sounds like the same crew. Did they have gas masks?"

Heathcliff shook his head.

Something clicked in my brain. "You said we. Did you see the footage?"

"Yes."

"Are you assisting on the case?"

"We are major crimes. Breaking into a medical supply warehouse and stealing knockout gas is something the major crimes unit should investigate."

"Nick told Thompson he was handling this himself. What changed?"

"The murder is all his. The rest is up for grabs."

"Even though they connect?"

Heathcliff glanced at me. "I know what you're thinking. Stop it."

"You wouldn't have shown up at Cross Security if you didn't want me involved."

"That isn't true. You were already involved. I know you, Parker. We all know you. You're a dog with a bone."

"Woof."

He parked in front of our usual watering hole. Good thing they had a decent menu to go with the booze. "All right, Lassie, tell me what I need to know."

"Uh-uh. It's your turn."

TWENTY

"Nick doesn't have any suspects?" I asked when Heathcliff finished filling me in. Unfortunately, nothing he said about the police department's investigation sounded that different from what I'd spent all day doing.

"He has suspects, but none that appear promising." Heathcliff sipped his beer. "Are you sure you don't want a drink?"

"I want to be sharp." I picked up the buffalo chicken sandwich and took a bite. Putting it down, I licked the dribbled sauce off my fingertips. "Nick's supposed to question the husband again tomorrow. Did he find anything to indicate Nathan York wanted his wife dead?"

Heathcliff handed me a napkin. "No."

After wiping my hands, I pulled out my phone and did a search on Nathan York. He had several projects in various stages of production. "I never heard much about this guy, but he has a lot of film credits to his name. Mostly arthouse and independent, but the projects he backs have gained critical acclaim, won awards, launched nobody actors into budding careers."

"The guy has an eye for these things. That's how he and Tabitha met." Heathcliff snagged a fry from the basket we were sharing. "She wanted to write a piece on him."

"Why? What was she investigating?"

"Nothing." Heathcliff pulled out his phone, brought up

the article, and handed it to me. "It was a human interest story."

I scanned the contents. "Do you know if she was assigned this piece or if she pitched it to her editor?"

"I don't know."

"Has anyone from the PD spoken to her editor?" Cross had the previous night, but I didn't want to volunteer that information when I hadn't learned anything useful from their encounter.

"Hubert Lunz." Heathcliff took another fry. "Huey to his friends. He says he let Tabitha do whatever she wanted. She was his star. He was looking forward to having her return. O'Connell figures maybe someone else wasn't happy to have the investigative reporter back on the payroll. The company had to downsize on account of industry changes. Assignments are coveted. If she came back, someone else would have to go."

I scribbled that down on one of the clean napkins to explore later. "Were her potential future coworkers questioned?"

"They were. No one acted like they knew she was coming back. Lunz vouched for them, said it was hush-hush. Everything was contingent on this article she planned to write. Whatever it was promised to be massive. If it didn't deliver some hard-hitting journalism with a major wow or shock factor, Tabitha York wouldn't get her old job back."

"Being dead makes it hard to get a job," I said, "unless you're auditioning for casket model, and even then, it's a short-term gig before they realize you stink."

Heathcliff snorted, nearly choking on a fry. "What are you thinking? Someone offed her to maintain their job security?"

"No." I ate the pickle spear and tossed the dirty napkins onto my empty plate. It was no wonder I rarely ordered this. It was too messy to eat. Next time, I'd have to remember to use a fork and knife. "Not unless one of them has ties to criminals."

"We'll look into it." He picked up his beer and finished what remained. "What's your theory?"

"We looked at everything. An inside job. An attempt at a

cash grab. A pissed off employee. I don't have a clue why any of this happened or who those men are. At this point, it could be anything."

"It's driving you crazy."

"Actually, you drove. But whatever you say, Crazy."

Heathcliff shook his head. "This is why I worry about you."

"You shouldn't." I drained my soda and motioned to the bartender for a refill. "Tell me what the deal is with the commissioner. You said we'd circle back to it, which means you were hoping I'd forget. Is it that bad?"

"Things have been different since you started at Cross Security. At first, it wasn't much. Moretti was asked about you, about your consulting, but he didn't think anything of it. After you left for California, it got worse. Lucien called in favors and got his dad to make some calls. I'm not sure what went down after that, but word is everything inside HQ is getting tightened up. No favors. No rule-bending. No appearances of impropriety. That's been having a trickle down effect on the rest of the department."

"I'd say that's a good thing, but…"

Heathcliff quirked an eyebrow. "But?"

"Do you remember when we first met? You were so rigid. A real rule follower. All spit-shined and polished." I gave him a bittersweet smile. "I ruined you, forced you to come over to the dark side."

"Things happened."

"I know. I was there. But I would have thought you'd be in favor of these more stringent rules."

"They're hindering, not helping,"

"Would Commissioner Cross really arrest Cross Security employees for interfering?"

"I'm not sure where you heard that. He never said it. All he said was he wouldn't approve of hiring a consultant for this case, not when the consultant was on the premises at the time of the invasion."

"Oh." I thanked the bartender for the fresh glass of cola and sucked half of it down in one gulp. "I was under the impression the commissioner's decree was in response to whatever favor or request Lucien made to have O'Connell named the detective of record for the case. Now I see how it is."

"Alex—"

"I'm a suspect."

"No one thinks that."

"Except the commissioner, even though I'm the one who called in the tip." I shook my head before Heathcliff could state the obvious. That didn't matter. Perps called in tips all the time, hoping it'd get them off the hook. Nine times out of ten, it backfired. "At least this isn't a family vendetta, which is how Lucien made it sound."

"I wouldn't know about that. You'd have to ask him or the commissioner."

My boss had a complicated relationship with his dad. "When O'Connell was handed the case on a silver platter, did he receive any other instructions other than to treat me as a suspect?"

"No, but he's expected to close the case. The commissioner wants the men responsible arrested ASAP." Heathcliff finished the fries and dug out his wallet. "Regardless, you're a witness. Our only eyewitness. You won't get paid, but we need your help."

"I guess that means I better decide on a theory."

"That would be nice."

I stared into nothingness, hoping the caffeine would kickstart my synapses, but my wheels were stuck turning over Tabitha York. "Do you think they went through the charade of invading the spa, knocking everyone out, robbing the guests, and searching the offices and computers just to cover up the murder?"

"It's possible, but there are easier ways to kill someone and make it look like an accident."

"Hit and run, poisoning, mugging gone wrong." I listed the possibilities. "Could York have been murdered to distract us from whatever else was going on?"

"You tell me. What else is going on?"

"I don't know. There have been some internal issues, but I haven't gotten deep enough to figure things out. It's possible they're cooking the books. It's also possible someone on the staff has a vendetta."

"Are you going back under?" Heathcliff asked.

"I wasn't planning on it. Lucien's decided we have enough to present to the insurance company." I drank the rest of my soda. "Regardless of what we find, Spa Alive will have dozens of claims. The insurance will be paying out, so they don't need us to warn them about it."

Heathcliff gave me an odd look. "Did anyone outside of Cross Security know you were investigating the spa?"

"Martin."

"He doesn't count."

I snickered. "He'd disagree."

"You know what I mean. How did you get hired?"

"Fake name. Fake background. Fake references. It doesn't take much to get a gig working as a cleaning lady."

"Management didn't know?"

"No."

"You don't think anyone found out?"

"I stuck to the script. You've seen me work undercover. I didn't compromise myself. What are you thinking?"

"I don't know." Heathcliff checked the time. "It's getting late. How about I drop you off at home?"

"We're staying at the apartment this week."

"I thought you were avoiding that place for a while."

"We were. Well, I was, but Martin's handling foreign business this week, so this made things easier."

Heathcliff laid a tip on the table, waved to the bartender, and waited for me to put on my jacket before leading the way to the door. Once we were outside, he looked around, as if expecting trouble.

"What's wrong?" I asked.

"The last time I let you pick the place, we ended up in a shootout."

I gave his arm a shove. "That happened yesterday. And you weren't there. I have a one shootout a week rule."

"I'm pretty sure that's not a thing." We got into the car. "Do you think someone on staff found out you worked for Cross Security and set things in motion to have you removed from the picture?"

"If the attack was a way to eliminate me, they killed the wrong woman."

"I didn't mean that."

"I guess it's possible, but that theory doesn't hold much water. For one thing, the police are involved now which is a lot worse than some private security firm snooping around. For another, the armed men didn't appear to be targeting me. They weren't even looking for me."

"They could have been. They were going through wallets. Maybe they wanted more than money. They could have been checking IDs."

"I'm not a high-value target. Compared to everyone else in that place, I'm nobody. And since I haven't found anything damning on the spa or its employees, at least not anything actionable, taking me out would be a waste of time."

"But they killed Tabitha York for a reason. O'Connell believes she was investigating the spa, same as you. If those men were hired to take care of the problem, you'd be the other name on their hit list."

"Only if they knew about me." I let out a sigh. "Dammit. This is why I keep going around and around. No matter what I do, I can't get off this stupid carousel. One minute, I'm convinced York was the target. The next, she was a distraction or collateral damage, but neither scenario makes much sense."

"Easy." Heathcliff pulled into a space a few blocks from my building. "O'Connell's on this. Major crimes is working the related angles, and another precinct's homicide unit is covering York's murder. Between their investigation and CSU's reports, we'll figure this out."

"Yeah."

"Alex," he forced me to look at him, "we got this."

"Uh-huh."

He looked down at the notes I'd taken from work. "It's late."

"Yep."

"Martin must be waiting for you."

"Martin's not even home yet."

Heathcliff turned off the car and pocketed the keys. "Do you want to invite me up?"

"I thought you'd never ask." With my notes in hand, I

hoped the quiet of my apartment and working side by side with the detective would lead to some grand insight. After all, we'd tackled plenty of cases and had an excellent closure rate.

Unlocking the door, I put my belongings down on one of the stools at the island counter and filled the coffeemaker. "Do you have an early morning?"

"I'm not expected in until the afternoon, unless something pops off." He pulled out his phone. "If we're going to do this, we should do it right."

"Are you ordering snacks? Not that I'm protesting, but we just ate."

"Not snacks. Reinforcements." He waited for whoever he called to answer. Then he said, "Hey, we're at Parker's apartment if you want to join." He waited a few seconds. "Yeah. We're working on it. See you in a few." He put the phone down. "O'Connell's on his way."

"He said we couldn't work together."

"Officially."

"Damn, I didn't just ruin you. I ruined the entire major crimes unit. Well, except for Thompson, who likes to pretend he doesn't like me."

Heathcliff played it straight. "He doesn't."

"See, this is why you need my help. Your detecting skills are getting rusty." I went to the closet and pulled the whiteboard out from where it was resting against the back wall. After setting it up on its stand, I grabbed a marker and opened the photos I'd taken on my phone. By the time I had recreated the boards from work, the intercom sounded.

Heathcliff went to the wall and pressed the button. O'Connell was waiting in the lobby. "Send him up."

I flipped through the pages of notes I'd made, scanning my theories and seeing if there was any additional details I needed to add or delete on the board, but I didn't know. Everything was a mess. Hopefully, O'Connell could shed some light on the situation.

TWENTY-ONE

Detective Nick O'Connell stood with his hands tucked in his back pockets while he read everything I had written down. "You've been busy."

"Told you," Heathcliff said.

O'Connell turned to me. "Is there anything else I should know? When I left you this morning, you didn't have nearly as much as you do now."

"You didn't call me when you got the autopsy report," I said.

"We aren't supposed to be sharing notes. That's why I didn't call. But you found some other way to obtain the information." O'Connell picked up the mug and blew on the surface of the too hot coffee. "You were right. She was suffocated with a towel." He pointed to the list of possible suspects I'd jotted down. "Lorna Pagano?"

"She's not the killer. She has an alibi for the time of the murder. Plus, I don't see her committing the crime herself." I thought about our encounter at the restaurant. "She has people who could do that for her."

"Assassins on the payroll?" O'Connell asked.

"Bodyguards."

"Cross Security bodyguards?"

"No. I don't know who they are. I ran into one of them this afternoon. He didn't seem particularly friendly."

"Did he shoot at you?"

"No, but he was armed."

"What kind of weapon?"

"I didn't get a good look."

O'Connell sipped the coffee, contemplating what I told him. "Did he have body armor?"

"Shit. The Kevlar. I didn't even consider that."

"Did Pagano's bodyguard have a vest?" O'Connell repeated.

"Not visible. I'm sure there was something in the car or trunk in case things got hairy, but whatever he wore beneath his shirt was light. I didn't notice any bunching." Going to the board, I wrote *body armor?*

"Why do you think Lorna Pagano would send men to invade Spa Alive and kill Tabitha York?" Heathcliff asked.

"I'm not sure she would, but we have reason to believe Tabitha York was interested in Pagano. However, I don't know the full extent of that interest. We postulated the two could have been working together to dig up dirt on the spa, but they had zero contact. We can't place them together, which makes finding a motive for murder more difficult. It's also possible York was investigating Pagano, but we didn't find many details on that either."

"Who's we?" Heathcliff asked. "You and your imaginary friend?"

"I wish he was imaginary. I'm talking about Lucien. He's been micromanaging me all day. It's a miracle I didn't shoot him."

"In the event we get a report, I'll pretend I didn't hear you say that."

"Thanks." I glanced at O'Connell. "What about you? Are you going to slap on the cuffs if Cross ends up dead?"

"As far as anyone else is concerned, I'm only here to follow up. We're not doing whatever this is, so I know nothing."

"That's why you're both my favorite."

"We can't both—" Heathcliff began.

O'Connell shook his head. "Yeah, we know." He put the coffee cup down and folded his arms over his chest, scrutinizing the whiteboard as if to scare the facts into submission. "Is there any other reason you can think of why Tabitha York would be interested in Spa Alive?"

"Possibly, but we ran through the other possibilities,

from the spa covering up some kind of outbreak to health and safety violations to creating an unsafe work environment. We don't have proof of any of those things occurring."

"But they're all possibilities?"

"Based on what we found in Tabitha York's search history and what I learned while working undercover, yeah. But no evidence surfaced to support any of those theories, which is why I think they're bogus. The spa has other issues, potentially, but York didn't have any research on them. Everything indicates her interest was in Lorna Pagano, but I don't know why."

Cross wouldn't be happy, but he was calling the insurance company in the morning and turning in our findings on Monday. Sharing our theories with the police shouldn't hurt matters, not when our job was nearly completed. Plus, Cross wanted O'Connell to play ball. This was about give and take. It was time I gave a little. So I told him everything.

"You could have mentioned this sooner," he said.

"You could have called me with the autopsy report."

"You already had it."

"Not the point, Nick." I rubbed my eyes and dropped onto the couch. "The men who came into the spa had gear. Between the Kevlar, gas masks, and guns, they looked like the real deal. But they had a breakdown in communications. One of them wanted to shoot me. The others didn't."

"That sounds like dissension in the ranks." Heathcliff studied something on his phone. "Do you think they were trained?"

"Not well enough. We were in close quarters. I was outnumbered and outgunned, and I still got away."

O'Connell hadn't taken his eyes off my notes. "I saw the bullet holes in the walls. You were lucky. They didn't intend for you to get away."

"Are you sure? Only Hazel Eyes pursued. The others didn't. If they had, I'm not sure we'd be having this conversation."

"They wanted you unconscious, like everyone else. When you didn't comply, they tried to force the point, but you fired at them and fled. Fight or flight. That would explain why Hazel Eyes went after you and the others didn't."

"To be fair, Hazel Eyes fired at me first."

O'Connell drummed his fingers absently against the coffee table. "Intentionally?"

"Not the first time. I surprised him. The gun went off. Everything happened so fast. But I'm almost positive he's the guy who came after me when I fled the room. Those shots were definitely intentional."

"Is that the one whose mask you peeled off his face?" Heathcliff asked.

"Yeah."

"That could have been why he panicked and why he wanted you dead."

"With all those shots you fired, he may have thought you killed his friends," O'Connell suggested.

"Maybe."

"But they already killed someone," O'Connell said. "Killing you shouldn't have mattered as much to them. They already crossed that line. Why stop their pal from shooting you when they had the chance?"

"Maybe they didn't know York was dead," Heathcliff said. "One person could have entered the spa to scout ahead. That could be the killer. Once he eliminated Tabitha York, he contacted his friends and had them join the party. He could have had his gear with him. Maybe he ducked into the bathroom, suited up, and waited for his buddies to give him the all-clear. No one else on the crew would have been the wiser."

"Which would mean the guy who wanted to shoot Parker is our killer," O'Connell reasoned.

My head spun with possibilities. "The only way we'll figure this out is to bring in someone on the team, and good luck convincing him to tell you the truth."

O'Connell picked up the marker and went to the board. "Regardless of the rest, there are three possibilities. One, the murder and the takeover are connected. The team went in, determined to kill Tabitha York and take whatever else they wanted while they were there. Maybe they agreed to keep the death toll to a minimum. Maybe they didn't want a body count. Maybe they hoped York's death wouldn't be ruled a homicide and would appear accidental, in case they were caught. Two, someone on the team went rogue or acted alone. Maybe the others knew. Maybe they didn't. Or three," O'Connell scribbled something else, making the marker squeak, "the crimes aren't connected. Someone else killed Tabitha York and got lucky enough to have armed men knock everyone out after the deed was done. That would mean one of the victims is also our killer."

"Not possible," I said.

O'Connell turned to me. "Why not?"

"Look at the timeline. Two unrelated crimes happening back to back. That's insane."

"Stranger things."

"No." I glanced at Heathcliff, hoping he'd back me up.

"It's possible, but not likely, not unless you have a suspect in mind," Heathcliff said.

O'Connell pointed to the name I'd written on the board. *Willa Garrison.* "According to what Parker said, Willa maimed Lorna Pagano and is engaged in a silent civil war with the cleaning crew. She was in charge of Tabitha York's treatment the day of her murder. Besides Parker, who walked in on York presumably after she was killed, Willa Garrison is the last person we know of who saw Tabitha York alive."

"It could be a frame job," I said. "Willa doesn't have a record, and she told me to go into that room."

"She knew you had interrupted another client's flotation therapy earlier in the week. She must have thought you'd do it again. That would mean you would find the body, which would make you our prime suspect."

"There would have been no evidence to pin it on me."

"Are you sure?" Heathcliff tapped on his phone. "You work for the cleaning crew. You folded the towels, which were used to kill York. Since we know she was suffocated and the murder weapon was returned to the chair, one could reason you went in there, did her in, and cleaned up the mess."

"It wouldn't hold up," I said.

"Probably not," O'Connell agreed, "but it'd be enough to

cast doubt. You are the newest hire. You'd already been warned not to interfere with a client's treatment session. Since you did it again, you'd want to make sure it couldn't be reported for fear of losing your job, so you took matters into your own hands. After all, you told your coworkers you were desperate for work."

"Great. I'm the killer."

O'Connell rolled his eyes. "Do you have any idea where Willa was prior to Tabitha York's murder?"

"I can't say for certain. I was busy cleaning another room, but usually, the staff member in charge of the treatment would return to the room to let the client know her time was up. After the client vacated the room, the staff member would tell someone on the cleaning crew the room was ready."

"Willa told you the room was ready," Heathcliff pointed out.

"Tell me again why you don't think she's the killer," O'Connell said. "She had means, motive, and opportunity."

"She was the first victim I found. She was unconscious on the floor of the break room. That's when I knew something was wrong and went to get help."

"Two separate crimes, back to back," Heathcliff said.

"I don't know."

"You didn't see anyone else down for the count before you found Willa?" O'Connell pulled out his notepad and clicked his pen. "When you took me through the place, you pointed out where you noticed others were unconscious. But Willa was the first."

"She's the first one I saw. I didn't see anyone else until after I spotted the men with gas masks. That's when I realized the people in the lobby, near the reception desk, were passed out too, and that's when I made a run for it."

"That's when you spotted more staff members and clients who had blacked out," O'Connell said. "Willa could be working with the team who invaded Spa Alive."

"Cross checked. He didn't find any suspicious calls, texts, or financial activity. I spent the afternoon looking into her records and internet activity, but nothing popped. That's why I don't think she's involved." Now I wasn't sure.

O'Connell had turned my sound reasoning on its head, but even as my brain mulled over the possibility, I knew the simplest answer was usually the right one. But my gut wasn't convinced. It'd be nice if the two could agree.

"I've only brushed the surface so far, but preliminaries didn't send up any red flags," O'Connell admitted. "When I spoke to her, she didn't remember what happened. But most of the victims I interviewed couldn't recall what they were doing immediately before they blacked out. The doctors said that's normal with the type of anesthetic used."

"Willa could have been lying. She could have used that as an excuse." I hated that I hadn't reached this conclusion on my own. Was I losing my touch? Or was this too easy, like I originally thought?

Heathcliff put his phone down. "Every account from the medical supply warehouse robbery said the assailants were men. I watched the videos again to see if someone may have been wrong or jumped to the wrong conclusion, but no one was built like her."

"She may not be connected to the masked men." I pointed to O'Connell's third theory. "Two separate, unrelated crimes seem highly unlikely, but what do I know?"

O'Connell looked at the time. "I'll pay Willa a visit in the morning and see what she has to say before I follow up with Nathan York." He put his empty mug in the sink. "Is there anyone else I should question?"

"Ralph Lively and Kathy Walters. They may be doctoring the books." I thought about our other theories. "You already covered the news outlet where Tabitha used to work and spoke to her editor. If anyone knew what she was investigating, it should have been him." I glanced at the board again. "Can you hold off on Lorna Pagano until after Cross finishes his business with the insurance agency? We don't want to tip our hand and force her to file before we have a chance to disclose what we found concerning a potential lawsuit."

"I'll try. It depends on where the evidence leads, but make sure he gets to that first thing Monday morning."

"I'll let him know." I wasn't sure how exactly to do that without getting reprimanded, but I'd figure it out. Given everything, that was the least of my worries.

O'Connell went to the door. "I know we're not used to working like this, but I didn't want to keep you out of the loop. Thanks for the leads. Can you stay out of trouble while I look into them?"

"Yeah, no problem."

O'Connell gave me a cockeyed look. "Get some rest. You look like shit."

"I love it when you tell me that."

He pulled open the door. "Night, Parker."

I moved to the doorway, waiting for him to get into the elevator. When it arrived, the doors opened, revealing Martin, who had his jacket over his arm and his face buried in his phone. He didn't even look up as he exited the elevator.

"This is why I insist he has a bodyguard," I said. "Zero tactical awareness. At least now I have witnesses."

At the sound of my voice, Martin looked up, surprised to see O'Connell standing in front of him and Heathcliff and me waiting in the doorway. "Gentlemen," he glanced from them to me, "is everything okay?"

O'Connell stepped into the elevator. "Don't worry, you didn't miss date night."

"Hold up, Nick. I'll ride down with you." Heathcliff grabbed his things. "You could have warned me before firing off that volley," he whispered while giving me a quick hug that involved minimal contact. "Before you get too self-destructive and blow your entire life up, remember there's a meeting Monday. I'll insist if necessary."

"Good night, Derek."

Martin bid the detectives farewell, made sure the elevator closed, and shut himself inside our apartment. "Ready for round two, sweetheart?" He put his things down, stopping to stare at the whiteboard in the center of our living room.

"I don't want to fight with you."

"You could have fooled me." He noticed the unfamiliar handwriting on the board. "That explains it."

"Explains what?"

Martin smirked, poured out the rest of the coffee, and put the empty carafe in the dishwasher. "You missed something." He jerked his chin toward the board. "You do this every time you mess up. I'm not playing along this time. If you want to punish yourself, find another way to do it."

"That's not what I'm doing."

"What are you doing?"

"Losing my mind."

TWENTY-TWO

I'd been parked outside Willa Garrison's apartment most of the night. Martin wasn't happy when I left, but we weren't fighting. I wasn't sure what we were doing, but it wasn't good. It was my fault. Most things were. It wasn't that I didn't want to talk to him, to explain, but I didn't know what to say. As usual, I wasn't sure what was wrong with me. But I had a strong suspicion it had something to do with finding a dead woman in the tub and getting shot. Maybe I would go to a meeting.

Willa got up bright and early. In fact, it wasn't even light out. Why would anyone get up this early on a Sunday?

She got into her car, a red four-door with a rusted bumper, and pulled away from the building. Since traffic was nonexistent, I waited until she passed the stop sign before pursuing. A few blocks later, she went through a drive-thru. Coffee and donuts, no wonder I had trouble believing this woman was a murderer. That was the breakfast of champions, but not something a Spa Alive employee should eat.

I circled while I waited for her to exit, hoping she wouldn't spot me. Getting recognized would not bode well, so I tried to come up with a cover story. However, since I didn't know where we were going, I couldn't come up with a decent excuse. Instead, I'd stick to the basics. I'd been out late drinking and was in desperate need of something greasy. Given how terrible I looked, it'd be an easy sell.

Luckily, Willa didn't notice me tailing her. A mile and a half later, she parked outside a church, grabbed the box of donuts and the drink carrier, and headed for the side entrance. I turned down the next street, glad to find plenty of empty spaces.

By the time I was situated, she had gone inside. I pulled up the church's information on my phone. *St. Anthony's.* Early morning mass started at 8 a.m. But no one I knew ever showed up an hour and a half early or took snacks with them.

I continued scrolling, finding an events calendar. The ladies' auxiliary was having an early morning meeting. None of my research indicated Willa was involved in church activities, but I had no reason to doubt it. This could have been a spur of the moment decision, a way to repent.

Settling into the seat, I stared at the church. My eyes tried to close, but I wouldn't let them. Instead, I turned on the radio and sang along. It was a good thing I'd parked on a quiet street. If anyone walked past my car, they were liable to make a noise complaint.

An hour and a half later, the rest of the congregation arrived. Now would be the perfect time for Willa to slip away, assuming she realized she had a tail, but her car remained where it was. As far as I could tell, she remained inside the church.

A little after nine, the doors opened. People poured out in their Sunday best. I watched and waited. The priest stood at the top of the steps, speaking to several parishioners. Black shirt. Black pants. White collar. I resisted the urge to make the sign of the cross.

Willa exited from the side door with two other ladies. They spoke, gesturing toward the rear of the church. I snapped a few photos, so I wouldn't feel like the entire night had been a waste. After three minutes of chatting, they parted ways. Her two counterparts headed for a green minivan which was parked in the opposite direction.

After jotting down the plate, I turned my attention back to Willa, who was getting into her car. When she pulled out of the space, I followed. This time, she didn't make any stops. She went straight home.

While I waited across the street, wondering if I should knock on her door or dig into her companions or the church, an unmarked cruiser came down the street. I checked the time. It was almost 10:30.

O'Connell parked four cars away and approached on the passenger's side. I hit the unlock, keeping my eyes glued to Willa's apartment. Out of an abundance of caution, O'Connell knocked on the window before pulling open the door and sliding in beside me.

"What are you doing here?" he asked.

"I couldn't sleep." I pointed to the travel cup in the holder. "Twenty-twenty hindsight being what it is, I shouldn't have made coffee last night." I gave him a look. "You didn't sleep either."

"Not with the brass breathing down my neck." O'Connell picked up the travel cup, disappointed to find it empty. "You didn't bring me one?"

"I wasn't counting on running into you."

"I told you my plans. Are you going to follow me to the Yorks' house after this?"

"Was that an invitation?"

O'Connell sighed. "How long have you been camped out here?"

"Since a little after four. Willa picked up breakfast, met with the ladies' auxiliary, and attended mass."

"Did she go to confession?"

"I have no idea. I didn't go inside. You know I'd burst into flames."

O'Connell rolled his eyes. "What church?"

"St. Anthony's." I handed him my phone. "It looked innocent enough, but I was bored. I thought I should do something to pass the time."

He forwarded the photos to his phone and copied the license plate number. "If nothing else, I can ask her friends if she was acting strangely or seemed off."

"We're really scraping the bottom of the barrel." I glanced at him. "If it helps, you can bring me in as a suspect. I won't hold it against you. It'll make the brass think you're making progress. It might buy you some time."

"Lt. Moretti would never believe that."

"This wouldn't be the first time I've been arrested. I've actually lost count. Remember that time Heathcliff arrested me? That was fun. Well, until I passed out in the middle of the emergency room."

"Parker—"

"I'm just saying."

"You're gonna be a buster until I find a way to get you onto this case. You know this isn't my decision. I'd hire you to consult if I could."

"It's not that."

"Tell me what it is. I know you. You don't sit on the sidelines."

"That's why I'm out here."

"It's more than that."

"Lucien's got me on a tight leash, and his father's backing his plays. Heathcliff tried to update me on their dynamics, but I'd need a compass and a roadmap. Even that wouldn't be enough. The only way I'd be able to figure out how we ended up here is with a Sherpa. That's what they're called, right? Not the blanket, but the guide that takes you up the mountain."

I hadn't seen that look on O'Connell's face since the last time I'd gone off the rails. "Do me a favor. Lay off the caffeine."

"It's the only thing keeping me upright." I turned to face him. "I'm fine. I'm just not sure what to do. Questioning anyone from Spa Alive will be frowned upon unless it directly relates to the insurance issue, and speaking to Willa won't help."

Since O'Connell had already talked to Ralph Lively, I should pay Kathy Walters a visit. I was scheduled to work Monday and she hadn't called to tell me otherwise.

"Okay, that look is more frightening than the last one." O'Connell pointed at my face. "What are you planning to do?"

"Talk to my boss."

"All right." He reached for the door handle. "I'll wish you luck with that."

"Thanks, Nick." I jerked my chin toward Willa's front door. "Same to you." Before he stepped out, I asked, "After this, you're going to the Yorks?"

"That's the plan, unless Willa Garrison confesses."

"Okay."

"Am I going to see you at the Yorks' too?"

"Not if I work on my timing. Hey, one other thing. Last night, I brought up the gear the masked men had. Any idea where it came from?"

"The only items we recovered were the ones you took off a suspect. Everything was basic. Nothing custom. It could have come from any place that sells tactical gear. We weren't able to run it down. Not with so many possibilities."

"But CSU has finished analyzing it?"

He nodded.

"And that information is floating around in the police database somewhere?"

O'Connell narrowed his eyes. "Why are you asking?"

"Do you think you could pull it up and share it with me?"

"It won't help."

"Is that a no?" Cross Security could find it on their own, but the fewer laws we broke, the better off we'd be. Perhaps that would convince the commissioner to remove the moratorium he placed on working with us.

O'Connell pulled out his phone, accessed the information, and held it out for me to see. I read it, thanked him, and copied it down on my notepad. If we were in kindergarten, we would have gotten gold stars for sharing.

"Thanks."

"Don't mention it." He gave me a look. "I mean it."

I pantomimed zipping my lip. "I'll see you around."

"Not too soon, I hope."

"Yeah, yeah. I'm working on it."

After pulling up Kathy Walters' home address, I drove to her place. Her car was parked out front. Knocking would come with a few questions, like how I got her address, but I was tired of observing. I'd done enough of that at Spa Alive.

Instead, I went up the walk and rang her doorbell. While I waited to see if she'd answer, I smiled at the doorbell camera. *Avon calling.*

Thirty seconds later, the door opened with a groan. Kathy stood on the other side, a plush, oversized robe wrapped around her. She didn't look like she'd been asleep, but I didn't think she was dressed either.

"Alexandra?" She made a face. "What are you doing here?"

"I wanted to know what was going on at work. I tried calling the main number, but no one answered. I thought about leaving a message, but figured by the time anyone checked them, it would be too late. I'm sorry. I'm rambling. Friday left me frazzled. I didn't know if I was supposed to report to work tomorrow."

She gave me an odd look. "That's why you're knocking on my door?"

"I just...I haven't...I spoke to Damon yesterday, but I haven't really talked to anyone else about what happened, except the police. I heard someone died."

"A client." She glanced behind her.

"Do you have company? I shouldn't have intruded."

"No, it's fine. I thought I heard the oven timer." But she didn't invite me in. Instead, she remained in front of the half-opened front door, blocking me from entering or seeing inside. "Everyone on staff made it out okay."

"Do you have any idea who the men were that attacked the spa or what they wanted?"

"No."

"Where were you when it happened?"

"I'm not sure. Everything from that afternoon is hazy. I was probably in my office."

No, she wasn't. "Do you have any idea what they wanted? Was it a robbery, a murder, or something else?"

"I don't know. But there's no reason to worry. The police will figure it out."

"Was the spa threatened? Maybe an employee had enemies? Maybe something shady was going on behind closed doors?"

She gave me a sideways look. "You're okay, right?"

"If that's what you want to call it."

She reached out to pat the side of my arm. "We'll be closed all week. Take some time to regroup and recenter yourself."

"That's it?"

"What else is there to say? The police are investigating. I'm sure they will catch the culprits." She peered behind me. "How did you get my address?"

"I found it online. Unfortunately, I couldn't find your phone number."

"Uh-huh." She wasn't buying it. "Someone on the cleaning crew should have notified you. I apologize for the oversight. It won't happen again, but this is highly inappropriate."

"Right." I held up my palms and backed away. "Sorry. I've always had issues with boundaries. Damon mentioned he was told to stay home, but I figured the cleaning crew would have to go in and get things tidied up after everything. I can't even imagine what Spa Alive must look like. Have you seen the aftermath?"

"No, but I'll make sure to call you when I need you."

"Okay." Before I could thank her, she slammed the door.

Aware of the camera aimed at me, I got off the porch. The camera covered the door, so I moved out of view. Since Kathy Walters lived on the end, I crept along the side of the house. Two voices sounded from inside. Despite being muffled by the building materials, I could still make out what they were saying.

"Who was that?" a guy asked.

"Someone from work," Kathy replied.

"What did she want?"

"I'm not sure."

I stopped beneath the window, but the blinds were closed. I couldn't see inside.

"I don't like this," the guy said. "She asked a lot of questions. Do you think she's working with the police?"

"She's part of the cleaning crew," Kathy said.

I moved to the next window, surprised when I found the blinds opened. From the looks of things, this was the bedroom window. The bed was unmade, the sheets and blankets rumpled and bunched.

"Shit." He stormed to the front door. His heavy footsteps stopped when the door opened. "What's her name?"

"Alexandra Bradley."

"How well do you know her?" The front door creaked as

he closed and locked it.

"Not well. She's a new hire."

The man entered the bedroom, but he kept his back to me. "Do you think she'll cause trouble?"

Kathy followed him into the room, opening her robe and revealing a slinky nightie. "She's only concerned with keeping me happy. A few days ago, she started crying before I could write her up. I'm sure that's why she came all the way here. She's a needy little thing."

"Kind of like you." He grabbed the hanging sash by both ends and pulled her to him. While they were kissing, he flipped their positions and tossed her onto the bed. Thankfully, he didn't see me, but I saw him. The bruise on his chest looked painful and fresh. He was one of the bastards I'd shot.

TWENTY-THREE

Busting inside and arresting him was the only thing I wanted to do, but I wasn't a federal agent. By now, I should have shaken that ingrained desire, but I hadn't. Instead, I called O'Connell. He had a badge to go with his handcuffs.

"Now what?" he asked.

"I found one of them."

"Are you sure?"

"Ninety-nine percent."

"Where are you?"

"Kathy Walters' house. I went to question her about the attack, but she shut me down. I didn't know she had company."

"Did he see you?"

"I don't think so. Even if he did, he wouldn't recognize me. I don't recognize him."

"How do you know it's one of the armed men?"

"He has a bruise on his chest from where the bullet impacted his vest."

"Do you think Walters is in danger?"

The man appeared volatile. I couldn't rule out the possibility he'd turn on her, but right now, she was safe enough. "Not at the moment."

"I'll send units to pick him up. Stay out of sight. Don't do anything stupid, Parker. I mean it."

"No problem." I disconnected and crept toward the front of the house, hoping to locate his vehicle. But I had no way of figuring out which one was his. How long would it take the police to arrive? Two minutes? Five minutes?

A phone rang inside the house. Before the second ring completed, it stopped. Did he answer? At this distance, I couldn't tell, so I crawled back beneath the window.

"Hang on. What?" He paused. "You're sure?" He paused again. "I'm on my way."

"Right now?" Walters sounded annoyed. "We're in the middle of something."

"I have to go. If anyone shows up, let me know immediately. Do you understand?" His tone didn't sound friendly.

"Fine," she said.

I thought about cautioning a glance through the window, but I didn't know where he was or if he'd see me. I couldn't let him get away again. Hoping he'd go out the front, I figured I'd get a head start by waiting for him inside my car, but then I remembered the doorbell camera. Would he avoid that exit for fear of being identified? Would he kill Walters for the same reason?

Someone on that crew was a killer. It could be him. Deciding that I couldn't live with allowing another murder to occur, I peered through the window. Walters remained on the bed, propped up on one elbow while she watched him dress. From this angle, I couldn't see much of him besides an elbow or a hand while he put his belt back on.

He didn't look familiar, and I didn't recognize his voice. But the men at the spa had on gas masks. That had muffled their voices. The bruise on his chest was the dead giveaway. Without that, I wouldn't have made the connection. Only one thing left a mark like that. I would know. I had a matching one at the back of my shoulder.

"Later," he said. The shadow disappeared out of the room. The closed blinds kept me from seeing in, but the shadow moved past the next window. The front door opened with a metallic scrape.

Ducking behind a shrub, I watched him go down the path and get into a black sedan. The paint on the roof was peeling in a few places, and the hood was faded from the sun. The plate was caked with dirt. From the looks of it, it had to be intentional. I could only get a partial 5-9-R.

Once he started the engine, I moved out of cover. The front door was closed. Thankfully, Walters didn't feel the need to wave goodbye. But he was leaving, and I couldn't let him get away. Not again.

As soon as he pulled out of the parking space, I ran to my car. Since I'd left the apartment in the middle of the night to conduct surveillance, I didn't have the company car. Even if Walters had looked, she wouldn't have known which car was mine. That meant this guy didn't know either. That was the only positive I could think of as I got behind the wheel and followed him.

Voice-dialing O'Connell, I put the call on speaker and shoved my phone into the cupholder. "He's on the move. Where are those units you promised?"

"They aren't there yet?"

"No."

"Where are you?"

"Following him."

"Call dispatch and update them on the situation. I will get to you as soon as I can. Be careful."

"Always."

O'Connell's words sent warning bells blaring in my brain. Normally, he'd drop everything to assist, especially with a murder suspect in my sights. Something was wrong. But I couldn't afford to be distracted by the endless possibilities. Instead, I kept my eyes on the black sedan.

Since he didn't know he was being followed, I had a little more wiggle room, but I couldn't risk tipping my hand. Once I got redirected to police dispatch, I gave them my current location, the direction we were traveling, and a description of the vehicle. Nearby patrol units were being informed of the situation.

Several blocks later, he turned. None of the vehicles between us made the same turn, so I slowed down. But I didn't want to risk losing him, so I couldn't leave too big of a gap between us. Did he know he was being followed? Was this a test?

I spotted brake lights near the end of the street. He had made his own parking space, half-blocking an alleyway.

There were no other places for me to park, so I had to keep driving. By the time I was beside his car, he was headed down the steps to the cellar.

"Dispatch," I said, "the suspect has gotten out of the vehicle. He's entering what may be a basement apartment." I gave them the address. "How long until units arrive?"

"Five minutes."

Resisting the urge to say something snarky, I parked at the end of the next block. This wasn't good. I couldn't see anything from here. He could have gotten into another car or disappeared. I didn't even get a photo of him. Determined not to let the bastard get away, I ignored the warning from the operator, telling me to remain in my vehicle, disconnected the call, and got out of the car.

Tucking my handcuffs into my jacket pocket, I took a deep breath. How many of them were inside? I grabbed the zipties from my glove box, shoved them into my back pocket, made sure my gun was secure in my shoulder holster, put my phone into my other jacket pocket, and crept toward the apartment.

I kept my head on a swivel, but no one was around. I didn't see any surveillance cameras. More than likely, this was their hideout. Maybe one of them lived here. Pausing beside the car, I scraped the caked-on mud off the plate with my keys and took a photo. Before doing anything else, I sent it to the Cross Security techs. *I need to know everything about the car and driver.*

This wasn't my investigation, but this guy and his crew had already pulled one disappearing act. I didn't trust them not to do it a second time.

Once I slipped out from my crouched position at the front of the car, there were no other cover positions between here and the basement steps. If someone inside was watching the windows, they'd see me if I went past. I needed to find a better vantage point.

The building looked like a lot of residences I'd seen. The above-ground units could only be accessed from the front door and the interior staircase. The basement had its own private entrance, as if it wasn't connected to the rest of the building. More than likely, it had been converted from a cellar into a rentable unit sometime in the last few decades.

The best thing to do would be wait for the police to arrive, point them in the right direction, and provide support if they needed it. So I waited. But the cops were taking too long.

A minute later, the basement door opened. Two men came out. I didn't recognize either of them. The bulges beneath their jackets warned me they were armed. Instead of heading toward the street, they moved down the alley and disappeared through the opening at the other end. They turned right. I could loop around and try to catch them.

We needed IDs. We needed to know who they were. It was the only way they'd be apprehended. But noise from the basement kept me from moving. Was that a scream? It didn't sound human.

I kept an eye on the windows. They wouldn't show much, nothing but legs walking past. But the man who left Kathy Walters' house was already on edge. Clueing him in to my presence wouldn't end well. Instead, I climbed over the railing surrounding the basement entrance and dropped down.

I landed softly, surprised to find the door ajar. It was dark inside. I leaned into the opening and listened. I didn't hear anything. Did I hallucinate the scream?

After waiting a few beats, I unholstered my nine millimeter and pushed my way inside. The door creaked, but no one came running. The limited light from the windows above cast eerie shadows over the place. Torn plastic and large metal gas canisters covered the floor.

The scream sounded again. This time, I found the source. An old motion sensor Halloween decoration sat in the corner of the empty room. The changing light patterns had triggered it.

What was this place? I'd been wrong. It wasn't an apartment. Shelves covered the entire rear wall. Lightbulbs, batteries, bullets, paper towels, duct tape, and tools filled the center shelves. The bottom had more interesting items, like gas masks and tactical vests. Besides the extra ammunition, I didn't spot a single weapon. Had they tossed their guns? Were they cleaning out their base of operations?

After checking the rest of the room, I wondered where the

man from Kathy Walters' house had gone. He couldn't have left unless he eluded me while I was parking my car. Even then, I'd been keeping an eye on the area. Had he snuck away and disappeared through the alley, like his two friends? I didn't spot any other way out.

"Dammit." I didn't know how I missed him. These guys were escape artists. They got away from Spa Alive without anyone noticing, and now they'd done it again.

I went outside and up the steps. The police were on their way. They'd find the car and the basement door open. Instead of waiting for them, I headed down the alleyway. Maybe I could pick up their trail. I wasn't sure how, but I had to try.

Emerging on the other side, I didn't find a parallel street. Instead, I found a gravelly driveway. Several tractor-trailers were abandoned in various states of disrepair. The gravel drive curved and looped. An old sign with half the letters missing declared this was a shipping company, one that had gone out of business five years ago.

The men who had disappeared in this direction could have followed the drive back to the main road and civilization, where they could have had a car waiting. I moved toward the parked derelicts, hearing the echoing crunch of gravel beneath my feet. If anyone was around, they'd hear me coming.

I made it to the first tractor-trailer, peered into the cab, and went around to the back. One of the trailer doors was missing. The sides and interior were covered in graffiti and garbage. It reminded me of a scene out of a post-apocalyptic zombie movie, except no one was around. This wasn't a nest with supernatural monsters. It was a rusted trailer.

Moving on to the next truck, I checked inside. Again, I found nothing. The wind picked up. One of the doors swung in the breeze, emitting a shrill creaking. If anyone was around, they'd want to make that sound stop as soon as possible. But no one came running.

I moved closer to the swaying door and peered inside. Besides trash, I spotted a ratty old blanket. Someone had used this place for shelter, but they were long gone. This was a waste. The men weren't here. Nothing indicated they ever had been.

Moving away from the rusted heaps, I hoped to find some indication of where they'd gone or what was so urgent that they called their friend to join them. I was halfway across the vacant lot when a second door started swinging in the breeze.

Turning, I could have sworn that trailer had been locked. O'Connell was right. I needed to lay off the caffeine and get some sleep. Since I came all this way, I crossed to that trailer and peered around. I didn't spot anyone, but I thought I heard the crunch of gravel mixed in with the squeaky doors.

Holding my gun down at my side, I looked around, but I didn't see anyone. Crouching down, I peered beneath the truck and the other trailers, hoping to see legs. But the ground was clear. Listening, I didn't hear the telltale crunch.

Carefully, I pulled open the rear door, half-expecting to find someone inside. Alive, dead, or undead. Instead, the items on the floor caught my attention. Was that a three-ring binder? Hoisting myself up, I ignored the sharp pinch along my side.

The interior was dark from where only the one door was opened. The other door left the rear corner in total darkness. Reaching for the flashlight on my keychain, I clicked the button at the same time something crashed into me from behind. My flashlight went flying, fire shooting through me. Another blow came immediately that knocked me to the ground.

"This is your final warning. Stay away, or next time, I'll kill you."

I reached for my gun, but the man shrouded in shadows moved too quickly. He knocked it away and hit me with the butt of his rifle. I blocked, which infuriated him even more. He tried to kick me.

I grabbed his shoe and latched on as he kicked me again. He tripped and fell forward. I scrambled to get a hold of a weapon. His. Mine. At this point, I wasn't picky. He shoved me into the side of the trailer, the door swinging closed and plunging us into total darkness.

Panic flooded my senses, but I kept my head. Muscle memory and close-quarters training took over. I'd spent hours running drills and sparring. Despite all that, given his size, it wouldn't be hard for him to overpower me.

He grabbed me, but in the dark, he was just as blind. He tried to ram me into the wall, but his aim was off. He didn't have a good enough hold, and I slipped away. He came at me again, more determined now, and pinned me to the floor.

Reaching into my pocket, I found the knife I sometimes carried, flipped it open, and stabbed it into his leg. He howled. I twisted the blade and yanked it out. Before I could stab him again, he got off me, moving backward.

"That's it," he snarled. "You're dead."

"You first." I found my flashlight and flipped it on. Spotting my gun, I lunged for it. But he disappeared into the shadows. I aimed, my flashlight and gun pointed together. Where was he? The trailer wasn't that large. Blood dripped down the wall. I pointed the beam of my light skyward.

The only thing I saw was the end of the rifle, and then everything went dark.

TWENTY-FOUR

"You're lucky he didn't kill you," O'Connell said.

"Tell that to my head and my side." I winced as the EMT pressed an ice pack against my temple.

"Hold that," she said.

I took it from her while she and her partner assessed the cuts and bruises that resulted from the fight. "He would have killed me if the patrol unit didn't arrive when it did. Next time, I'd prefer if they had less dramatic timing. Backup would have been nice. This isn't some prime time police drama."

"Breathe in," the EMT said.

I did. "Ouch."

She finished taping a cut on my side. "You should get x-rays to be on the safe side."

"I'll add it to the to-do list."

"A CT scan is also in order to rule out a concussion. You took a nasty hit to the head. You lost consciousness." The other EMT checked my pupils again. "Are you nauseous or lightheaded?"

"I'm fine."

"I'll make sure she gets checked out," O'Connell promised.

"Oh, so you finally decided we're on the same team?" I asked.

The detective shook his head, his eyes going skyward. "We've always been on the same team."

"It hasn't felt like it these last forty-eight hours."

O'Connell helped me down from the back of the ambulance. "As soon as we finish up here, I'm taking you to the hospital. If they say you're okay, I'll have a talk with Moretti about making other arrangements."

"Planning on putting me in a holding cell?"

"Only if I can find one that's padded." O'Connell crossed the vacant lot and pointed to the blood trail. "You got a piece of him."

"Trail ends a hundred feet that way." The crime tech pointed toward the main road.

"He had friends waiting. At least one. Possibly more. I don't know. I followed one guy to the cellar. I never saw where he went. But two other men led me here," I said.

"Did they know you were following them?" O'Connell asked.

"I have no idea."

O'Connell nodded to the back of the trailer where several items of interest had been found. "They led you here. This looks like a trap. Are you sure Walters didn't tip off her boyfriend?"

I doubted he was her boyfriend. More like some bad boy one-night stand who overstayed his welcome. "He didn't make the call. He received the call."

"He could have sent a text," the tech offered.

I glared at her. "He didn't send a text. He had no way of knowing I'd show up at Walters' place to ask questions."

"Why do you think he was there?" O'Connell offered me a pair of latex gloves, which felt like a waste since I'd already been all over the crime scene before it turned into a crime scene.

"To make sure she kept her mouth shut."

"Did he threaten her?"

"Not in so many words. It was his tone."

"Is that the same man who attacked you?"

"Voice sounded similar, but I never saw him. It was too dark." I pointed to the blood spatter. "I got you DNA evidence and a license plate. Find someone with a stab wound to the upper thigh, and you'll be in business."

O'Connell picked up the evidence bag that contained the

binder. "Was this taken from Spa Alive?"

"I'd say so, but you should ask Ralph Lively. Maybe he'll tell you the truth."

"Do you think he's involved?"

I shrugged and shifted the ice pack from the bump at my temple to one of the knots on my side. "What did Willa say when you questioned her?"

Something flitted behind O'Connell's eyes. "Come on, we've seen all we can here. Let's get you checked out while CSU finishes evidence collection." He led me to the unmarked and opened the passenger door for me. "Willa Garrison's in custody. That's why it took me so long to get here." I knew there had been a reason. "She confessed."

"To what?"

"Assaulting Lorna Pagano."

"That was months ago. Why would she confess now?"

O'Connell waited for me to get inside the car before closing the door and getting in on the other side. "She thought doing so would get her off the hook for Tabitha York's murder."

I couldn't follow that logic, and I was pretty sure it had nothing to do with the blow I took to the head. "The assault gives her motive for murder. She wanted to cover up one crime by silencing the person investigating it."

"Yeah, well, she didn't think that through. Instead, I presented a theory to her, and she admitted to one while adamantly denying the other."

"You told her you had proof the chemical burns were intentional."

O'Connell smiled. "I am a decorated major crimes detective."

"Damn. That changes things."

"Does it?" O'Connell eyed me. "How so?"

"I haven't figured that part out yet, but Kathy Walters should be able to help us with it." I pulled out my phone and called the office. Even on the weekends, techs and experts were always around. "Hey, with all that digging we did into Willa Garrison, did you find any outside communications between her and Kathy Walters or the main line of Spa Alive?"

"We didn't find much of anything. They're friends online but have no interactions, aside from the occasional like on a photo or inspirational quote," the tech said.

"All right, thanks."

"While I have you, we got the information on the plate you sent," the tech said.

I pressed the speaker button. "Go ahead."

"Archie Hudson." The tech rattled off his home address and phone number. "He has a record. Two counts of armed robbery."

"Where does he work?" O'Connell asked.

"Ms. Parker, who is that?"

"Detective O'Connell," Nick said before I could answer.

"Lucien won't like this," the tech muttered.

"Lucien knows we have an arrangement. In fact, he insisted on it," I said. "Now answer the question."

"He works at a hardware store." The tech gave us the name and address.

"Known associates?" I asked before O'Connell could cause the tech more agita.

"I don't know."

"Find out," I insisted, hanging up. Turning to O'Connell, I asked, "Was that helpful?"

He followed the signs for the hospital and found a reserved space near the emergency room to park. It was one of the perks of being a public servant and driving a police car. "We had the name. We didn't have the rest." Reaching for the mobile data terminal, he brought up Hudson's mug shot. "Is this the guy you saw at Kathy Walters' place?"

"That's him."

"All right." He reached for the radio. "Go get checked in. I'll have a BOLO issued."

"Are you planning to ditch me?"

"I'll meet you inside," he promised.

"You better, or I'll tell your wife."

I made my way to the entrance. The doors slid open. No matter how much they disinfected these places, they always had a smell. I hated it.

"Here," the woman at the desk pushed a clipboard toward me, "fill that out." She eyed the bump on my head.

"Did you lose consciousness?"

"It's best if we don't talk about that."

"Ma'am—"

"It'd also be a good idea not to call me that. Not in this place. Not today."

She wouldn't give up that easily. "What happened?"

"Ask the asshole with the rifle. He'd know better than I would."

"Did you call the police?"

"That's how I got here. A detective gave me a ride. He said he'll meet me inside. Between the two of us, I think he's planning on taking off so he can follow up on the lead I gave him."

She looked down at the form, where I filled out my name and the reason for my visit. "Ms. Parker, take a seat. Someone will be with you momentarily. Are you feeling dizzy or like you might pass out?"

"I'm fine." I turned, scanning the waiting area for an empty seat away from everyone else. Against the side wall, halfway down the row, was a man with a bloody towel wrapped around his leg. I snorted. I should have realized today was going to be one of those days. "Call security," I said quietly. "That man over there, the one with the leg wound, he's wanted by the police. You should consider him armed and dangerous."

Her first reaction told me she didn't believe a word I said. Then the dots connected, and she picked up the phone. I leaned in, shielding most of me behind the separator, and called O'Connell. "Cancel that BOLO. I found your suspect. If you don't do something about it in the next ten seconds, I will."

I kept an eye on the guy to make sure he didn't plan on making a break for it. As far as I could tell, he wasn't armed. He'd ditched the rifle somewhere. But he could have a piece behind his back. Given my last two encounters with him, I wouldn't put it past him to try to shoot his way out of this mess.

Security arrived, two patrol officers who looked around warily. Before the woman at the check-in desk could wave them over, I headed in their direction. The last thing we needed was to make our suspect anxious.

"Hey," I said, "how's it going?" I communicated with my eyes where the man was. "Staying cool?"

"Yes, ma'am," the one on the left said.

It was definitely one of those days. I nodded to them, spotting O'Connell coming through the double doors. "Be prepared for anything." Turning, I headed for our suspect.

The seat to Hudson's right was empty. The one on his left wasn't. That could be a problem.

"Sir," I said to the man cradling his purple wrist, "the lady at the desk needs to speak to you."

"Sure, thanks." He got up.

Hudson hadn't looked up. He was staring at his leg, probably coming up with an excuse as to how he got stabbed that wouldn't cause the doctors to alert the police. That, or he was devising another escape plan to get in and out without anyone noticing.

"Hey." I kicked his ankle. "I didn't expect to see you again so soon." Moving my hand inside my jacket, I gripped my holstered weapon. If he pulled a piece, I'd drop him. "How's the leg?"

Recognition shone in his eyes. "Fuck."

"Don't try anything," I warned. "Are you armed?"

"Are you a cop?" Hudson asked.

"No, but I am." O'Connell came up beside me, his badge on display, his hand on his side arm. The two patrol officers had joined us. One cleared the waiting room while the other provided backup. "Archie Hudson, you're under arrest. Stand up." O'Connell frisked him and cuffed him before dropping him back into the chair. "We'll get that wound taken care of, and then you're coming with me."

TWENTY-FIVE

I opened my eyes to find Martin standing beside me. "I told you I was fine. You didn't have to come down here."

He leaned down and kissed me. "I wanted to hear it from someone with a medical degree."

"You didn't believe me?"

He smiled. "I didn't mean to wake you."

"I wasn't asleep. I just had my eyes closed."

"For the last two hours."

"You've been here that long?"

"No." But I didn't believe him. "Your CT scan was clear. No broken bones. No brain bleeds."

"Did O'Connell leave?"

"Not yet."

I sat up slowly, the ache in my back duller. Whatever they gave me had worked wonders to ease the tension. I rubbed my hand along my side, surprised to find it barely hurt. "Hey," I got off the bed and put my hands on Martin's waist, "I'm sorry about last night and the other night."

"It's okay." He tugged on the loops of my pants, pulling me closer and kissing me again.

"Is it?"

Martin nodded before pressing his forehead against mine. "We're okay, sweetheart. I'm not saying it out of guilt or fear. We're okay. You're dealing with some things. So am I."

I wasn't sure what that meant, but I was glad he wasn't

angry or freaked out. My hands tangled in his hair. "Are you working late tonight?"

"The nurse said to keep an eye on you. I can rearrange some things. Conference from home." He ran the tip of his nose along the bridge of mine.

"That's not why I was asking. You don't need to take care of me."

A glint developed in his eyes. "I like taking care of you."

A knock sounded behind him. "I'd say get a room, but you're already in a room. So maybe wait until you're in a room you own."

I peered over Martin's shoulder at O'Connell. "Is Archie Hudson in one piece?"

"They stitched him up and gave him an otherwise clean bill of health. He should be discharged in a few minutes. He'll be processed and booked before I take a crack at him."

"What about me?"

O'Connell glanced at Martin. "Are you sure you don't want to go home? It looks like I interrupted something."

"Nick," I warned.

"It can wait," Martin said, his eyes searching mine. Something playful flitted behind them. We really were okay.

The detective shrugged. "Fine. Are you free to go, Parker?"

"Am I?" I asked Martin, who nodded. "Let's rock and roll."

* * *

After I finished providing my statement, Lt. Moretti called me into his office. He rubbed a hand over his mouth. He didn't look pleased, but he didn't look surprised either. "Do you want to explain to me what happened today?"

"I had insomnia."

"How does that lend itself to where we are now?"

"I couldn't sleep, so I got antsy."

"Jablonsky warned me what happens when you get bored."

"I'm sure he's not the only one."

Moretti glowered at me, so I shut my trap and stared at

G.K. Parks

the paperwork on his desk. "The commissioner didn't want anyone from Cross Security involved in this investigation. As far as I'm concerned, no one in the major crimes unit should be involved either. But somehow, because of you and the strings you pulled, we're all in this mess together."

"I never meant for any of that to happen."

"I know." He rubbed his mouth again. "I could sign off on you consulting, but it's not worth the headache. The way I see it, you're a witness which means we need you to stick around and cooperate. Furthermore, you're our best shot of IDing these guys, and since you already have an investigation into Spa Alive in the works, we would appreciate any assistance or details you want to share."

"So I'm consulting without the paperwork or getting paid?"

"Who are you kidding? You don't need the money. You'd do this anyway." Moretti shrugged. "Do you promise not to sue the department in case of injury or death?"

"Sure." Martin and Cross might have other ideas, but Moretti asked for my word, not theirs. Plus, if I was dead, I wouldn't be around to deal with the repercussions.

"All right." He jerked his chin toward the door. "It's O'Connell's case. Do what he says. And don't cause problems."

"I never cause problems."

Moretti glared at me. "Get out of my office, Parker."

"Yes, sir."

I took a seat in front of O'Connell's desk and scanned the sticky notes for anything interesting. I was leafing through his files when Thompson joined me.

"Stop that," he scolded. "That's not your seat."

"Nick doesn't mind."

Thompson pointed to the empty desk across from Heathcliff's workstation. "That's your seat."

"I'm not consulting."

"The hell you aren't." He pointed more emphatically. "Don't hold your breath for a nameplate because that isn't happening." He waited for me to get up and take a step toward the computer. "It should already be logged in. Check whatever you need. Nick's making sure Hudson's squared

- 191 -

away. Once he's settled, you can watch the interview."

"Can I go in?"

"You just said you're not consulting. It must be me or that blow you took to the head." He winced and pointed to his own temple. "Nick said it looked like a golf ball when patrol first found you. Are you sure you don't have a concussion? It would explain a lot."

"Remember when you used to not talk to me? Let's go back to that." I winked. "Or is this your way of saying you're glad I'm okay?"

"Yeah, yeah." Thompson sunk into his chair.

Rubbing my palms together, I stared at the blinking cursor in the search box. Starting with the basics, I brought up everything I could find on Archie Hudson. His prior arrests involved armed robberies. They were simple in and out jobs. No grand conspiracy. He didn't work with a crew. In fact, the weapons he'd used during both robberies hadn't been loaded.

"Did anyone find the rifle he had today?" I asked.

Thompson shook his head. "He must have taken it with him."

"Is patrol searching for it?"

Thompson's look told me to stop asking stupid questions. "Of course, they're looking for evidence. It's what we do."

"What about the items in the cellar?"

He reached for the files on O'Connell's desk, picked one up, and held it out in my direction.

"See, this is why you shouldn't have made me change seats." I took the file and scanned the inventoried items. Archie Hudson rented the cellar. "No one ever taught our suspect not to shit where he eats." I held up the photo of the metal canisters. "Were these taken from the medical supply warehouse?"

"The lot numbers match."

"What about surveillance footage from nearby cameras? We may be able to ID the rest of the crew that way." I held up my hand before Thompson could give me another one of those looks. "Yeah, I know. You're on it."

"Right."

Rocking back in O'Connell's chair, I fished out my cell

phone and called the Cross Security tech I'd spoken to earlier. "Hey, did you find anything else on Archie Hudson?"

"Are you hoping for something in particular?"

"Known associates."

"A deep dive into his socials didn't reveal much. He's careful. He doesn't have a lot of friends. The ones he does have appear to be bots. The photos he's posted are mostly of himself. He's never with anyone. We're working on getting a look at his phone records and internet activity. So far, all I can tell you is he had an active dating profile which he hasn't accessed in the last two months."

"Did he match with anyone?"

"I can't tell. Getting behind their walls is a little trickier."

Which is why so many people used dating sites. "Does Kathy Walters use the same service?"

"Let me check."

More than likely, this was how they met. I snapped my fingers at Thompson. "Hey, has Walters been brought in?"

"She's waiting in an interview room. No one's questioned her yet."

"They could have devised the plan to take over the spa together. But if Walters wanted to up the insurance, why would she tell Hudson to execute the plan now? She should have waited until the added coverage went into effect. Then she could have sued and made even more money."

The tech came back on the line. "A+, Ms. Parker. Kathy Walters has used that dating site on and off for the better part of three years. Her last log-in was the same day as Archie Hudson's."

"They're dating," I said. "Any idea when they first met?"

"I'll have to dig deeper."

"E-mail me whatever you find."

O'Connell and Heathcliff emerged from the double doors. Heathcliff hovered over me, checking the welt at my temple. He didn't say anything, but I knew what he was thinking.

"I wasn't being self-destructive," I said. "I was working."

O'Connell went into Moretti's office, returning a moment later. "Looks like we could use a witness to help our investigation."

"I told you so," I said.

O'Connell checked the intel that had piled up on his desk. "All right. Let's get to it."

I followed O'Connell back to the double doors. From there, we made our way to the interrogation rooms. Archie Hudson was seated at a table with his lawyer, a public defender.

"We know some but not enough," O'Connell said. "Any weaknesses I should exploit?"

"He's screwing Kathy," I said. "Cross Security discovered they use the same dating app. I assume that's how they first met, but he didn't seem all that interested in her. She's a means to an end. If given the chance, he'd throw her under the bus."

O'Connell came to a decision. "All right. We go at her first. I want you in there with me."

That surprised me. Witnesses weren't part of interrogations, but Moretti's declaration made me a consultant, albeit one who didn't get paid. "Has she been arrested?"

"Not yet. We don't have anything to hold her on. That may change once we speak to Hudson."

"You'll blow my cover."

O'Connell looked me in the eye. "Does that matter? If it does, you can wait out here. But I wanted to shake her up, make her think we know things we don't. If she is involved, knowing someone was watching her from the inside will make her more forthcoming. She'll want to save her own skin."

"All right, but if she admits to anything and you have reason to hold her, do it."

"You think whoever killed York will come for you if word gets out?"

I hadn't thought about that, even though that should have been my first thought. I laughed. "I've been working for Lucien too damn long."

"You're afraid you'll get in trouble at work."

"That knock to the head scrambled my brains. I'm back now. We're good to go."

"Are you sure? You don't have to."

I headed for the interrogation room and pointed to make sure I had the right one. "This is what I've wanted since the beginning. I'm not backing down now."

TWENTY-SIX

"Ms. Walters, I'm Detective O'Connell. This is—"

"Alexandra?" Kathy Walters stared, flummoxed. "What are you doing here?"

"Surprise," I said.

O'Connell took a seat, pushing out the chair beside him so I could sit down. "I see you've met."

"Alex is on the cleaning crew at Spa Alive." Kathy's brow furrowed. "She was at my house this morning. I don't understand."

"I'm not a cleaning lady," I said. "I'm a private investigator. My firm was hired to look into Spa Alive and find the dirt, so to speak."

"Is that why you were on the cleaning crew? Who even hired you?"

"You did." I cocked my head to the side. "Did you suffer a blow to the head too today?"

Her eyes narrowed at the mark on my face. "How did that happen?" She looked at O'Connell. "I didn't do that."

"No, but your boyfriend did." I sat back in the chair, regretting that move instantly when the metal bar at the top hit against my bruise.

"Boyfriend?" Kathy looked to O'Connell for help. "I don't know what she's talking about. I don't have a boyfriend."

"Archie Hudson." O'Connell produced a photo. "He was at your place this morning. Your doorbell camera can prove it. He has an interesting bruise right here." O'Connell indicated the place on his own chest. "Do you know how he got that?"

"He said he got pelted by a football when he was playing with friends at the park." Kathy looked sincere, but I couldn't be sure. "And he's not my boyfriend. We don't do labels."

"But you're sleeping with him," I said.

She nodded.

"Are you sleeping with anyone else?"

"Why does that matter?"

"Answer the question, please," O'Connell said.

"No, only Archie."

O'Connell clicked his pen and wrote something in his notepad. "How long have you been involved with Mr. Hudson?"

"About two months. Did he do something wrong?"

"You could say that. Do you know his friends?" I asked. "Specifically, the ones who allegedly hit him with the football?"

"I met a few of them once or twice when we were out for dinner or drinks. They never stuck around very long. I'm not even sure I got their names."

O'Connell pulled out the photo of the masked man I'd incapacitated. "Do you recognize him?"

Kathy covered her mouth. "Oh my god. Is he dead?"

"No, ma'am. We're trying to identify him."

"I don't know who that is." She studied the photo more carefully. "That's the sauna at Spa Alive. What's he doing there? Napping?"

"That's from the incident on Friday. He's one of the men responsible for the attack. Do you recognize him?" O'Connell asked again.

She stared at the photo. "Didn't you show me this when I was in the hospital?"

"So you do remember something," I muttered.

Kathy glared at me. "That was a very trying day."

"I know. Your boyfriend or one of his buddies shot me."

"Archie did what?" Her eyes went wide. "I can't believe he'd do something like that. You must be mistaken."

"He has a record. Two armed robberies." O'Connell

produced Archie's mug shot and rap sheet. "I take it he didn't tell you about this."

She stared at the paper, her mouth open, shock in her eyes. "I had no idea."

"How well do you know Mr. Hudson?" O'Connell asked.

"We met online. We went out a few times. He seemed like a nice guy. We were having fun. It was casual. Dinner, drinks, movie, whatever." Kathy rubbed a hand over her face. "He always had a rough edge. I asked him about it once. He said growing up was hard. I dropped it after that."

O'Connell tucked the photo back into the folder. "We found evidence linking him to the attack at Spa Alive. We found the gear he wore and the equipment used to knock everyone out. He didn't do this alone."

"Do you think I had something to do with what happened?" Kathy stared at him, horrified, before turning her attention to me. "You know me. You said you were investigating the spa. Surely, you can't believe I had something to do with this. Tell him that."

O'Connell bumped his leg against mine, a silent way of urging me to keep my mouth shut. "Ms. Walters, I am not in the business of blaming victims. That is not my intention, but you must see how this looks. Your boyfriend and his crew took over the spa, robbed your clients, killed one of them, and fled. Today, we find him at your apartment. He didn't skip town. Instead, he was with you. Tell me what I'm missing."

"I don't know. I had no idea he was planning this."

"He's in the next room. When I speak to him, will he tell me the same thing? That you had no idea any of this was about to happen?"

"I don't know what he'll say." Tears welled in her eyes. She shoved the edge of the folder farther away. "I don't know anything about him."

O'Connell nudged me again. Obviously, I was here to play bad cop.

"Why did you go to Mr. Lively and suggest Spa Alive increase its liability insurance if you didn't know something like this was going to happen?" I asked.

Kathy stared, as if she couldn't believe I knew any of that.

"We needed more coverage. If a client were to sue, we'd go under. We needed added protections."

"Why?"

"Things happen." She gestured emphatically at the folder. "Obviously." Realizing she'd put her foot in her mouth, she shook her head. "I didn't know any of this would happen. I had no idea. I was worried about angering and injuring our clients, like you did the other day with Mr. Chesterfield."

"I didn't injure him. He didn't have grounds to file suit. There were no damages."

Kathy snorted. "You're a lawyer now too?"

"No, ma'am. And I don't play one on TV either." I leaned forward, stabbing at the tabletop with my pointer finger. "Did you know of any clients who had been harmed?"

She bit her lip, her head nodding slightly, even as she said, "No." That wasn't true.

"What about Lorna Pagano?"

Her cheeks reddened. "I don't want to discuss that."

I pointed to the door. "What Detective O'Connell failed to mention is Willa Garrison is also in one of these fine interrogation rooms. She admitted to assaulting Lorna Pagano."

"Maybe you should discuss that with us," O'Connell suggested, unsure where I planned to go with this but willing to play along anyway.

"Spa Alive was trying to cut corners and save money. Our profit margins have been in decline for nearly a year. The cleaning crew wanted higher wages and better benefits, which hurt our bottom line even more. So we started experimenting with our treatments. Everything we use is custom-made, proprietary blends. We started changing up the formulas and using cheaper, lower quality ingredients. Lorna Pagano had an unfortunate reaction."

"She was covered in chemical burns," I said.

"Why would Ms. Garrison confess to an assault if it was an accident?" O'Connell asked.

"Willa didn't know what caused the reaction. She'd been annoyed with the situation and not paying attention to what she was doing. She blamed herself, and I let her. Only management knew the truth. We didn't tell anyone on the staff what was happening. We thought we'd test out some changes, see if anyone noticed the difference or if we received any complaints, and go from there." Kathy looked nervous. "No one else had any issues."

"That's not making much sense," I said.

"Even with clinically tested products, reactions happen. Read reviews on any beauty product on the market, and you'll find someone who had a breakout or rash or something happen. Everyone is different. Sensitivities, allergies, a person's chemistry all play a part in these things. It's why perfume smells different on different people." Kathy sighed. "That's why I wanted the increased liability. Lorna's an influencer. She threatened to post what happened online. Hundreds of thousands of people would have seen it. It would have spread. Others would have reposted it or shared her story with their friends, and so on and so forth. We convinced her not to do it, to take the photo down, but things change."

"You mean she and Damon were no longer dating, so you thought she'd go through with the lawsuit," I said.

Kathy looked away, nodding. "I didn't want to see Spa Alive go down. We hit a rough patch. Lots of businesses do, but we can bounce back. We replaced our expensive ingredients with cheaper alternatives. We were boosting our numbers, finding new clients. We were planning additional marketing campaigns. The bachelorette party ordered one of our new packages. And then this happened." She scowled. "Archie ruined everything I've been working so hard to save and you have the audacity to think I'm part of it. How dare you?"

"That's the spin you put on it," I said. "Maybe all your hard work didn't pay off. Maybe you were tired of trying to salvage a failing business, one where you were only the manager. You don't own the place. Maybe Ralph Lively threatened to fire you. Maybe you arranged this to get revenge or so you'd have grounds to sue and claim as much as possible. After all, you were a victim in Friday's attack. You may have wanted the increased liability to weasel your way into a larger settlement."

"This is outrageous."

O'Connell put his hand on my forearm, again proving he was the good cop who had to rein me in. "If you're telling the truth, Ms. Walters, it shouldn't be hard to get to the bottom of it. I'm curious, though, how the men who invaded the spa knew how to access the ventilation system so easily."

"They also took over the computer system, cut the phone cords in the offices, and stole a very specific binder," I said.

O'Connell studied her. "Did you provide Archie Hudson with any of those details?"

Kathy's face went ashen. "I complained about the lack of Wi-Fi one day. Another day, I must have mentioned the A/C was overactive. Work's a big part of my life. I talk about it a lot. He must have been paying attention to every little detail."

"Why would he take a binder from Ralph Lively's office? What did it contain?" I asked.

Kathy snorted. "You mean there's something you don't know?"

"We recovered the binder," O'Connell said. "It's written in code. We will crack it, but I would appreciate it if you could save us some time."

"The binders contain formulas for what we use in our treatments. They were written in shorthand because they are proprietary. We don't keep that information on the network. We also used it to compare the price of ingredients, carrier oils, things like that, and see how we could modify or tweak to save more money. I don't know why anyone would want that? It's useless unless you run a wellness center."

"Which is why it's hard to believe you aren't involved in this," I said.

"I already had access to the binders and the formulas. I did that work myself. The price comparisons, the ingredient searches, all of it. Why would I need someone to steal something I could have taken anytime I wanted?"

Kathy made a fair point. I didn't have an answer.

"Why wasn't it saved on a computer or stored on the network?" O'Connell asked.

Kathy sighed again and waved her hand at me. "Hard copies could be destroyed without anyone knowing. If a client decided to sue, they'd have no evidence we switched out the ingredients. We advertise only organic, plant-based, natural ingredients are used in our treatments. Discovering we were using other things would not have gone over well."

"The binder was in Ralph Lively's office. Did he tell you to do this?" O'Connell asked.

"Ralph left me in charge of everything. The only thing he wanted me to do was keep us in the black by any means necessary. He didn't ask questions, and I didn't tell him anything he didn't need to know."

"Do you think he got suspicious when you suggested he increase the spa's liability coverage?"

Kathy thought about it for a moment. "I told him it'd be more profitable in the long-run. That was enough to pacify him."

"So you don't think he set the incident in motion?" O'Connell asked.

"I don't," Kathy said. "Ralph Lively isn't that kind of man."

"Ralph Lively might not be that type of man, but Archie Hudson is." I pointed to the file on the table. "Even if you didn't mean to help him, you did. You could be facing accessory charges, at the very least."

"I didn't know," Kathy insisted. "What can I do to prove it? I want to help."

"Did Archie leave anything at your place?" O'Connell asked.

"A toothbrush. Maybe a shirt. Nothing important."

"Would you mind if we looked around? Maybe he left a phone or other device, something that would point us in the direction of his accomplices. If one of them masterminded this or had a connection to the spa, you'll be off the hook. We'd also like access to your doorbell camera and home security system."

"Yeah, fine. Whatever you need. I want this cleared up. And when you talk to Archie, tell him we're done."

O'Connell patted her forearm and stood. "Will do. Thanks for your help, but I need you to hang around here a while longer, until we get things sorted. An officer will take you somewhere more comfortable, get you some coffee or soda, whatever you want."

"Do you have herbal tea?" she asked.

I hid my chuckle, turning away as I got up from the table. I saw that one coming a mile away.

"I'm sure we have some around here." O'Connell held the door, waiting for me to exit. Once we were alone, he gave me a look. "Do you believe her?"

"Herbal tea's all the rage."

"Not about that."

"I hate to say it, but I think I might. We should check her place before she changes her mind."

O'Connell lingered outside the door to the other interrogation room. "Update Moretti on the situation. I'll be there in a minute."

"Are you sure you don't want me to sit in?"

"Not on this one. You already put a knife in this guy's leg. His lawyer will have a field day if I let you in that room. They'll call it intimidation, especially since you aren't here in an official capacity."

"Yes, sir."

TWENTY-SEVEN

I looked around Kathy Walters' bedroom. The bed remained rumpled. She hadn't bothered to make it before the police came knocking. That surprised me. She seemed the type to want everything neat and orderly. That's how she ran Spa Alive, but her house had a homey, lived-in feel.

Opening her closet, I peered inside. No winter coats. O'Connell had checked the coat closet, but it was filled from floor to ceiling with a door-to-door cosmetics line.

"Find anything?" I called.

"Not yet." O'Connell went into the kitchen while I checked the attached bathroom.

"I got a toothbrush. Blue is for boys, right?" The other one was a fancy electric brush. I didn't think Archie Hudson would leave a two hundred dollar toothbrush at his hookup's house. I also didn't think he'd waste two bills on a toothbrush.

"I'll bag it in a second."

I slid open the shower door. The shelf contained a single bottle each of shampoo, conditioner, and body wash. The two bars of soap on the ledge may have belonged to Archie or were part of Kathy's routine. I had no way of knowing, but it didn't matter. None of this would lead us to Archie's accomplices.

"Why are you bagging the toothbrush?" I asked.

"In case compelling DNA turns problematic." O'Connell wrote on the bag and tucked it into his pocket for safe keeping. "Did you find anything else?"

"You mean the blueprints to Spa Alive that are rolled up beneath the bed?"

O'Connell gave me a dead eye stare. "Why do you tease me like that?"

"I have to tease someone."

He knew I was joking, but he checked under the bed anyway. "It looks like you and Martin made up."

"I'm not sure we were ever fighting. He got weird after he found out what happened on Friday."

O'Connell surfaced from beneath the bed. "He doesn't like learning you were in danger. We've had this conversation before."

"Several times."

"So why are you confused by the way he was acting?" O'Connell moved to the dresser, which I'd already searched, scanned the items on top, and peered behind it. "Help me with this."

I went to the other side and gripped the top. "You know I strained my back moving that washing machine on Friday."

"You're supposed to lift with your legs." He waved me off and scooted his side forward before coming around and scooting my side forward. Behind the dresser was a scrap of paper. Snatching it off the floor, he examined it before handing it to me. It contained a photo of Tabitha York printed from the internet. Given how small and grainy it was, I had to assume it had been posted online with an article she had written.

"This can't be a coincidence."

"I'm sure it isn't." O'Connell tucked it into an evidence bag. "But it's circumstantial at best."

"Do you think Kathy Walters printed that?"

O'Connell looked around the room. "I didn't find a printer. Did you?"

"She could have printed it at work."

O'Connell examined it through the clear plastic. "It's creased and torn."

"You think it's Archie Hudson's." I pointed to the dresser. "He could have emptied his pockets before he and Kathy got down and dirty. More than likely, he would have put his belongings on her dresser."

"And that fell behind." O'Connell considered the possibilities. "Given the attack, the PD has been granted access to Spa Alive's database. Let me make some calls and see if this photo was stored on their system."

"I think it came from one of her articles."

"If that's the case, I'll have them check and see if any of them had been accessed on a Spa Alive computer. They have printers, right?"

I nodded.

While he made a few calls, I did the same.

*　　*　　*

"This was in your bedroom." I showed the folded scrap of paper that had been used to print the photo of Tabitha York to Kathy Walters. "We found it behind your dresser. Were you a fan?"

Kathy took the evidence bag from my hand and looked at the photo. "A fan of what?"

"Tabitha York's."

"Was she famous? I know her husband's a big time director."

"Producer," I corrected.

"Oh-kay." Kathy put the bag down and scooted it closer to me. Since O'Connell had gone into the interrogation room to ask Archie Hudson about it, I had wandered into the empty conference room where they'd left Kathy to stew. There was no reason we couldn't have a friendly conversation. "Was she a starlet?"

"You really don't know who she was?"

"No." Kathy peered down at the photo again. "Should I?"

"Did Archie ever ask you about her?"

"No."

"What about your other clients?"

"I really don't remember. Like I told you and the detective earlier, I always spoke about work. It took up most of my time."

"What about your cosmetics line?"

Kathy blushed. "You found that?"

I nodded. "Is that your side hustle? Were you not making enough managing Spa Alive?"

"Actually, I invested in that damned pyramid scheme before I ever started at Spa Alive. You may not know this, but I planned to be a cosmetologist. I went to beauty school, learned tricks of the trade, and worked at the makeup counter in a department store for a while. After that, I got a job in a beauty supply store. While I was there, one of the girls told me she was making bank selling this line on the side. She convinced me to get involved. I invested heavily. It never worked out. When I first got the job at Spa Alive, I tried to sell off the excess stock to clients, but that didn't go over big with them or Mr. Lively. I still have no idea what to do with the stuff."

"How deep in the hole are you?"

"I'm not anymore. That investment was a decade ago. I've written off the loss since. There's not much I can do. Occasionally, I make an effort to move some of it by hosting parties, but no one wants that shit."

"I'm surprised you didn't start using that for Spa Alive's treatments." I laughed until I saw the look on Kathy's face. "Shit. You actually did that?"

"A few times, but Mr. Lively wouldn't reimburse me. It was a losing battle. So I moved all of that back home."

"Is that why your winter coats are in your closet at work?"

"Yeah."

I popped the top on a can of soda and took a sip. "Would you like one?"

"That's battery acid for your insides."

"Plus caffeine," I said.

Kathy looked appalled. "No. Thank. You."

I took another sip. She was right, but the caffeine and sugar were keeping me upright. And the coffeepot in the break room was empty. Thompson gave me a dirty look when I asked where the filters were. Heathcliff said he'd make a fresh pot, but I'd wandered away before he had the chance.

"Water?" I pointed to the vending machine outside the room.

"I'm okay." She looked at the clock on her cell phone.

"Has Archie said anything yet? The detective said I could go if he cleared me."

"He's being tight-lipped. This may take longer than we anticipated."

"Is Willa still here?"

I hadn't spoken to her. Heathcliff had been handling that. And to think, this was another precinct's problem. No wonder the boys upstairs hated it when I came around. I really ought to do something to make it up to them. Last poker night turned into a disaster. I'd have to come up with something better.

An officer poked his head into the room. "Parker, they want you upstairs."

I got up from the table. "If you change your mind about that water, let him know." I thanked the cop keeping an eye on her and went back to the major crimes unit.

Heathcliff had a cup of coffee waiting on my desk. I put my soda can beside it. No reason I couldn't drink both, but if I ended up with an ulcer, that would explain it.

"Lab only pulled one set of usable prints off the photo. They belonged to Archie Hudson. Hudson hasn't admitted to anything, but he told O'Connell Kathy had nothing to do with anything. In the same breath, he said he had nothing to do with anything either."

"That's not particularly convincing. How did things go with Willa?"

Heathcliff rolled his eyes. "She's...something."

"If you need leverage, confront her about the donuts. That'll make her crack. Or even better, tempt her with a donut. That would also do the trick."

He ignored my rambling. "You were right about her. She's a perfectionist who is far from perfect. Self-sabotaging with a guilty conscience. Takes one to know one?"

"What did she say?" I had wanted to observe that interview. It would have been relevant to the Cross Security investigation, but O'Connell had other priorities. Since Moretti said I was to follow O'Connell's orders, I did what I was told, for once.

"She confessed. When I asked her to elaborate, she ran through everything that had happened that day. How annoyed she'd been at her clients. How demanding they were. How she couldn't properly do her job when the cleaning crew refused to cooperate. How she had been expected to clean up and administer beauty treatments and be friendly and bubbly. How Lorna was bitchy that day because her massage had been rescheduled, and how everything she did was wrong. Lorna complained the wax was too clumpy, the face mask was too gritty, and the seaweed smelled weird. Willa said she kind of snapped. The only thing she wanted to do was get Lorna out of there as quickly as possible. She said she wasn't paying attention. She mixed whatever, slathered on whatever. She said she didn't care what happened to Lorna. She wanted to pour the paraffin down her throat."

"But she didn't do that."

"No. Instead, she turned up the heat on the paraffin. Originally, she thought that was what had burned Lorna. She believed she'd done it intentionally, but when she learned they were chemical burns, Willa figured that was due to her own negligence and not paying attention. She's copped to it and wants to take full responsibility. After what happened on Friday, she wants to clear her conscience. She wants to make amends. Life's too short and all that."

I pointed a finger at him. "Don't you dare make another comparison of her to me."

Heathcliff held up his palms. "Why would I do such a thing?"

I wasn't buying his innocent act. "Has she reached out to Lorna Pagano? Apologized? Posted on social media?"

"She wants to make amends, but she's not willing to throw herself on that grenade."

"That's why she went to church. She wants to make cosmic amends."

"It's all about forgiveness," Heathcliff said.

I sent a text to Cross, updating him on the situation. At least something I'd done today was relevant to my day job. "What about Tabitha York? Did Willa want to pour paraffin down her throat too?"

"Willa said she loved Mrs. York. She was one of her favorite customers. Always friendly and respectful. Mrs.

York was never rude to her and always tipped well."

"But Willa was the last person to see her alive."

"Besides the killer." Heathcliff picked up a legal pad and slid it toward me. "That's the blow by blow of every move Willa made that afternoon. According to that, she went into the flotation therapy room to let York know her session would be over in five minutes. After that, Willa took Mrs. Byrne back for her massage. She showed her into the room, brought her a sheet, notified Damon his next appointment was waiting, and went to grab a snack."

"Willa never mentioned telling me to clean the flotation therapy room." I put the legal pad back on his desk and picked up the coffee to take a sip. The soda was better, but I didn't have the heart to tell him that. "She left out everything that happened in the ten minutes leading up to the attack."

"She said that's everything."

"Can I talk to her?"

"I don't think that's a good idea."

"Probably not, but can I do it anyway?"

"How about I do it for you? You can watch from the observation room."

"O'Connell says I shouldn't be on the sidelines."

"Are you sure that's what he said?" Heathcliff led me down the hall and back to the interrogation rooms. He pointed to the connected observation room. "Wait in there. If you think I'm botching it, knock on the window. I'll come out, and we can discuss." But he knew damn well I wouldn't interrupt unless there was a question that needed asking.

I watched through the other side of the glass while he confronted her, saying he spoke to me and I had a different story to tell. Willa stuck to her guns. She didn't remember telling me anything. At first, she insisted I had gotten it wrong. That I was mistaken and someone else had told me to clean the room, but when Heathcliff asked what snack she had, she froze. Either she was an excellent liar, which seemed apparent given her initial denial about what she'd done to Lorna Pagano, or she didn't remember.

"Why would someone else ask Alex to clean the room? Wasn't Tabitha York your client? Wouldn't it have been your responsibility to make sure York vacated the room?"

Heathcliff asked.

"Yeah, but…" Willa's eyes narrowed, her brow furrowing. The deep wrinkles in her forehead would require Botox to iron out.

"What?" Heathcliff waited. It was the same trick he pulled on me the other night. Damn, if he wasn't good at interrogating suspects.

Willa blinked a few times, as if the information wouldn't compute. "When I was told what happened, after waking up in the hospital, the police officer said everyone had been robbed."

"Okay." Heathcliff gave her a confused look.

"But I had my wallet and phone. No one took those things from me."

"They may have missed you. The Spa Alive clients were a priority."

"Figures," she muttered, sounding jealous. "I still had the money in my pocket and my phone. I keep that with me in case a guest wants to tip using a card or online cash transfer. The cash in my pockets was from the tips I'd collected."

"Uh-huh."

"Tabitha York always tipped well. At least twenty-five percent, sometimes close to forty. But when I counted my cash, I never collected her tip."

"What does that mean?"

"I never went back into the room. If I had, she would have paid me."

"Then why did you tell Alex to clean the room?"

"I didn't."

"She says you did."

"She's a liar."

"Not when it comes to things like this. She said you told her to clean the room." But Willa wouldn't budge. "You had a vendetta against the cleaning crew. You may have even had an issue with Alex in particular."

"I did not."

Heathcliff gave her a look that made her cower in her chair. "There's a theory floating around that you killed Tabitha York and told Alex to clean the room in the hopes we'd pin the murder on her."

"I'm not a killer."

"You hurt Lorna Pagano."

"I feel terrible about that."

"So you say, but you never came forward or admitted what happened until now."

"I already explained that."

"You had everything necessary to murder Tabitha York. She'd never suspect you. She trusted you. She liked you. If she didn't, she wouldn't have tipped so well. All you had to do was sneak up behind her and suffocate her."

"I didn't do it."

"Can you prove it? All the evidence points to you."

"What about the men who knocked us out? Why aren't you looking at them?"

"We are, but they were working with someone on the inside."

"It wasn't me." Willa started to cry.

"Your story isn't making a lot of sense. Are you sure you don't remember how any of this happened?"

"I told Alex the room was ready when it wasn't to get her in trouble. She worked for the cleaning crew. She needed to learn her place. But I'd never hurt Mrs. York. You have to believe me."

TWENTY-EIGHT

I stood in the observation room, my arms folded over my chest. Heathcliff had made Willa Garrison crack. Unfortunately, she didn't confess to the murder or conspiring with the armed men to commit the murder. Meanwhile, the photo O'Connell and I found behind Kathy Walters' dresser indicated someone else was out to get Tabitha York. Did they plan this to cast enough reasonable doubt that no one could be blamed for the murder?

I didn't think any of them were criminal geniuses. Escape artists, yes. But we had yet to figure out why Tabitha York was killed. My gut said it was because of one of her investigations. Sure, she had been looking into Lorna Pagano and the spa, which may have given Willa Garrison a reason to eliminate her, but now that Willa confessed to temporarily maiming Lorna, I didn't think she was our murderer.

On the other side of the glass, O'Connell questioned Archie Hudson. Archie wasn't stupid. He didn't offer extra details. He knew he was caught, if for nothing else than assaulting me. The knife wound in the leg proved it. Surveillance footage from around the cellar showed he had gone inside and left. In fact, he was the first one out. I'd missed it.

"Did you know you were being followed?" O'Connell asked.

Archie stared at him, the anger evident on his face. "Why

does that matter?"

"I'm trying to figure out why you would leave evidence behind." He held out the bag containing the binder recovered from the trailer. "This was found at the site of today's assault. Why put it there? Why give us proof you were also involved in the attack at Spa Alive?"

"I didn't put that in there."

"You were in the trailer. You were waiting for the woman who was following you to step inside. Did you use the binder to lure her there? Were you planning on picking it up and taking off after you killed her?"

"I've never killed anyone," Archie insisted. "I wouldn't."

O'Connell circled, glancing at the mirror as if he could see me. "We'll get to that, but answer my question first. Did you use the binder to lure the person following you into the trailer?"

Archie looked at the attorney. "I'm not answering that."

"You don't have to," the attorney agreed.

"Let's talk about the cellar. A witness and security footage put you inside. We found the equipment used in the attack. We found canisters of medical-grade anesthetic stolen from a medical supply warehouse. And we found ammunition. Add to that this photo." O'Connell pulled out the crumpled scrap. "I have everything I need to build a case against you. Multiple counts of armed robbery, assault, and murder. Keeping quiet won't help you. I have everything I need. But what I'd like to know is who helped you. You didn't do this alone. There were other men involved and someone on the inside. Give me their names, and I'll see what I can do about lessening the charges."

"First of all," Archie said, his temper getting the best of him, "the rifle wasn't loaded."

"The rifle today?"

"And the one inside the spa. In fact, ask the prosecutor and the other cops who nabbed me for those prior offenses. They'll tell you the guns weren't loaded. The armed robbery charges were bogus. I wasn't armed."

"You had a rifle," O'Connell said calmly.

"It wasn't fucking loaded."

"That doesn't matter." O'Connell looked at the attorney.

"I would have thought someone should have explained that to him."

"It shouldn't count." Archie pushed away from the chair, his hands bound to the table, but that didn't stop him from leaning forward and banging his palms against the flat surface with a loud thud. "I never killed anyone."

"Tabitha York is dead. You had her photo at your girlfriend's place." O'Connell leaned across the table, getting in his face. "Sorry, she said you don't do labels."

"Leave Kathy out of this."

"Is she your accomplice? Did she tell you and your friends how to incapacitate everyone inside the spa and who to target? I bet she told you which binder to steal and who to kill too."

"You're not listening." Archie lurched forward, the table groaning.

"Sit your ass down," O'Connell said. "Or I'll have you tied to the fucking chair."

"Detective," the lawyer warned, but O'Connell ignored him.

"I said sit."

Archie dropped, letting out a disgusted breath. "Kathy didn't know."

"Tell me who did. Someone on your crew accessed the Spa Alive security system. The surveillance footage was wiped. How would someone know the codes and how to access the system if Kathy didn't tell you?"

Archie stared at the table, his lip twitching. I wouldn't be surprised if he started spitting or biting. O'Connell might threaten to muzzle him next. *Show him the photo*, I thought.

"We have surveillance footage of the two men you met at the cellar. It's only a matter of time before we ID them. It's not snitching when we already have the information."

"I don't care about that," Archie insisted.

"What do you care about?"

Archie let out a huff.

"There has to be something," O'Connell wheedled. "How about food that isn't prepared by a prison chef? Walking around free? Sex?"

Archie's cheek stopped twitching. That last one got him.

O'Connell picked up on it as quickly as I did.

"Dating sites are nice. They're even better when you don't have to make plans ten years in advance. Tell me what I want to know. Like you said, you didn't kill anyone. Tell me who did, and maybe we can make the rest of this go away."

"That's a lie," Archie said.

"Minimum sentencing. You said your weapon wasn't loaded. Maybe I'll knock armed robbery off the table. The assault with a deadly weapon can be bumped down to misdemeanor assault. Tabitha York is a wealthy lady with a powerful husband. Finding her killer is the department's top priority. Give me that and I'll make sure you get a fair deal."

"Tabitha York may be wealthy, but she pissed off someone with a lot more money. I was told we were supposed to scare her. That's what Friday was supposed to be. We go in. Knock everyone out. Take whatever we want, and leave everyone shaken. That was supposed to take care of things. I didn't know she was going to die. If I had, I would have said no. I wouldn't have been there."

"Who told you to scare her?" O'Connell sat down.

"I don't know."

"That's not good enough."

"I don't," Archie hissed. "My pal, Winslow, heard about a big payday. Easy money. Everything was planned. The crew needed a few experienced guys. He asked if I wanted in. I said yes, and that was that."

O'Connell tapped the pen on the page a few times. "Winslow?"

"Winslow Smith." Archie looked uncomfortable. "He was my cellmate during my last stint."

I entered the name into my phone, hoping to find something. No social media. But I found a dated article, which was a press release issued when he'd been convicted for knocking over a string of gas stations. Unfortunately, I couldn't find a photo. But since he was a convicted felon, he'd be in the corrections database.

"Where did Winslow hear about it?" O'Connell asked.

"I don't know. You'd have to ask him."

"Where can I find him?" O'Connell asked, but Archie shrugged. "Why give him up?"

"Like you said, Detective, you already have proof he was at the cellar with me. I'd say getting an ID from the footage won't take you too long. Just do me a favor and say that's how you found him. In case we end up in the joint together, I don't want him to hold this against me." The anger burned in Archie's eyes. He said he wasn't a killer, but I wouldn't put it past him to shiv his pal for causing him all this grief.

"What about the other man who met you this afternoon? What's his name?"

"I don't know."

"C'mon, you can't expect me to believe that." O'Connell quirked an eyebrow. "I'm going to get the information regardless."

"I. Don't. Know. Winslow called him Chief. We all called him Chief."

"Was he calling the shots?" O'Connell asked.

"No."

"Who was?"

"Someone else. One of the other guys. I didn't catch his name either."

"Of course, you didn't." O'Connell showed Archie the photo of the man I'd taken down at Spa Alive. "Who is he?"

"That's Guido. We met for the first time that day."

"Did he have an accent?"

"Why would he have an accent? That's racist."

O'Connell let out a frustrated sigh. "Does he have a last name?"

"I'm sure he does, but I don't know it."

"How did he escape Spa Alive when he was unconscious?"

"We carried him out."

O'Connell turned his head and rubbed his mouth to hide the smile. "How did you get away that day? The police were outside."

"As soon as that woman got out of the room, we cleared out."

"Why take Guido with you? Shouldn't it have been every man for himself?" O'Connell stabbed at the photo. "Dragging a full-grown man around would be slow going."

"We couldn't leave him behind."

"Why not?"

"He would have turned on us."

"Why not kill him?" O'Connell asked.

The attorney made an agitated sound, uncomfortable with the question.

"I already told you. I don't kill people." Archie leaned back in the chair. "Clearly, you're not listening, so I'm done talking."

*   *   *

"I haven't found anything on Guido or Chief." I swiveled my chair from side to side. "What did you find on Winslow?"

"Winslow Smith." O'Connell turned in his chair, so he could see me while we spoke. From this angle, I had a clear view of his monitor, which made things easier for both of us. "Several robbery convictions but not much else on his rap sheet. He and Archie make the perfect pair." O'Connell checked the time. "Uniforms went to Winslow's last known address, but he wasn't home. We checked his place of business, but he wasn't there either. He must have known Archie got caught when they didn't meet up after clearing out the cellar."

"Except they didn't clear out the cellar," I said. "Evidence remained. It's why you have such an airtight case against Archie."

"They went there for a reason. Archie didn't say what it was, but it was important. You saw two of them leave. Area footage shows they had a couple of backpacks with them. I'm guessing they took the loot."

"Pirates," Thompson muttered from his desk.

I snickered, but O'Connell wasn't amused.

"Why leave the binder behind?" I asked.

"They could have removed a few pages or they could have copied whatever information they needed out of it. I don't know. All I know is what we found and what I've been told. You're supposed to be a brilliant private eye. Dazzle me."

"I'll need glitter."

O'Connell snorted. "At least we have names. It's more than what we had before."

"The names aren't getting us anywhere." I checked my phone for the eight hundredth time. Cross Security hadn't gotten a hit on the photo of Guido. They tried running it against the name, but that wasn't helping. "Honestly, Chief and Guido sound made up."

"Archie gave us Winslow Smith. That was real."

"But that was his cellmate and accomplice. He knew we'd find him. The other two we haven't found." I clicked the mouse and checked the fingerprint analysis that had been conducted from the items "Guido" had touched. Copying down the case number and file information, I picked up my phone and sent the information to Cross. If he wanted to hack into the police database and gain access to the prints, I wouldn't stop him. But since I didn't ask him to do it either, I was in the clear. And if it led to the suspect's actual name, O'Connell wouldn't complain too much. "Guido sounds like a mob hitter, and Chief sounds like a football fan's beloved hound." I leafed through the transcripts from the other interviews. "There is so much shit here."

"You can never do anything easy." O'Connell spun around to face his computer. "We have enough to hold Kathy Walters and Willa Garrison, at least for tonight."

"They won't like it," Thompson said, his eyes on his screen.

"Too bad." O'Connell hit the button on his monitor and put on his jacket. "I'm gonna pay Ralph Lively a visit. On the way back, I'll make a dinner run. Does anyone want anything?"

Thompson and Heathcliff made their requests while I drummed my fingers on the desk. Even now, I couldn't figure out why Tabitha York had been murdered. Archie Hudson claimed to have no knowledge that was going to happen. Until Winslow was brought in, we couldn't ask him, and I had little faith we'd ever ID Guido or Chief.

"Parker, you coming?" O'Connell towered over me, one hand on his hip, the other gesturing toward the door.

"Yep."

Ralph Lively didn't have much to say that we hadn't heard a million times. He stuck to the previous script. He didn't deviate. He didn't offer any other information. When confronted with what Kathy Walters was doing to cut costs, he seemed genuinely clueless. Not appalled or angry, just surprised.

"This binder was found today. The men who invaded Spa Alive had it in their possession. Any idea why someone would have wanted to steal this?" O'Connell showed him a photo. "It was taken from your office. They specifically went looking for it."

"For that particular volume," I added.

Ralph Lively shrugged. "You'd have to ask Kathy. She runs the place, organizes the offices, keeps everything going. If she says those are formulas we use for our treatments, that's what they are."

"It's your business. Your office," I said. "Shouldn't you know a little more than that?"

Lively looked at me. I hadn't been introduced as a witness or cleaning lady. O'Connell said I was assisting on the case and called me by my last name. "Do I look like a spa guy?" He held up his hands. His fingernails were chewed and grimy. "I wouldn't know the first thing about mani-pedis or massages. I leave that up to people who know what they're talking about. People who can tell you the difference between Shiatsu and hot stones because I don't have a freaking clue."

"Is it true you told Kathy Walters to do whatever it takes to make the spa profitable?" O'Connell asked.

"Yeah. I'm in this for the money. She runs the place. I pay the overhead and everyone's paychecks." Lively studied us closely. "Since Kathy was cutting corners, practically scamming our customers, I guess it's possible her insistence on the insurance increase was another scam she planned to run. Maybe you're right. Maybe I don't know my manager as well as I thought. You said her boyfriend was part of the crew who invaded the spa. Do you think she planned this?"

"I was hoping you could tell us." O'Connell tucked the pen into his breast pocket. "Do you recall any suspicious activity or any mention of problems arising or potential problems?"

Lively shook his head. "I preferred the hands-off approach. As long as we were operating in the black with healthy margins, I didn't worry too much. The only thing I reviewed was the money angle. Sure, we've been struggling against dwindling returns, but things were picking up. If this was a scheme, it backfired. We'll be lucky to recover from this. Right now, I'm looking at losing every client who had been there the day of the incident, plus paying out whatever the insurance won't cover, not to mention several employees who are considering quitting. If Kathy is responsible, it wasn't to help the spa. It may have been to help herself."

TWENTY-NINE

"Do you think they would have improved their profit margins?" I asked.

O'Connell glanced at me. "Lively sounded convinced. The only thing I don't buy is that he didn't know what was being kept inside his office."

"He denied it, but I'm sure he knew they were ripping off customers. I also think he believed it was working. I don't think he intended to abandon ship when Spa Alive had a plan in place to turn things around. The only reason he'd orchestrate the attack would be if he knew it wasn't working."

"Maybe it wasn't." O'Connell stopped at the light. "I've seen their business portfolio, the projections, their accounting. The situation wasn't dire. Not yet. I don't think he had anything to do with what happened on Friday. More than likely, Archie Hudson cozied up to Kathy Walters to gain the intel necessary for the crew to pull it off."

"There's just one problem."

"It doesn't explain why Tabitha York was killed." The light changed, but instead of going straight, O'Connell turned. "Since our plans this morning got ruined, what do you think of paying Mr. York a surprise visit now?"

"I thought you didn't want to run into me at York's place," I said. "If you bring me with you, you're definitely going to see me there."

"Circumstances changed."

"Don't they always." I looked at the time. Showing up this late would be considered impolite, but it was a homicide investigation. Etiquette was the first thing that went out the window, unless you were in Russia, in which case the first thing that went out the window was usually the body.

"You've never been good with change," O'Connell said after a time.

"Why do I feel like I'm about to get sandbagged?"

"How are you holding up? A few weeks ago, your entire life got derailed. Martin was accused of assault. Someone else was shooting at you."

"People always shoot at me. I never should have gotten a target tattooed on my back."

He laughed. "Given the givens, I'd think you'd prefer change."

"What do you want, Nick? Besides the two hour nap in the hospital, I haven't slept. I don't have the bandwidth to figure out why you're beating around the bush."

"I'm wondering what happens if Commissioner Cross retaliates for the way we've been bending the rules on this case. Will you be okay working private sector without consulting?"

"That *is* my job."

"Yeah, but ever since you started at Cross Security, you've been in and out of the precinct. Moretti thought about having a revolving door installed. Jablonsky warned us about that."

"That's how it was when I was a federal agent, but you know the private eye biz. We're going to cross paths. I can't help that. I didn't volunteer for this assignment so I could become a suspect or witness. I never wanted any of this."

"What do you want?"

"Since when do you ask me questions like that?"

"I'm just making conversation."

"No, you aren't. You're trying to get in my head. Who put you up to it? Was it Heathcliff?" I narrowed my eyes. "Martin?"

"Neither."

I snorted, shaking my head. "It was Jen."

"She's my wife. I'm obligated to do what she says."

"No, you're not. Remember the tacos you snuck when she insisted you eat healthier?"

"Tacos aside, happy wife, happy life. Have you not heard the saying?"

"Why is she asking questions? Is this because I canceled our last double-date night?"

O'Connell parked in a space near the York's apartment building. "She knows losing a parent can be hard. You didn't have a funeral or wake. She wanted to do something for you, but she didn't know what. She was hurt you didn't call or mention it."

"You know why I didn't." Faking my adoptive father's death was the easiest way to get him off everyone's radar and into WitSec. Very few people knew the truth. I hadn't shared those details. My gut said my pals in major crimes knew, but maybe they didn't.

"Regardless, she's worried about you. We've seen you spiral. She wanted me to make sure that wasn't happening again. I figured the personal stuff wasn't the problem, but the professional stuff," he shrugged, "that eats at you. I know it does."

"What did you tell her?"

"I said you didn't want to talk about it."

"And yet, you brought it up anyway."

He held up his hand and pointed to his wedding ring. "I didn't have a choice. She'll make my life hell. You don't want that."

"You didn't seem so concerned when you were sneaking tacos." I laughed. "I'm okay, really. As far as I'm concerned, my parents have been dead to me since they kicked me out fifteen years ago. Nothing's changed. As far as work, I always figure something out. Cross and I will reach a compromise, or you'll have another homicide on your hands."

"All right. I'll pass that along." He opened his door, and I gave him a look. "Seriously, it's dropped. I won't bring it up again."

"Thank you."

The doorman announced our presence and escorted us to Nathan York's front door. The bereaved husband stood in the doorway in a smoking jacket and slippers. I'd never seen someone wear one of those outside of old movies.

"Mr. York, we're sorry to show up so late." O'Connell held out his identification. "I spoke to you the other day."

"I know who you are, Detective." Nathan moved away from the door, heading into the living room. "You said you'd be here this afternoon."

"Another lead surfaced concerning your wife's murder."

Nathan cringed at the word before easing into his chair and taking a sip of whatever was in his glass. "I hope that means you made some progress."

"Not as much as I'd like." O'Connell sat across from him, leaning forward and resting his elbows on his knees. "One of the men involved in the attack is in custody. He's given us the name of his accomplice, and the alias for two others involved." O'Connell pulled out his notepad, as if to demonstrate he wanted to get the facts correct.

While he asked Nathan if he knew any of the men involved, I looked around the room. The Yorks had four children, but I didn't see or hear them. Moving one of the pillows on the couch, I found a doll tucked between the cushions.

"That's Myra's. We always tell her to take better care of her things." Nathan held his hand out for the item. He brushed the ragdoll's yarn hair back and placed it on the coffee table.

"Where are your children?" I asked.

"Their nanny took them to their grandparents' house for the weekend. They don't need to see me like this." He indicated his odd attire. "Losing Tabitha," he twitched, his eyes searching the ceiling for a second, "is taking a toll. I need to figure out how to deal before I can help them deal."

"I'm sorry for your loss," I said.

"At least you have one of the men in custody. Do you think he's the one who...y'know?" Nathan asked.

"He denied it. However, there are other possibilities to explore. The cosmetologist Tabitha booked confessed to harming another client a few months ago," O'Connell said.

"Do you think she had something to do with what happened to my wife?"

"It's unlikely, but we are exploring every possibility."

O'Connell glanced at me. It was time I took over.

"Mr. York, a private security firm was hired to investigate Spa Alive. Do you think your wife may have been doing the same thing?"

Nathan stared at the doorway. "She was always so dedicated to her work. So dogged in her determination. She used to receive threats regularly."

"Did any of them come directly to her?" O'Connell asked.

Nathan shook his head. "They were sent to the media outlet where she worked. That's why she never published under her own name. She didn't want the crazies to find her."

"Still, secrets get out," I said.

"We have security in this building. Our children attend private schools. We take precautions. We don't have our own set of bodyguards, but I always hire people whenever we attend public events. I'm not without my share of enemies. But this is unfathomable."

"Did anyone threaten you recently?" O'Connell asked.

"My publicist would have dealt with any correspondence, but I don't recall anything in particular."

O'Connell jotted down a note.

"Where did your wife conduct most of her research?" I asked.

"She always tried to go directly to the source," Nathan said, "but when she was getting started, she used her laptop."

"May I see it?"

Nathan went into the other room and returned with a large machine. "Her passcode is 2-1-6-3."

Turning it on, I changed the log-in option and entered the code. Her background was set to a family photo from a few years ago. Her youngest was two at the time. They were all dressed in matching holiday pajamas. I should have done something to save her. The pang of guilt hit hard.

Swallowing it down, I checked the list of recently created files and her search history. Her browsing data didn't reveal much of anything, which I should have expected since Cross Security had already performed a deep dive. However, Tabitha had saved snipped images from a few websites she'd visited and several pages of notes.

"May we take this with us?" O'Connell asked. "It could aid in our investigation."

Nathan seemed hesitant. "She kept everything on there. All our photos, videos, everything."

"We'll bring it back in the same condition we found it. We won't delete anything," O'Connell said.

"Do you think it'll help?"

"It can't hurt," O'Connell said.

I skimmed more of the files she'd created. Most of it looked like background on Lorna Pagano. She had details on Pagano's bodyguards, her daily activities, her posting schedule, how she posted, the automation software she used, her list of check-ins, everything. Beyond that, Tabitha had pulled data on the brewery Lorna stood to inherit. She had basic research on the process of fermentation, bottling, and distribution. I skimmed some more, finding a profile on Ed Pagano, Lorna's father and head of the brewery.

"Your wife was thorough in her research." I glanced up from the screen. "Did she ever mention Lorna Pagano to you?"

"Not that I recall," Nathan said.

"What about Ed Pagano, her father? Do you know either of them?"

"Not personally. We may have crossed paths at an event, but I can't be sure." Nathan quirked an eyebrow. "What does that have to do with the spa?"

"I don't know," I admitted.

O'Connell asked a few more questions while I searched for deleted files. When I couldn't find a smoking gun or something that would point me to motive, I asked, "Would you mind if I looked around your wife's office and went through her things?"

At first, Nathan looked like he wanted to protest, but that was a knee-jerk reaction. Instead, he pointed to the doorway where he'd gone to fetch the computer. "You should start in there. When you finish, I'll show you to the bedroom."

O'Connell got up and followed me inside. "How did you get him to agree to that?"

"It's easy. He didn't kill his wife. He wants to find out who did. We want the same thing."

"He wasn't this forthcoming when I spoke to him the other day."

"Do you think he destroyed evidence?" I asked.

"No." O'Connell leafed through the files and pages on top of the desk while I went through the drawers. "Nothing indicates he's responsible. There hasn't been any odd financial activity or oddities when it comes to his phone records. He's cooperated thus far."

"He's not responsible," I said.

"Probably not."

In the middle drawer, I found an investor's pamphlet, complete with glossy photos, future projections, overhead percentages, and the like regarding the brewery. Beneath that was more documentation from other breweries, not owned by Ed Pagano. Maybe Tabitha wasn't that interested in Lorna. Maybe she was interested in the Pagano empire.

"Anything?" O'Connell asked.

I held up what I found.

"Did you find something?" Nathan asked from the doorway, a drink in his hand.

"Maybe. What do you know about breweries?"

"Not much. Beer-making has always been a pet project of mine. Tabitha even bought me one of those home kits. The results were disgusting. It all started a few years ago when we toured several vineyards. Wine isn't the same, but I'd thought about buying one of them. I thought it'd be a fun side project. A film I was producing at the time had run out of budget. We were almost through, and they needed a place to shoot the last few scenes. It would have been a great write-off, but I found the funding another way. After that, I looked into brewing my own beer, and it turned into a joke between us. Why do you ask?"

"Tabitha has a lot of research on several breweries. Could that have been what she intended to write her latest piece on?"

"I guess, if she found dirt."

I checked the top of the desk while O'Connell went through the drawers. But I didn't find any notes. "If she had a lead, would she have written it down somewhere?"

Nathan led me into the bedroom. Her dresser and mirror were covered in drawings and notes from her kids. Again, the sick feeling returned. "Check her jewelry box. That's the only place I can think where she'd put anything." He indicated the ornate box in the center.

I looked through it, but I didn't find anything. Once I finished with that, I checked the notes and drawings her children had made, but she hadn't defaced any of those with her own notes. After checking the rest of her dresser, her closet, and beneath the bed, I found a shoebox. Inside was a memory card. "Any idea what this is?"

"I've never seen it before." Nathan studied it for a moment. "That looks like it could have come from her phone."

"We have her phone in evidence," O'Connell said. "It wasn't missing a memory card."

"That doesn't mean she didn't have a spare." Reluctantly, I handed the tiny object to O'Connell for closer inspection.

"We have the same model phone." Nathan pulled his from his pocket. "I want to see what's on here."

THIRTY

The three of us huddled around Nathan York's phone. Tabitha's hidden memory card contained hundreds of photos of Lorna Pagano. Some were taken outside Spa Alive, which violated their terms of service, but Tabitha was never caught. That must have been before she started going to the spa, or they'd doctored their records.

Several videos had been taken of Lorna getting into her waiting car after her massage or facial. Tabitha had everything from shots of the bodyguard, to the license plate, to the driver.

Other footage, much more recent, had been taken away from Spa Alive that showed Lorna Pagano enjoying lunch with friends or stopping to pick up a matcha latte. If I didn't know what Tabitha York did for a living, I would have thought she was a stalker.

"Fine line, Parker," I mumbled.

"Huh?" O'Connell gave me a sideways look.

"Nothing."

Nathan flipped through several more photos. Those were taken of the Pagano estate. More bodyguards. More security. "I had no idea my wife was doing any of this." Other photos showed Lorna at the yoga studio in various poses. "I didn't even know Tabitha did yoga."

"She may have just started." I checked the date. The photos were taken two months ago.

"Tabitha was into kickboxing. That had been her exercise of choice." Nathan lowered the phone and rubbed his face. "Do you know what she hoped to expose by following Ms.

Pagano around town?"

"We're working on it." I picked up the phone and flipped through more photos. Near the end were videos of Damon Thoreau. Most were with Lorna. Tabitha had even caught a few money shots of the couple stealing a kiss or sharing an intimate embrace. "Your wife would have made a wonderful private investigator."

"That never would have satisfied her. She only did this so she could tell a story. Paint a picture." Nathan sighed and wandered into the other room. "Take the card, but leave my phone. I'm sure you'll find some use for it."

"Sir?" O'Connell moved to follow, but I put a hand on his forearm and shook my head. "Is there anything you need? Anyone we can call for you?"

"I'll be okay," Nathan said from the other room.

After removing the memory card, I gave the bedroom one last look, but there was nothing else to find. By the time I emerged, O'Connell was standing near the front door. He kept an eye on Nathan, but the man didn't appear suicidal or dangerous. He looked like his world had ended, and he was tired of our snooping.

"We'll be in touch as soon as we make progress." O'Connell clapped him on the shoulder.

"Thank you for your time," I said. "I'm sorry for the intrusion."

Nathan nodded.

Once we were outside, O'Connell took the memory card from me, as if he didn't trust me to hold on to it. I wondered if he would have done the same thing if I was an official police consultant. Maybe he knew I wanted to copy the files and send them to Cross Security for further analysis. This sneaking around behind his back felt underhanded and dirty. I didn't like it, but I wanted answers and had a vested interest in finding the truth.

"Do you think he'll be okay?" I nodded toward the apartment.

"Eventually. Tonight, he'll eat a gummy and drink himself into a stupor." O'Connell opened the car door. "Lorna Pagano hasn't set foot in Spa Alive in months. That means Tabitha York has been investigating her even longer than that. I wonder what triggered it. What set Tabitha York after her?"

"I don't know. But she took photos and videos of everything. The answer has to be here. We must be looking right at it."

"Do you have dinner plans?" O'Connell asked.

"No. Why?"

"Now you do."

*   *   *

O'Connell rocked in his chair. The burger he'd picked up had gotten cold two hours ago. But he didn't care as he ate what remained. "I don't get it."

"Join the club." I had gone through the photos and videos again. "From what I can tell, Tabitha was following Lorna before the mishap at Spa Alive even happened. This can't be about the spa's practices or the injury. This has to be about Lorna."

"Unless there were other victims before."

"Cross Security checked. I checked. It's possible they were covered up, but when we found Tabitha's notes on flesh-eating bacteria, I was thinking class action. Lucien knows where to dig to find things. Since that didn't hold water, we had no reason to believe anyone had been harmed prior to that incident."

"Someone's been harmed since." O'Connell flicked the photo of Tabitha. "Someone was killed."

"But why?"

"Tabitha must have seen something she wasn't supposed to or planned to expose something someone wanted buried. You heard what Archie said. Tabitha York pissed off someone with a lot of money."

"You think Lorna Pagano had her killed?" I asked.

"She has the means. All she would have to do is find someone willing to commit the crime."

"Why stage something so elaborate? Let me guess. Lorna figured she'd kill two birds with one stone. That's why the masked men stole the binder. In case she wanted to file suit and prove Spa Alive had lied to her and intentionally caused harm."

O'Connell put the burger down, wiped his mouth, and grabbed a post-it. He scribbled something on the sheet and stuck it to the corkboard we were using to dissect the murder.

"Why didn't she get revenge on Willa Garrison while she was at it?" I asked.

"Maybe you interrupted the men before they had time. Or Lorna feared that would lead us directly to her. Or," O'Connell's eyes lit up, "she thought framing Willa for Tabitha's murder would be the best revenge of all."

"Except she couldn't predict how the investigation would turn out. She couldn't have counted on me being at Spa Alive. The situation would have played out differently if I wasn't there. I'm not sure I want to know how much worse it would have been, but we could be looking at multiple bodies or mass casualties."

"True, but if you hadn't interfered, the men would have had more time to make Willa look guilty. They could have carried her into the room, put the murder weapon in her hand, or who knows what. Maybe they would have drowned her in the same tub where Tabitha was killed."

I jerked my head toward the double doors. "We could take another run at Archie and see if he has any insights to share."

"Let's give him time to stew." O'Connell looked at the clock. Heathcliff and Thompson had gone home twenty minutes ago. We were the only ones still working on this. "I don't see him being forthcoming, not until we locate Winslow."

"Are you hoping to play them off each other?"

O'Connell smiled and tapped the tip of his nose. "That's what makes you a fancy private eye."

"I'm pretty sure being forced out of the OIO is what made me a private eye. But I'll take what I can get." I stretched, wincing when I moved my shoulder. "Dammit."

"Still sore?"

"What do you think?"

"Jen said to use heat on everything below the bruise. Your muscles were knotted and tensed when the doctors examined you. That's what put a strain on the rest."

I wiggled my shoulders a little, shimmying slightly. "Leave the medical advice to your wife."

"You could call her and ask for recommendations," he wheedled. "It'd make her feel better."

"Fine, but if I slip and mention your taco obsession, you'll just have to deal with it."

"You don't play fair."

"Why would I? No one else does." I pointed to the computer. "Any chance I can get a copy of that memory card?"

O'Connell sighed dramatically. "I'll pretend I didn't hear you ask that. In fact, you've upset me so much I need to walk this off." He opened the top middle drawer on his desk, where a few blank USBs were kept. "I'll be back in ten minutes. You better be on your best behavior when I return."

"I'll try." I winked. "Maybe I'll even call Jen."

"You better. And no taco talk either."

Once he was gone, I took the USB out of the drawer, checked to make sure it was blank, and copied the files from the memory card to the external drive. As soon as the transfer completed, I tucked the device into my pocket and dialed his wife.

"Hey, Jen. It's Alex. We haven't had much girl time lately. I was thinking if you're off one night this week, we could catch up. There's a new wine bar Kellan was raving about. What do you say?"

"Did Nick put you up to this?"

"No."

"You're a worse liar than he is," she said.

"Regardless, he's right. I've been neglecting my friends. And I could use a night with my gal pal. What do you say?"

"Just us?"

"Yeah. Martin and I are...I don't even know."

"Now, you know I can't say no to that. I saw him earlier today. He seemed okay, considering. Are you fighting?"

"We had a fight. But I think we're finished fighting."

"Did you make up?"

"Not in so many words. I apologized, but it's like he's

waiting for something else or doesn't care what I have to say."

"He cares."

"You know what I mean. He didn't care that I apologized. I do it so often, he's become immune. But he doesn't seem mad either. It's weird."

"All right, this sounds like a two bottles of wine kind of problem. How does Tuesday sound? Say nine o'clock?"

"Great, unless Nick needs me."

Jen laughed. "He won't. I'll make sure of it."

I wasn't as confident. This case took priority, but since Nick let me copy the memory card, I had to do something to make his life easier. I just wasn't sure when I became Jen's pet project. Usually, she'd swoon over Martin and spend most of the night conversing with him when the four of us went out, while her husband and I talked shop or debated if the person in the corner had nefarious goals in mind.

Before I could hang up, O'Connell returned from his walk. He gave his computer a look, shutting the open drawer in the process. As far as he could tell, I hadn't done anything. But he knew better. Just like how I knew the reason he left was so he'd have plausible deniability.

"I should go. He's giving me that look, like I'm wasting time," I said.

"Let me speak to him," Jen insisted.

I held out my phone. "It's for you."

O'Connell took it, "Hey, honey. No, I'm leaving now. Alex is being a buster. You know how she gets."

I stuck my tongue out at him.

"Do you need me to bring anything home?" Reaching for the sticky notes, he wrote something down. "Is that the one in the blue container?" He wrote something else. "Okay. I got it. I'll see you soon." He hung up and handed me my phone. "We're calling it. With any luck, Winslow will be brought in tonight, and tomorrow's interviews will go better than today's."

"I'd hope so."

"I'll call you if I need you. But you said you and Cross had a meeting tomorrow with the insurance agency. You should take care of that instead."

"You don't want me to sit in in case you have questions?"

"I said I'd call." He pointed toward the break room. "Don't forget to grab your food from the fridge. If you don't take it with you, someone will eat it."

"Thanks for reminding me."

"I figured I should. You did take a nasty hit to the head."

I made a face. "I'm fine."

"Are you sure? What's the square root of 983?"

"31."

"Seriously?"

"No, but you're not the only one who's ridiculous." I grabbed the takeout containers from the fridge and slipped them into the folded brown paper bag. The Italian place Martin loved had been nice enough to deliver. But instead of sending the food to the Martin Technologies building, I had it brought here so I could hand-deliver it myself.

"Good night, Parker."

"Night, Nick."

I went down the stairs and found my car waiting in the rear lot. An officer had been nice enough to pick it up from where I'd left it a block away from the cellar. Again, I wondered what made the men return. It wasn't the scene of the crime, but given what was hidden inside the cellar, it was close. If they were there to clear out their ill-gotten gains, as O'Connell suspected, the two men who left Archie to take the fall must have known we were on to them. But how did they find that out?

I pondered that while I detoured to Cross Security. Since I wasn't planning on sticking around, I parked on the street and went through the front door. Building security knew me by name. It was late but early by my standards.

Instead of stopping by my office to look for notes or requests, I went straight to the lab, handed Amir a copy of the USB, and told him what it was. "Is there anything else I should know?"

"Have you spoken to Lucien?" he asked.

"Not since this afternoon. What's up?"

"Did he tell you he arranged a meeting with the insurance company at eleven tomorrow?"

"Yeah, but the photos and videos on that drive I just

handed you may change his mind."

"I doubt it. After you told him the binder was stolen and what it contained, he did some digging."

"You mean he read the interview transcripts off the police servers?"

Amir looked uncomfortable. "I don't ask questions like that. But whatever he found led him to some cold hard evidence to back his theories. Spa Alive was lying to its customers. One of them, Lorna Pagano, had a negative reaction because of it. It's only a matter of time before the truth comes out. Now, with the cosmetologist admitting responsibility and the internal documents which are in police custody, there's no way Spa Alive gets out of this unscathed. Their clients will be filing suit or threatening too, which will force the liability clause of their insurance policy to come into play, and the insurance will be forced to pay out."

"Glad you're the expert."

Amir cocked an eyebrow, unsure if I was being flippant or serious. "Lucien consulted Mr. Almeada. The attorney agrees with that assessment."

"What does Lucien want me to do? Provide a song and dance? Draw pictures to illustrate what's going to happen?" I grinned. "I've been practicing drawing stick people and money bags. I'm sure I could come up with something to emphasize our point."

"He said he would leave a report for you to review." Amir pointed skyward. "Justin should have a copy at his desk."

"He's still here?"

"He's been waiting for you."

"Shit."

THIRTY-ONE

"I know I said we'd do lunch, but when I didn't show up, you shouldn't have stuck around."

Justin provided a pity laugh. "Lucien wanted to make sure you were prepared for tomorrow."

"He made you stay here and wait for me? You should go to human resources. Go on strike. Quit, even."

Justin laughed again. This time, it didn't sound like it was out of pity. "I had other things to do, which is why I stuck around, but we were pretty sure you'd stop by before calling it a night."

"I have to work on being less predictable."

He held out a printed copy. "I sent the digital version to your dropbox."

My phone chimed the second he finished saying that, but I read the hard copy instead. "I wrote half of this." There were no surprises. Cross had been intentionally vague when it came to our findings. He postulated several different causes for possible pending lawsuits and provided facts to back up his belief that Spa Alive knowingly engaged in underhanded practices which left them open to lawsuits. Assuming the insurance agency wanted us to pursue this and the police department found more supporting evidence that Ralph Lively was involved in Kathy Walters' scheme, the insurance wouldn't be responsible for issuing payouts due to Spa Alive misrepresenting themselves.

"Lucien wants to know if you think there's enough here

for fraud charges," Justin said.

"Against Spa Alive?"

"Yeah."

"Possibly. It depends on how the company is structured. As of this moment, Kathy Walters is the only one we can prove committed fraud. For criminal charges to stick, we'd need more than this."

Justin made a note and centered his keyboard before typing something, which he'd presumably send to the boss. "Do you have any contacts in the FBI who could help?"

"Possibly, but for something this small, I don't think they'd waste their time."

"That's assuming something doesn't blow up."

I cringed. "Don't say that. With the way things are going, words like that are asking for trouble. The next thing you know, we'll find a bomb hidden somewhere."

"I didn't realize you were superstitious."

"I'm not. I'm cautious."

He pointed to my temple. "I'd never know by looking at you."

"I'm working on it."

"Good night, Ms. Parker."

I gave him a look. "Does Lucien make you sleep here too? I know people in HRT. I can call them. They can mount a rescue. We can get you out. Blink once for yes. Blink twice for no."

He blinked twice.

"What about ESU? I know a guy. Several, actually. We don't have to involve the Feds. We can keep it local."

"Is there anything else?" Justin asked.

I pushed the button for the elevator, deciding it'd be best to give up while I was ahead. "Good night." Once the doors closed, I texted him Rafael Dominguez's number, in case he changed his mind on being rescued.

He didn't respond, but I didn't expect him to.

After leaving Cross Security, I went to the Martin Technologies building. I wasn't as well acquainted with the night crew as their daytime counterparts, but since I had been responsible for most of their hiring and training, I recognized the two men at the desk.

"Evening, Ms. Parker," Ivan greeted me. "He's in his office." He handed me a visitor pass with elevator access. "You can go on up."

"Is he expecting me?" I hadn't made plans with Martin, which made me suspicious why security didn't seem surprised to see me. Was I really this predictable? Did everyone on the planet know what I was doing and when I was doing it?

"Not that I'm aware. He didn't mention anything to me, but we have standing orders to let you upstairs."

"Great, thanks." I slid the card and pressed the button. The elevator doors opened, and I went inside.

When they let me out on the seventeenth floor, I was surprised to find Martin's glass wall set to opaque. Usually, he liked to see out into the hallway. I checked the time, hoping to recall how many hours ahead Australia was. For them, it was Monday, sometime midday. Maybe Martin was in the middle of a call.

I thought about texting but figured that would be just as distracting. Instead, I entered the unlock code, bypassing the biometric features, and quietly opened the door. Martin was behind his desk. One hand ran through his hair while he leaned forward, jotting down notes in the side margins. At the intrusion, he looked up.

"I should have knocked. But I didn't know if you were in the middle of a call." I held up the brown paper bag with the Giovanni's logo on the side. "I thought I'd drop off dinner."

He put the pen down, rubbed his eyes, and got up to greet me. "Hey, sweetheart." He snagged the bag from my hand while he leaned down to kiss me. "How are you feeling?" His green eyes teased me. "Did you hit your head? You never bring me dinner."

"Fine. I'll take it home." I reached for it, but he pulled it away, stealing another kiss in the process. The bag dropped onto his desk, and he pulled me to him with both hands. One found its way into my hair and the other pressed against the small of my back, drawing me closer. I pulled away, nearly breathless. "Martin—"

He stared into my eyes before kissing me again, less demanding but somehow more intense. "Did you eat yet?"

"I had a few of O'Connell's fries."

Martin gave me a confused look. "Giovanni's doesn't sell fries."

"We picked up burgers. You almost got a cheeseburger instead." I searched his eyes. "Maybe that would have been better."

"No. This is perfect." He turned away, rummaging through the bag and pulling out container after container. "I hope half of this is for you."

"It is, but I wasn't sure if you wanted to eat together. I can take mine home."

"Nonsense. I have forty-five minutes. You should stay. I can't remember the last time we had dinner. It's been at least a week." He thought back. "Nine days."

"If you insist."

His eyes blazed. "I do."

"All right, I'll heat those up in the microwave." I reached for the two entrée containers. "I'll be right back."

"I can do it."

"You're busy." I pointed at the notes he'd been making. "Finish whatever that is while I'm gone."

The Martin Technologies break room contained a vending machine, a fridge, microwave, and several tables. It hadn't changed since the first time I stepped foot inside the building, which surprised me. Given how attentive Martin was to his employees, I was shocked he didn't put out a spread every morning or afternoon. Some kind of breakfast bar or a food truck for lunch. Did Cross Security have a perk Martin Technologies didn't?

I shook the thought away. The digital timer on the microwave counted down as the plate spun and the contraption hummed. Once my chicken was heated, I put Martin's dinner inside and set the timer.

The microwave beeped. I removed his dinner and headed back to his office. Martin had cleared off the table near the leather couches and placed cushions on the floor. He put two glasses of sparkling water down and assessed his handiwork.

"You didn't have to set the table," I said.

He took the warm containers from my hands. "I was

hoping to find candles. Maybe I should have been more concerned with silverware."

"The utensils are in the bag." I pulled out the two sets of neatly packaged fork, spoon, and knife combos. "Look, they even stuck a napkin in there. It's everything we could possibly need."

"What about real plates?"

"We don't need plates. No reason to be pretentious."

"I wasn't. I just thought plates would be nice." He took a seat on the nearest cushion. Unbuttoning his cuffs, he rolled up his sleeves, loosened the knot on his tie until he could slip it off over his head, and unwrapped a set of flatware. "Eat. You don't want it to get cold. Again."

Taking a seat on the other cushion, I freed my own flatware from the cellophane, my eyes on him the entire time. He wanted everything to be perfect. Martin was always a little like that, but to go to these extremes meant one thing. An uneasy feeling gripped my insides, but he had a few more hours of work. Now wasn't the time for this conversation.

I cut my chicken and popped a piece into my mouth. The microwave hadn't done it any favors. As a rule, Italian food was one of the worst to microwave, even if I had been known to gnaw on rubberized pizza crusts or shovel reheated pasta into my mouth as if I were starving.

"How is it?" I asked.

Martin looked up from his dinner. "This really hit the spot. Plates and wine may have made it better, but I'll take whatever I can get. It's better than stale sandwiches from the vending machine."

"Is that what you've been eating every night?"

"Not every night. Once, I had sushi."

"Places do deliver. It's how I survived as long as I have."

He turned his attention back to his plate. "By the time I realize I'm hungry, most places have closed. Things have been hectic around here. Worse than usual."

We ate in silence for a time. When my plate was nearly empty, I asked, "Are you mad at me?"

"No. I told you this afternoon, we're okay. Everything's okay." He pointed the fork in my direction, his brow furrowing. "Don't do that."

"Do what?"

"You know what. You're looking for a lie, a secret. Stop it."

"I wouldn't be looking if you weren't hiding something." I didn't want to bring this up now. I forced myself to look at my chicken while I cut the rest of it into bite-sized pieces. "Even when Giovanni's is bad, it's still pretty good."

"You ordered the same thing the first time we broke up."

I hadn't expected that. "Excuse me?"

"Before we even got started, when we were figuring things out, we went to dinner at Giovanni's."

"We've eaten there a hundred times since. I order this dish every other time we go there. I didn't realize this was problematic for you."

"It isn't."

I put my utensils down. If I didn't, I might stab him. "Talk to me. This afternoon, you said we were going through some things. That you were going through something. What is it? What's wrong? Tell me what I did or didn't do. Tell me how I can make it better."

He smirked, devious thoughts lighting up his eyes. "Can I ask for anything?"

"Dammit."

The look in his eyes assured me my annoyance had hit a nerve and triggered something because he turned serious. "You were shot."

"It doesn't count. I had on a vest."

"Where did you get it?"

"I took it off a guy with a gun. It's the same damn place I got the gas mask."

"Why weren't you prepared?"

I didn't like the interrogation. It reminded me of the other morning. I had been tired then, and I was tired now. "I was working undercover as a cleaning lady in a luxury spa. My gun was in my locker, along with my phone. None of this was supposed to happen. Cross Security was hired to look into an insurance scam. Everything that happened was unexpected. We already discussed this."

Martin blew out a slow breath. He wanted to keep his cool. He didn't want to yell or fight. That was a first. "I love you. This has nothing to do with you."

"What the hell does it have to do with?"

He wiped his mouth on a napkin. "Lucien begged me for the research on biotextiles. If he hadn't gotten involved, if my project hadn't gotten derailed, I wouldn't have had to scramble. We never would have gone to L.A. Bruiser wouldn't have gotten hurt. None of that shit would have happened. But all of that was supposed to be for a good reason. It was so I could do something to help keep you safe. The biotextiles research, all of that, was necessary to create bullet-resistant fabrics. You even gave me the first prototype. It's hanging in my closet." He held up his hand before I could interject. "Lucien promised you'd be the first person who got outfitted at Cross Security. Yet, it hasn't happened yet. And even if it did, he's missing the bigger picture. The point was so you'd always be protected. It shouldn't matter if you're doing corporate work or something dangerous. The material should be versatile and comfortable enough for all of it. He swore up and down it'd be like a uniform, an everyday outfit. Why hasn't he done anything yet? What is taking him so long?"

"Martin, I'm okay."

"You were lucky."

"I've never been lucky. But I know how to handle myself. Do not belittle that."

"That's not what I'm doing." He shook his head, his nose crinkling. "Jones almost died. He's helping the day shift out, but he's not back at full capacity yet. He should be in a few more weeks, but it was touch and go."

The memories hit like a solid punch to the gut. "I know. I was there. For a few agonizing minutes, I thought it was you."

"It could have been." He stared at the ceiling. "That can't be for nothing."

"It won't be. Cross will figure it out. He said he needs more." I told Martin about the conversation I had with my boss a few nights ago. "I thought he would have approached you about it."

"We have a meeting on the books for next week, but he should have said something sooner. Done something sooner. Lives are on the line. Your life is on the line."

"Martin—"

He sighed. "I know. You can take care of yourself. But your panic attack the other night woke me up. Then I see the mark on the back of your shoulder."

"A silk shirt couldn't have done much better."

"Maybe not." A stray thought crossed his mind, and he went to his desk. "Then again, with the tensile strength of the material and the grid pattern from the weaving, it may have been able to absorb more of the impact and disperse it over a larger area."

"So I'd have a bigger bruise. How is that better?"

"It wouldn't be as severe." He entered something into his computer, reread it, and hit enter. "I'll have to run more tests."

"I thought you weren't developing your own body armor."

"I wasn't planning on it, but now I'm worried Cross dropped the ball."

"This is Lucien Cross we're talking about. He must have come up with something grander than whatever he originally imagined. That's the only reason he'd be delayed. I'm sure that's why he wants to talk to you. He needs greater access, more research, whatever."

"We are not going back to L.A."

"Agreed. I'm pretty sure I'm banned from entering the city."

"Good." He returned to the table and sat on the floor beside me. Gently, he brushed my hair back, revealing the bump at my temple. "Did you have a vest today?"

"I didn't need one. He didn't have a loaded gun."

"But he had a gun?" Martin asked.

"What have I told you about reading between the lines?"

"You can't tell me you don't need protection."

"That's why we buy condoms in bulk."

"Alexis, be serious for a moment." He put his fingers under my chin and forced me to look at him. After searching my eyes, he pulled me into his chest and hugged me, careful to keep his hands away from the sore spots. "You had a panic attack the other night. You were assaulted today. How are you, really?"

I melted into him. "A woman was killed. I can't worry about anything else right now. All that matters is finding out why it happened and who's responsible."

"That's not your job."

"It doesn't matter." I pulled back, a little shakier now than before. "It's what I have to do."

He ran his thumb across my cheek, his eyes sad. "I know."

THIRTY-TWO

"I hope everyone had a restful weekend," Cross said from his spot at the head of the conference table. Somehow, I resisted the urge to lunge out of my seat and strangle him. Instead, I sipped my cappuccino. "As you may recall, our firm's been particularly interested in the happenings at the luxury spa, Spa Alive."

"More like Spa Dead," Renner mumbled.

It was gallows humor. In his previous life, he'd been a homicide detective, but it grated on my nerves. Not enough sleep. I took another sip. It was my new drinking game, only without the liquor. As long as I caffeinated every time something irritated me, eventually I'd be awake enough not to be annoyed. That seemed reasonable to my sleep-deprived brain.

"Alex and I will be providing our conclusions to our client in a couple of hours. If anyone has anything to add or share on the situation, now's the time." Cross peered at the group assembled around the table.

Crickets.

"On to our next order of business." Cross handed out a stack of blue folders, presumably containing new clients and cases.

"Whatever happened with the massage therapist?" Kellan asked while he leafed through his newest piece of business.

"Damon?" I shrugged. "He and Lorna had a fling, but as far as I know, it's over now."

"Did he have anything to do with the attack or murder? He had motive."

"He was out cold."

"That doesn't mean he couldn't be your inside man."

"Did you find something?" Cross asked.

"No. I researched everyone and everything like you asked, but I didn't find any dirt on the sexy massage therapist," Kellan said. "Nothing surfaced on Willa either. No one paid them off. As far as I can tell, neither benefitted from what happened."

"Do we know for sure Kathy Walters was our inside man?" Cross asked.

"I haven't heard from O'Connell this morning," I said. "But everything points to her. The suspect he arrested started dating Kathy after he was asked to join the crew planning to knock over the spa. I'd say he sought her out on the dating site and used her to get whatever information he needed."

Kellan made a tsk sound. "That's cold."

"Are we all set?" Cross asked.

"Sure," I said. We had more than enough to appease the insurance company. The rest the police would handle, possibly with my help.

Cross answered a few questions concerning the new assignments, dismissed everyone, and waited for the conference room to empty. When I didn't move, he rocked back in his chair, rolling his eyes and sighing when it squeaked. "I told someone to fix that."

"You should have done it yourself." I took another sip from my cup. Drink first, bitch second. But after my conversation with Martin the previous night, my boss was even lower on my list of people I liked.

"That is what they say." Cross glanced at the blue folder in front of me, which I hadn't touched. "Now what's the problem?"

So many things, but I refrained from saying it, which meant my caffeine plan was working. "I need a few days off."

"No, you don't."

"Justin needs a vacation."

"He can have one, but I'd like to hear it from him."

"I'll pass that along."

"I will let him know." Cross got up. "We leave in an hour and a half. The car will be waiting out front. You are familiar with the report."

"I wrote half of it."

"Great, you can present that half. I'll present the rest. If they ask anything about the police investigation, I'll let you handle that. In the meantime, I have other business to attend." He pointed at the folder in front of me. "For the record, so do you."

"Oh, I know."

I watched him leave the conference room and head for the stairs. The door swung closed. Martin would fight his own battles. He could handle his business, just like how I could handle mine. Lucien Cross wasn't my enemy. But the blue folder in front of me which demanded my time was.

"You're coming with me." Scooping it up, I went down the hall to Bennett Renner's office and knocked. "Hey."

"Let me guess. You want me to cover your case."

"I don't know. I haven't looked at it yet." I hefted it in the air, balancing it on my palm. "Feels light. That should mean there's not much to it."

"It could also mean the research hasn't been started or it'll require in-person surveillance."

"Do you want it?" I asked.

Renner chuckled. "Explain that logic to me."

"Coin toss. It could be the easiest assignment you ever get."

"No way. Cross handed it to you. That automatically qualifies it as a giant pain in the ass."

"Please, Bennett." I held it out to him. "Whatever you want. Name it."

He looked at the stack of folders on his desk. "I would if I could, but I'm swamped."

"All right. Thanks, anyway."

He pointed at the folder. "Why don't you see what it is? Maybe it can wait."

"It doesn't matter what it is. It has to wait."

Renner pointed to the phone. "Do you want me to make some calls for you? My buddy Jake owes me a few favors.

Since you're interested in the homicide investigation, he's your best bet at getting details and updates."

"O'Connell's on it."

"I'm surprised this is a major crimes case."

"It isn't. It's his case. Homicide's looking into it. Different precinct, but O'Connell is overseeing everything."

"And Nick being Nick, he's putting in the legwork himself." Renner held out his hand, crooking his fingers for me to come closer. "Which means you're helping." He took the blue folder away from me. "I'll give it a look and take care of the preliminary interview, if there's one scheduled. If not, this goes on the backburner until you wrap things up at the precinct." He opened the folder, lifted the first sheet, and scanned the rest. "On second thought, you can make time for this."

Confused, I looked to see what was inside. The folder was filled with blank pages. "I don't understand."

"Lucien's letting you pick your next case. I guess he figured arguing would be pointless."

"He's the boss. He doesn't argue. He commands."

"Sure, but he knows you won't listen." Renner nodded at the blank sheets. "And he accepts that."

Now I felt like an even bigger ass. I turned in the doorway. "Once I finish with O'Connell, I'll help you tackle that mess." I pointed to the stacks of files on his desk.

"Most of the investigations are finished. I just have reports to write."

"I figured as much. Lucky for you, that's my favorite part." It wasn't, but I'd help anyway.

"I always said you'd make a great assistant."

"In your dreams."

After leaving Renner's office, I went into my office to see if any progress had been made. Being on the outside looking in meant I didn't know if Winslow Smith had been arrested or if the police identified any of the other men involved. For all I knew, Kathy had cracked under the pressure and confessed. But I didn't think she was guilty.

Instead, I went over the files contained on Tabitha York's memory card for the fourth time. One thing was clear. She had Lorna Pagano under surveillance. She followed the woman everywhere.

I twisted to grab the legal pad, and my side cramped. "Jeez." I pressed my thumb into the knot, hoping to get it to release, but it only made it hurt worse. "Come on." I stretched backward, forcing the muscles to lengthen and loosen. Once the cramp eased, I sighed and sat forward.

Pausing on a photo of Lorna in triangle pose, I pulled up Tabitha York's financials. She wasn't a member of that yoga studio, so how did she get that photo?

To make sure I wasn't missing anything, I called the yoga studio, pretended to be Tabitha York, and asked when my next payment was due. The woman on the other end said I wasn't in the system and went into detail on how to become a member.

"Oh, that's right," I said. "Maybe I bought a day pass."

"We don't offer those, but you could have come as another member's guest."

"That must have been it. I'll have to sign up for my own membership." I studied the photo again, but my yoga knowledge was limited. I couldn't recognize the type of practice from the photos alone. "What's offered on Wednesdays at nine a.m.?" That was the timestamp on the photo.

"That's our intermediate class." She used a few words after that that weren't English, but I'd moved on to the other saved photos. "I can sign you up over the phone."

"That's okay. I'll be by later. Namaste." I hung up.

Zooming in, I studied the man in the background. Lorna had been the focal point of the photo, so he wasn't easy to see. His hair didn't look as greasy, and with those sunglasses, I couldn't be sure, but he looked like the man I'd knocked out and left in the sauna. Was that the same small scar on his cheek?

I called Amir. "Any progress?"

"Nothing since the last time I updated you."

"What about the memory card?"

"There's a lot here. Tabitha York would have made a great private eye."

"What about the man in the background?" I gave him the file name. "Does he look familiar?"

"Um..."

"Is it the same guy I knocked out?" I asked.

"This doesn't give me much to go on."

"Do your best to find out." I put the phone down, itching to do something. I didn't know if my assumption was correct, but this could be the break I needed. Except, I didn't know what it meant.

Cross stood in my doorway, clearing his throat. "Are you ready?"

I waved him over. "Take a look at this." I showed him the enlarged photo from Tabitha's memory card before pulling up the photo I took. "Is that the same guy?"

"Possibly." He reached for the mouse, zooming out a little. "Facial rec should be able to tell us something. His eyes are covered, so it won't be definitive. O'Connell won't be able to use it."

"That doesn't matter."

He reached for my phone, but I put my hand on top of his. "I already passed this on to Amir."

Cross ignored me, picked up the phone, and told him to make this a priority. "It's time to return the favor."

Picking up my copy of the report, I gave the computer a final look, sent copies of the files to my phone, so I could review them on the go, and met him at the door. "You didn't assign me another case."

"What would have been the point?" He pressed the button for the elevator. "If you can't beat them, join them. And beatings are prohibited. They create an unsafe work environment. Then I'd have to up our liability insurance, and the company would hire someone to investigate me."

"They could get Ace Darrow."

He glared at me. "That's not funny."

"It's a little funny."

The elevator was crowded. With all the extra stops, it took five minutes to get to the lobby. Our driver was waiting out front. Cross opened my door before going around and getting in on the other side. Who knew he could be a gentleman?

We ran through our presentation once. I may not mind writing reports, but performing for clients didn't make me happy. I was too brass tacks, not enough sparkle. But Cross had been a money guy. He knew how to sell things and how to present facts to gain the spin he wanted.

The meeting didn't take that long. Our client only wanted to know about the dollars and cents. How much would this cost? How much did they stand to lose? Could they get out of it? We spent more time speaking to their legal counsel than anyone else. At least that was over.

"Ms. Parker, wait," the lawyer called. He had followed us out of the building. "You spoke to Tabitha York's family. Do you know if they have any intention of suing?"

"They could," Cross said.

The lawyer ignored him. "What did Mr. York say?"

"He's dealing with a lot right now," I said.

"What does that mean?"

I shrugged. "You can't expect him to know much of anything at this point. He's reeling."

"That's understandable." The lawyer nodded his thanks and headed back inside.

Cross put his hand on the small of my back and pulled open the car door. "Do you think York will sue?"

"They don't need the money. It depends on if the police find the party responsible and who that party is. Right now, the only thing Nathan York needs is for his life to make sense again. For that to happen, he'll want to know who killed his wife and why. After that, I'd imagine retribution or justice will be next on the list, but everyone's different. He may go nuclear and blow up at everyone."

"Either way, we gave them what we could. It's up to their legal counsel to find a solution the insurance company will like."

"If they get out of paying because of a loophole, it'll be bad publicity," I said.

"They know that. They're also in the business of making money, not spending it. My guess, they'll use what we provided as reasons why they don't have to pay out, but instead of refusing all together, they'll offer a smaller portion in good faith. That way, they look like the good guys, and everyone will know Spa Alive was responsible."

"The luxury wellness center's going under."

"The ship's been sinking since the masked men knocked everyone out."

I thought about it, but no one on staff benefitted from losing their jobs. Unemployment wouldn't last forever, and it wouldn't cover what they'd been making, not when tips were factored into the equation. Now with the insurance being less than it was, their best hope would be suing the owner for negligence, maybe fraud. Again, I wasn't a lawyer. Ralph Lively wasn't worth enough for this to be life-changing for any of his employees or customers. They didn't stand to make enough to warrant hiring a team of masked men to invade the place, let alone commit murder.

"It wasn't an inside job," I said. "Kathy Walters was used. She's not innocent, but she wasn't part of this." I flipped through Tabitha's files. O'Connell had her laptop at the precinct. I hadn't asked to copy her hard drive. Even if I had, that would have taken too long. He never would have agreed to that, especially when he handed it over to the lab techs when we first arrived. "The men invaded the spa because of Tabitha York or something Lorna Pagano had done or wanted to do. York must have known what that was. That's why they killed her."

"That's incredibly vague."

I held up the photo I showed Cross earlier. "That's the same guy I knocked out. I don't care what facial rec says. I know it." I flipped through a few more photos. Other men were in the background. They all wore suits and sunglasses. Our suspect blended in, probably to avoid being recognized. Given where the photos were taken, at upscale locations, I figured he didn't want to stand out. When I got to the videos Tabitha had shot, I paused. Lorna and Damon had snuck behind the shrubbery outside Spa Alive to steal a kiss. The footage was taken from a distance. Near Lorna's waiting car was the same man from the other photo. He tilted his head forward, his sunglasses sliding down the bridge of his nose, while he glared in their direction. "Could that be her bodyguard?"

Cross scooted closer, so we could watch the video together. "He's not in the system. No record. You said the police didn't recognize him. That would explain why." He pulled out his phone. "Ed Pagano uses Precision Protection for security. They cover his company, his plants, his offices, everything related to his business. I think he has them providing personal protection as well. Let me see what I can find out." He spoke for a few minutes, getting shuffled from assistant to assistant. Finally, he made some progress.

"Well?" I asked.

"This will require meeting face to face. Where can I drop you? Back at the office?"

"The precinct." O'Connell said he'd call if he needed me, but he didn't know about my hunch.

"I figured as much." Cross leaned forward, telling the driver to drop me off before rerouting to Precision Protection.

When the car came to a stop, I pushed the door open. My side knotted again, so I did another exaggerated stretch. Stress would kill me, eventually. And to think, this had started before I even got shot.

"I'll call as soon as I know something." Cross cocked an eyebrow at my posture. "You should call Damon and take him up on his offer. You never know what you might learn. It's not like you have to keep your identity a secret any longer." He winked and pulled the door closed.

THIRTY-THREE

"You're not supposed to be here," O'Connell said when I appeared at his desk. "Didn't I say I'd call you?"

"I have a lead."

"Is your phone broken?"

I gave him a look. "Did the PD's AV club find anything on Tabitha York's laptop?"

He pointed to a thick file sitting on the edge of his desk. "They cataloged her files. The problem is she used the laptop for everything. Family photos, videos, grocery shopping, research. Parsing through the data and determining what is and isn't relevant could take forever."

"Shouldn't you be helping?"

"Don't you think I have enough to do?"

I looked around. The bullpen was quiet. "It's a slow day."

He shook his head and sighed. "Winslow's still in the wind, if that's why you're here."

"It's not. I'm here about Tabitha York's hidden memory card. Tell me you at least went over that."

"She had Lorna Pagano under surveillance. We looked at everything yesterday. What more do you want me to see?"

"Not Lorna Pagano." I leaned over, reaching for his mouse. "Do you mind?"

He held up his palms and slid his chair to the side. "By all means, help yourself."

After a few clicks, I brought up the images. "My interest is in this guy." I drew a circle around him with the mouse.

"He pops up in a few of the shots. Always in the background. Always unobtrusive."

O'Connell checked a few more images, finding him lingering in some of the others. "Do you think he was stalking Lorna Pagano or Tabitha York?"

"He was at Spa Alive on Friday. He was the guy nice enough to let me use his body armor and gas mask."

O'Connell rocked forward, his hand resting on top of his desk phone. "Are you absolutely certain?"

"I am."

He squinted at the computer screen. "These aren't the best photos. Did Cross Security run a comparison through their facial rec?"

"It's processing."

"So you can't be sure."

"I'm sure. But Lucien said it's not enough. You won't be able to use it."

"Do you have a name?"

"No." I gave him a look. "You don't buy Archie's story that this guy's name is Guido?"

"Do you?"

"No, which is why I want to look at Tabitha York's computer. If she had other photos, maybe non-surveillance photos, we can determine how long he was following her, or even if he was following her."

"He could have been on Pagano."

"He could also be responsible for killing Tabitha York."

"That's a lot of conjecture."

"Actually," I zoomed in on the unidentified man near Lorna Pagano's waiting car, "I was thinking he could be security. Lucien's looking into it."

O'Connell rocked back in his chair and rubbed his mouth. "That would change things. It may even explain why they stole the binder from Spa Alive. Though, it wouldn't explain why they left it behind."

"It's in police evidence. If it's used in a court of law, it becomes part of the record, including the information it contains, which Lorna could use in her lawsuit against the spa. But that wouldn't explain why Lorna would have had members of her security detail kill Tabitha York."

"Tabitha was stalking her. Clearly, the investigative reporter was on to something. Assuming that something had nothing to do with the spa and everything to do with Lorna Pagano, it might make sense." O'Connell got up. "It's time I have another chat with Archie and the others we're holding. If you want to see Tabitha York's computer, I'll tell the techs to give you access. Do not delete anything. In fact, don't touch anything. They'll do the touching. You can tell them what you're looking for."

I clutched my chest. "Knife through the heart, Nick. I thought you trusted me."

"I do. But this investigation has to be clean."

After forty-five minutes of watching the techs sift through birthday photos on Tabitha's laptop in the hopes of finding the unidentified man lingering in the background at the restaurant or park, I gave up. "What about saved articles and documents?"

"There are hundreds."

"Any mention of some guy named Guido?"

"None."

"Let me see the file names." I scanned the list, but nothing stuck out. However, Tabitha York was smart enough to hide her research behind an innocuous name that no one would ever think to check. "Try that one." I pointed to *Coupon Club*.

The tech opened the file. Inside were York's notes on the rise of mommy bloggers, coupon queens, and the history of counterfeiting and committing fraud.

Instead of wasting the entire day banging my head against the wall, I handed the tech my card. "I'm looking for anything to do with Lorna Pagano and her family's business. If you find something juicy, let me know."

"This is Detective O'Connell's case."

"Great, let him know too." I headed for the door. More than likely, someone would update me. My money was on O'Connell, but there was an even better chance Amir or someone at Cross Security would find the data we needed faster. I didn't put it past my boss to have hacked the PD's database and copied everything for our perusal, but since I hadn't heard anything yet, I wasn't sure. Since the files were on a non-regulation machine, Cross may not have had access. I guess I'd find out soon enough.

After leaving a note on O'Connell's desk, I called Damon. "Hey, is that offer for a massage still on the table?"

"Uh, yeah. I guess."

"I have some things to tell you. I'm on my way to your place."

"Okay, Alex. I'll see you in a few."

I returned to the office, picked up my car, and headed to Damon's. This had the potential of being a terrible idea. For all I knew, Damon Thoreau had played a part in Tabitha York's demise. He was her massage therapist. He knew when she had an appointment. He could have provided that information to the team who took over the spa. In fact, he could have been the one who killed her. After all, Tabitha was dead before the men gassed the place. She wouldn't have given it much thought if Damon showed up in her treatment room. She trusted him.

I knocked on Damon's door, the thoughts running rampant through my mind. Maybe I should leave. Maybe I should be armed. Or I should stop letting my imagination run wild.

He opened the door, raising an eyebrow. "Hey, are you okay? You look worried."

"Did you kill Tabitha York?"

"What?" He stepped backward, either out of habit or because the accusation struck him as hard as a physical blow. "I'd never do anything like that. No fucking way. Why would you even think that?"

I stepped inside. "Did you know she was asking about Lorna because she was looking into your ex-girlfriend?"

"Are you serious?" He looked uneasy, like he'd just gotten to the twist and realized he was in the Twilight Zone. "I thought you wanted a massage."

"I could use one, but I have issues letting strangers touch me." Cross's words played through my mind. My boss better be right, or I'd be the next homicide the police were forced to investigate. "I'm not a cleaning lady."

"No shit." That was the first thing I said that didn't surprise Damon. "I'm guessing you're a cop."

"Private."

"Did you know what was going to happen on Friday?"

"No."

"Why were you at Spa Alive? Don't tell me it's because business was slow and that was your side hustle."

"The insurance company reached out. Spa Alive wanted to massively increase their coverage. It made the money guys worried. They thought a lawsuit might be in the works."

"That's why you kept asking all those strange questions."

"Hazard of the job."

He scowled. "You played me. Do you even have a brother?"

"No. That was my boss. If it makes you feel any better, we did go to a meeting the next morning. It just wasn't the kind of meeting you assumed."

Damon stared at me. "Is your name even Alex?"

"Alexis Parker." I tried to look contrite. "It's nice to meet you."

"Jesus." He scrubbed at his forehead while he circled a few times, unsure what to do or say. "Why are you coming clean now?"

"I have questions that only you can answer. The police will come knocking eventually. I hoped to beat them to the punch." I looked him in the eye. "I want to know who killed Tabitha. She had kids and a husband. I went into that room and didn't even bother to check on her. I didn't want to get in trouble. I didn't want to risk my cover."

"You feel guilty."

I nodded.

"Tell the police what you know," he said.

"I already did. I used to consult for them. I'm the reason they showed up Friday. When everyone else was knocked unconscious, the mask I wore bought me a tiny bit more time. I would have gone down eventually, but I got to a window before that could happen. When one of the men came into the sauna, I jumped him and took his mask. That's when I called for help."

Damon studied me. "You put the towel under my head and covered Mrs. Byrne. The police asked me about that, but I didn't know how it happened."

"You were hurt. I wanted to make sure you were okay, and I didn't want her to get cold. Those sheets are thin."

He came to a decision. "All right. Tell me how I can help. What does any of this have to do with Lorna or our relationship?"

"Tabitha York was a journalist. She was looking into Lorna. Do you have any idea why?"

Damon puffed out his cheeks and blew out a breath. "Lorna's an influencer and an heiress."

"Any skeletons in the closet?"

"Not that I'm aware." He gestured to the chair across from the couch, and we sat. "She didn't engage in a lot of drama. She wasn't a reality star."

"But there was drama. Lorna had sued several companies."

"I wouldn't know about any of that."

I believed him. "Did Tabitha ever ask anything specific?"

"I already told you she wanted to know about our dating life. Where we went, the things we did. It always sounded innocent enough."

"Where you went," I repeated, mulling that over. "Did Lorna have any favorite spots?"

"I couldn't afford those kinds of places," Damon said, "and mooching off her wasn't part of what we did. With me, she got to experience how the rest of the world lived. Movies, grabbing a slice, chilling at a dive, hanging out here or at her place, those are the kinds of things we did." He smiled. "We went bowling once. She'd never been before. Can you believe that?"

"I saw the photos," I said. "Not everything you did was low-key."

"She took me to a few fancier places. We went away one weekend. From the private jet to the five-star accommodations, it was insane. But I never told Tabitha about that. I kept that stuff quiet."

"I get it." Damon had no idea how much of that I understood. "What about security?"

"Security?"

"Did Lorna have a bodyguard or a protection detail?"

"She has a driver and one bodyguard. Her father insists.

For the most part, they keep their distance."

I took out my phone and brought up the suspect near Lorna's car. "Do you recognize this guy?"

Damon's eyes grew wide. "Where did you get this? That's me with her."

"Tabitha had this."

"That was months ago. How could she possibly have this photo? No one was supposed to know about us, that was before we went public, before Lorna stopped going to Spa Alive."

"Relax, Damon. No one cares. This isn't a cheating spouse situation. You're both single. It doesn't matter."

"It does." Damon looked panicked. "I could lose my job, possibly my license."

"Spa Alive's going out of business. Other things have come to light. Don't worry about this." I enlarged the photo of the man, forcing Damon and Lorna off my screen. "What do you know about this guy? Does he work for Lorna?"

"Spa Alive's going out of business? How do you know that?"

"Answer my question first."

He studied the photo carefully. "I'm not sure if he works for Lorna, but that's the uniform her bodyguard and driver wear. Well, I call it a uniform. It's a navy blue suit with a white shirt and navy blue tie. I teased her they wore that color so she couldn't call them the men in black."

"Do you know any of their names?"

"I can't remember."

"Does Guido sound familiar?"

Damon quirked an eyebrow. "I would have remembered that."

"Have you spoken to Lorna recently?"

"Not since we broke up."

"Before you broke up, you said she would ask questions about the spa. Did she ever ask about your clients? Did she bring up Tabitha?" Those were leading questions, but this wasn't a court of law.

"Once in a while, she'd ask if I thought any of them were prettier or sexier than she was. I never went into specifics. You know Spa Alive's policies. I never mentioned anyone by name, but she seemed a little jealous of my female clients, whether they were eighteen or eighty."

"She was your girlfriend. Rules don't always apply when it comes to matters of the heart. Are you sure you never mentioned anyone by name to put her mind at ease? When I pressured you, you gave her up."

"That was different. I thought you worked at the spa." He looked me in the eye. "I never said a word to her."

I wasn't sure I believed that, but if he told her, I didn't think he'd gone into much detail. "So Lorna didn't know about Tabitha York?"

"Nuh-un." He shook his head for added emphasis.

"Did you ever notice anyone snooping around you or the spa?"

"Nope."

"What about guys wearing navy blue suits?"

"Not that I recall. Not without Lorna."

I brought up a photo of the bodyguard I'd encountered when I confronted her at the rooftop restaurant. "What about this guy?"

"That's Lorna's guy. He'd always glare at me whenever I picked her up. He reminded me of a disapproving father, except he's not old enough to be her father."

"Do you think he had a romantic interest in her?"

"Possibly, but his presence never felt like rivalry. I got more big brother vibes than jealous ex-boyfriend vibes from him."

"Okay." I was running myself in a circle and not getting anywhere. All I knew was the man in the photo wore the same suit as Lorna's security. On a whim, I searched for Precision Protection. Their website boasted a few large, muscle-bound meatheads in navy blue suits. I scanned the rest of the photos, but the average guy with the greasy hair and scar was nowhere to be seen. Precision Protection only showed their most impressive looking hires. I was sure Cross Security did the same.

"It's your turn," Damon said, pulling me from my search. "Why am I out of a job?"

"Management was cutting corners. They replaced the expensive, organic, non-toxic ingredients with cheaper alternatives. It may have been what caused Lorna's reaction."

"Did Kathy know about this?"

"Kathy's the one who instituted the changes. According to what she told the police, this wasn't widely held knowledge. She stands to take the fall for it."

"How could I not know this was going on?" Damon asked.

"Why would you know?"

He thought about it. "What about the cosmetologists? Janet, Willa—"

"You'd have to ask them, but don't. Please. The police won't be happy if this information gets out. They want to question everyone first to determine who knew what and when they knew it."

"You weren't supposed to tell me any of this, were you?"

"I owed you an explanation. I really am sorry for deceiving you."

"When this is over, how about that movie?" He looked around. "When you called, were you serious about the massage?"

"My side's knotted, but I wasn't kidding when I said I don't like to be touched."

He wasn't that easily deterred. "Can I see it?"

"What?"

"Your back. I want to see if the knot is visible."

"Does that matter?"

"If it's that severe, it'd be easy to pinpoint. You could get a massage gun and do it yourself." He held up his palms. "Professional courtesy, but it's up to you."

Something told me this was a test, like he didn't fully believe me, that he said what he thought he should. But maybe if I let my guard down a little, he would too. "All right."

I took off my shoulder holster, leaving my gun close in case he tried something. After removing my jacket, I unbuttoned my shirt and slid it off on my injured side. I turned in the chair, so he could see my back. "Well?"

He moved closer to get a better look. I tensed, which made my side cramp.

"Shit."

He put his fingers above the cramp, working them back and forth. For the first few seconds, I saw stars. Shooting him wasn't out of the question. But then the knot released, causing the ache in my ribs and along my shoulder to ease. "The massage gun can help with that. Hang on. I have one here."

If he returned with an actual gun, I would shoot him. Instead, he came back, pressed the percussion massager to the sore spot, and let it run. The remaining tension dissipated and everything felt better.

"I'm sold," I said. "That's going on my Christmas list."

"How did you get this bruise? Is this where you fell on something?"

I turned back around, pulling my shirt on and buttoning it. "The men who invaded Spa Alive shot me. I had on one of their tactical vests. That's the mark it left."

"But you were tense before that happened."

"I'm always tense. Hazard of the job." Though, I suspected it was a hazard of being me.

Damon held up his palms and backed away until he was seated on the couch again. "You're the reason we survived."

"I didn't do much. I don't think they planned to hurt anyone else."

"You said they killed Tabitha."

"Someone killed Tabitha. My money's on them, but she was down for the count before they gassed the place. Any idea who could be responsible, if they aren't?"

Damon thought about it. "I don't know."

"What about Lorna's security? Is there anything else you can tell me about them?"

"Lorna always had the same two guys following her. She was familiar with them. But when they were driving us somewhere, I remember her bodyguard talking to someone through his earpiece. It sounded like there was a second team keeping an eye out."

"Did you ask Lorna about it?"

"She said her dad liked to send a few of his guys to help when he thought things might get out of hand."

"Where were you going?"

"That night, we were going to a club. A famous DJ was

performing. Lorna begged me to go. It wasn't my usual scene, but she really wanted to see him."

"Did you ever meet Ed Pagano?"

"Her father? Yeah, a few times. He treated me like the help. He made it clear he didn't think I was good enough for his daughter."

"What about his business?"

"He kept that to himself. Lorna always got upset when he talked about it, which I assumed was why he didn't."

"She didn't approve?"

"She hated it. She would spend hours ranting about wastewater, emissions, and byproducts. Lorna's an environmental activist. It drove her crazy that her father wasn't doing more to clean up his business."

I opened my dropbox and checked the profile we had on Lorna Pagano. The other lawsuits she'd filed had to do with services and products failing to live up to their claims. She'd been allegedly harmed by each of them. What none of us had realized was every one of them had to do with something "clean" failing to live up to the claim.

"Could Tabitha York have reached out to Lorna?"

"How?" Damon asked.

That was a good question. "Did Lorna ever report any of the things her father's company was doing?"

"You mean like a whistleblower?" Damon shook his head. "She may not like it, and she is serious about making an impact. But she isn't all or nothing. There's no way she would give up her leather handbags or trips on the private jet. She likes what she likes. And Lorna likes being wealthy. Everything else was second."

"So she didn't turn the mirror on herself, just the rest of the world?"

"Yeah, something like that."

Tabitha could have been planning to expose Lorna for being two-faced, or she intended to shine a light on Ed Pagano's brewery. Either would have made a splash, one in the gossip columns and on social media, and the other with the news and business outlets. Tabitha could have caused quite the shakeup. In fact, she could have planned to write an article that exposed both.

THIRTY-FOUR

After leaving Damon's apartment, I checked Lorna's social media accounts. No wonder her father didn't think a sole bodyguard and driver were enough. Even after our confrontation the other day, Lorna continued to post her check-ins and whereabouts. Part of the celebrity lifestyle was showing it off to make others envious.

Cross had told me in no uncertain terms to stay away from Lorna. For once, I thought I'd listen to him. However, I couldn't help it if the coffee shop I chose to visit happened to be in the vicinity of the boutique where she was trying on outfits.

While I sat near the window, keeping an eye out for men in navy suits, I kept one eye on her page. Damon said she was into saving the environment, but she wasn't particularly outspoken about it. Besides several photos of her modeling a cute baseball cap or t-shirt she received from one charity or another, she didn't post a lot about her cause. Less than five percent of her posts were about the environment. The rest were about her trips, her shopping, and what she ate for breakfast, lunch, and dinner.

Maybe she didn't give a shit about any of it. Maybe she was as shallow as her profile indicated. Or she cared deeply and everything she posted online was a persona, an act. Something to appeal to the masses. But why bother building a platform without using it?

Tabitha York had never commented on any of Lorna's

posts or photos. In fact, her browsing history showed she had a limited interest in Lorna Pagano. No DMs. No nothing. How did Tabitha get on Lorna's radar, assuming Lorna had wanted the journalist killed?

When Lorna exited the shop, her bodyguard followed beside her. It was the same man I'd encountered the other day. As far as I knew, he hadn't been involved in the attack at Spa Alive. I snapped a few more photos of him for good measure and zoomed in on the driver. I didn't recognize him.

Once Lorna was settled into the back of the SUV, hidden behind the tinted windows and reinforced doors, they pulled away from the curb. Tossing my coffee cup into the trash, I kept my eye on them and got into my car. Given midday traffic, the SUV wasn't going anywhere fast. In fact, it had only moved a few feet before getting stopped at the intersection at the end of the block.

As soon as they started moving again, another SUV pulled out from where it had been parked several car lengths away. It looked identical to the one Lorna had gotten into. Same tinted windows, same thick outer shell. Either Damon was right and Lorna had a second team keeping an eye out, or someone planned to kidnap or kill her. My money was on a second protection detail, but I'd be remiss if I wasn't prepared for every possibility.

Pulling out of my space, I kept a safe distance and followed the cars. The second SUV remained a few cars away from the first. That wasn't normal procedure, unless they were keeping an eye out for a tail. Were they expecting trouble?

I thought back, but when I confronted Lorna at the rooftop restaurant, there hadn't been a second vehicle. Only the one. Was I the reason for the added security, assuming that's who they were?

A few streets later, the lead SUV pulled to a stop. The bodyguard got out of the car and opened Lorna's door. The second SUV parked at the end of the street. I stopped at a yellow light, hoping they wouldn't notice me. The car behind me honked angrily. By then, the light had changed, and cross traffic started to move. With any luck, Lorna's people wouldn't think much of this.

Lorna entered the gym. Her bodyguard followed. The driver remained in the SUV. The doors on the second SUV opened, and two men in navy blue suits exited. They checked the area. When they turned in my direction, I snapped their photos, but I didn't recognize either of them.

The two man team moved toward the gym. One of them remained near the front. The other went around the side, presumably to keep watch on the other exit.

The light changed, and I drove through the intersection, squeezed into a spot, and took a few photos of the license plate on the second SUV. After sending those to Cross Security, I zoomed in on the other bodyguards and snapped more photos.

While I waited for Lorna to finish her workout, my phone rang. *Cross.*

"Hey, boss. Did you find out anything interesting?"

"You're spending too much time with Justin," Cross said. "I IDed the man you photographed at Spa Alive. His name is Pete Berenson."

"Not Guido?"

"Where the hell did you get Guido?"

"It doesn't matter." Archie Hudson had lied. Big surprise.

"Berenson is on Pagano's payroll. He provides security for the brewery. My contact at Precision Protection said Ed Pagano moves his guys around to keep them from getting complacent. On occasion, he has them provide protection for his daughter. Looks like I was right."

"We were right," I corrected. "Any idea why he was at Spa Alive? Was he hired to kill Tabitha York?"

"Again, this is not in our job description," Cross reminded me. "Tell O'Connell. He can take care of it."

"Right. Yeah. I got it."

"Uh-huh." He didn't believe me. "I had Amir put together a background. Pete Berenson doesn't have a criminal record. No military or law enforcement training. He has a degree in criminal justice. Precision hired him, and he got assigned to Ed Pagano's account three years ago. He's been there ever since. No complaints. No issues. No incidents."

That didn't tell me anything. "What about known

criminal ties? Can you connect him to Archie Hudson or Winslow Smith?"

"Amir's looking into it. Again, this is not our job."

"Yep. Thanks."

"Parker, I'll see you back at the office."

"Sure thing, boss." Except I had no intention of going back to the office.

I called O'Connell and updated him on the situation. He needed approval and court orders. Since Precision Protection didn't have Pete Berenson's photo posted online, O'Connell would have to do things the hard way. The easiest would be to go straight to the source, talk to Ed Pagano, and meet Pete Berenson face to face. Once O'Connell got a look at the guy, he'd have every reason to arrest him. But if Ed Pagano was behind the murder, he wouldn't hand over his guy that easily. So I headed to Pagano's brewery.

Operations were in full swing. Security covered the entrance. There was no getting in or out without someone noticing. Instead, I kept my distance, choosing to watch from afar.

Since I'd only seen two of the masked men without their masks, Pete Berenson, a.k.a. Guido, and the guy with the hazel eyes, I had no idea if Archie and Winslow had been hired to assist or if Pete had gotten involved in the scheme for some other reason. However, my hunch about Tabitha's investigation indicated this had everything to do with the Paganos, which could mean more than one member of the security team was involved.

I had to be careful. I couldn't go up to the guard stand, flash my P.I. license, and ask about Pete Berenson. Actions like that could tip him off or get me shot, and since I wasn't wearing one of Cross's fancy prototypes and my tactical vest was in the trunk, I didn't want to anger Martin by getting another hole in me. So I remained in my car, watching and waiting.

Security didn't do much. Two men covered the front gate, checking IDs and waving deliveries through. The rest of the place looked like a manufacturing plant. There had to be a security office within the building where more guards monitored the surveillance feeds to make sure no one was committing any heinous acts.

Since Berenson wasn't stationed outside, I had to assume he was inside. When I grew tired of waiting, which didn't take long, I found the phone number for the brewery and asked to speak to Pete Berenson. She told me he couldn't be reached, but she'd be happy to take a message.

"That's okay. I'll try again later." Did that mean he wasn't at work?

I went back to monitoring the area, watching whenever a door opened and someone stepped out. No one lit up, so they weren't taking smoke breaks. But the workers who exited were definitely on a break. They wore all white, including their hair nets. A few ate energy bars or candy bars they'd squirreled away in their pockets. Some would pull out their cell phones. Breaks never lasted more than fifteen minutes. Every worker was exceptionally punctual.

Not a single navy blue suit exited from the doors. No rest for the wicked, I assumed. But security probably had a nicer place to relax and lounge than the workers on the floor. I wasn't sure exactly what went on inside the building or how breweries were run. The commercials I'd seen on TV always showed a lot of horses and frogs. Neither of which had anything to do with anything.

The rumble of an approaching engine caught my attention, and I turned to see a police cruiser pulling up.

O'Connell slowed beside my car and rolled down the passenger side window. "Any sign of him?"

"Negative. If Pete Berenson's in there, he hasn't come out. I tried calling, but he wouldn't come to the phone."

"Get in."

"Moi?" I pressed my fingertips to my chest. "You want me to ride along with you?"

"What did I tell you about being a buster?"

"I don't remember."

"Get in before I change my mind."

I saluted. "Yes, sir." After closing my window, I climbed in beside him, wondering if I should have grabbed my vest from the trunk. Surely, O'Connell had a spare.

He drove up to the main gate, leaned out the window, and held out his credentials. "Detective O'Connell, major crimes." He peered at the security guard over his sunglasses. "I need to have a word with the person in charge."

"Do you have a warrant?"

"To have a conversation?" O'Connell stared at him. "I can come back with one, but if I do, I'll be arresting someone for the trouble. This has nothing to do with the brewery. This has to do with a worker wanted in connection with a robbery. So what's it gonna be?"

"Wait one second." The security guard spoke to his partner before picking up the phone. He returned a moment later. "Go on through. You can park over there." He pointed to some spaces near the building. "That door will lead you inside. Someone will be waiting to take you to the manager."

"Great. Thanks."

O'Connell parked where he was told.

"Here's the thing, Parker. You're necessary to this investigation. You are the only person who saw the second man, the one with the hazel eyes. You didn't get a photo of him, so I need you to see if you can recognize him."

"That's what I'm doing here?"

"That's why Moretti said I had to pick you up on the way."

I gave him a look. "Are you sure you want to do this? I don't want to get you or Moretti jammed up."

"We'll be okay."

"Nick—"

"It's all good. No worries."

"All right." I got out of the car, made sure my weapon was concealed, and followed O'Connell inside.

A woman with a severe bun and dark-rimmed glasses was waiting for us. "What can I do for you, Detective?"

"I'd like to speak to the plant manager. It's about an employee, possibly more than one."

"I'm the head of human resources. Tell me who you want to see."

"Pete Berenson."

"He's a member of our security staff. Are you sure you have the right man? Security goes through a rigorous background check. They aren't even brewery employees. They are third party contractors."

"I'm hoping he can clear some things up for me,"

O'Connell said. "Since he's not one of your employees, you shouldn't have a problem showing me to his office."

The woman wasn't expecting that. "Right this way." She led us up the stairs. "It's the first door on your left. You can't miss it."

"Thanks." O'Connell took lead.

I followed him down the narrow hallway. At the office door, O'Connell stopped, knocking against it. He pushed his jacket aside, revealing his badge, which gave him better access to his gun. The two men inside turned at the sound.

"He's not here," I whispered.

O'Connell introduced himself. "I'm looking for Pete Berenson. Any idea where I might find him?"

"Berenson's dealing with an issue on the floor," the blond-haired guard said.

"What kind of issue?" O'Connell stepped into the office while I remained outside, keeping an eye out in case Berenson returned.

"A worker was injured. It happens from time to time. Security always responds. We write incident reports, if nothing else."

"Is it serious?" O'Connell pointed to the monitor. "Do you need to call an ambulance?"

"That won't be necessary. It's a minor injury. Another worker will drive the injured to urgent care to get checked out."

"I'd like to see for myself. Would you be kind enough to show me the way?"

The guards exchanged a look. "Sure thing, Detective." The other guard headed to the door. "But you'll have to get outfitted first. No one's allowed on the floor without the proper gear."

"Okay." O'Connell gave me a look. "Stay here. I'll be back soon."

Once he was gone, I entered the security office. The blond-haired guard pointed to the coffee machine. "Would you care for a cup?"

"I'm okay." I looked around the office. Snack wrappers and fast food containers covered most surfaces. "What's it like working security? Do you deal with a lot of issues?"

"It's usually quiet. Once in a while, someone gets burned or cut on the equipment. We deal with that. Otherwise, we get the occasional individual who wants to break in. Usually, they're teenagers or drunks. Y'know, the kinds of people who get it in their heads that if they get inside, they could have all the beer they want."

"Isn't that the case?" I pointed to the shiny silver vat on the screen.

"That's the brew kettle." He directed my attention to more silver containers with pipes running to and fro. "That's the mash tun and lauter tun. This," he pointed again, "is the fermenter. Until the process completes, the stuff inside wouldn't be very good. In fact, it could be pretty dangerous between the gasses and high temperatures. It's our job to keep people safe."

"That's admirable. Do your coworkers feel the same way?"

"We're a tight bunch. Mr. Pagano treats us like family."

"That's great, but don't you work for Precision Protection?"

"We do."

"So how does that work? Who do you report to?"

"Mr. Pagano's in charge. He determines our shifts and where we work. Precision Protection provides our paychecks based on the information Mr. Pagano submits to them."

"Isn't it weird he doesn't have his own security teams? Why go through a third party?"

"It didn't start that way. Mr. Pagano wanted personal security. He hired Precision Protection to provide that to him and his daughter. Since he was always at the brewery, so were we, which is why we started handling brewery issues in addition to Mr. Pagano's personal issues, and one thing led to another."

"Do you know his daughter?" I asked.

"I never met her."

"What about Pete Berenson?"

"He's been assigned to her detail several times." The guard snickered. "Between you and me, I think he has a crush on her."

"Does she reciprocate his feelings?"

"He'd say yes, but I don't think there's anything to it."

I filed that away for later. "Was Pete working this past Friday?"

"Let me check." The guard went to the clipboard tacked to the wall and flipped the coffee-stained sheets backward. "He didn't have any duties assigned that day. Not here or at the Pagano estate."

"Who else had off that day?"

"Milo, Richard, and," he used his finger to follow the line across the page, "George."

"Can I get their last names?"

"Why? What do you think they did?"

"I'm not sure they did anything." Except for Pete Berenson, who was guilty as sin.

"But you're investigating something. A robbery, was it?"

Before I could answer, the sound of rubber-soled boots against the metal stairs echoed from outside the room. I glanced at the monitor. O'Connell and the guard were on the floor, but Berenson was gone.

"Hey, Danny, we need to reorder med kits for—" Berenson stopped, his eyes on me. "Shit."

"Take it easy." I could see the panic on his face. He'd either run or fight. So he ran.

THIRTY-FIVE

I raced down the steps after Pete Berenson. If there had been any doubt this was the same man I'd left in the sauna, his running alleviated it. He recognized me and knew he was in trouble.

"Stop," I yelled, but he didn't.

Bursting out the front door, he disappeared from view. I shoved my way through the door. He wasn't in front of me. I paused only long enough to look from right to left. The navy blue jacket disappeared behind a heavy white door.

I ran as fast as I could along the side of the building, shoving my hand against the door as it came into contact with the jamb. Thankfully, I'd been fast enough to stop it before the lock reengaged, or I would have lost him.

Inside, dozens of barrels and shiny metal containers filled the cavernous room. The screech from his boots sounded from somewhere in front of me. Pulling my nine millimeter, I held it at my side while I moved through the room, checking between the rows of barrels and behind the shiny metal containers. But they were too large. It wouldn't matter if I circled around. As long as Berenson moved at the same pace, I'd never spot him.

"Pete," I called, hoping he'd respond, "I only want to talk. Running makes you look guilty. You don't want that, do you?"

"Fuck you," he yelled. "How did you track me down?"

"It wasn't that hard." It was harder, but he didn't deserve

the satisfaction. "Why don't you tell me your side of things?"

"Leave me alone or else."

"I can't do that. The police are—"

A gunshot rang out. I dove behind the nearest row of barrels. "Next time, I won't miss," he said.

"Killing one woman wasn't enough for you?"

Two more shots rang out. One hit the barrel in the row behind me, above my head and to the right. I should have grabbed the vest out of the trunk. Martin wouldn't be happy about this, which meant it was better if he never found out.

"I'll take that as a no." I aimed in the direction where the shots had originated. But I couldn't see him. I crept toward the other end of the row of barrels. A bullet hit the one in front of me, letting out a solid ting that reverberated to the point I thought my teeth might be vibrating along with the sound waves. "Why'd you do it, Pete? Why'd you kill Tabitha York?"

He fired again. This time, I spotted his reflection in the large metal container. What was that? A giant mixer? A fermenter? It didn't matter. I kept my eye on the mirrored surface. Berenson's contorted reflection made it harder for me to tell where he was. I edged around the side of the row, moving closer.

His next shot almost clipped me. Aiming where I thought he was, I returned fire, confused how he had me in his sights when I couldn't get a bead on him.

Glancing up, I spotted a mirror hanging from the walkway above. I flipped him off and scurried to the opposite end of the row, rolled across the exposed walkway, and came up behind one of the metal vats. I pressed my back against it, relieved when it didn't burn me. At least it wasn't hot.

Slinking around the side, I ducked beneath the thick pipe that ran into the vat and crawled to my next cover position. From there, I scanned my surroundings, straining to hear Pete moving around. He didn't move or make a single sound. More than likely, we were both operating blind, which put us on an even playing field.

But since this was his place of business, he had the home court advantage. I had to find a way to even the score.

Tossing a coin from my pocket across the room, I waited for it to land with a ting. Unlike the last shot he fired, it didn't echo. He didn't open fire, and he didn't move. Damn him for being that smart.

The door behind me banged open. Was he getting away? I half-stood to see if he was escaping, and another shot flew in my direction. Luckily, his aim was off. It hit the pipe, causing it to hiss. The escaping steam whistled and spit. With any luck, that wasn't the toxic gas Lorna had ranted about.

"Police," O'Connell announced. "Throw down your weapons and come out with your hands up."

Breaking cover, I rushed toward O'Connell and dove on top of him before the next shot put him down. "Are you okay?" I asked, the whistling from the escaping steam getting worse.

"Where is he?" O'Connell peered around the side of the vat we were using as cover.

"Over there." I jerked my chin in the direction the shots had come.

"No shit." O'Connell used hand signals, and we split up. If we could flank him, we could take him.

The shrill whistle drowned out any noises we made as we crept toward Berenson's cover position. Unsure where exactly he was, I kept my head on a swivel. My gaze swept side to side and up and down. At least there were no mirrors on this side, but all these shiny objects provided dozens of reflections.

Halfway across the room, I spotted a navy reflection. This was worse than a carnival funhouse. Moving along the curve of another metal container, I found Pete Berenson on one knee, his gun held near his head while he peered around the side, searching for us. He fired off a few shots. Since O'Connell was distracting him, I was in charge of the takedown.

Silently, I approached, the whistling becoming louder. I'd heard sounds like that in action films before things exploded. That worried me almost as much as the armed man in my crosshairs.

Once I was close enough to touch him, I pressed my gun

against the back of his neck. "Drop it."

Berenson did as I asked, his gun clattering to the floor. "Too bad we're all dead." He lunged to the side, spinning and knocking my gun hand away.

I held onto my weapon, but he didn't care. He pushed off the floor, leaping at me and knocking us into the side of the nearest metal container. Unlike the other one, this one was hot, just not enough to scald.

Breaking free from his grip, I clocked him with my gun, grabbed his arm, twisted it behind his back, and held him face-first against the side of the container. I holstered my weapon and hooked the handcuff onto his wrist and made quick work of the second bracelet.

"O'Connell?" I called, unsure how he missed the fun. When he didn't answer, my heart leapt into my throat. I didn't hear a scream or a pained grunt. But it was hard to hear anything over the escaping steam. "Nick?"

Dragging Pete toward the exit, I spotted O'Connell behind the barrels. He had taken off his belt and secured it around his upper thigh. A small rivulet of blood ran down his leg.

"You son of a bitch." I wanted to smack this guy into the nearest metal container or shove his face into the escaping steam, but I didn't. "Nick," I said louder, hoping to be heard over the whistling, "how bad is it?"

"It's a scratch. I'll be fine." O'Connell used the shelves to pull himself up. I moved closer to help, fighting with Berenson who struggled to get away. I kicked him in the back of the knee and moved to offer O'Connell some assistance when the whistling turned into a shriek and the pipes blew.

The sudden whoosh rocked us backward, making the shelves teeter. The barrels on the nearest shelf crashed to the floor. One cracked open while the other rolled toward us. The entire building rumbled. And the noise only got louder.

"We have to hit the automatic stop, or the whole place will blow," Berenson said.

"Where's the shut-off?" I asked.

Berenson grinned. "I'm not telling."

"Let's get out of here before something else goes boom." O'Connell grabbed our suspect by the other arm, and we dragged him toward the exit.

We were almost to the door when it burst open and several brewery specialists in their white uniforms and the two security guards we spoke to earlier entered. I aimed at them, unsure whose side they were on. The men in white ignored me while they hurried to hit the emergency shut-off. The two security guards raised their hands.

"More police cars are on the way, and an ambulance is en route," the blond-haired guard said. He cocked his head at Berenson. "I can't believe you did it."

"Shut up," Berenson snarled.

I looked at the blond-haired security guard. "Did you know about this?"

"No, but we saw what was going on in the security office."

"And it took you this long to get here?"

"I told them not to interfere," O'Connell said.

"What happened to calling for backup?" I asked.

O'Connell snorted. "I did." And just like that, sirens sounded outside the door.

THIRTY-SIX

Pete Berenson didn't look happy to be in police custody. Once he was brought in, Archie Hudson identified him as the man he'd been introduced to as Guido, the one he and Winslow had to carry out of Spa Alive.

"Why the alias?" O'Connell asked.

"Why do you think?"

O'Connell pulled out Archie's statement. "You were afraid your accomplices would turn on you."

"They aren't my accomplices," Berenson said.

"Really?" O'Connell sighed dramatically. "Explain that to me. We can place you inside Spa Alive during the attack. We have your gas mask and body armor. We even have a photo of you passed out in the sauna. Archie Hudson explained how he and his pals carried you out of the spa. If you don't think that qualifies them as your accomplices, I'll get you a dictionary because you don't know what the word means."

"Fine. Whatever."

"They aren't his accomplices," I said. "They weren't there to kill Tabitha York. Only Mr. Berenson was."

"It's nice you don't want them to take the blame for her murder," O'Connell said.

Berenson glared at me. "That wasn't my fault. Killing that lady wasn't my idea."

"Whose idea was it?" O'Connell asked.

Berenson glanced at his attorney. "Not unless I get some kind of deal."

"You've got to be kidding. You tried to kill us," I said.

O'Connell held up his hand. "Tell me what you know. Leniency is on the table. The DA's office is willing to deal, but only with good intel. Who wanted Tabitha York dead?"

Berenson looked uneasy. "Mr. Pagano."

"Ed Pagano?" O'Connell asked for clarification.

"Yep."

"Your boss wanted Tabitha York killed," I said. That went along with everything I'd discovered, but I had zero proof. Hopefully, Berenson could change that.

"He didn't just want her killed. He ordered us to do it. He didn't give us a choice. We'd either do it, or we were done. And I don't think he was talking about looking for another job, not after that."

"Us?" O'Connell slid a pen and pad across the table. "Who else did Pagano order to commit the hit?"

"It was me and Milo Regant. We were providing personal security that night, and when things didn't go his way, Mr. Pagano took us into his home office and told us what we had to do. He didn't give us a choice."

O'Connell turned, gesturing at the two-way glass. Heathcliff was on the other side. He'd bring in Regant. "The two of you are employed by Precision Protection, right?" O'Connell asked. "Why didn't you report Pagano to them?"

"It's not that simple. We work for Pagano. We do double-time between his house and the brewery. It's been like that since the beginning," Berenson said. "We eat dinner together. We stay at his house more than any other security guards. He'd be able to destroy us, our careers, our reputations, everything. Pagano knew he had us where he wanted us. We were his to do with as he liked."

"You could have said no," I said.

Berenson scoffed. "He would have found a way to end us. An accident at the brewery. A drive-by. Something. But not after running damage control. After all, that's exactly why he wanted Tabitha York taken out. It was damage control."

"What do you mean?" O'Connell asked.

"Mr. Pagano said Tabitha York was causing trouble. She had found something on him, on his brewery, maybe even on Lorna. Stan and Gary had seen Tabitha York following

Lorna around, having chance conversations with staff from the brewery, and asking questions of the inspectors assigned to the brewery. Mr. Pagano tried to dissuade York. He offered to pay her off, to set up trust funds and scholarships for her kids, to finance her husband's next movie, but she wouldn't give in. So Pagano threatened her."

"Why didn't she report it?" I asked.

Berenson chuckled. "You don't get it. Mr. Pagano never delivered a direct threat. They were all veiled warnings. Nothing actionable."

Receiving threats was part of Tabitha York's business. She wouldn't have backed down or shied away. She must not have believed Pagano posed a danger, or she would have done something. At least, I hoped she would have tried to protect herself and her family.

"After we returned from an event where Pagano made one last attempt to persuade York to back off, she turned the tables on him. She threatened his family, his daughter."

"How?" I asked.

"York said he better back off or she'd bury his daughter right beside him. That's when he ordered us to eliminate the problem. He wanted it to look like an accident or like she'd been the victim of a random act of violence. None of this was supposed to link back to us." Berenson glared at me. "You fucked this up."

"That's kind of my job."

"Tell me what happened at Spa Alive. Whose idea was it to take over the wellness center?" O'Connell asked.

"That was Milo's idea. We'd been keeping tabs on York. She started going there soon after Lorna stopped. Lorna had told us all about the place, how the skin treatment gave her blisters, and how much she hated the people who worked there."

"What about Damon Thoreau?" I asked.

Berenson rolled his eyes. "He was a flavor of the week."

"Does she hate him?"

"No."

"Do you hate him?"

"Why would I?"

"Your buddy said you had a crush on Lorna."

"We all had a crush on Lorna. Milo worse than any of us. He wanted to be her knight in shining armor. To tell you the truth, I think that's why Mr. Pagano asked us to do this. He knew Milo would do anything to protect Lorna."

"Is that why someone on your crew took the binder from Ralph Lively's office?" I asked. "Did Lorna ask you to do that?"

"I don't know what you're talking about."

O'Connell gave me a look, reminding me I wasn't supposed to be asking questions. "Take me through your role at Spa Alive."

"I didn't kill Tabitha York," Berenson insisted. "In fact, I wanted to try to scare her off. That's when Milo came up with the plan to knock everyone out and create a hostage situation. He thought a near-death experience like that would hit the point home. Milo knew a guy from his gym who had a record. They came up with the scheme to get some knockout gas, rent a van, and pretend to be there to service the HVAC. Milo went in first. He said he had to check the system. As soon as everyone started dropping, he gave us the all-clear."

"How many of you were involved?" O'Connell asked.

"There were four of us. Milo and me. His ex-con pal and one of his buddies."

I opened my mouth to object, but O'Connell kicked me in the shin. He knew there were more than four, but he didn't want me to point that out to Berenson.

"After we joined Milo inside, I started searching the rooms for York. She was already dead."

"Do you think Milo killed her?" O'Connell asked.

"He must have."

"Why didn't you leave then?"

"We couldn't. This had to look like a robbery, like a planned attack. York was supposed to look like an accidental casualty. No one left a mark on her."

"How would you know that?" I asked.

Berenson squinted at me. "I didn't kill her. I was outside."

I wanted to point out how he couldn't prove that since the cameras were knocked out, but O'Connell's icy stare forced my mouth shut.

"Then what happened?" O'Connell asked.

"Milo's buddy told me to check the rest of the rooms and see if anyone had any valuables for the taking. That's what I was doing when this one," he pointed at me, "jumps on me, and the next thing I know, I'm waking up in the cellar."

O'Connell took the pad back from Berenson. "This name here," he pointed to the shaky scrawl, "Winslow Smith, who is that?"

"That's Milo's buddy."

"The ex-con?"

"Yep."

"What about the other man?"

"I never got his name," Berenson said.

"Did he get yours?"

"I used a fake name. I didn't want them to turn on me in case things went south and one of them got caught. They had records. Obviously, they'd done this before and hadn't been successful. I didn't want to take that chance."

"But Winslow Smith knew who Milo was."

"No. Milo hates his name. He said it makes him sound like a pussy. When he went to the gym, he introduced himself as Mike." Berenson shrugged. "Don't ask me. That's his hang-up, not mine. But they didn't know who we were. And I didn't want to know who they were either. The less information we exchanged, the better."

O'Connell rubbed his forehead. "Let me make sure I got this straight. You didn't kill Tabitha York, but you were involved in the conspiracy to kill her. So when I showed up at your place of business to ask about the incident, you decided to open fire on a police officer and a witness."

Berenson pointed emphatically at me. "She could ID me. She knew I was there. She's the reason you ruled York's death a homicide."

"How would you know that?" I asked.

Berenson closed his mouth and looked the other way. His attorney said, "He has no obligation to answer that question."

"So you didn't kill Tabitha York. You didn't steal the binder from Spa Alive. And you didn't rob any of the clients who were on the premises." O'Connell tapped his pen against the pad a few times. "Besides being hired to perform the hit, you had nothing to do with any of this."

"My client will not incriminate himself. He's named names. You have what you wanted," the attorney said.

"We have footage of the break-in at the medical supply warehouse," O'Connell said. "Things will go easier if you confess to the part you played."

"I was there," Berenson said. "We didn't hurt anyone. We got in and out. We didn't take anything but the gas. No pharmaceuticals. Nada."

"All right." O'Connell used the table to help himself stand. He hadn't been shot. He had caught a ricochet which hadn't penetrated beyond the muscle, but it was fresh and sore. On the bright side, it wasn't bleeding. "I'll see what Milo Regant and Winslow Smith have to say. Then we'll figure out what to do with you."

"Hey," Berenson objected, but his protests fell on deaf ears as we exited the interrogation room.

THIRTY-SEVEN

Milo Regant wasn't hard to find. He was at home when uniformed officers showed up with an arrest warrant. Unlike Pete Berenson, Milo didn't resist arrest. He went willingly, without inflicting any unnecessary bloodshed.

Heathcliff and O'Connell put him inside an interrogation room. I watched from the other side, but I didn't recognize him. He had brown eyes, not hazel.

"The reporter lady was following Lorna around, watching her, watching Mr. Pagano. She would speak to people from the brewery at the most random places. Mr. Pagano said she was conducting an investigation, finding sources, gaining evidence, and that she needed to be stopped. She was going to hurt him, hurt Lorna, and put us all out of a job." Milo stared at his hands. "Mr. Pagano gave us an order. There was no questioning him. We did what he said. End of story."

"Have you ever heard of free will?" Heathcliff asked.

"The reporter lady was going to hurt all of us. The Paganos were like family. I had to protect them. Protect her."

"Who?" Heathcliff waited.

"Lorna. She didn't deserve any of what was happening. She never had a job, not a real one. If her inheritance dried up, if she lost the family business, how was she going to survive? As if that wasn't bad enough, that bitch was stalking her. I didn't like her messing with Lorna. Lorna had enough going on. She already had plenty of obsessed fans. She didn't need a stalker watching her every move."

"What did you do?" O'Connell asked.

"I did what I had to."

"Tell us about the crew you assembled," O'Connell said. "Did they know what was going to happen?"

"The only one who knew was Pete. Mr. Pagano asked us both to take care of the problem. We were in it together." The rest of Milo's story backed everything Pete Berenson had said.

"Who killed Tabitha York?" O'Connell asked.

Milo shifted his head from side to side, realizing he shouldn't answer. "I'd rather not say."

"How many guys were on the crew?" O'Connell asked.

"Six."

"Berenson said four."

"He didn't know about the other two. They showed up to assist on the robbery. That wasn't my doing. That was Winslow's. He had this vision we'd be hauling gold bars out of the spa."

"Did any of them know the real reason you were there?" O'Connell asked.

"No. They thought it was a robbery. That we were pulling a Robin Hood, stealing from the rich and giving to ourselves."

"Did Pete Berenson kill Tabitha York?" Heathcliff asked.

Milo shook his head. "No." That left only one possibility, even if Milo hadn't planned on incriminating himself for the murder.

I knocked against the two-way glass. Even though the detectives couldn't see me, they knew what I wanted them to ask.

"Did you take a binder from Ralph Lively's office?" Heathcliff asked.

Milo nodded. "Lorna had been burned. She swore it was their fault. According to her boytoy masseur, it had been an accident. But Lorna was adamant it wasn't. She needed proof. I promised myself I'd get it for her. All I ever wanted to do was keep her safe." He smiled. "At least she's safe now."

*   *   *

"What about Winslow Smith?" I asked. The homicide detectives from the other precinct had found him and brought him in for questioning. He was being held there, but O'Connell had already put in a transfer request. In the meantime, he and Heathcliff had reviewed the transcripts. I hoped to get the Cliff's notes version.

"He didn't know anything about the murder. All he knew was they were supposed to rob Spa Alive. Winslow, Archie, and two of his other acquaintances hoped to clear the place out. They broke in to the medical supply warehouse, took what they needed, and hit the spa. According to Winslow, no one was supposed to get hurt. After things went sideways, they cleared out, using the van they rented with the HVAC maintenance decals as their means of escape," O'Connell said.

"DOT footage tracked the van. They ditched it near the cellar you found." Heathcliff showed me stills from nearby traffic cams. "There's Berenson, getting carried to the building."

"So he wasn't lying," I said.

"Not about that." O'Connell rubbed his leg.

"I guess it would have been best if you hadn't taken me with you."

"If he didn't start shooting, I'm not sure I would have had grounds to arrest him. So it all came out in the wash." O'Connell turned to Thompson. "Has the warrant come back for Ed Pagano?"

"It should be here any second."

"Let's hope so."

Thompson pointed at me. "We could always send Parker. When he shoots at her, we'll arrest him. That is how we do things now."

"Hardy har." Reaching for the file, I reviewed Archie Hudson's transcript. "They reconvened at the cellar, stashed their gear and loot, and split up. Winslow, Archie, and the other two robbers were waiting for the heat to die down before getting rid of the incriminating evidence. But when it turned into a homicide investigation, Winslow panicked. He called his friends, and they went to clear out the cellar. That's when I followed Archie from Kathy's house back to the cellar."

"They should have known better," Heathcliff said. "Criminals always panic. That's how they get caught."

"It's the guilt," O'Connell said. "It's also why catching psychopaths is so difficult."

"No guilt," I said. "But why did Archie leave the binder behind?"

"They had no use for it. That was what Milo stole for Lorna. It had nothing to do with Winslow's crew. If anything, it placed them inside Spa Alive. It proved they were guilty. It could even lead to a murder charge hanging over their heads." Heathcliff glanced at the phone, as if hoping it would ring.

"What about Kathy Walters and Willa Garrison?" I asked.

"We have nothing to hold them on, but they were instructed not to leave town. Patrol cars have been assigned to keep tabs on them in case of anything, but I don't think they had anything to do with Tabitha York's murder. As far as I can tell, Kathy Walters was an unknowing participant. She didn't realize talking about work is how the team gained such easy access to Spa Alive," O'Connell said.

"So the only thing left to do is bring in Ed Pagano." I looked at the time. Cross expected me back at the office hours ago. By now, he and everyone else had gone home.

"Don't even think about it," O'Connell warned.

I held up my palms. "I wasn't. I was thinking it was late. I'm ready to call it a night."

"You're getting soft on us," Thompson teased.

Heathcliff gave me an uncertain look. "Are you okay?"

"I'm fine."

"All right. I'll walk you out."

I was almost home when my phone rang. It was my boss. Had I said his name three times in a row? I didn't think so, yet here he was.

"Hey," I answered, "any progress?"

"On what?"

"I don't know. We had a million things in the works."

"Didn't you share those findings with O'Connell? Didn't

he take care of it? Isn't that why you spent half the day outside Pagano's brewery and the other half at the precinct?"

"This is why I hate using the company car."

Even though I couldn't see it, I knew Cross rolled his eyes. "Where are you going now?" he asked.

"Home."

"Why? Martin's at the office."

"Are you tracking him too?"

"No, Alex, I'm not, but am I wrong?"

He wasn't. "What do you want?"

"You were supposed to meet me at the office?"

"Do you want me to come in now?"

"No, but I'd like you to meet me at a private club. I'm texting you the address."

Before I could ask any more questions, he hung up. Curiosity always got the best of me, and unsure what he wanted or why he thought meeting this late at night was a good idea, I drove to the address, parked near his Porsche, and headed for the front door.

This wasn't a typical nightclub. It was quiet. Subdued. Upon entering, the smell of cigars and spirits assaulted my nostrils. Had I known, I would have worn the N95 in here. The maître d' didn't ask for my name. Instead, she said, "Right this way, Ms. Parker."

Halfway across the low-lit dining hall, I spotted my boss. He sat at a round booth, a drink on the table in front of him. His back was to me, but I knew that suit and haircut anywhere. He didn't turn even as I slid in across from him.

"What do you want, Lucien?" I asked. "It's been a long day."

"It's about to get longer." He nodded at something behind me.

Turning, I spotted Ed Pagano seated at the bar. "What are we doing here? Why are you keeping tabs on Pagano?"

"He's responsible for Tabitha York's murder. At least, that's what the police think. What do you think?"

"Evidence backs it. Two members of his security detail gave him up."

"They could have lied." Cross glanced at me for the first

time. "Do the police have proof besides the word of killers?"

"That's enough for now. Once they arrest him, they'll get a search warrant."

"You always have so much faith in the system."

"And you don't. What are we doing here? You do not concern yourself with these things."

"You're right." He sat back in his chair and picked up his glass, as if toasting to me. "I don't. But Nathan York came to me earlier today. He wanted to know what we could do to speed up the police investigation. Apparently, he looked you up, which led him straight to me. Had you been in the office, like you were told, you could have taken the meeting and assured him of all the wonderful things the police department was doing on his wife's behalf. Instead, he had to talk to me."

"The poor man."

Cross smirked. "Let's just say Cross Security has not changed its policy on murder investigations. However, helping the police locate and apprehend a suspect would be performing a civil service, specifically since my father didn't believe we were capable of doing anything but fucking this up."

"Which is why you're here."

"We're assisting. I don't want him blackballing us, not when you keep insisting we need to have a good working relationship with our blue brethren."

"Did Bennett say that? That sounds like him."

"He may have mentioned something along those lines." Cross took another sip of his drink. "Amir did a deep dive into Pagano's financials. Milo Regant and Pete Berenson got a substantial bonus in this month's check. We're talking five figure bonuses. He tried to cover it by promoting them to co-presidents of security operations, but that's not a real position, and even if it was, they wouldn't get paid like that."

"He paid them to murder Tabitha York."

"That may not be enough for the police. So we're going to have a friendly chat with Ed and see what he has to say."

"Lucien," I warned, but Cross had already made up his mind. Was he really that self-destructive? Was I?

Cross drained his glass and took the empty to the bar. He

took a seat beside Ed Pagano. I had a choice. Walking away would be the smart decision. But my boss needed backup. And I was the only person he called.

"Mr. Pagano," Cross held out his hand, "I'm Lucien Cross, owner of Cross Security."

I dialed O'Connell, left the line open, and took a seat on the other side of Pagano. This was a one-party consent state, which meant the conversation could be recorded and shared since Cross was a willing participant.

Pagano shook his hand. "What can I do for you, Mr. Cross?"

"Actually, it's what I can do for you." Cross gave him the business smile, which reminded me of the cat who ate the canary. "I spoke to my friends at Precision Protection earlier today. They said they handle your security needs. Any interest in changing companies? I only hire the best. They'd put the men you have working for you to shame."

Pagano looked annoyed. "I'm happy with who I have." He turned, bracketing his drink with his forearms and hunching over, hoping to put an end to the conversation.

"Are you sure about that? The police arrested the two men you just promoted. The same men you paid substantial five-figure bonuses to."

"How do you know that?" Pagano asked.

"It's my job." Cross held the smile. "It's Cross Security and Investigations. I'm in the business. I know people, so I hear things. The men who were arrested, Berenson and Regant, they told the cops you hired them to kill Tabitha York."

"I don't know where you heard that, but when I find out who's spreading those lies, I'll sue them for slander."

"I already told you who said it. The bonuses make you look guilty. Let's add to that the story Tabitha York was putting together on you."

"I don't know what you're talking about."

"Sure, play it that way," Cross said. "The only problem is I was hired to look into Tabitha York. She had a lot of enemies. More than just you."

"Exposing companies and ruining lives will do that to a person." Pagano swirled the cubes around his glass. "She should have found a safer profession. She was a mother. She should have stayed home and cared for her children. I'm sure she was warned."

I resisted the urge to retort. Instead, I remained on the seat, half-turned away from him while I recorded the conversation.

"I bet you warned her, but that's not important." Cross smiled. "I'm here to make you an offer. Hire my firm for your security needs. We're the best. Everything from personal protection to corporate overhauls. You won't be disappointed. In fact, for the same five-figure bonus you paid the men who I'm guessing won't have jobs once they're serving life sentences, I'll make sure the police find out exactly who is responsible for Tabitha York's murder. The files she had, the information, it could lead to several different possibilities. I'll make sure it leads to the right one, if you know what I'm saying."

Pagano looked up from his glass. "I think I do."

"Do we have a deal?" Cross asked.

"Yeah, okay."

"Great." Cross threw his arm around Ed. "We both know you had York killed, so this may take some work. How many other people did you involve in your scheme?"

"Only Berenson and Regant. I trusted them. They'd been with me for years. They weren't like the others. They didn't have ties to law enforcement or that whole honor thing my military guys have. They weren't supposed to turn on me."

"Next time, you should contract out," Cross said. "They did, which is how you ended up in this jam."

"Is that why the police came to my brewery?"

"They found part of the crew your men assembled to make York's death look like a robbery gone wrong, except ex-cons will say or do just about anything to stay out of prison."

"You'll have to take care of them too."

"How would you like me to handle it?" Cross asked. "I can make it look like they were vengeful employees, like they tried to blackmail you."

Pagano grinned. "You make it look like they killed York and tried to make me take the fall, forcing me to pay them those bonuses, and you have yourself a deal. If that doesn't work, find another way. Things happen in prison," Pagano said. "You said you'd take care of my issues. I don't care how you do it. I need the rest of it to go away. I'll pay whatever you want. I just need this mess cleaned up quickly."

"You should have thought about that before you sent your guys to do your dirty work."

"I tried to take care of it myself, to get York to back off, but she wouldn't listen," Pagano hissed. "I didn't have a choice. She wanted to destroy me. I had to destroy her first."

"All right. I'll take care of it. There's just one problem. Actually, two." Cross held up his fingers. "First, you paid them before York was killed. I could make that go away. Say they blackmailed you and then tried to bury you. The vengeful bastards. If not, we move on to plan B."

"What's the second problem?" Pagano asked.

"You just admitted to contracting a hit on Tabitha York, and since her husband came to me first to find the person responsible, taking you on as a client would be a conflict of interest."

Pagano reached into his pocket, pulling out a twenty-two. He aimed it at my boss. "You fucking asshole. You set me up. I'll kill you."

Spinning on the stool, I grabbed Pagano, sliding one hand down his arm toward the gun, while I slammed my elbow into the inside of his bicep, where the nerves and veins were concentrated. That instantly numbed his arm, and I grabbed the gun from his grip before he could fire or drop it.

Then I slammed his chest against the bar, beside the drink he'd been nursing. "Thanks for confessing. You just made everyone's job a million times easier."

Cross cuffed Pagano while I held him down. By the time we had him bound, police cars had arrived outside. I didn't recognize the officers, but two of them nodded to Cross.

"Your father will be proud," the older one with the mustache said.

"I need another drink." Cross gestured to the bartender, who looked as shocked as everyone else inside. "What the hell? Can I get a round for everyone?"

THIRTY-EIGHT

"I thought you were going home," O'Connell said when Cross and I were escorted to the bullpen by uniformed officers.

"Blame him." I pointed to my boss. "Heathcliff even walked me to my car. I was almost safely back at my apartment when this one calls and tells me to meet him. It's not my fault he came up with the bright idea to—"

"Make the PD's case for them." Cross took a seat in the straight-back chair beside Thompson's desk. "You're welcome, Detective."

"I was going to say entrap Pagano," I corrected.

"It's only entrapment when the police do it." Cross picked up the folder and flipped through it. "I hope you thought to record the conversation in case there are questions."

"I recorded it," I said.

"So did I." O'Connell snatched the folder out of Cross's hand. "What I'm not sure about is how you possessed the information you did."

"It's Cross Security and Investigations. People always forget the second part." Cross picked up a paperclip and straightened the metal before folding it in half, as if he expected to need it to free himself from a pair of handcuffs.

"Parker does the investigating," Thompson muttered. "You only provide the name."

I smiled at him. "I knew you liked me."

Thompson rolled his eyes. "I'm calling it. Nick, have fun

dealing with this circus."

"Yep." O'Connell watched his partner leave. "Your father called, Lucien. He wanted to say thank you. Getting a confession out of the man responsible for Tabitha York's murder will go a long way to making sure he pays for his crime."

Cross looked sick. "Are we back in the department's good graces? Any shadow of doubt regarding Cross Security or Alex's involvement in what happened at Spa Alive has been eradicated, right?"

"As far as I know, but no one here ever thought differently," O'Connell said.

"What about Dominguez and Sgt. Wu?" I asked. "They weren't my biggest fans."

"The other precinct had some questions, and a few issues," O'Connell admitted. The look on my boss's face said he already knew. Again, no one bothered to share any of this with me. "But that's been cleared up."

"Is consulting back on the table?" I asked.

Cross glared at me. "I told you this is not what we do."

"It's fine by me. Moretti signed off. Whenever we have something for you, we'll let you know," O'Connell said.

"The city better pay our rates," Cross said.

O'Connell gave me a look as if to say, *Do you believe this guy?*

* * *

When I finally made it home, I was so far past exhausted that I was once again wired. Martin wasn't home. Around two a.m., I had texted him that I was pulling an all-nighter, so he did the same.

Part of me considered making a pot of coffee, taking a shower, and going to work, but I needed a break. My back was starting to ache again, so I ordered the percussion massage gun Damon had used, sent him a text, thanking him for the suggestion, and decided to indulge in a nice hot bath.

As soon as I sunk into the water, thoughts of Tabitha York bombarded my mind. She was just doing her job. She wanted to protect people by exposing harmful practices, and that got her killed. No matter how hard I tried, I couldn't help but draw parallels to my own life. It was no wonder Martin worried.

Last night proved one thing. Cross was reckless to the point his actions may have rivaled mine. This was why Mark Jablonsky never wanted me working for him. He knew how destructive Cross was and how destructive I was. In the short time I'd been working there, we'd encountered far too many deadly situations. Despite my new designation, nothing had changed. In fact, it may have gotten worse. No wonder Martin wanted to know what the holdup was with the body armor.

"Sweetheart?" he called.

"In here."

A moment later, the door opened. Martin stood, looking a little rough around the edges. "Is your back bothering you still?"

"Not as much, but I wanted to head it off before the spasms start."

He leaned down and kissed me. "Mind if I join you?"

"I was going to insist."

After he stripped, he slid into the tub behind me. I leaned back against his chest, resting my head against his shoulder and burying my face in the crook of his neck.

"You deserve better from me. I can do better. Try harder. I won't let you be the next Nathan York."

"Hey," he kissed my forehead, "all I want is for you to be careful. I never want you to stop doing what you do. It took a long time for me to accept it, but it's who you are, and I would never change that."

DON'T MISS THE NEXT INSTALLMENT IN
THE ALEXIS PARKER SERIES.

CHECK OUT DAMAGE CONTROL (ALEXIS
PARKER #27).

ABOUT THE AUTHOR

G.K. Parks is the author of the Alexis Parker series. The first novel, *Likely Suspects,* tells the story of Alexis' first foray into the private sector.

G.K. Parks received a Bachelor of Arts in Political Science and History. After spending some time in law school, G.K. changed paths and earned a Master of Arts in Criminology/Criminal Justice. Now all that education is being put to use creating a fictional world based upon years of study and research.

You can find additional information on G.K. Parks and the Alexis Parker series by visiting our website at
www.alexisparkerseries.com

www.ingramcontent.com/pod-product-compliance
Lightning Source LLC
Chambersburg PA
CBHW021314250626
47155CB00002B/539